"CAN I . . . HELP YOU WITH SOMETHING?"

Her voice betrayed the effect he was having on her.

He took his time, his gaze flicking over her white linen blouse, unbuttoned at the throat and sheer enough to show the outline of the pink lace bra beneath. His mouth twitched as if holding back some forbidden comment.

"As I recollect, you and I never finished what we started." He spoke in a slow drawl. "And I'm not a man to walk away from unfinished business."

Pulse skittering, Lauren rose and walked around the desk. She wanted to put him in his place, to inform him that the half-drunken floozy he'd picked up in the bar wasn't her real self. She had an education. She had goals and standards. And if Sky Fletcher thought he could just walk in here and expect her to fall into his arms . . .

They stood almost toe to toe. Hands on her hips, she glared up into his impossibly blue eyes.

Lord help her, she wanted the man. . . .

Don't miss any of Janet Dailey's bestsellers:

TEXAS TOUGH

JANET DAILEY

ZEBRA BOOKS
KENSINGTON PUBLISHING CORP.
http://www.kensingtonbooks.com

ZEBRA BOOKS are published by

Kensington Publishing Corp.
119 West 40th Street
New York, NY 10018

All Kensington titles, imprints, and distributed lines are available at special quantity discounts for bulk purchases for sales promotion, premiums, fund-raising, educational, or institutional use.

Special book excerpts or customized printings can also be created to fit specific needs. For details, write or phone the office of the Kensington Sales Manager: Attn.: Sales Department. Kensington Publishing Corp., 119 West 40th Street, New York, NY 10018. Phone: 1-800-221-2647.

Zebra and the Z logo Reg. U.S. Pat. & TM Off.

First Kensington Books Hardcover Printing: June 2015
First Zebra Books Mass-Market Paperback Printing: April 2016
ISBN-13: 978-1-4201-3376-9
ISBN-10: 1-4201-3376-4

eISBN-13: 978-1-4201-3377-6
eISBN-10: 1-4201-3377-2

10 9 8 7 6 5 4 3 2 1

Printed in the United States of America

In grateful recognition of Elizabeth Lane.

CHAPTER 1

The sun burned blood red through a lingering haze of dust. As it sank behind the buttes and turrets of the Caprock Escarpment, shadows stretched long across the heat-seared landscape. With each minute that passed, the two riders grew more anxious. If they didn't find the missing man soon, they'd be searching for him in the dark.

Jasper Platt, the Rimrock's retired foreman, had gone hunting early that morning. When he didn't show up for supper, Sky Fletcher and Beau Tyler had saddled their horses and set out looking for him. Armed with pistols and flashlights, they rode out across the flat toward the dry alkali lake where the old man liked to shoot quail and wild turkey.

"I don't like this." Beau scanned the horizon with his binoculars. "The old man's got no business out here alone, driving that ATV God knows where, maybe rolling it in a wash, or even running into those smugglers who've been leaving tracks all over the place. We need to make some rules and insist that he follow them."

"And how do you think Jasper would take to your rules?" Sky spoke softly, sharp ears alert for any unfamiliar sound. "He may be old, but that's no reason to treat him like a child. After all, he practically raised you and Will after your mother died."

Beau exhaled a tension-charged breath. "Somebody had to do the job. Our dad sure as hell didn't have the patience. Jasper was more of a father to Will and me than Bull Tyler ever was. I just hope we find him safe."

Sky let the words pass. It was no secret that Beau Tyler and his domineering father, Bull, had clashed bitterly at every turn. After their last quarrel, Beau had left for the army and stayed away eleven years.

Sky, however, had nothing but respect for the hard-driving rancher who'd taken in a starving half-Comanche teenager and given him a job. In the fourteen years Sky had worked for the Rimrock, he'd learned that Bull could be harsh but never unfair. The man's death this past spring had been a genuine loss. Sky was still reeling from the legacy Bull had left him in his will—the deed to 100 acres of prime ranchland, the first thing of real value he'd ever owned.

"Maybe we should've brought the dog." Beau's words broke into Sky's thoughts. Tag, the black and white Border Collie, was about Jasper's age in dog years. The two were close companions.

"I didn't see Tag at the house," Sky said. "Jasper might have taken him along in the ATV. If anything happened to Jasper, that dog would stay right with him. Keep your ears open. Maybe we'll hear something."

Both men fell silent as the twilight deepened. Sky's ears sifted through the night sounds—the drone of flying insects, the faraway wail of a coyote, the rhythmic *ploof* of shod hooves in the powdery dust. With scorching temperatures and no rain since spring, the land was drier than he'd ever seen it. The drought was a constant, gnawing worry. But right now the more urgent concern was finding Jasper.

"Listen!" Beau hissed. "Do you hear that?"

"Sounds like a dog!" Sky had caught it, too. Urging their horses to a gallop, the two men thundered toward the sound.

Minutes later they found the ATV. The open vehicle had careened and landed on its side in a hollow, where a minuscule spring seeped out of the ground. Protected by the roll bar, Jasper was sprawled belly down, one side of his face pressed in the water-slicked mud. The Border Collie stood guard, barking at their approach.

"Get the dog out of the way." Cursing, Beau dropped to a crouch beside the old man, who was as much a part of the Rimrock Ranch as the land itself.

Gripped by dread, Sky held the dog's collar, stroking and soothing the agitated animal while Beau, who'd had some medical experience as an Army Ranger, checked for vital signs.

"Is he alive?" Sky asked, steeling himself against the answer.

"Barely. His pulse feels week. Sounds like he might have some fluid in his lungs, too." Beau worked a hand beneath Jasper's head to lift his face clear of the mud. "I'd guess he's been here awhile. Damned lucky he didn't drown."

Sky's free hand whipped out his cell phone. "I'll get Life Flight. Want me to call the house, too? Will and Bernice will be worried. And they'll need to tell Erin."

Beau was probing for broken bones. "Go ahead and call Life Flight. Then you can help me push the ATV off him and turn him over. I'll phone Will when we've got him more comfortable."

By the time Sky had finished the call, the dog was calm enough to stay put. Between them, Sky and Beau tipped the light vehicle back onto its wheels and pushed it out of the way. Jasper was semiconscious, muttering and moaning, his Stetson gone, his muddy white hair plastered to his scalp.

"I'll take his head and shoulders," Beau directed. "You support his hips and spine. On the count of three, we roll him onto his back."

Crouching low, Sky worked his hands beneath the bony old body and waited for the count. Jasper had been on the Rimrock since before Will and Beau were born. By the time Sky showed up, he was already a silver-haired elder. Arthritis had ended his days in the saddle, but he remained a treasure trove of wisdom, humor, and experience. If he didn't make it, his loss would devastate the ranch family.

Between advanced age and dehydration, Jasper's body felt almost weightless. After lifting him like a child, they rolled him onto a patch of dry grass. By then the twilight had deepened to dusk. But even without the flashlight, they could see the dark stain spread around the hole in the front of his faded plaid shirt. Sky's heart slammed. Beau cursed.

Jasper had been shot.

Will Tyler had left for the hospital within minutes of Beau's call, taking Bernice, Jasper's widowed younger sister who'd run the Tyler household for the past thirty years. Beau had gone with Jasper in the helicopter, leaving Sky to take the dog and horses to the barn and return in the pickup for the ATV.

Sky had decided against going to the hospital. Somebody had to look after things at the ranch—and even though he thought the world of Jasper, Sky was aware that he wasn't family. Not like the Tylers were family.

He was helping with early-morning chores when the call came from Will. "The old man's barely hanging on." Will's voice was gritty with exhaustion. "He's got pneumonia now, as well as the gunshot wound. He's a tough old man, but the doctor isn't sure he'll make it."

"Anything I can do?" Sky spoke past the knot in his throat.

"Yes. Jasper's conscious and asking for you. Get here as soon as you can."

Still in his work clothes, Sky piled into his ten-year-old Ford pickup and set out on the hour-long drive to the hospital in Lubbock. He couldn't think of any reason why Jasper would ask for him, but if that was what the old man wanted, he would be there. If the worst happened, it would at least give him a chance to say good-bye.

The rising sun, a fireball above the rolling plains, promised another day of blistering heat. On either side of the road, the grassy landscape stretched as dead as broom straw, dotted with clumps of dry mesquite. Buzzards, a half mile distant, flocked around a dark, bulky shape. A dead cow, maybe even a horse. At least the scavengers were eating well.

Sky had seen droughts before, but never one as

bad as this. With the summer not half over, things were bound to get even worse. Will had already talked about selling off the cattle early, which made Sky's work training horses to sell even more vital to the ranch's survival.

But concerns about the drought would have to wait. Right now what mattered most was Jasper's life.

As Sky swung the pickup into a parking spot, a white Toyota Land Cruiser pulled up next to him. Beau's fiancée, Natalie Haskell, flew out of the driver's seat to join Sky on a fast walk to the waiting room. Doll-sized, she was dressed for her work as a vet in jeans and a tan cotton shirt.

"Beau said I didn't need to come, but I couldn't stay away. I've known Jasper all my life." She brushed back her mop of dark curls. The diamond on her finger scattered rainbows where it caught the sunlight.

Sky didn't reply as he held the door for her. There were no words for a time like this.

The small waiting room was crowded. Beau, who'd been awake all night and looked it, hurried forward to pull Natalie in his arms. The two held each other, taking and giving comfort.

Bernice, red-eyed and disheveled, huddled on a couch, needles clicking with each stitch of the brown afghan she was knitting. Will's ex-wife, Tori, a willowy blonde, sat next to her with an arm around their twelve-year-old daughter, Erin. Tears stained the girl's pretty, young face. Jasper was like a grandfather to her.

A wall-mounted television in the far corner was blaring an early-morning talk show, but no one in the room was paying it any heed. As he looked around for Will, Sky found himself wondering if the sheriff's men had been here, or if the press had caught wind of the shooting. If Jasper didn't make it, the authorities would be looking for a murderer.

Unshaven and haggard, Will stood alone by the window. Dark, blue-eyed, and muscular, he was the near image of his late father. Seeing Sky come in, Will crossed the room to join him.

For the past six years, since Bull Tyler's paralysis in a riding accident, Will had run the Rimrock. After Bull's recent death, Beau had come home for the funeral and stayed on as foreman, freeing Sky to manage the horses full time. But it had been Jasper's deep knowledge of the ranch—the how and why of things—that had sustained them all. Much as Jasper would be missed by the ranch family, Sky suspected Will would miss him most.

"He's down the left hallway. I'll show you where." Will opened the swinging doors that led from the waiting room to the ICU.

"Do we know who shot him?" Sky asked.

"Jasper says he didn't see a soul. When the bullet hit, he lost control of the ATV, and that's the last thing he remembers. The doctor thinks he may have a concussion." Will's lips tightened. "He'll have an oxygen mask on, but he can take it off long enough to talk to you. Just make sure you don't tire him."

"Don't worry. I'll make the visit a short one." Sky had long since accepted Will's need to manage things. Bull's nature had been much the same.

Alone now, Sky opened the door to Jasper's room and walked in. Propped in bed with a thin blanket covering his legs, the old man looked as frail as an ancient skeleton, ready to crumble at a touch. Monitors and IV lines formed a web around him, beeping and flashing. Anchored by a clip, a catheter bag hung over the side of the mattress.

Growing up among his Comanche mother's people, Sky had learned to accept age and death as a natural process. To truss up an elder in such a way, denying him the dignity of a good death, struck him as demeaning. But who was he to question the wisdom of the doctors?

A plastic cup, supplying oxygen, covered Jasper's nose and mouth. Above it, his pale eyes were open and surprisingly alert. One hand gestured feebly toward the oxygen mask, signaling that he wanted Sky to move it aside—easily done, since it was held in place by a strip of soft elastic.

"Isn't this a pickle? For two cents I'd yank off all this fancy rigging and walk out of here." Jasper's voice was weak. Will had been right about not tiring the old man. Every word seemed to cost him strength.

"Will said you wanted to see me," Sky said. "I got here as soon as I could."

"Thanks. Feelin' like hell. If the good Lord's ready to take me, I'm willin' to go. But I won't rest easy till I've told you a secret—" Jasper's voice dropped to a labored breath. "A secret I've kept all your life."

"You need to rest, Jasper." Why did Sky feel that he was about to hear something he was better off not knowing? "The secret can wait."

"No. You deserve the truth. And I'm the only one left who knows to tell you." Jasper's gaze flickered toward the open door. "Close it," he rasped.

Sky closed the door and returned to the bed. Jasper seemed to be struggling to breathe. Sky touched the oxygen mask in a silent question. The old man shook his head. "This won't take long," he said. "Lean closer. . . . That's better. You never knew about your father, did you, boy?"

"Only that he was white. And that he wouldn't marry my mother."

"Listen, then." Jasper was fighting to breathe. "I swear this is God's truth. Your father was Bull Tyler."

CHAPTER 2

Leaving Jasper in the care of a nurse, Sky walked back down the hall toward the waiting area. He passed through the swinging double doors into a roomful of strangers—Will and Beau, his half brothers; Erin, his niece; Tori and Natalie, his once and future sisters-in-law.

None of them knew the truth, of course. And he would never tell them—Sky had made that decision by the time he left Jasper's hospital room. Life would go on exactly as before. But whether he liked it or not, he would be looking at the family through different eyes. Tyler eyes.

"You're leaving?" Beau stopped him on his way to the outside door.

"Somebody needs to look after the ranch, and I can't be much help here. Keep me posted on how Jasper's doing." Sky turned aside. Right now all he wanted was to get away and sort things out for himself.

But what difference did it make now that he

knew? Sky wrestled with that question as he drove home. Bull Tyler hadn't wanted anybody to know he'd slept with a Comanche woman and fathered her son. Yet, when young Sky had wandered onto the ranch and asked for work, Bull had kept him on and, years later, left him a parcel of land. Had Bull been moved by affection—or, more likely, by guilt?

The more he thought about it, the darker Sky's mood became. Jasper had been too weak to tell him how it all happened. But any way you looked at it, the bottom line was, Bull Tyler had been too ashamed to acknowledge his half-breed son. And he hadn't cared enough to reach out and help the mother who'd died of cancer when Sky was three. Maybe if he had, things would have been different. She might even have lived.

The pickup's wheels spat dust as he pulled up to the long barn that housed the mares and foals. Across the yard, the rambling stone house appeared empty with the family gone.

But not quite empty.

Parked next to the porch, with the dust still settling around it, was a sleek black Corvette.

Sky struggled to ignore the jolt he felt. He'd met Lauren Prescott face-to-face just once. But that meeting stuck like a cholla spine in his memory. He'd picked her up in town at the Blue Coyote, half drunk and looking for trouble. The lady, who'd declined to give her name, had invited him to drive her car. They'd parked on an overlook and things were heating up when he'd realized the time and place wouldn't work for what they had in mind. He'd driven her back to town, bought her coffee, and set her on the road home. End of story. Or so he'd thought.

A few weeks later he'd learned she was the visiting

daughter of their jackass neighbor, Congressman Garn
Prescott. She was also a capable accountant. Beau had
hired her part time to create an online spreadsheet
and enter the data for the ranch accounts. That
would explain what she was doing here today.

So far, Sky had made himself scarce when she was
around. Any meeting between them was bound to be
awkward as hell. And her being Prescott's spoiled
princess daughter was a complication he didn't need.

But that hadn't stopped him from thinking about
her, picturing that tousled red hair and those thor-
oughbred legs. It hadn't stopped him from remembering the taste of her luscious mouth and the cool,
firm silk of her breast in the hollow of his hand.

Now she was here—alone. And the pain of what
he'd learned from Jasper was eating a hole in his gut.
The urge to break the rules and do something crazy
surged like wildfire in his veins. Damn it, *he wanted
her.* And if having her was a risk, so much the better.

Kicking caution into the dust, Sky raked a hand
through his black hair and strode toward the house.

Lauren was entering a line of data into the com-
puterized studbook and double-checking the numbers when she heard the creak of a floorboard. She
looked up.

He stood in the doorway, leaning against the
frame as if he'd been there awhile, just watching her.

Heat flooded Lauren's face, staining her cheeks
with crimson. "Can I . . . help you with something?"
Her voice betrayed the effect he was having on her.

He took his time, his gaze flicking over her white
linen blouse, unbuttoned at the throat and sheer
enough to show the outline of the pink lace bra be-

neath. His mouth twitched as if holding back some forbidden comment.

"As I recollect, you and I never finished what we started." He spoke in a slow drawl. "And I'm not a man to walk away from unfinished business."

Pulse skittering, Lauren rose and walked around the desk. She wanted to put him in his place, to inform him that the half-drunken floozy he'd picked up in the bar wasn't her real self. She had an education. She had goals and standards. And if Sky Fletcher thought he could just walk in here and expect her to fall into his arms . . .

They stood almost toe to toe. Hands on her hips, she glared up into his impossibly blue eyes.

Lord help her, she wanted the man. . . .

He waited with a knowing look that told her it was only a matter of time. Damn his complacency. It would serve him right to get his gorgeously chiseled face slapped hard enough to leave a bruise.

Even when her hand shot up, poised to strike, he didn't turn away. His steady gaze was strong but disturbingly gentle. Lauren felt something break loose inside her—the shards of her resistance as she gave in to what she wanted. Her arm caught his neck. She strained upward, yearning for the kiss she'd remembered since that night in her car—the night that had left her burning for more.

Unfinished business, he'd called it. And now their bodies demanded that they finish what they'd started—here and now.

His lips crushed hers with a savage tenderness, demanding all she had to give. As he jerked her close, a hot, hungry ache surged inside her. His erection pressed her belly through layers of denim. She tilted her hips to heighten the tingle, molding her thighs to the solid ridge—demandingly hard and so big that she found herself wondering how he would fit inside her.

With a low mutter he slid his hands into her jeans, cupping her buttocks to rock her against him. She moaned, shuddered, and gasped. The burst of sensation that ripped through her was a release that left her wanting more. Moisture soaked her panties. In every way, she was ready for him.

Drawing back, she reached down and fumbled with his belt buckle. With a rough laugh, he moved her hand aside and finished the job himself, dropping his Wranglers and sliding on protection in a blur of movement. Her hip-hugging designer jeans came down with a single jerk to scrunch around her boot tops, along with her lace thong panties. There'd be no time to undress all the way; no caresses, no tender words. Nothing but raw, hot sex.

Right now it was all she needed.

Bracing her against the desktop, he tilted her back at a low angle. Her hands gripped his shoulders as his swollen length slid deep inside her. "Oh . . ." she gasped as her body clasped his heat. "Oh, sweet . . ." Her voice trailed off into incoherent mutters as he pulled back and thrust in again and again. Her eyes closed. Her head fell back. "Don't stop," she whispered as her muscles spasmed around him. "Don't stop, don't stop, don't stop . . ."

When she spiraled back to earth and opened her eyes, he was grinning down at her. "Okay if I stop now, Miss Prescott?" His dark blue eyes held a mischievous twinkle.

"I think . . ." Lauren fumbled for words. Despite feeling warm, rumpled, and deliciously wicked, she could sense reality closing in. She sat up as he turned away to reassemble himself. "I think what you'd better do is leave," she said.

"That's exactly what I plan to do." He tucked in his shirt and fastened his belt buckle. "We've both got work, and I don't know how much longer this house will be empty—so I suggest you pull up your britches before somebody comes home."

He walked to the office door, then paused to look back at her, one black eyebrow quirked upward. "About that unfinished business . . . This was a lot of fun, but whether it happens again is up to you. You know where to find me."

As the door closed softly behind him, Lauren squelched the urge to pick up the nearest heavy object and fling it after him. Furious tears stung her eyes as she pulled up her jeans. She'd had enough experience with men to know that once they'd scratched that itch, it was back to business as usual. But Sky had been so abrupt, almost cold. She felt as if she'd just been doused with ice water.

Well, never mind, she'd learned her lesson. And if he was expecting her to come around begging for more, the man would grow old waiting. There'd be ice skating in hell before she let down her guard with Sky Fletcher again.

All the same, his brusqueness had stung her.

Walking back around the desk, she sank into the chair and stared at the computer screen. She didn't feel much like working. But she wasn't ready to go home and face her father. And in her present frame of mind, driving into town was probably a bad idea.

She'd taken this job, in addition to accounting work for the Prescott ranch, in order to add experience to her skimpy résumé. But on the days when her father was at home—browbeating her about her reputation and the need to take an active part in his campaign, the Tyler office had become her refuge. At twenty-two, she was determined to build her own future. And that future didn't include becoming a pawn in Garn Prescott's political game.

On her first day here Lauren had recognized the steel blue Ford pickup—the one she'd first seen parked outside that honkytonk in Blanco Springs. She'd learned from Beau that its lean, dark, and oh-so-hot owner was Sky Fletcher, the Rimrock's legendary horse whisperer.

That night at the Blue Coyote she hadn't even known his name. She'd known only that she'd hit bottom, and the fast-track cure for the pain was to get drunk and get laid. She'd been partway to drunk when the sexy cowboy had shown up in her booth. Sin-black hair, cobalt eyes, and a slow, melting smile . . . It was as if the devil had read her mind and granted her wish.

But nothing had happened—except that she'd thrown herself at him and made a fool of herself. And now she'd done it again.

It wasn't supposed to be like this. She was supposed to have married the man she loved and settled down to raising the family she'd wanted. But Mike's suicide, just a year ago, had sent her into a downward spiral from which she was still crashing.

That's why she'd come to Texas, a place she barely remembered, with a father she hadn't seen in years. She'd hoped the change would help her heal. But she should have known better. The bouts of reckless behavior had followed her here.

Until she'd regained control of her life, the last thing she needed was another man—especially a blue-eyed heartbreaker with a knack for pushing her libido over the edge and then walking away.

Clicking the mouse to refresh the computer screen, she forced herself to focus on her work. Sky Fletcher may have shot her over the moon, but she'd fallen back to earth now. The sexy horse whisperer had made a fool of her for the last time.

CHAPTER 3

It was late afternoon by the time the black Corvette pulled away from the house and sped down the dusty lane toward the highway.

Sky was in the smaller of the two round pens, working a year-old bay gelding on a lead. He heard the growl of the engine and the crunch of tires spitting gravel, but he didn't turn around and look. After the way he'd walked out on her, telling her she'd know where to find him, Miss Lauren Prescott wouldn't be throwing him any good-bye kisses.

Not that he was proud of the way he'd treated her. For the most part, he liked to think of himself as a gentleman. But today he hadn't been in a gentlemanly frame of mind. He'd needed a rush to fill the aching void inside him. And Lauren, so sexy and vulnerable—and so damned willing—had been there.

Was there any excuse for having treated the congressman's daughter like a common tramp? Had he wanted to make somebody—anybody—hurt like he was hurting? Had he wanted to prove that he could have sex with a snooty, rich white girl and walk away without feeling a thing—the way Bull Tyler had walked away from his mother?

A powerful yank on the lead rope reminded him that he needed to stay focused. Sky's method of starting young horses demanded concentration. This promising colt deserved the best he had to give.

"Easy boy . . ." he murmured, using touch and voice to create a sense of safety. "That's it. You're doing fine. . . ."

He ended the training session by rubbing the horse down with his bare hands and turning it into the paddock. By now the afternoon was getting on, and he still hadn't heard how Jasper was doing. Sky had worried about the old cowboy all day. He'd asked Will to call if there was any news. But if Jasper had taken a turn for the worse, Will would have more urgent concerns on his mind.

Deciding to make the call himself, Sky reached for his cell phone. But no sooner had he fished it out of his pocket than it rang. The caller was Will. Bracing himself for bad news, Sky pushed the answer button.

"Will? What's happening? How's Jasper?"

"He's one tough old buzzard." Will's voice sounded tired but upbeat. "The doctor says his vitals have stabilized and his lungs are starting to clear. He's grumpy as hell, but I guess that's a good sign."

"Thank God." Sky felt himself breathe again.

"Bernice wants to stay the night at the hospital, and Erin's going with her mother. But Beau and I will be coming home before long to get some rest."

"Anything I can do?" Sky asked.

"You've done plenty, staying to take care of things.

Since Bernice won't be there to cook, we're picking up a couple of pizzas on the way home. We'll make a bachelor night of it, maybe unwind by watching some baseball for as long as we can stay awake. We're hoping you can join us."

Could he handle that? Sharing an evening with his half brothers? But nothing had changed except what he knew, Sky reminded himself. He'd already made the decision to carry on as usual. That would include joining Will and Beau in the house for pizza and beer.

"Thanks, I'll plan on it," Sky said. "And tell Jasper I'll stop by and see him tomorrow."

After Will ended the call, Sky stood by the paddock fence studying the colts. He could learn a lot just from watching them—which ones were bold, which ones were docile, which ones were light on their feet . . . Knowing each horse was essential to training. Most days he had no trouble staying focused on his work. But today was different.

Your father was Bull Tyler.

Jasper's words burned like a fresh brand, still smoking from the iron. When he saw the old man again, should he ask for more details? Or would he be wiser to let those secrets stay buried for good?

Beau and Will drove in around six, bone tired but in good spirits. Jasper was doing better. The bullet wound had missed his vital organs, and his pneumonia was responding to treatment. If he continued to improve, the doctors would let him go home sometime next week.

"Did the sheriff come by?" Sky asked as Beau slid the pizzas into the oven to reheat them.

"*Acting* Sheriff Sweeney showed up this afternoon."
Will fished three cold Tecates out of the fridge and
popped the tab on one of them. "He asked Jasper a
few questions and took the slug as evidence—from
what I could tell it looked like a 32-20 from one of
those old lever action rifles. I told him about the tire
tracks and cigarette butts I'd found on ranch property, but all I got from him was one of those blank
looks. Hell, I don't even know if he recognized the
bullet."

"Abner Sweeney isn't exactly the brightest bulb in
the pack," Beau said. "Axelrod may have ended up a
crook and a murderer, but at least he wasn't stupid.
He caught some bad hombres over the years, before
he crossed the line."

Sky nodded his agreement. Sweeney, a former
deputy, had been appointed to replace longtime
sheriff Hoyt Axelrod, who was awaiting trial for mul-
tiple murders—including the deaths of Natalie's es-
tranged husband, Slade, and Sky's young cousin,
Lute. Axelrod had shot Sky as well and nearly killed
him. The wound, from a high-powered sniper rifle,
had left a scar that still throbbed after too many
hours in the saddle.

If convicted, Axelrod could face the death penalty.
But there were rumors that he might take a plea
deal—a life sentence in exchange for what he knew
about organized crime activities in the county. Not
that a man with Axelrod's law enforcement background could expect to live long in a Texas prison.

"I hear Sweeney's running for the permanent job
this fall," Will said. "My vote's going to whoever runs
against him."

"Sweeney and Garn Prescott. The cream of our
fair county's political crop." Beau took his beer and

wandered into the office. He came out a moment later with something in his hand. "Looks like Lauren was here," he said. "I recognize this little gold earring of hers. What I can't figure out is what it was doing *behind* the computer."

Sky willed his expression to freeze. "She was here most of the afternoon, working on your spreadsheet. I stopped in and said hello to her."

Beau grinned. "So the two of you finally met. It's about time. That young lady's been mighty curious about you, asking me all sorts of questions."

"Don't get any ideas, Beau. Lauren's a sharp girl, and damned good-looking. But I know better than to mess around with Garn Prescott's daughter."

The lie made Sky cringe, but he could hardly tell the truth. Beau and Will would split their sides laughing if they knew. He might not mind making himself the butt of their jokes, but he couldn't do the same to Lauren.

"Sure you do." Beau tossed the dainty earring in the air, catching it in his fist. "I'll leave this in the desk drawer. If you see her before I do, you can tell her it's there."

"Fine." Not that he expected to see her again—even though the memory of that afternoon triggered a disturbing heat rush to his jeans. Hanging around when she came over to work would only make her uncomfortable. Annoy her enough and Beau would lose the help he needed. Even if she wasn't Garn Prescott's daughter, Sky knew he'd be smart to keep his distance.

"Pizza's hot. Let's watch the game a while." With Will carrying the flat cardboard boxes and Beau lugging an extra six-pack of Tecate, they trailed into the den. Beau switched on the 48-inch flat-screen TV. Sinking into the big leather sectional, they put the boxes on the coffee table and wolfed down the pizza without the bother of plates. The baseball game was in its seventh inning, with a wide spread in the score and not much action. After a while the commentary faded into the background.

"So who do you figure shot Jasper?" Sky asked.

Will shrugged. "My money's still on drug smugglers. But cartel types would've used a heavier weapon, like an M-16 or a Glock. And they'd have made sure Jasper was dead. Given the small slug the doctor dug out of the old man, I'd say our smugglers are kids, or lowlifes using whatever gun they can get their hands on. Whoever they are, they're dangerous. Nobody's going out there alone till they're stopped."

Beau set his beer on the table. "Well, since we can't count on Sweeney, I'd say that's our job. Who's for riding out to where we found Jasper tomorrow morning for a look around?"

"I'll go with you," Sky offered. "Then, after chores are done, I want to run into Lubbock. I can check on Jasper and bring Bernice home. She must be worn out."

"Then I'll stay here and keep an eye on things." Will finished the last slice of pepperoni pizza. "What about the shotgun Jasper was using? Was it still on the ATV when you found it?"

"No sign of it," Sky said. "Either it fell out or it was taken—which could mean our shooter would have to get close enough to grab it. If we could find tracks, that would at least give us something to go on."

"Let's plan to go at first light. The earlier we get there, the fresher any clues will be." Beau glanced toward the TV. "Hey, look, Rodriguez is up with two on base."

By the time the game had progressed two more innings, Beau and Will had both fallen asleep. Sky gathered up the remains of the pizza and beer and took them to the kitchen trash. When he came back, they were still snoring, Will with his head sagging forward, his dark-stubbled chin resting on his chest, and Beau sprawled over one end of the sectional, head back, mouth open.

A strange tenderness crept over Sky—the realization that if he'd had his choice of all the brothers on earth, these men were the two he would have picked. But as things stood, they would never know. The truth would change everything, and not likely for the better.

Dismissing the thought, he switched off the game, dimmed the lights, and left the house.

The next morning Sky stepped outside to a leaden dawn. For a moment he stood on the porch of the brick duplex he shared with Jasper, gazing southeast, toward the hundred acres Bull had left him in his will. The land wasn't part of the Rimrock. It lay along the ranch's eastern border, like the heel of a boot. Bull had bought the prime section from the absentee neighbor for what must have been a handsome sum—bought it as a legacy for the blood son he'd never acknowledged in life.

Sky had ridden across the land in the past, admiring its grassy, wooded hills and spring-fed creek, never dreaming it could be his. But since the reading of the will he had yet to revisit the place. He was still coming to terms with the gift Bull Tyler had left him.

Except for Jasper, no one else, not even Will and Beau, knew about the land. At first Sky had questioned whether he deserved it. Now he found himself wondering if he even wanted it. He could sell it for a good price, return the money to the ranch, and be free of any obligation to the father who'd been too ashamed to claim him as his own. He had his pride, after all.

But the decision would have to wait. This morning he'd agreed to ride out with Beau to look at the place where Jasper had been shot. It was time they got moving.

He was walking out to get the horses when Will hailed him from the front porch. "Sky! Get in here! You've got to see what's on the news!"

Spurred by the urgency in his voice, Sky sprinted across the yard to the house. Will was already headed back inside. "Hurry," he said. "The TV's on in the den."

The commercial break was just ending when Sky walked in.

Beau, still rumpled and unshaven, was perched on the edge of the couch, drinking coffee and staring at the television screen. Will, freshly showered and dressed, handed Sky a steaming cup.

"Back to our breaking news story." The Amarillo newscaster was a fiftyish man with a bad toupee. "Former Blanco County Sheriff Hoyt Axelrod, awaiting trial for murder, assault, and conspiracy, was found dead inside his cell this morning. The cause of death has yet to be determined, but there appeared to be no sign of foul play. For more, let's go to Mindi Thacker outside the Blanco County Jail."

The curvy blonde looked as if she'd done her hair and makeup in the news chopper, which sat on the landing pad behind her. Her porcelain smile seemed out of place in the grim dawn light. "The story's still unfolding here, Bill. A guard, making a routine check of the prisoners early this morning, found Axelrod lying on the floor of his cell. Paramedics were called, but the former sheriff was unresponsive. He was declared dead at 4:43 a.m. Preliminary assumption, pending the medical examiner's report, is that death was due to natural causes."

"Natural causes!" Beau slammed his cup on the table, sloshing his coffee. "That's a joke! Somebody got to the bastard before he could make a plea deal and talk."

"In his cell? That would take some doing," Will said.

"That doesn't mean it couldn't be done. A man Axelrod's size and age is a likely candidate for high blood pressure or diabetes. A switch in his meds would do the trick, or something in his food, even some kind of injection if they could incapacitate him first. Not that much to it—just a matter of enough money changing hands."

Sky's gaze met Beau's across the room. Nobody in the ranch family would grieve over Axelrod's death— least of all Beau, who'd nearly gone to prison when the sheriff tried to frame him for killing Slade Haskell, Natalie's abusive husband.

"You know this isn't over," Beau said. "Hoyt Axelrod died for the same reason Slade died, the same reason Lute and that poor little waitress died. He knew too much, and he would've spilled his guts to save himself from the death penalty. That's why he had to be silenced."

"But it was Axelrod who killed the others." Will seemed to be playing devil's advocate.

"This is bigger than Axelrod," Beau said. "Whoever's pulling the strings is still out there."

Stella Rawlins turned away from the big-screen TV above the bar and lit a Marlboro to celebrate. Hoyt Axelrod was dead and couldn't implicate her. She could breathe easy again.

"You gonna tell me how you pulled that off?" Her husky half brother Nick was perched on a bar stool, sipping coffee and munching a stale doughnut. The morning sun, slanting through half-closed plastic shutters, gleamed on the black Maori-style tattoos that ringed his shaved head.

Stella blew a lazy smoke ring. "The less you know, the better, Nicky. For you as well as for me."

"Gotcha." Nick carried his cup behind the bar to rinse it.

Nick, who went by Nigel these days, had been a runner for the Romanian mob in New Jersey. After snitching on them in a plea deal, he'd been forced into hiding. Stella had taken him in two years ago when she'd bought the Blue Coyote Bar in Blanco Springs. He'd proved his worth as her bartender and bouncer. But she knew better than to trust him—or anybody else—with her secrets.

She'd done pretty well for herself here in Blanco. The town was off the beaten track but with easy access to the Mexican border. Trading Texas guns for Mexican drugs had made her a tidy profit. But if she'd learned one thing, it was to keep her hands clean and leave the dirty work to others. So far it had worked. As far as the law was concerned, her record was spotless.

Her business depended on connections and the exchange of favors. Money, sex, and fear were valuable tools, and Stella knew how to use them all. But there'd been some collateral damage along the way—Jess Warner, the waitress who'd stumbled on one secret too many; Slade Haskell, who'd become a useless, wife-beating drunk; Lute Fletcher, the half-breed boy who'd gotten too greedy for his own good; and now Hoyt Axelrod, the sheriff whose one big mistake had been getting himself arrested.

Hoyt had been a wheezing walrus in bed. But his skills with a long-range rifle had come in handy. He wouldn't be an easy man to replace.

Turning back to stub out her cigarette, Stella caught her reflection in the mirror behind the bar. Without makeup she looked old and tired. Her flame-colored hair needed a fresh dye job, and the crow's feet were deepening at the corners of her eyes. She was forty-six years old. How much longer could she work this racket and get away with it? She needed something more. She needed security.

A Dallas crime family was looking to expand its reach. They'd sent out feelers about her Mexican ties—a tentative invitation for her to join them. Stella had always prided herself on flying solo, but having an organization to back her wouldn't be all bad. They'd demand a cut, of course, but in return she'd get protection and, if needed, access to a reliable hit man.

But she couldn't go begging to them, or give them the keys to an operation they could easily take over.

She needed something to offer them—some sphere of influence uniquely hers, to keep power in her own corner.

The early-morning newscast had ended. Stella was about to switch off the TV when a paid political ad came on the screen. The ad was a low-budget job, just some talking head running for reelection to Congress. The candidate, a silver-haired man, wasn't bad looking, but he could have used better lighting and a decent makeup artist. And why would he be plugging for votes at an hour when so few voters would be watching? Maybe his campaign was short on funds. Prime time had to be expensive.

Nick was watching her from behind the bar. "I've seen that look," he said. "Why are you smiling?"

"Because I just got one helluva good idea."

"What kind of idea?" he asked.

Laughing, Stella poured herself a fresh cup of coffee. "As I said, little brother, the less you know, the better."

Sky and Beau had taken the ranch pickup to check the place where Jasper had been shot. At this early hour, a whisper of coolness lingered on the morning air. They rode with the pickup windows rolled down, the air blasting their faces, drinking in the freshness before the rising sun could burn it away. Beau was at the wheel, Sky scouting the parched landscape for anything that looked out of place.

"We don't even know for sure if we're dealing with smugglers," Sky said.

"True," Beau said. "But somebody's been leaving tracks and cigarette butts out here. Something's going on—I'd say either drug running or illegal immigrants. Whatever it was, Jasper must've gotten too close."

"So why didn't they make sure he was dead?" Sky argued. "I'm with Will. I'd bet on a bunch of fool kids who got scared and ran when they saw what they'd done."

"Maybe we'll find some answers this morning." Beau steered the pickup around a jutting rock. A collared lizard skittered clear of the wheels. In the near distance, swallows skimmed and darted above the muddy seep where Jasper had been found. They scattered as the truck drew closer.

"Tell me something." Beau's voice had taken on a mischievous note. "How did that little earring really manage to fall out of Lauren's ear and roll behind the computer?"

Sky glanced away to hide a flush of heat. "None of your damned business," he said.

Beau guffawed as he pulled the truck to a stop. "Have it your way. Your secret's safe with me. But if the congressman gets wind of it, you'd better have a place to run."

"I wouldn't back down from Garn Prescott—not even if I wanted his daughter, which I don't."

"Then you've got more pride than sense."

"Leave it alone, Beau." Sky opened the door and swung out of the truck. He hadn't been here since the night before last, when they'd found Jasper. He was curious to inspect the spot by daylight. And he was anxious to escape Beau's ribbing.

"I see plenty of tracks." Beau studied the ground. "But most of them look like yours and mine."

"We had to free Jasper. And then I had to come back and load the ATV. If I'd been thinking about clues, I'd have been more careful." Sky crouched to look closer. "The paramedics left tracks, too. See, here and here? They were wearing sneakers. But unless the shotgun fell off the ATV, somebody had to get close enough to steal it. Here's where the roll bar landed. They would've had to reach—"

He broke off as he found the track. A dozen paces short of the seep, it was almost obscured by the others. It was the shallow imprint of a cowboy boot, the toe long and pointed, the sole and heel worn around the edges, maybe a narrow size 8. Not a big man; maybe even a boy. Or . . .

A sense of unease crept over Sky. He didn't like what he was seeing. And he didn't like where his thoughts were leading him.

"Let's see what else we can find," he said, rising. "Maybe we'll get lucky."

"Here." Beau had started a wider circle of the spring. He'd dropped to a crouch and was gazing at the ground, where the crushed stub of a marijuana joint, hand-wrapped in brown paper, lay in the dust.

"We'd better collect this." Beau had worked for the DEA between his army stint and his return to the Rimrock. This was his area of expertise. He whipped out his cell phone and snapped a photo. "If they were smoking weed, they could've been dealing it, too."

"I saw a sandwich bag in the truck." Sky found what he was looking for and returned. After turning the plastic bag inside out, Beau used it to scoop up the joint.

"With luck it'll have some traceable DNA on it," he said.

"You're not going to turn it over to Abner Sweeney, are you?" Sky asked.

"Sweeney wouldn't know DNA from his own rear end." Beau rose, slipping the bagged evidence into the pocket of his shirt. "I'll hang on to this until we learn more. It'll come in handy for matching if a suspect turns up."

Sky bit back what he'd been about to say. It was too soon to borrow trouble, too soon to make assumptions. He'd need to do more investigating on his own before he voiced his suspicions. But in the end he knew where his loyalties lay. Somebody had trespassed on ranch property and shot an irreplaceable old man—and somebody, whoever it might be, would have to pay.

"Maybe I can find the casing from the shot," he said. "If we don't collect it now, it's liable to end up in some pack rat's midden."

"Good luck with that," Beau said. "It could be anywhere within a couple of hundred yards, and we need to get back before long."

"Give me fifteen minutes."

"How about a bet? If you don't find the casing, you'll tell me about your encounter with the delicious Miss Prescott."

"And if I do find it? Forget the bet. There's nothing I want." Sky started with the place where Jasper's ATV had wrecked and backtracked from there. Before shooting into the seep, the tire tracks zigzagged erratically in the dust, bouncing against rocks and flying over hollows. Twenty yards back, the tracks changed to form a controlled line. This, then, would most likely be where Jasper had been when the bullet struck him.

Sky studied the spot, calculating where the shot would have come from. The bullet had struck Jasper from the front, which would eliminate most of the area behind him and to the sides. Since Jasper claimed he hadn't seen anyone, the shooter had probably hidden behind something—all guesswork, but if it led him to the casing, he would know he'd been right.

By now the sun was coming up, its rim a blinding streak above the plains. Jasper had gone out early. Had he been facing into the sun when he was shot? Shading his eyes, Sky scanned to the horizon. A big clump of mesquite stood within easy shooting distance. Sprinting toward it, he circled and came in from behind.

This had to be the place. There were plenty of tracks—the smaller, worn cowboy boots he'd noticed earlier and a larger pair that looked more like a motorcycle boot. There were motorcycle tracks as well. Sky studied the tread pattern, setting it in his mind. He thought about calling Beau over, but Beau was impatient to leave. He would look around for the casing and call it good.

Just behind the mesquite clump, he could see a cluster of tracks, as if someone had crouched there. Most of these tracks were made by the smaller boots. But the larger tracks were here, too. Had the shot been fired from this spot? Following Beau's example, Sky used his cell phone to snap a picture.

At the base of a rock, the sunlight glinted on a bit of brass. It was the casing from the bullet. Sky photographed it in place, then picked it up with his clean handkerchief. Maybe he should have made that bet with Beau after all.

Only as he was turning to go did he notice another object, lying in the dust. As soon as he saw it, Sky realized what it was.

Without remembering to take a picture, he picked it up. His stomach clenched. It was a folded two-blade pocket knife—small, cheap, and old. The handle was covered in plastic made to look like mother of pearl. Sky turned the knife over, knowing what he would see. Two initials, darkened from years of handling, were scratched into the plastic.

S.F.

They were Sky's own initials. He'd carved them himself, with the point of a nail, as a boy of ten.

CHAPTER 4

"May I join you, Lauren?" Congressman Garn Prescott pulled out a chair and sat down at the dining room table. Lauren smeared a dab of strawberry jam on her wheat toast. She'd hoped to finish her breakfast and escape before he came downstairs. So far this wasn't her lucky day.

The Mexican cook who came in part time brought him a fresh carafe of coffee and a plate of bacon, fried eggs, and grits. This morning the congressman was dressed in a baby blue shirt with a bolo tie. His striking silver hair was carefully overcombed to hide the thinning spot on top. He was only fifty-two, but up close he looked older. Too much Texas sun had splotched his fair skin. Too much social drinking and greasy food had left him with an old man's belly on his lanky frame.

"I understand you spent yesterday afternoon working for the Tylers," he said. "I was hoping maybe you and Beau—"

"Beau's engaged—and he's in love with his fiancée."

"Well, you're spending a lot of time over there."

"So? The Tylers pay me decently and the experience will look good on my résumé. Besides, Bernice makes the best coffee in the whole blessed state of Texas." Lauren glanced away to hide the blaze in her cheeks. If her father knew what she'd been up to yesterday with Sky, he'd have her on the next plane back to Maryland.

If she'd dropped her panties for a man with money and influence, the congressman might have secretly approved. But Sky Fletcher had no fortune, no pedigree, and no political clout. The fact that he was part Comanche and worked with his hands for somebody else would be a total strikeout in her father's book.

Could that be one reason she found Sky such a compelling challenge?

Yesterday, after he'd left her steaming, she'd vowed never to go near Sky again. But she'd been angry and hurt. Now that she'd had time to lick her wounds, damned if she wasn't intrigued. She found herself wanting to know more about the fabled horse whisperer of the Rimrock, and wondering whether any woman alive could corral him.

"Why should you bother with a career, anyway?" her father was saying. "You're pretty enough to snag a rich husband and be set for life. And right now I could use your help with my campaign. A lovely young thing like you could get me more attention from the press, as well as opening doors and wallets. Take that fund-raising barbecue I'm staging tomorrow night in Lubbock—the one where the former Secretary of Agriculture will be speaking. You could make an impression on some important people. I hear the governor's stepson will be there. He's good-looking and newly single."

Lauren stifled a groan. "Please don't start on this again, Dad. I've earned a college degree, and I *want* a career. I came here to get some work experience so I can apply for a real job. Between keeping the books for this ranch and what I'm doing for Beau Tyler, I don't have time to get involved in your campaign. And husband hunting isn't even in the picture. I'm still getting over Mike."

"How long does that take? It's been a year, dammit! It's high time you were moving on, getting married. You need a man to satisfy your needs and keep you respectable. Otherwise you'll end up like your mother—"

"Stop it!" Lauren rose, quivering. "Whatever my mother did, you probably drove her to it. And if you say one more word against her, I'll go upstairs, pack my bags, and be on the next plane east."

He sagged in his chair, shaking his head. "Oh, hell, never mind. I still maintain I'm right, but it's not worth spoiling the day. Sit down. Finish your breakfast, and we'll say no more about it."

Lauren exhaled and surrendered, knowing that storming off would only make things worse. She'd been four years old when her mother had left Garn Prescott and moved back to Maryland to be near her family. In the years that followed, Fiona Wentworth Prescott, blessed with stunning beauty and family money, had flitted from party to party and from lover to lover. But she'd always been there for her daughter. Lauren had never wanted for affection or any material thing that caught her fancy.

Fiona's death in a car crash when Lauren was fifteen

had been the most shattering event of her youth. Her cold, practical grandparents had finished raising her, while the father she barely remembered had remained a stranger.

In most ways, Garn Prescott was still a stranger.

"What are you looking at?" he asked her, switching to a less volatile subject.

"That photograph above the sideboard. I've never paid attention to it before. When was it taken?" Lauren was making small talk now, but the picture, mounted in a rustic knotted pine frame, was intriguing. The faces and figures were slightly blurred, as if the image had been blown up from a smaller photo. It showed a summer gathering—a party or picnic—on the front steps of the ranch house.

Rising with her coffee, Lauren moved in for a closer look. One figure was unmistakable. Standing in the center of the photo, dressed in hunting clothes and holding a glass in one hand, was a smiling Ronald Reagan.

"He was still president then," her father said. "Some party bigwigs invited him to come bird hunting, and my dad volunteered to host a picnic here afterward. See, that's me standing next to the great man. I was still a pup, not even married yet, but that was the day I decided I wanted to go into politics. That's why I hung the picture, to remind me."

Lauren studied the photo. Her father would have been about twenty. She recognized the wavy blond hair and slightly receding chin. His parents, both of them gone now, were standing on the other side of the president—Ferguson Prescott, short and thickset, with a bristling mustache and a gaze fierce enough to cut steel; his pale wife, Edith, looking drained as always. Ferg had made her pregnant five times. Only Garn had survived.

There were other people in the photo—neighbors, party dignitaries, and Secret Service agents skulking in the background. At the edge of the picture, a tall, slender young woman in an apron held a tray of cocktail glasses. It appeared she'd meant to step back out of camera range but hadn't moved far enough.

"Who's that woman?" Lauren asked.

"The dark one? Nobody. Just the maid."

"She's beautiful. Look at those dark eyes, and those high cheekbones. She could have been a model. What ever happened to her?"

Prescott shrugged. "Who knows? After this picture was taken, I went away to school. When I came home for my mother's funeral, she was here, but the next time I came back she was gone. I never asked about her. Why should I?" Prescott slathered butter on another slice of toast. "That fund-raiser tomorrow night—is it negotiable?"

"What do you mean, negotiable?" She turned back toward him, setting her coffee cup on the table.

"I don't have the time or energy to spend the whole summer fighting with you, Lauren. So I'm prepared to bargain. Tell me something you want, within reason of course. Go to the fund-raiser with me, and it's yours."

Lauren took a moment to think. Much as she disliked giving in, her father's offer made sense. The constant friction was wearing them both down. Why not go to the fund-raiser if it meant getting something she wanted?

But what did she want? The idea—so bold that

it kicked her pulse into high gear—sprang out of nowhere.

"Only this one fund-raiser, right?"

"For now," he said. "So what do you want in exchange?"

A thoughtful smile tugged at her mouth. "I haven't ridden since high school," she said. "I want to take it up again. And I want my pick of any horse on the ranch."

Garn Prescott remained at the table after Lauren left, sipping his coffee and sopping up his eggs with his bread, the way he'd liked to do as a boy. He reached for the carafe to refill his empty coffee cup, then changed his mind and pulled a thin silver flask out of his hip pocket. He was sipping the bourbon he'd poured when his cell phone rang. The name on the display was that of Ted Abernathy, his campaign manager.

"Howdy, Ted." His voice took on the folksy tone he used with his constituents. "Yup, I'm good to go for the fund-raiser. Even bringin' my pretty daughter along to sweeten up the contributors. Are we set with the barbecue?" He paused as the voice crackled on the other end of the call. "What? They want payment in advance? The hell you say!"

Prescott's fingers snapped the handle on his late second wife's Limoges cup, spilling a trickle of bourbon on the table. He'd planned to reimburse the caterer out of funds raised at the event. To pay in advance would drain his war chest down to pocket change at a time when he needed every penny. Hoyt Axelrod's arrest had taken care of his most worrisome opponent, but other candidates were crawling into the open like rats out of a haystack—and one of them was even a damned war hero. Prescott was fighting for his political life. And the one weapon he desperately needed—cash—had become as scarce as rain in this drought-ravaged summer. Once he got the nomination, the party machine would kick in. But until then—with the nomination in peril, the conservatives deserting him and the primary less than two months away—he was on his own.

All the more reason word mustn't get out that his campaign was hard up for money.

"Pay the bastards, Ted," he sighed. "If there's not enough in the account, let me know and I'll dig into my own pocket. Let's hope we can make it up at the fund-raiser."

"Will do." Abernathy's voice came through as the static cleared. "Did you hear that Hoyt Axelrod died in his cell?"

"What? Hell, no!"

"It's been on the news all morning. Since he was set to run against you, making a statement would get you some press. I can write it up for you—good lawman gone bad, the final tragedy, whatever."

"Fine. E-mail it to me and set things up with the TV station—maybe that hot little blonde, Mindi Thacker, could do an interview. At least she's good-looking." Prescott hung up the phone and poured himself another three fingers of bourbon. The way the day was starting out, he was going to need it.

Sky pulled the pickup into the hospital parking lot and switched off the ignition. As he turned sideways to swing down from the driver's seat, he felt the press of the little pocketknife he'd slipped into his jeans. All the way to Lubbock, he'd been wrestling with his conscience. Sooner or later he'd have to show the knife to Beau and Will and tell them what it meant. But did he have to do it today, or could he leave it till he'd had the chance to check things out for himself?

Either way, Sky knew the conclusion would likely be the same. Jasper had been shot and left for dead by a member of his own family.

For years Sky had struggled to put his ugly childhood behind him. But there could be no denying who he was and where he'd come from—especially when pieces of his past kept resurfacing in the present.

After losing his mother, young Sky had gone to live with her brother's family in Oklahoma. His aunt had descended from a long line of Comancheros—border bandits who'd dealt in guns, liquor, and slaves. Their lawless traits had filtered down through the generations. Smuggling, theft, forgery, grift, and abuse were a daily part of life in the Fletcher household. At fifteen, Sky had run away, his back scarred by blows from his uncle's belt.

Two of the children, a girl and a boy, had been born after Sky's arrival. Years later, hoping to save at least one of them, Sky had invited the boy to come to work on the Rimrock. But the intervention had come too late. Lute had proved as rotten as the others.

As for the girl . . .

Sky's thoughts scattered as he stepped into the hospital waiting room. Bernice, looking like she'd aged ten years, was dozing in the rocker, her knitting in a tumble on the floor. The poor woman had been here ever since Jasper was brought in. She needed to go home and get some rest.

Scooping up the yarn and knitting needles, Sky laid them gently in her lap. She opened her pale eyes. "Oh, hullo," she mumbled. "Is it daytime yet?"

"Yes, and I'm here to drive you home," Sky said. "How's Jasper?"

"All right, I think. He had some pain in the night. But they gave him some pills that seemed to help. When I looked in on him early this morning he was sleeping like a baby."

"What do you say we go check on him? Then we can head home." Sky helped her to stand. He could have gone to see Jasper alone, but he knew Bernice wouldn't leave until she was sure her brother was all right.

She took his arm as they moved down the hall. They found Jasper sound asleep. His color was good, the oxygen mask replaced by a tube with a clip. Bernice tiptoed to his bedside and touched his hand, as if to reassure herself that her brother was still warm. Turning, she gave Sky a tired smile. "We can go now," she said.

In the truck she was quiet. "He'll be all right, Bernice," Sky said. "Your brother is one tough old cowboy."

"I know that. But we can't all be tough forever."

"How come Jasper never had a family? I've wondered, but I never asked. Figured that was his own business."

"His sweetheart died—drowned in a flood three days before their wedding. Pretty little thing—Sally was her name. Jasper never got over her. But he has a family—Will and Beau, you and me, Erin, and everyone on the ranch. That's his family."

Ignoring the tightness in his throat, Sky swung the truck onto the main highway. "Did you know Will and Beau's mother?" he asked.

"I never did. She died a few weeks before I came to cook and take care of the boys. You know how it happened, don't you?"

Sky had heard the story—how Bull's wife, Susan, had been driving home from town and blown a front tire on her car. Out of control, she'd crossed the median into the path of a speeding semi-truck and died in the crash.

"And Bull—I know he never remarried. Were there other women in his life?" Sky sensed he'd strayed onto dangerous ground.

"Not that I know of. When I met him he was still half-crazy with grief." Bernice shook her head. "Jasper told me a little about Bull's wife. She was from quality folk back East. They disinherited her when she married Bull, but the two of them were too much in love to care. I don't think Bull ever got over losing her."

"I see." Sky sank into silence. He wouldn't be asking Jasper any more questions about Bull and his mother. He already knew the answers. Marie Joslyn Fletcher had been there when Bull needed a woman. When he was done using her, he'd walked away without a thought.

Had his mother been in love with the grieving rancher? But why even wonder? The past was dead and couldn't be changed. And Sky had more pressing concerns in the here and now. Like the knife he'd found and the story behind it—a story he was duty bound to share with Will and Beau. He would tell them tonight, before things got any more complicated than they already were.

Glancing over at Bernice, he saw that she'd fallen sound asleep.

Bernice had offered to cook supper that night, but Will and Beau insisted that she put her feet up and take it easy. They could drive into Blanco Springs for burgers and shakes.

"Come with us, Sky," Will said as they walked out to the truck. "I'll be dropping Beau at Natalie's after we eat, and then picking up Erin at Tori's place, so it won't be a long night. But it'll be a nice break."

Sky could've warmed some leftover chili in his own small kitchen, but an evening in town did sound like a good idea. And it would give him a chance to tell the brothers about the pocketknife. They might wonder why he hadn't told them earlier. For that there was just one honest excuse—he'd needed time to think.

Blanco Springs, the county seat, was a twenty-minute drive from the ranch. Its population of 3,082 souls, not counting those who lived on surrounding farms, was served by a gas station and garage; an old-fashioned movie theatre; a grocery store; the Burger Shack, which served sandwiches, shakes, and pizza; and the Blue Coyote, which welcomed cowboys, truckers, and anyone else old enough to drink. Will's ex-wife, Tori, a lawyer, lived in Blanco. So did Beau's fiancée, Natalie, who had her veterinary practice there.

Sky had thought about telling his story in the truck. But with the oversized tires rumbling over the rough asphalt and the radio blaring country music, serious conversation wasn't worth the effort. He would have to wait for the restaurant.

Even for a weeknight, the Burger Shack was quiet. The three ordered cheeseburgers with fries and shakes at the counter and took a seat in one of the empty booths. In the interval while they waited for their meals, Sky drew the folded knife out of his pocket, laid it on the red Formica tabletop, and forced himself to speak.

"I've been waiting for the right time to show you this. It was lying on the ground, close to the place where Jasper was shot."

Will picked up the knife, frowning as he examined it. "Looks like something a kid might have dropped. Are you thinking it has something to do with our shooter?"

"Turn it over," Sky said. "Look at the initials on the back."

Will stared at the crude carving on the handle. His dark eyebrows came together in a puzzled scowl. "I'll be damned. Those are your initials."

"I know. I carved them myself."

"You've already lost me," Beau said. "I hope you're going to fill us in on the whole story."

Sky took the knife from Will, balancing it on the flat of his palm the way he'd done years ago. Except for the fact that his hand was bigger now, it felt much the same.

"I was in third grade when I found this on the way home from school," he said. "It was lying in the road, like somebody'd dropped it. Just a cheap little knife, but I'd never had anything much of my own. To a boy like me it was a treasure. I scratched those initials on it and kept it hidden so my older cousins wouldn't take it."

"Your older cousins? You mean Lute's brothers?" Beau asked.

Sky nodded. "They were big enough and mean enough to take anything they wanted. Lute was just a toddler when I found the knife, and his sister, Marie, the only girl, named after my mother, wasn't much older."

Sky had always felt protective of the two young ones and tried to shield them from the brutality that was life in the Fletcher family. Not that it had done much good. Lute was dead now, and the last he'd heard of Marie, she'd run off with a boyfriend.

"I hung on to the knife till I was fifteen," Sky said. "You already know some of this. My uncle had whipped me pretty bad, and I'd had enough. I packed my clothes and a little food in a pillowcase and waited till the middle of the night when the family was asleep. Then I snuck through the house to the back door. I thought I'd made a clean getaway, but I was wrong."

The story was interrupted by the waiter with their orders. The cheeseburgers were hot and fresh, the men hungry after a long day of work. For the first few minutes they enjoyed filling their bellies in silence.

Finally Beau spoke up. "So tell us the rest."

Sky downed the last of his chocolate shake. "I was about to unlock the kitchen door when I heard a noise. I turned around and there was little Marie in the old ripped T-shirt she wore for a nightgown.

Tears were running down her cheeks. 'Don't go, Sky,' she begged me."

"Let me guess," Will said. "You gave her the knife to keep her quiet."

"And that's the last you saw of the knife till you found it this morning," Beau finished.

"You two really know how to ruin a good story," Sky said. "She'd always wanted that knife. She promised to take care of it and not to tell anybody she'd seen me leaving."

"So you're thinking she could be the one who shot Jasper?" Will had never been one to beat around the bush.

"I don't know." Sky stared down at the knife in his open hand. "I saw boot tracks small enough to be a woman's. But I can't imagine Marie shooting an old man. Maybe somebody else had the knife. Maybe she wasn't even there. I know I could be wrong, but . . ." His voice trailed off. He shook his head.

"You were wrong about Lute," Beau reminded him.

"I know. This time I just want to be sure before I ruin somebody's life." Sky laid the knife on the table again. "When I found this I knew I'd have to tell you about it. But I'm hoping you'll give me some time before you call in the law. I need to learn the truth, and I can best do that on my own."

Will and Beau exchanged glances. Beau gave a barely perceptible nod.

"Since the law around here is Abner Sweeney, it's an easy choice," Will said. "But Jasper was almost killed by these people. Promise you'll be careful and that you'll keep us in the loop. If we cut you some slack, we'll need to know what's going on."

"And promise you'll ask for our help if you need it," Beau added.

"You've got my word on it. Thanks for understanding." Sky rose from his seat in the booth. "I'd like to wander over to the Blue Coyote, maybe see what I can find out about who's new in town. Will, can you stop by and pick me up on your way back to the ranch?"

"Sure. But be careful. Some folks might not take too kindly to your asking questions."

"I mostly just plan to keep my ears open. Call when you're there, and I'll meet you outside. That way you won't have to leave Erin alone in the truck."

"Thanks. I appreciate that." Will was protective of his daughter. Now that school was out, Erin was spending most of her vacation with him on the ranch.

After leaving his tip on the table, Sky walked out of the Burger Shack and into the summer dusk. Beau would be spending the night with Natalie, who'd drive him home in the morning. The two planned a fall wedding but had yet to figure out where they were going to live. Beau had his responsibilities on the ranch. Natalie had her clinic in town and didn't want to give up her practice.

Doubtless they'd work it out. Natalie and Beau were too much in love to let that kind of roadblock stand in their way. Sky had noticed the secret glances they exchanged and wondered idly if a woman would ever look at him with that kind of tender passion. Not likely, he conceded. But if he had to settle for something less, the naked lust that had flashed in Lauren Prescott's copper-flecked cat eyes wasn't a bad substitute. She'd looked at him as if she wanted to eat him alive. And she damn near had. He wouldn't mind giving her another chance. But chasing after a woman wasn't his style. Any rematch would be up to the lady.

With the sun gone, the night air was, if not cool, at least tolerable for walking a few blocks down Main Street to the Blue Coyote at the far end. There wasn't much traffic, either on the road or on the sidewalks. Probably some big sporting event on TV, which would mean customers crowding around the 52-inch screen above the bar in the Blue Coyote. At least he'd be able to circulate without drawing much attention.

As Sky had expected, the Blue Coyote's parking lot was full and the bar was jammed. On the TV screen was a regional championship bull riding competition. Since some local cowboys were involved, there was a lot of whooping, cheering, and informal betting. There was no place to sit. Sky found an empty place to stand near the door and looked around.

Nigel, the tattooed skinhead who served as bartender and bouncer, was filling glasses as fast as his customers could empty them. Stella, who owned the bar, was busy playing hostess.

"Hello, Blue Eyes! Where've you been keeping yourself?" She'd spotted Sky through the crowd and was working her way toward him. A handsome, buxom female in her forties with flame-dyed hair and overdone makeup, she looked—and acted—like the town floozy. But Sky knew better than to underestimate her. Nothing escaped those sharp, absinthe eyes.

"What's your pleasure? I'll see that you get it pronto. And if you'd like to stick around till after closing . . ." She winked, then laughed, leaving a wisp of doubt that her outrageous flirting had been a joke. For a woman who'd been sleeping with Hoyt Axelrod, and who surely knew he was dead, she didn't seem to be grieving much. Sky wouldn't put it past her to have ordered the ex-sheriff killed.

But as he already knew, there wasn't a shred of proof against the woman.

Sky fished a bill out of his wallet. "I'll have a Corona," he said. "No need to bring the glass."

"You've got it, honey!" Turning, she snapped her fingers to catch the ear of the busy waitress. "Over here! A bottle of Corona for my handsome friend!"

Following her gaze through the crowd, Sky glimpsed the waitress from behind. Tall and boyishly lean, her stringy, black hair twisted up with a plastic clip, she was dressed in ragged jeans and a black T-shirt. He didn't remember having seen her before, but he hadn't been to town in a while. Waitresses tended not to last long at the Blue Coyote. Stella drove them hard, and the men, some at least, considered the girls fair game.

The new girl had vanished in the direction of the bar. Stella lingered next to Sky, greeting people as they walked in the door. She was a shrewd business-woman and made it a point to know her customers. Some she gave nicknames. Sky had been "Blue Eyes" from the first time she noticed him.

The waitress was coming back, balancing Sky's beer, along with other drinks, on a tray held above the heads of the crowd. Sky's gaze traveled from the tray, down her upraised arm to her face—strong-boned with fierce, black eyes and a thin, white scar, like the slash of a knife, running down the left side from temple to chin.

Years had passed since he'd last seen her, but Sky's heart slammed with the shock of recognition. His eyes searched for, and found, the tiny white mark in the center of her forehead, a souvenir of the time she'd fallen as a toddler and struck a sharp rock. The years had changed her, and not for the better. But there could be no room for doubt.

It was Marie.

CHAPTER 5

Sky waited for some sign of recognition, but Marie's scarred face was a mask of indifference. There was no way she wouldn't know him, but for some reason she kept it to herself. Until he learned more, he'd be wise to play along.

Lowering the tray, she handed him the open bottle. He passed her the ten-dollar bill in his hand. "Keep the change," he said.

"Thanks." Something flickered in her eyes as she turned away—a cold, animal wariness.

Stella lingered beside him, a sphinxlike smile on her painted face. Did she know her waitress was the sister of Lute Fletcher, the twenty-one-year-old boy she'd hired and likely set up to be murdered by Hoyt Axelrod? Stella Rawlins was a master manipulator who played her cards close to her ample bosom. If she suspected the truth, Marie could be in more danger than she knew.

With a saucy parting smile, Stella sashayed off to

tend to other customers. Finding a newly emptied table, Sky sat down to finish his beer and wait for Will's phone call. He glimpsed Marie weaving her way through the crowd, but she didn't try to come near him or even to make eye contact.

Whatever cards life had dealt her, she must've had a rough time of it. The nervous eyes, the slashing scar, and the fact that she'd taken this menial job spoke more than words about her condition.

There was no way her showing up here could be a coincidence. But had she come to Blanco Springs to avenge her brother, or for some even darker purpose? Had she dropped the pocketknife by accident, or had she left it for Sky to find, knowing it would lead him to her?

And what was her connection to Jasper's shooting?

So many questions. And his only hope of getting answers was to talk with Marie alone. But that wasn't going to happen tonight—not with the bar packed, Stella on alert, and Will due to pick him up soon. His best chance would be to come back here tomorrow, before the night crowd gathered, maybe pass her a note and arrange a discreet meeting somewhere.

And then what? If he didn't like her story, he would have some hard decisions to make. Blood cousin or not, his first loyalty was to the Tylers. But when he thought of Marie, it was that sad-eyed little girl, begging him not to leave, who came to mind. If the ugly truth demanded it, could he turn his back on her again? If she gave him her trust, could he use it to betray her?

He needed to decide now, before he got pulled in any deeper. If the answer was no, he'd be better off walking away tonight and forgetting he'd seen her.

* * *

Will dropped Beau off at Natalie's house on the far edge of town. As he watched his brother stride up the walk, a spring of anticipation in his step, he couldn't suppress a twinge of envy. It had been a long time since he'd spent a night making love to the woman he adored, drifting off to sleep in her arms and waking up to the sweet sight of her face on the pillow.

But Tori had made her decision. So had he, and there was nothing more to be said. At least they had Erin to show for their train wreck of a marriage. Their daughter had been worth it all.

Tori's split-level frame house was ten minutes from Natalie's. The two women had gone through school together and were fast friends, along with Beau, who was the same age. Will, six years older, had never been a part of their tightly knit gang of three. Even as a teenager his duties on the ranch had come first, before friends, fun, sports, and social life. In the end, that had been part of the problem with Tori. But not all of it.

Forcing the thought aside, he pulled the pickup into the driveway. Switching off the ignition and the lights, he mounted the porch steps and rang the front doorbell. Over the years, he and Tori had arrived at an armed truce, which they maintained for their daughter's sake. They rarely clashed these days, but the tension Will felt every time he was about to see her would never go away.

By mutual agreement, Erin's summers were spent on the ranch with Will. This week, however, a dentist appointment and a friend's birthday party, along with Jasper's crisis, had made it more convenient for her to stay with her mother. Will had missed her. In a

life of responsibility and hard work, Erin was his sunshine.

"Hello, Will." Tori opened the door, wearing faded
jeans and a striped cotton shirt, unbuttoned far
enough to show the barest glimpse of cleavage. Her
blond hair was caught back in a loose ponytail. The
wire-rimmed glasses she wore for close reading were
perched on her nose. Her feet were bare. She looked
damned sexy, Will thought. But that notion was best
kept to himself.

"Come in," she said, shifting her glasses to the top
of her head. "Erin's upstairs getting ready. She'll be
down in a few minutes. Meanwhile, we need to talk."

"Is something the matter?" Will followed her into
the kitchen and took a seat at the table, which tonight
was cluttered with open law books and legal briefs.

"Not really. Just a change you need to be aware of.
Would you like some iced tea?"

Will shook his head. *What change was she talking
about? Was she planning to move? Maybe even get remarried?* He braced himself as she puttered in the kitchen,
putting a carton of milk in the fridge, a glass in the
open dishwasher. Was the woman trying to drive him
crazy?

"How's Jasper?" she asked.

"As feisty as an old badger. Bernice talked with
him on the phone a couple of hours ago."

"So Bernice isn't at the hospital now?" She added
two spoons to the rack in the dishwasher.

"No, she's home. For God's sake, stop fussing and
sit down!"

Tori closed the dishwasher and took a seat across
from him. "I tried to talk Erin into staying here the
next few days, but she doesn't want to be away from

her foal. I guess she'll be all right as long as Bernice is handy."

"Erin can pretty much take care of herself. Why would Bernice need to be there?" His chest constricted. "Is something wrong with Erin?"

She looked at him as if he were a backward child. "Erin got her first period today. Since she insists on going to the ranch, I want her to have a woman around in case she needs something or has any questions. Asking you or Beau would be awkward, don't you agree?"

Will stared at her, thunderstruck. "But isn't it too soon for that? Erin's just a little girl."

"She's twelve, Will. It's not uncommon for girls to start that early."

"But she's—" Will shook his head, feeling old and foolish. "Never mind. It's just the idea of her growing up. It'll take some getting used to."

"For her, too." Tori's hand reached toward him, then withdrew as if she'd had second thoughts. "Young girls are very private about such things. I'm only telling you so you'll understand if she's uncomfortable and out of sorts. But don't try to talk to her about it. Leave that to Bernice."

"You'll let Bernice know?"

"I'll call her after you leave." Tori rose from her chair, as footsteps pattered along the upstairs hallway. "Shh, here she comes. Don't tell her what I said."

After listening to Tori, Will expected his daughter to be changed somehow. But as she bounded down the stairs with her backpack, her grin was as happy as ever. She loved the ranch and everything on it, especially Tesoro, the palomino foal Sky was helping her raise and train.

"Let's go, Daddy!" Giving her mother a quick kiss, she dashed out the door to the truck.

Will followed his daughter as far as the front porch, then turned back to Tori. "See you at the ranch for Sunday dinner?" he asked.

"Sure." She reached up and plucked her glasses off her head. After he left, she'd probably go back to reading up on her current court case. If her life involved anything besides work, her daughter, and her friendship with Natalie, Will hadn't seen any sign of it. Tori was a beautiful woman. She could marry again any time she chose to—hell, that bastard Garn Prescott would have her in a minute. But she and Will had been divorced for eight years, and she was still alone.

"Call if there's any problem," she said, meaning a problem with Erin.

"Don't worry about it." He turned away and went down the steps to join their daughter in the truck.

While Erin buckled her seat belt, Will made a quick call to Sky to let him know they were coming. Then he backed the truck out of the driveway.

For a few blocks they drove in awkward silence. Then Erin spoke. "Well, I guess Mom told you my big news," she said.

"I guess she did." Will touched the brake at the stop sign and swung the truck onto Main Street.

"I'm not the first girl in my class to get my period. Michelle Hawkins got hers right after school started. And Emily White got hers two months ago. And there are probably some I don't know about. I'm just glad not to be the last. That would be humiliating."

"Well, congratulations, I guess," Will said.

"Thanks. How's Tesoro? Does he miss me?"

"He always misses you. Just like I do." In the darkness of the cab, Will allowed himself a smile. Even after twelve years, he and Tori had a lot to learn about being parents.

Lauren speared a morsel of steaming beef from the plate someone had set in front of her. Taking a bite, she forced herself to chew. She didn't mind good barbecue, but this piece was tough enough to make her wonder if the steer had died of old age. And she could hardly spit it out in front of the guests who'd paid extra to share the round banquet table with the congressman.

"Nothing like good old-fashioned Texas barbecue," her father was saying. "Now if only I could get my colleagues in the House to sit down to a meal like this, we could solve all the country's problems in one afternoon!"

"And the next day you could invite the Senate!" Josh Hardesty, the governor's stepson, glanced around the table, waiting for a response to his joke. Garn Prescott obliged him with a hoot of laughter. Her father was trying too hard, Lauren thought. For that matter, so was Hardesty.

Representing his stepfather at the fund-raiser, Josh Hardesty was handsome in an overblown way, his Armani suit and silk tie too formal for the countrified setting with hay bales and red-checked tablecloths. He had a way of raising his wrist to check the time on his diamond-studded gold Rolex, as if to display the vulgar piece for Lauren's eyes. He'd arrived at the party in a red Maserati, and Prescott was practically drooling over him. Lauren was under strict orders to be gracious, in the hope of coaxing an extra digit onto his contribution check.

"So what do you think of Texas by now, Lauren?" Hardesty flashed a set of flawless veneers. He was leaning so close that Lauren could have counted the pores on his nose.

Lauren toyed with her food, pretending to eat. "I suppose it has its charms, but I've yet to discover them." True, she thought. Sky Fletcher was one of the least charming men she'd ever met, but even here she couldn't get him out of her thoughts.

"I'll be in Lubbock for the next few days," Hardesty said. "I'd be delighted to help you discover some of those charms you're missing."

"Thanks for the invitation, but I'm a working girl," Lauren said. "I'm keeping the accounts for two different ranches. People are depending on me to get my work done."

He shook his head. "I can't understand why a pretty little thing like you would choose to be an accountant."

"Why not? I've always been good with numbers, and I like the challenge of putting things in order."

"But all you'd have to do is bat those gorgeous eyes at the right man and you'd be set for life. You could have anything you wanted."

"Funny," Lauren said, "that's just what my father tells me."

Prescott had made it clear that he was hoping for some sparks between his daughter and one of the state's richest single men under fifty. Hardesty seemed interested, but he was far from her type. She would be polite and pleasant for as long as this dreary event lasted. Then she would slip away without giving him her phone number.

Tomorrow she would demand the payment she'd earned—her pick of any horse on the Prescott ranch.

Garn Prescott surveyed the banquet hall as the seventy-two-minute address from the former Secretary of Agriculture ended. People were pulling out their chairs, standing up to stretch their cramped limbs. A few were already dashing for the exits. Lord, where had his staff dredged up the old dotard? He'd requested a speaker who could fire up an audience. Instead, the former cabinet member, who looked as if he'd served under Warren Harding, had put most listeners to sleep with his droning monotone. Too late, Prescott realized he should have hired a band with a singer to keep things lively. He couldn't afford a celebrity, but there were groups out there who'd perform for the chance to be heard.

The crowd was up and milling now, some headed for the open bar, more leaving. On the far side of the vast room, Prescott glimpsed Lauren, a fetching sight in jeans, boots, and a western-style shirt. He'd noticed how the cameras flashed when she entered the hall on his arm. Now Josh Hardesty had cornered her, and the two appeared to be deep in conversation. If those two clicked, he would count the event a success. Otherwise it was a near fiasco. He'd be lucky to cover what he'd already paid for the hall rental and the damn-blasted caterer.

"Congressman." The female voice, coming from somewhere behind his shoulder, recalled the taste of aged bourbon—rich and mellow, with a subtle kick.

He turned to meet a pair of absinthe eyes framed by mascara-slathered lashes. The woman wasn't young—well into her forties, he guessed. But there was a sensual quality about her that defied age. Her hair was dyed a flamboyant carmine, her makeup applied with a lavish hand, giving her face an exotic look that brought to mind some ancient Egyptian queen. Her black silk jumpsuit, worn with high-heeled red boots, hugged her generous curves.

"Have we met?" he asked, knowing he'd remember her if they had.

She gave him a slow smile. "Not until now. I just wanted to shake your hand and make a small personal contribution to your campaign." She drew a plain white envelope from her purse and held it out to him. "Stella Rawlins. My phone number's written on the inside flap of this envelope. Call me if you need more. Call me, in fact, if you need anything at all."

Some instinct made him hesitate. She thrust the envelope into his hands. "Take it. No strings attached. I just want to see the best man win the nomination—and the election in November."

The envelope was thick and heavy between Prescott's fingers. He'd expected a check. This felt more like cash, probably small bills. Never mind, the lady meant well, and every little bit counted.

"Thank you," he said, switching the envelope to his left hand and extending his right for the handshake. Her palm was warm, her firm grip lingering a few extra seconds.

"You're *very* welcome." She turned and walked away, her hips doing a little shimmy as she disappeared into the crowd.

Curious, but not wanting to be observed, Prescott made his way to the men's room and shut himself inside a stall. Mindful of the phone number—not that he planned to contact the woman—he ran his index finger under the sealed flap and opened the envelope.

His pulse cartwheeled.

Inside was a thick bundle of hundred-dollar bills. Prescott's hand quivered as he ruffled through them, keeping a mental count. There were two hundred of them, if he hadn't lost track. Two hundred even.

Stella Rawlins had just handed him twenty thousand dollars cash—and told him to call her if he needed more.

Three days had passed, and Sky had yet to find the time for an afternoon trip to town. With drought conditions getting worse and no rain in the forecast, Will had ordered a crew up to the summer range to collect the cattle into one fenced pasture where the herd could be fed. The windmills pumped enough drinking water from the vast aquifer under the caprock to fill the tanks, but in the rainless heat the grass on the high plain was crumbling into dust. The cattle would need daily rations of hay to keep the animals from starving.

Sky had been pressed into service with the rest of the hands. Managing the remuda, riding herd with the other cowboys, and delegating care for the young horses he was training kept him so busy that even his worry about Marie had been pushed to the back of his mind. Cattle were the lifeblood of the Rimrock.

No job was more vital than keeping the herd safe and healthy.

Sky was scanning the flat horizon for strays when Will rode up beside him. "The Boss," as his hired men called him, had barely slept in days. His face and clothes were gritty with dust, blown by a wind that was like the heat from a blast furnace.

"You look like hell," Sky said.

"I'm guessing I look about the same as you." Will pulled down the red bandanna that protected the lower part of his face. "At least we got most of them penned. The first truckload of hay should be here any time. It'll cost us a blessed fortune to feed this many head of cattle."

"Better than watching them waste and die," Sky said. "How long do you figure we can afford to keep the hay coming?"

"According to Beau's numbers, we can feed them for another three weeks—maybe a month if the rains come and we know there'll be grass. Otherwise, we'll have to sell them off cheap and see them trucked away to feed lots."

"So this is a big gamble."

"Damned big. I've lost nights of sleep wondering if we shouldn't just go ahead and sell them now. If it doesn't rain, every cent we're spending on hay is just money down the hole."

The two men sat in silence, watching dust devils play across a landscape so flat that early Spaniards named it the *Llano Estacado*—the Staked Plain—because they had to mark their trails with stakes in the ground to keep from getting lost.

Will lifted his Stetson and raked a hand through his sweat-soaked hair. "Those colts you're breaking to sell could keep us from going under. How many can you have ready for auction before the fall roundup season?"

"The yearlings are barely halter broke," Sky said. "But I've got at least twenty good two-year-olds that are partway there. It'll take a lot of work to get them to where they should be. But I'll do my best."

The furrow deepened between Will's dark eyebrows. Sky could imagine him doing the math in his head. A well-bred, well-trained young cow pony could go for as much as $30,000. An exceptional horse, trained by a man of Sky's reputation, could fetch more. With luck, they could count on more than half a million dollars for the lot of them—minus what they'd paid for the unbroken colts in the first place. Would that be enough to make a difference?

Given what the ranch would lose if they had to sell off the cattle, it didn't seem like much. But that wasn't Sky's decision to make. All he could do was give the young horses his best and trust to luck.

"The boys and I can look after things up here," Will said. "For now, I want you to get back to those colts. Go home, get some rest, and start again as soon as you're ready."

"You're sure? There could still be strays out there."

"I'll send somebody to check. Go on now." He wheeled his mount, then paused, turning back. "About that cousin of yours. I know you need to check out what she's doing here and whether she had something to do with shooting Jasper. Take the time you need, as long as it's not too much. Those colts have to come first."

"I hear you." Sky had been working with the Tyler men since he was fifteen, and Will's controlling style sheeted off him like water off a stone. Beau, on the other hand . . .

Letting the thought trail away, Sky swung his roan gelding back toward the corral where the spare horses were kept. He'd brought his own pickup, which he would drive back down the winding road through the escarpment to the heart of the ranch. The horses not needed up on the caprock would be trailered down later—a task the cowboys could easily handle.

Meanwhile, Sky would resume training the prime colts he'd brought to the ranch, and try to squeeze in time, tomorrow maybe, for an afternoon visit to the Blue Coyote.

He was unsaddling the roan when Beau rode up to the gate, dismounted, and led his bay mare into the corral. "Will wants me to ride back to the ranch with you," he said. "I just found out he made an appointment for me with a banker in Lubbock. I'm supposed to go and talk with him about a backup loan to tide us over in case we need it."

Beau's face was a thundercloud. Sky guessed that Will had made the appointment without consulting his brother and foreman. The stress of the drought was putting everybody on edge. Unlike Sky, Beau chafed visibly under the weight of his brother's authority. Sooner or later, Sky feared, there'd be a showdown—one that could end badly. Beau had left once after a clash with their father. If Will pushed him far enough, he might leave again.

Sky had vowed that nothing would change for him after Jasper's revelation. But some things couldn't be helped. The depth of his concern for his two blood brothers had come as an unsettling surprise. Whether he liked it or not, the Tylers weren't just his employers. They'd become family even before he knew of their shared blood.

Beau said little as Sky drove down the gravel road that zigzagged among flat-topped mesas and red sandstone hoodoos to emerge above the ranch. As the view opened up, Sky caught himself glancing down toward the house, to the open area beyond the porch where visitors parked their cars. There was no sign of the black Corvette.

"She hasn't been around." Beau seemed to read his mind. "The computer hasn't been touched, and that little gold earring is still in the desk drawer. What did you do to the woman, anyway?"

Sky muttered a noncommittal reply. He'd tried to wall Lauren out of his thoughts, but she'd crept back to haunt his unguarded moments—that lush mouth, that lithe willing body, those sharp little whimpers as he'd brought her to climax. . . . He'd been crazy to take her—and even crazier to keep wanting her. She was the spoiled daughter of a man the Tylers barely tolerated. If he passed her on the street, she'd probably turn and look the other way.

"Whatever the hell's going on with you two, I need Lauren's help with the books," Beau said. "If she doesn't show up soon, I'll have to go to her on my knees, offer her the moon, and promise to slug you if you get within a hundred yards of her."

"Do what you have to," Sky said. "Lauren doesn't take orders from me."

"Getting testy, are we?" Beau prodded.

"Just don't push me. Get her back here and she's all yours. I've got better things to do than fool around with Garn Prescott's little princess."

"Fine. Let's keep it that way."

"Are you going to see Jasper on the way back?" Sky changed the subject.

"Of course I am," Beau growled. "You and Will don't have to remind me of every little thing."

Sky drove on in silence. Both men were saddle sore, hungry, sleep deprived, and on the ragged edge of snapping. But they made it to the house without an all-out clash. Sky let Beau off by the porch and drove around to his own quarters out back. Once they'd had a chance to rest and clean up, things would be all right between them, Sky knew. But anxiety over the drought was eating away at everyone on the ranch. And the blazing afternoon sun promised nothing but more of the same.

Jasper, at least, was doing better and would soon be coming home. Sky was counting the days. If ever there was a time when the ranch could use Jasper's salty wisdom, experience, and gentle humor, it was now.

Sky showered, dressed, and washed down a turkey sandwich with a cold beer. There wasn't enough time to go to town today, but if he got right to it, he could work with the colts for several hours.

Twenty minutes later, he was in the corral, saddling a two-year-old gray gelding, when he heard Beau's Jeep peel out of the yard and head down the long gravel lane toward the main road. Even without looking, he could tell that Beau's mood hadn't changed. As Jasper might have put it, dealing with bankers was like dealing with coyotes. They were quick to take advantage of a weakness, and any rancher with his back against the wall was fair game. Will had sent Beau in early to negotiate a possible loan before it was needed so they could get better terms. It was a wise move, but Sky could understand Beau's annoyance at being treated like an errand boy—just as he understood that Will had been too preoccupied to make sure Beau was involved in the plan.

Sky eased into the saddle, lowering the brim of his Stetson to shade his eyes from the burning sun. The dwindling money, the hungry cattle, the flaring tempers—a good spell of rain would wash away all those troubles. But the heat-seared land was dying, and the heavens were merciless.

The dappled gray gelding—named Quicksilver by Erin—was a small horse with an elegant head that showed his Arabian blood. Smart as a fox and agile as a cat, Quicksilver had the makings of an ideal cow pony. Sky had singled him out for extra training in the hope of getting a premium price. Today he'd decided to introduce backing and turning, an essential maneuver for working a cow. The sharp little horse responded to the pressure of Sky's knees and the slight shifts in his weight, performing the moves as if they'd come naturally. Some lucky buyer was going to get their money's worth out of this boy.

Sky was paying no attention to anything going on outside the corral. A shrill whinny from the direction of the house shattered his concentration. He looked up to see a spectacular black horse dancing across the yard toward him, battling its rider all the way.

Sky swore out loud.

Clinging to the saddle, fighting for control of the reins, was Lauren.

With Quicksilver distracted by the newcomer, there was no way the training could go on. Taking his time, Sky freed the colt from the saddle and bridle and loosed him into the paddock. Emotions warred as he walked slowly back to the corral fence. Lauren Prescott was nothing but trouble in high-heeled boots. So why was he so damned glad to see the leggy, red-haired hellion?

More to the point, what was she doing to that poor horse?

CHAPTER 6

Battling the reins, Lauren managed to pull up short of the log fence. The Prescott cowhands had warned her not to ride the tall black gelding they called Storm Cloud. He had a rebellious streak and a tendency to nip and rear. He was nothing but trouble, they'd told her. Only a strong man could control a horse like that.

Which was exactly why Lauren had chosen him.

It had been all she could do, getting Storm Cloud the six-mile distance from the Prescott Ranch. He'd fought her every step of the way, shying at the wind in the brush, sometimes rearing, sometimes balking or fighting the bit with his tossing head. If Lauren had been a less experienced rider, or a less deter-mined one, she might have been thrown.

There'd been moments when she'd been ready to give up and abandon this crazy idea. But she'd stuck it out, and here she was—sweaty, dusty, sore, and windblown, but still in the saddle, bracing herself for the most challenging moment of all.

Sky was at the fence—glaring up at her as if he'd caught her beating the wretched animal with a whip. So far this didn't look good.

"What in hell's name do you think you're doing?" he demanded.

"I'm trying to ride this horse," Lauren said. "And since I brought him all the way here to ask for your help, the least you can do is be civil."

He shook his head, his breath easing out in a long exhalation.

"I can pay you," Lauren said. "I'll pay as much as you want."

"I don't need your money, Lauren." His low, flat voice was more withering than if he'd shouted at her. "I don't have much time to spare, but I'll do what I can—not so much for you as for this poor horse. Look at him, he's overheated and scared half to death."

"Scared? This brute? Now, that's hard to believe."

He swung over the corral fence in one easy motion. "Horses in the wild are prey. Fear helps keep them alive. It's part of their nature to be scared. You can climb down. I've got him."

Gripping the bridle with one hand, he stroked the horse's damp neck, murmuring words Lauren couldn't understand—Comanche perhaps. She felt Storm Cloud's taut body begin to relax. Swinging her leg cautiously over his hindquarters, she slid to the welcoming earth. The last time she'd ridden had been in her teens, when she'd competed in dressage with her grandfather's gaited American saddle horses. She remembered the basics, but her thigh muscles were screaming.

You know where to find me.

It had been a gamble on her part, choosing a difficult horse so she could ask Sky for help. There was something aching and restless in her that yearned to see him again and take a chance on what might happen. But after what he'd said to her before he walked out of the ranch office, she had too much pride to simply show up and say, *Here I am.*

Did he feel the same? Sky took a step toward her, leaning close. Lauren's pulse skittered as she readied herself for a kiss, but he only sniffed the air above her head. "I can tell you one thing right now," he said. "You're wearing perfume, and this horse hates the smell of it."

"Oh, I hadn't thought—" Lauren swore silently. She had dabbed her earlobes, the back of her neck and the hollow between her breasts with a pricey fragrance that, according to the ads, was supposed to make men melt. Evidently it didn't work on horses— or on Sky Fletcher.

A smile teased the corner of his grim mouth. "In case you're wondering, I think you smell fine," he said. "But if you're going to be around this horse, you'd better get rid of that scent. There's a faucet outside the barn door. Go and rinse off as much as you can."

So much for seduction. Reaching the barn, Lauren found the faucet, turned it on, and began splashing cold water on the spots where she'd dabbed perfume. It was good perfume, formulated to last. Even after she'd finished dousing herself, she could still smell the sweet, musky aroma.

By the time she made it back to the corral, Sky had a second horse, a drowsy-looking bay mare, saddled and waiting. "We're going for a ride," he said. "I'll take your horse, and you can tag along on this lady. Her name's Belle."

"Is she the one you save for seniors and children?" Lauren tried a feeble joke.

"She's a great cow pony, and her foals are some of the best on the ranch. You should be honored to ride her." Evidently, where his horses were concerned, the man had no sense of humor.

"Then I'll treat her as the lady she is." Lauren moved past Storm Cloud to get to the mare. The big black horse snorted and laid back its ears. "I'm starting to take this personally."

"If I can still smell that perfume, so can the horse. We'll need to camouflage that. Come here." Beckoning her close, Sky turned and ran a finger under the edge of the saddle pad where the gelding's warm hide was soaked with perspiration. "Hold still," he murmured, stroking his moist fingertip along the side of her throat and up behind her ear.

"You're making me smell like horse sweat!" Lauren hissed.

"Urine works even better. So does manure, if you'd rather have that. Hold still." Collecting more of the dampness, he circled the back of her neck, working the horse smell into the base of her hair. The strangeness of it—the pungent aroma and the light pressure of Sky's touch—awakened whorls of subtle sensation. The feeling shimmered downward to pulse like a glowing current in the depths of her body. Her lips parted. She stifled a moan as his fingers spread the scent over her damp chest and slid downward to the deep vee of her wet shirt front, where she'd tried to splash the perfume away from the hollow between her breasts.

His breathing had gone rough. She could feel the tension in him, the conflict as he struggled against the urge to move his hand lower. Blast the man! He must know what they both wanted. Why didn't he just give in?

Driven by impulse, she seized his wrist and tugged his hand down to cup her breast. He groaned. A shudder passed through his body as his fingers closed on her tingling softness. His free hand caught her waist and jerked her close, grinding her hips against him as his mouth crushed hers. The ground seemed to spin under Lauren's feet. She closed her eyes, losing herself in the waves of torrid heat that surged through her body. . . .

But only for a moment. Then Sky was shoving her away from him, holding her at arm's length. His hooded eyes burned as hot and blue as gas jets.

"Not here." His voice was a growl. "We've got an audience."

His head jerked in the direction of the yard, where one of the cowhands was strolling toward the bunkhouse. Only the horses, blocking the view, had kept him from getting an eyeful.

"And not now," he said. "I promised Beau that if you came back to work on the books, I'd keep my distance."

"You told *Beau*?" Lauren's cheeks blazed.

"He guessed after he found your earring behind the computer. It'll be in the desk drawer when you want it back." He turned toward the black horse again. "Come on, let's ride. We'll take it slow for the horses."

Sky headed southeast, keeping the late afternoon sun at their backs. They rode single file across the brushy landscape, Sky in front on Storm Cloud, Lauren on Belle a few yards behind him. He'd warned her to keep the mare at a distance so she wouldn't distract the big black. But he suspected that Lauren's silence had little to do with the horses. He'd done it again—wounded her womanly pride. If he was getting the silent treatment now, it was no worse than he deserved.

Lord, did she have any idea how hard it had been to push her away? All he'd really wanted to do was drag her into the barn, throw her down in the hay, and thrust his sex deep into that lush, willing body. He knew she'd wanted it, too. That was why she'd shown up smelling like a high-class French cathouse, with her blouse unbuttoned to the point of luscious indecency.

The horse had been nothing more than an excuse. He understood that. But Storm Cloud was a magnificent animal, and his trust issues were real. If anything could be done for him, Sky resolved to do it. He kept his touch light but firm, guiding as much with his knees as with his hands. He could sense the resistance in the big gelding. What was the creature afraid of?

"What do you know about this horse?" he asked Lauren. "Where did he come from?"

"Sorry, can you say that again, louder?" Her voice came from a dozen yards back.

Sky glanced over his shoulder, making sure she could hear. "Bring the mare up even with us. Not too close. Let's see how he does with the two of you next to him."

Nudging the mare to a trot, she came up alongside, keeping a safe distance between the two horses. The gelding tensed and snorted but kept to his brisk walking pace. Heat waves shimmered in the distance, blurring the air above the sunbaked land. A lone vulture circled against the blazing turquoise sky.

"Storm Cloud's behaving just fine for you," Lauren said.

"But not because he wants to. I can feel the fear in every step he takes. It would help to have some idea of what's bothering him."

"It's not just the perfume," Lauren said. "He misbehaves with the cowboys, too."

"What do you know about his history?"

"Not much. The foreman told me he wasn't raised on the ranch. One of the syndicate men brought him in last year. He'd bought the horse for his wife, but things hadn't worked out."

"With the horse or with the wife?"

Lauren's laugh was deep and real—a sexy laugh, not a ladylike giggle. "I'm not sure. But could that explain why he hates my perfume?"

"Maybe. That, or he just plain doesn't like the smell. If you're bound and determined to ride this horse—"

He broke off as a jackrabbit exploded out of the mesquite, almost under the gelding's hooves. Storm Cloud squealed and reared.

"Easy, boy. . . . That's it." Sky soothed the quivering horse, keeping firm control as the rabbit streaked away. "As I was about to say, if you're determined to ride this horse, I'd like to keep him here for a week or two, keep an eye on him, ride him a little and see how he does. When you're helping Beau in the office, you can come out afterward, and I'll work with both of you."

"Is this a bribe to get me working on Beau's spreadsheet again?" Mischief danced in her copper-flecked eyes. They'd be tempting fate, and they both knew it. Alone together, there'd be no way they could keep their hands off each other for long.

"Beau really does need your help," Sky said. "He thinks you've stayed away because of me. We had a few words over it today. Sorry, but this drought's got everybody on edge."

"My staying away had nothing to do with you. It's just that I've been busy."

"So you'll come back?"

"I've meant to come back all along."

"And the horse?"

"I'm with you. He deserves better than to be so miserable. Do whatever you can for him, and I'll give Beau some free hours in exchange."

"You don't have to do that." But it would please Beau, Sky thought. Given the ranch's limited cash flow, even that small saving would help.

"Please let me. I took the job for the experience, not for the money. And it's a great excuse to get away from my father."

Yes, her father. Sky had actually begun to like the woman before she reminded him whose daughter she was. Garn Prescott was everything that gave politicians a bad name—two-faced, double dealing, and greedy. At least his late father, Bull's archenemy Ferg Prescott, had been up-front with his meanness. But Ferg's congressman son hid everything behind a genial mask.

How did Jasper put it? *Trust a rattler before you trust a Prescott.* Wise words, Sky knew. But kissing Lauren by the corral had lit a bonfire inside him. He wanted her—any time, any place he could get into those damned two-hundred-dollar jeans of hers.

But having her would mean walking a fine line—maybe even a dangerous line.

They were almost there before Sky realized where he was taking her. Without conscious thought, he'd been headed toward the southeast boundary of the ranch—and the hundred acres Bull had left him in his will.

Torn by conflict over his father's motives, Sky had avoided coming here. But he'd seen and admired the place before without knowing it was to be his. It was a choice piece of land, rolling, wooded in spots, and watered by a deep spring—perfect for horses.

Even now, as they crossed the boundary, something resisted in him. It would serve his pride to sell the land and donate the money to the ranch. He didn't need it. And he didn't want a guilt offering from the man who'd left his mother pregnant and alone. If he saw the land, if he rode across it, he might begin to think of it as his—and he wasn't ready for that.

But something in him had wanted to see the place again; and being here with Lauren made it easier. He wouldn't tell her about the land, of course. He didn't plan to tell anybody until he'd made a final decision. For now, at least, her company kept the darkness from his thoughts.

They talked about safe things. She told him about growing up in Maryland and competing in dressage. He explained the fine points of riding a Western cow horse. Heat lay like a blanket on the land. Insects droned in the long grass. The horses had slowed to a plodding pace. Even Storm Cloud was too hot to misbehave.

A bead of sweat trickled like a liquid jewel down her cheek. Sky checked the impulse to reach out and brush it away with his fingertip. With Lauren, one thing was apt to lead to another. Maybe it was time they turned around, before they found themselves in trouble.

"There's a spring here somewhere," he said. "We'll water the horses and then head back. If you want to leave Storm Cloud with me, I'll stable him and drive you home in the pickup."

"Fine." Lifting her hat, she raked her fingers through her coppery hair, holding it off the back of her neck. The motion tugged her thin shirt against her breasts. "I don't think he's up to a ride home in this heat. I know I'm not. Tell Beau I'll be back tomorrow to work on the spreadsheet."

Sky willed himself to ignore the tightening of his body. "I can hear the spring. It should be just beyond that clump of mesquite." He swung the gelding toward the sound. The mare followed without any urging.

The spot where the cold spring formed a shallow pool was overgrown with watercress and ringed with moisture-sucking tamarisk bushes, which would need digging out if the water was to be of much use—but what was he thinking? Why make plans for a property he didn't plan to keep?

The horses lowered their heads to drink. Lauren slid off the mare, flung back her hat, and crouched to splash water on her hot face. Sky eased off Storm Cloud, looped the reins around a branch, and joined her, wetting his face with his hands and slicking back his hair. "Now this is more like it," he muttered.

Lauren shot him an impish glance. Lifting her hat free, she scooped the crown full of water and dashed it over his head.

"Why, you little—" Grinning, he made a grab for her. She laughed and scooted out of reach.

"I'll show you a thing or two!" Sky lunged to his

feet. In a lightning move, he caught her up in his arms. He'd meant to toss her in the water. But her closeness put entirely different ideas in his head. Her wet shirt clung to her half-exposed breasts. As his body responded, he lowered his head and nuzzled their softness. Lingering traces of her perfume crept into his senses, rousing him to a fevered ache. He cursed silently. The woman was driving him crazy.

She arched against him with a little purring sound. Her hand dropped to brush his swollen sex. "Sure . . ." she whispered.

He'd tucked a condom in his wallet, so the only problem was where. Lifting his gaze, he glanced around for someplace that wasn't either wet or prickly. Damn it, he'd take her standing up if he had to, but there had to be a less awkward way.

As he turned with her, he felt his boot heel come down on something slick and rigid that gave beneath the pressure of his weight. Sky tensed, his danger instincts quivering.

"What is it?" Lauren had sensed the change in him.

"Something isn't right." Sky had an idea what it was, but before he checked it out, he needed to make sure Lauren was safe. "I'm going to put you on the mare," he said quietly. "Ride out of here the way we came, slow and easy, like nothing's wrong. If you hear anything—a voice, a gunshot—get away fast. Otherwise just keep going easy till I catch up with you."

"And if you don't show?"

"Don't worry, I'll be fine." He boosted her into the saddle. "If something goes wrong, don't take any fool chances. Just go. Got it?"

She nodded, her eyes wide and questioning. Sky gave the mare a light slap on the haunch to get her

started, then watched until she was clear of the brush
and headed back toward the ranch. Only then did he
crouch to examine what he'd felt on the ground.

What he found was what he'd expected—a length
of three-quarter-inch black PVC pipe, lightly buried
under a layer of dirt and leaves. Emerging from
under the water in the spring, the pipe ran back
through the tamarisk and beyond. Keeping low, Sky
followed it through the scrub to a battery-operated
siphon pump, duct taped to a half-dozen black hoses,
running off in different directions like the legs of a
spider.

Too bad he hadn't brought a gun. Unarmed as he
was, it would be risky to go on. In any case, there
could be no doubt what he'd find if he followed
those black hoses far enough.

Somebody was farming marijuana on his land.

Right now he needed to get back to the horse and
make sure Lauren was all right. But he planned to return and investigate when he was better prepared.
Something told him he'd stumbled on the missing
piece of a jigsaw puzzle—a piece that could connect
to Jasper's shooting and to Marie's appearance in
Blanco Springs. But he couldn't be sure of anything
until he had more evidence.

Picking up a broken branch, he began brushing
out his tracks as he backed away. At the same time, he
scanned the ground. There were no horse signs and
no vehicle tracks, which meant that the weed growers
were coming and going by some other route. But marijuana plants needed water, especially in this drought.
Somebody would need to maintain the pump and
make sure the pipe was clear.

The tracks, when he found them, appeared to be
several days old. But they were distinct enough for

Sky to recognize the same motorcycle boot and the worn, narrow print he'd seen near the spot where Jasper had been shot.

Sky used his cell to snap quick photos of the pump and the tracks. He had just slipped the phone back in his pocket when a faint but unmistakable sound reached his ears. It was the metallic rumble of a big motorcycle—a Harley, he guessed—approaching fast from the direction of Blanco Springs. The rider might have a camp near the marijuana patch. For a fleeting second, Sky was tempted to sneak back for a look at him. But he'd left the horse by the spring, and there was Lauren. If she was headed for the ranch, she'd be in the open, exposed and vulnerable.

The sound of the approaching bike had grown to a roar. Abruptly it stopped, the silence more unnerving than the noise had been. Sky reached the horse and freed the reins. Springing into the saddle, he kneed Storm Cloud to a lope. For once the unruly gelding behaved. Soon they were clear of the brush and headed back toward Rimrock land.

Had the biker heard him ride away, or even seen him? If so, the marijuana growers would be on high alert. Anyone getting too close would run the risk of being shot—like Jasper had been shot. Except that Jasper hadn't been anywhere near this place. One more missing piece of the puzzle.

Slowing the horse to a walk, he scanned the parched grassland ahead for Lauren. Taking the mare at an easy pace, as he'd told her to, she couldn't have gotten far. But there was no sign of her.

Sky's throat jerked tight. How much time had passed since he'd sent her off? Five minutes? Ten at most. Even riding away at a gallop, she'd have left a trail of dust that would linger in the air.

Where was the woman? Had one of the bastards grabbed her? He'd seen no one, heard no one except the biker. But anything could have happened.

So help him, he would kill anybody who'd laid a hand on her.

He was about to go back and look for her when he heard the rapid pounding of hooves coming up behind him. Turning, he saw Lauren on the mare.

He waited for her to catch up. By the time she did, anger had flooded the hollows worry had left.

"I told you to get away," he snapped. "What the hell were you doing?"

"Hiding in the brush while I waited for you. Did you really think I was going to ride off and leave you when I knew something was wrong?"

"Blast it, Lauren, don't be stupid! Anything could've happened to you back there. And it would've been my fault. The next time I tell you to do something, just do it."

Lauren's silence told him what she thought of that idea. "What did you find back there?" she asked after a long pause.

"Nothing." Sky was mad enough to lie to her. "Just a place that looked like some homeless people were camping out. Since they weren't on ranch property, I decided to leave them alone."

"I heard the motorcycle. Did you see anybody?"

"No, that was when I decided to leave. You know about Jasper getting shot, don't you?"

"Everybody does. It was on the news. Do you think the people back there might have done it?"

"Maybe. But since I didn't have a gun, I decided not to stick around and find out the hard way. I don't want you going near the place again."

"Why should I? What reason would I have to come

back here?" Lauren's response made it clear that his orders meant nothing to her. "How is Jasper, by the way?"

"Mending." Sky was relieved to change the subject. "He should be home in the next couple of days. From what I hear, he's really put the hospital staff through their paces."

"He sounds delightful. I've never had the chance to meet him, but I'm looking forward to it."

"Fine, but be warned. Jasper says exactly what he thinks—and he doesn't think much of your family."

"Sometimes I don't think too much of them, either. We'll get along fine." Lauren laughed—that low-pitched, sexy laugh that sent Sky's thoughts spinning in all the wrong directions. He'd had sex with her on a desk and almost had sex with her on the bare ground. A bed would be a nice change. Maybe he should ask her out on a real date—dinner in Lubbock followed by an adventurous night at a first-class hotel. If she was worried about her father, they could always come home earlier—but Lauren was over twenty-one and accustomed to running her own life. Beau had even mentioned that she'd been engaged once. Why should it matter?

The more he thought about the idea, the more sense it made. He'd bring it up when he drove her home, after he'd put the horses away.

They'd made it back to the corral and were just climbing off their horses when a low-slung red Maserati came speeding up the lane toward the house. As if the driver had spotted them, the car made a sudden swerve toward the corral and braked in a cloud of dust. The man who climbed out appeared to be in his early forties, his health club body dressed in a tailored blue suit with a silk shirt open at the throat. His thick, sandy hair was sculpted into a pompadour that would hold up in a norther. Sky had never set eyes on the man before. But he certainly seemed to know Lauren.

"Here you are!" His grin showed movie-star-perfect veneers. "I hope you don't mind my coming by. Your father said I might find you here."

Sky glanced at Lauren, trying to gauge her reaction. She was cool, unreadable.

"Hello, Josh." She wiped her dusty hands on her even dustier jeans. There was mud on the knees where she'd knelt by the spring to splash her face—and to splash *him*. "This is Sky Fletcher. He's been giving me a . . . riding lesson."

So that's what she wanted to call it. Fine.

"Sky, this is Mr. Josh Hardesty. I met him at a fund-raiser for my father."

"Hardesty." Sky offered a hand.

Hardesty pumped it vigorously, a politician's hand-shake. "This girl made quite an impression on me, Fletcher. So much so that I just dropped by the Prescott Ranch to give the congressman a nice little contribution to his campaign—I suppose it would be bad form to say how much."

"That was very kind of you, Josh." Lauren spoke as if she were reading lines from a play. "I know how much my father appreciates your help."

Hardesty grinned. "Well, he did tell me that if I came over here and found you, you might consent to have dinner with me."

Lauren glanced down at her dirt-stained clothes. "I appreciate the invitation, but—"

"No problem. I'll just run you home and visit with your dad for a bit while you change and freshen up. I got us a table at the Texas Tower. Best prime rib in the country, but it's a down-home place, so no need to dress fancy. If Fletcher here doesn't mind putting up your horse, we can leave right now."

Sensing Lauren's hesitation, Sky looked away. She wasn't his property. He hadn't even asked her out, though he'd meant to. If she wanted to go to dinner with a rich older man, why should he give a damn?

And why should he want to dump a bucket of fresh manure all over that fancy red car?

"Your dad was *mighty* grateful for my help," Hardesty added, no doubt pushing Lauren's guilt buttons. "And since I have the governor's ear, I promised to see that he endorsed the nomination."

"Fine," Lauren replied with a toss of her hair. "Sky, now that you don't need to drive me home, you won't mind taking care of the horses, will you?"

"It's my job." Sky's tone was flat with indifference. "Can I still tell Beau you'll be back here tomorrow?"

"Of course." Head high, she strode over to the open door of the Maserati and lowered herself to the leather seat.

By the time the red car roared off down the lane, Sky was already leading the horses toward the long barn. After turning the mare over to a stable hand, he found an empty stall for Storm Cloud, unsaddled him, and gave him some hay and water. The gelding was too warm and too tired to misbehave. A sigh of contentment eased through the big body as Sky began rubbing him down with a towel. Sky usually found the job relaxing. But right now his thoughts were tumbleweeds in the wind.

Lauren's departure had left him smarting, but she was the least of his worries. The discovery he'd made today had to be dealt with. That would mean involving Will, Beau, and ultimately the law—most likely the DEA, since Abner Sweeney didn't seem competent to handle anything more serious than a traffic ticket.

But first he needed to talk with Marie. He'd hoped for a free afternoon to drive into town and catch her before the bar got busy. But it hadn't happened, and now he couldn't wait any longer. He would go back to the Blue Coyote tonight before closing time, and he wouldn't leave until he found out what she was doing in Blanco Springs.

The little girl he remembered was long gone. He could only hope the hardened woman who'd taken her place would tell him the truth.

CHAPTER 7

It was ten-fifteen when Sky pulled his pickup into the parking lot at the Blue Coyote. The bar closed at eleven on weeknights, and the lot was already thinning out. As Sky switched off the engine he saw Abner Sweeney, still in uniform, stroll out the front door, cross the crumbling asphalt, and climb into a gleaming maroon Ford Explorer, so new that it still had the temporary license permit stuck to the rear window. Either Abner had been saving his pennies, or his promotion to sheriff had given him a nice bump in pay. Or maybe he'd just done somebody a big favor.

Never mind, Sky lectured himself. Having a new vehicle wasn't against the law. And the reason he'd come here had nothing to do with Abner.

Marie was working. As Sky stepped through the door she glanced up to meet his eyes, then tore her gaze away. She looked drawn and harried, the scar a white slash against the olive skin of her face. Except for that scar and her grim expression, she looked much the way Sky remembered his mother.

Stella was nowhere in sight, but her half brother, Nigel, was on duty behind the bar. Sky remembered the boots and the tracks. There weren't many biker types in a cowboy town like Blanco Springs. But the bar would have been open at the time Sky had heard the motorcycle. Nigel would have been working. So, most likely, would Marie.

Finding an empty booth, Sky sat down to wait. Marie was the only one serving seated customers. Sooner or later she would come to him. When she did, he'd have the twenty-dollar bill, with the note folded inside, ready to give her.

Blue pickup, parking lot, after closing—or tell me when and where.

Stella wandered in from the back hallway, tugging down her skin-tight denim skirt. Sky turned away, shifting his face toward the back of the booth. If the woman decided to corner him, that could keep Marie at a distance.

"What'll it be, mister?" Marie stood next to the booth. Sky kept his eyes lowered as he fished the money with the note out of his pocket.

"Corona, no glass." He handed her the bill. "Bring me back ten and keep the rest."

"Thanks." Her voice betrayed nothing as she turned away and headed for the cash register at the end of the bar. Sky cautioned himself not to watch her. Stella had sharp eyes and a suspicious nature. If Marie wanted to treat him like a stranger, he'd be smart to play along. It was clear that she didn't want her boss to know about her connection to the Fletcher family.

Marie came back with the beer, along with ten dollars that she laid on the table. No reply note and no eye contact. Did that mean he was to wait outside for her, or was she blowing him off?

Sky sipped his beer, taking his time. Stella gave him a wink and a wave but didn't sidle over and join him, which was all to the good. At ten minutes to eleven, he walked outside and sat in his truck with the lights off. Twenty minutes later the parking lot had emptied and he was still waiting. He watched the blue neon sign above the door flicker off. His fingers toyed with the keys that hung from the ignition. Maybe he'd struck out.

He was about to start the engine when a shadow peeled away from the dark shape of the building and moved across the parking lot toward him. Making sure the dome light was off, Sky opened the passenger door. Marie slid into the cab beside him, slumping low in the seat as if she didn't want to be seen from outside.

"You haven't changed much," she said.

"I can't say the same for you."

Her fingers traced the ugly scar. "A little present from my ex-husband. He came at me with a butcher knife. I don't have to tell you he'll never do that again. Mind if I smoke?"

"Not as long as you blow it out the window."

While Marie fished for a cigarette and lit it with a cheap, pink plastic lighter, Sky lifted the pocketknife out of his vest. "This belongs to you. I couldn't help wondering if you dropped it on purpose." He waited for her to answer. When she simply took the knife, he continued.

"Somebody out there shot a fine old man, Marie. Then they went off and left him to die—it's a miracle he survived. Before I pass judgment and decide what to do, I want to hear your side of the story."

Marie puffed on her cigarette. "It wasn't me, if that's what you're thinking. It was Coy."

Coy.

Another piece of the puzzle slid into place. Coy Fletcher, the second oldest of Marie's brothers, was the bully of the family. Slow-witted and mean, he took pleasure in tormenting anything—or anyone—smaller and weaker than he was. After receiving some nasty bruises and a dislocated shoulder, Sky had learned to stay out of his way.

"It was an accident," Marie said. "We were short-cutting across the ranch when we heard the ATV coming right toward us."

"The old man wouldn't have hurt you," Sky said.

"Maybe not. But we didn't know that. And we didn't want to be seen and identified. Coy's got some warrants back in Oklahoma. If he got arrested here, even just for trespassing, he could be in a lot of trouble.

"Coy grabbed the gun off the bike and we ducked behind the bushes. Afterward he told me that he'd meant to shoot over the old man's head, just to scare him off. But right when he fired, the ATV hit a bump. The old man bounced up far enough to catch the bullet."

Could he believe her? Sky had always had a soft spot for his younger cousin. But the story sounded pretty far-fetched. Given the evidence, he'd be crazy to trust her.

"So after he crashed, you took his gun and left him there." Until he spoke the words, Sky didn't realize how angry he'd been—and was. Whether her story was true or not, there was no excuse for leaving Jasper wounded and half-drowning in the seep.

"I wanted to go to him. But Coy said that he was dead and we had to get out of there before somebody else came. The dog was barking at us. Coy was going to shoot it. I promised that if he wouldn't, I'd get the old man's gun where it had fallen off the ATV and go with him. That was when I dropped the knife, on the chance that you'd find it. I wanted to let you know I was here, in case we needed your help."

Needed his help? Something went cold in the pit of Sky's stomach. Whatever he'd stumbled into, it wasn't good.

"You said you were shortcutting."

"We'd picked up some supplies in town. I was driving, and Coy was sitting behind, hanging on to the stuff we'd bought. It was awkward going, so we took the shortest way there."

A battered Ford Ranchero pulled into the parking lot, radio blaring Mexican music. Its headlights made a sweep as it turned around. An empty Dos Equis beer can flew out the window and clattered to the asphalt. Marie shrank lower in the seat as the vehicle swung close, finished turning, and roared out the way it had come in.

Sky waited for Marie to say more. When she didn't reply, he broke the silence. "I found the marijuana operation, Marie. Did you know it was on my own land?"

She stared down at her hands. Slowly she nodded. "I went to the county recorder's office to check the maps for an out-of-the-way spot with water. It was perfect—especially with your name on the deed. With it being yours, we figured if you caught us, you'd let us off easy. You *will* let us off easy, won't you, Sky?"

When she looked up at him, Sky glimpsed the sad-eyed little girl he'd left behind in the kitchen all those years ago. But there were limits to how soft-hearted he could be.

"The marijuana has to go," he said. "If it's cleared off my land by the end of tomorrow—plants, hoses, tools, and whatever you and Coy are living in—I won't call in the law. But if you get caught somewhere else, you're on your own. And one thing more. You're never to set foot on Tyler land again. Understand?"

She tossed her glowing cigarette stub out the window. "It was Coy's idea to grow the weed, not mine. Once it's gone, maybe he'll get a job or something."

"I'm hoping he'll be smart enough to go back to Oklahoma. You too. What are the two of you doing here, anyway?"

"Lute used to call me sometimes. He said there were ways to make good money here, if I wanted to come. When I told Coy, he said he wanted to come, too."

"Well, you know what happened to Lute."

"Yes. And I heard that the bastard who shot him died in jail. Thanks, by the way, for paying to have Lute's body sent home."

"Lute was family. So are you," Sky said. "Let me drive you back to your camp. We can talk to Coy together."

"I'm not sleeping out there. I'm staying in the back room above the Blue Coyote. Stella takes the rent out of my pay. It's just Coy who's camping on your land. But don't go out there tonight. He's got guns. If he hears somebody coming, he's liable to shoot first and ask questions later. You know Coy."

Sky did. Meanness and stupidity made for a dangerous mix.

"If you can come back for me in the morning, I'll ride out with you. Coy won't be happy about leaving, but he'll be more apt to listen to reason if I'm there."

Sky thought about training the colts and all the

work he needed to do. Will wouldn't be pleased by his absence. But this mess involved the safety of the Rimrock and everyone on it. It had to be taken care of.

"How early can you be ready?" he asked her.

"As early as you want."

"Eight?"

"Fine. But not here. Pick me up outside the Shop Mart." She opened the door and swung her legs to the ground. "Good to see you, Sky. Maybe we'll get more time to catch up."

Sky watched her walk around to the back door of the bar, where the stairs led up to the second floor. Some, maybe most, of Stella's waitresses had used that room to make extra cash as prostitutes. He wouldn't put it past Marie to be doing the same. The thought saddened him, but she was a grown woman, and after what had happened with Lute, he wasn't in the rescue business.

After she'd gone inside, he started up the truck and headed out of town. The marijuana was one thing. But Jasper was another. If the old man had died—as he nearly had—Coy would be guilty of murder, or at least manslaughter.

There was no way Sky could keep this secret from Beau and Will. Tomorrow he would tell them about the marijuana and how Jasper had supposedly been shot. Jasper would need to be told, too. If he chose to press charges, Coy's fate would be up to a jury.

He would have to tell the brothers about his property, too, Sky realized. It shouldn't be a big surprise, since they knew Bull had left him something in the will. But he'd hoped to keep it secret until he decided what to do with the land. No doubt they'd have plenty of suggestions.

Glancing down at the dashboard clock, he saw

that it was after midnight. Had the red Maserati delivered Lauren back to her doorstep, or was she still
"thanking" Josh Hardesty for his contribution to her
father's campaign?

Sky cursed the rage that crackled like summer
lightning through his veins. Jealousy was a waste of
time and energy. If Prescott's spoiled princess daughter wanted to go out with an old *cabrón* in a fancy car,
that was her business. He had more urgent worries,
enough to drive a sane man crazy. Lauren Prescott
was just one more distraction—one he didn't need.

He would work with her horse because he'd
promised, and because a good horse deserved better
than to live in fear. But if she expected any more
than a friendly fist bump from him, the lady was in
for a letdown.

If he told himself he didn't want her, he'd be
lying. The memory of pressing her against the desk,
thrusting into that tight, hot silk while her voice
urged him on, would burn him alive if he let it. But
he was a man, with a man's pride and a man's responsibilities. Lauren could play her little games with
somebody else.

Marie dragged her feet up the wooden stairs, bone
weary after her grueling eight-hour shift. The dark
stairwell smelled of cigarette smoke and stale urine.
God, how she hated this place. But never mind that.
She'd come here for a reason, with a plan she'd already set in motion.

Getting Sky's sympathy had been part of that plan.
It was easily done. Sky had always been generous to a
fault, too willing to see the good in people even
where there was no good to be found. He'd believed

in that dumb-ass Lute, and if she played her cards right, he would believe in her.

Not that she meant him any harm. Unlike her brothers, Sky had always been good to her. She wasn't ungrateful. But she wasn't above using his influence and his protection to her advantage. Tonight she'd fed him just enough truth to gain his trust—including the part about the recorder's office. The lies—and there'd been a few—would need fixing before she saw him again.

She'd never meant to bring Coy to Texas with her. But he was wanted in Oklahoma, and he'd insisted on coming. So far his presence had been a disaster. If she hadn't been hauling his lazy ass back from town on the bike, they would never have run into that old man and Marie wouldn't have had to shoot him. Now she feared Coy's big mouth would get them both in trouble. And trouble was the last thing she could afford right now.

From the upstairs hallway, she opened the door to her room. The day's heat came rushing out, along with the lingering odors of stale sex that rose from the mattress on the rusty metal bed. Marie hated that smell and what it meant. She'd done things she wasn't proud of, but she'd never been a whore.

Stepping inside, she opened the only window. With no cross-ventilation it didn't let in much air, but it was better than nothing. The room above the Blue Coyote was a shitty place to live—there was no better word for it. The only bathroom was downstairs in the bar. Needing it now, she took her key and went down the hall to the inside stairway.

Nobody else was in the bar at night. Stella and her brother lived in an apartment across town—probably a palace compared to this dump. Marie used the toilet and bent over the sink to wash. The single 40-watt bulb gleamed on the mirror that reflected her scarred face. Someday she'd have the money to get that scar removed. She'd have money for other things as well— a hot car, pretty clothes, and her own condo. Lute had wanted those things, too. He'd died trying to get them. But she was a lot smarter than Lute. She had a plan—one she was about to take to the next level.

She'd figured there was no hurry. But now that Sky was involved, time was running out. She would have to act tonight.

"You're home late. I hope that's a good sign." Garn Prescott set his bourbon glass on the coffee table and rose as his daughter walked in through the front entry.

"Hardly." Lauren sounded annoyed. Her rumpled blouse was missing a button. "We had a flat tire on the way home. I offered to help him change it, but he insisted on calling his auto club. We were stuck in the middle of nowhere for over an hour, waiting for them to show up."

Prescott sighed. "Well, at least the time must have given you a chance to get better acquainted."

"Oh, we got acquainted, all right, if that's what you want to call it. The wrestling match ended when I slapped his smarmy face! I hope you cashed that check he gave you. After tonight, I wouldn't put it past him to stop payment."

Prescott had put the check in his wallet for his next trip to the bank. The thought that the funds might be blocked was enough to make his stomach churn. Maybe it was time he got one of those high-tech phone apps that let you snap a photo of the check and send it to the bank.

He squelched the urge to rail at his daughter. Didn't Lauren realize how much he needed the goodwill of the governor's family, to say nothing of the money?

At least Stella Rawlins's cash was safe in the bank. It wouldn't be a bad idea to call and thank her, maybe take her out to dinner. He preferred his women younger, like Tori Tyler, who'd been turning him down ever since his wife's death had made him a widower. But Stella's air of knowing sexuality intrigued him—almost as much as her offer of more money for his strapped campaign.

"Did you have to antagonize the man, Lauren? Not that I expected you to sleep with him, but couldn't you have given him a little encouragement, maybe left him hoping for more?"

Lauren's shoulders sagged for an instant. Then her head came up. "God, I'm not even going to dignify that question with an answer!" She flung him a look of defiance. "What are you doing up so late, anyway? It's not like I'm still in high school."

Prescott picked up the TV remote and clicked it on. "The local station gave me a deal on some airtime. I just want to make sure they're running my ad."

He settled back on the sofa to watch. The ad was a rerun from his previous campaign two years ago. But what the hell, he hadn't changed that much and neither had his message. Anyway, who was going to see it in the middle of the night? When he got more money coming in, he'd shoot a new ad and buy some decent time to run it. But right now this was the best he could manage.

"What do you think, Lauren?" he asked. "How

could I improve on this for the new ad? Would you be willing to say a few words on camera, maybe give the boys something to look at?"

There was no answer.

"Lauren?" He looked back toward the entry, where she'd been standing. His daughter was nowhere to be seen.

Lauren switched off the floodlights that illuminated the swimming pool behind the house. Cloaked in darkness, she walked to the water's edge. The night air was stifling, her skin sticky with sweat. Worse, she felt dirty, as if she'd just allowed herself to be sold. Maybe she hadn't delivered the goods. But Josh Hardesty had assumed she would. After all, he'd paid the price. He'd even implied as much the first time she'd shoved him away.

The smell of expensive leather, from the Maserati's sweat-dampened seats, clung faintly to her clothes. Her fumbling fingers peeled away her blouse and bra, her slacks and underwear. She kicked off her sandals, stepping free of the clothes that had bunched around her feet.

Never again, she vowed as the dark heat of shame crawled over her skin. This was the last time she would let guilt, filial duty, or even the need for peace goad her into playing politics for her father.

Maybe if she'd been born male, he would have cared more for her growing up. But Garn Prescott had never shown much interest in his daughter. And now that she was here, all he wanted was to use her. To hell with him.

Curling her toes over the tiled edge, she knifed into the pool. The water closed over her, cool, dark, and welcoming, shutting out the ugliness in the world. She swam deeper, lungs bursting with the urge to breathe. Was this how it had felt to Mike when he—

But she mustn't think about that. Dwelling on the memory would only send her into another downward spiral. She couldn't let it happen again. She had to move on.

Like a fighter pilot pulling out of a dive, she kicked for the surface. Breaking free, she filled her lungs with air and stretched out to float on her back. High overhead, framed by an ocean of stars, the Milky Way spilled across the heavens. Starlight gleamed on her breasts where they rose above the water. Chilled by the deep dive, her nipples were darkly swollen, like ripe blackberries.

She imagined Sky looking down at her, touching her body with hypnotic hands as gentle as water. The thought lingered, triggering delicious twinges of memory. . . .

If she were to make a list of reasons she should stay away from Sky Fletcher, it would be a long one. And Sky's list of reasons to avoid her would be even longer.

They'd grown up in different worlds. She was a city girl. Sky was wedded to his life on the ranch with the horses he loved.

She was an heiress who loved designer clothes, gourmet restaurants, and posh surroundings. Sky's wealth lay in his utter lack of need for material things.

She was in limbo—reaching, searching for something she couldn't even name. Sky knew exactly who he was and what he expected from life. She was an emotional train wreck. He was as solid as a granite boulder.

If discovered, their relationship would send her father into a screaming rage. Lauren couldn't care
less. But she knew what the Tylers thought of Garn
Prescott. A liaison with Prescott's daughter was a
complication Sky didn't need—and wouldn't want.

Red flags and roadblocks all the way. Common
sense told Lauren to heed the warning signs. But
how could she, when she craved Sky's arms around
her the way she'd craved air when she was underwater,
holding her breath?

Would she see him tomorrow when she went to
the Tylers', or would he find reasons to avoid her?
They hadn't exactly parted on good terms. She'd
sensed something was wrong earlier when they'd ridden away from the spring. Then, when Hardesty had
shown up at the ranch house, she'd not only stood
there and let the man treat Sky like a common hired
hand but she'd joined in, dismissing him with an
order to put away her horse.

What had she been thinking? Had she wanted to
avoid a showdown? Protect Sky? Protect herself? Any
way you looked at it, she'd handled the situation like
a jerk. Sky was a proud man. What were the odds that
he would never forgive her?

Early the next morning, when Sky stopped by the
house to talk with Will and Beau, the brothers were
gone. He found Bernice in the kitchen, spooning
pancake batter onto a cast iron griddle for Erin's
breakfast.

"They left twenty minutes ago in Beau's Jeep," she
told him. "Will said they were going up to check the
cattle pens on the caprock. From there, they planned
to drive to Lubbock and bring Jasper home."

"Great news. This place hasn't been the same without him. Did Will give you any idea when they'd be back?"

Bernice scooped three golden pancakes off the griddle and dropped them onto Erin's plate. "They were hoping it might be before noon. But you've been in the hospital, Sky. You know how long getting out of there can take—waiting for the doctor, signing all that blasted paperwork. Want some pancakes?"

"Thanks, but I can't stay," Sky said. Telling Beau and Will about the marijuana on his land would have to wait till tonight. Meanwhile, he had to pick up Marie in town and prepare for a nasty confrontation with Coy. He could only hope he wouldn't need the Smith and Wesson .38 he kept under the driver's seat of his truck.

Erin buttered her pancakes and drowned them in a lake of maple syrup. "Sky, can you help me work with Tesoro this morning?" she asked between bites.

Most days Sky enjoyed helping Will's daughter handle her precious palomino foal. But today the timing was wrong. "Sorry, but I need to go into town," he said. "Remind me when I get back. I'll see what we can do then."

"Okay. But promise me you won't forget."

"I won't forget if you remind me, will I?" He flashed her a grin as he ducked out the kitchen door. Erin was a great kid. He liked knowing she was his niece, even though he'd never tell a soul. Later in the day he would try to make time for her. But right now he had darker concerns on his mind.

Marie was waiting outside the grocery store when he pulled up. She slid into the passenger side of the truck and slumped in the seat, her battered Stetson pulled low to shadow her face. "Let's get going," she said.

Sky pulled onto Main Street and headed back toward the highway. "I think it's time you told me what all the sneaking around is about," he said.

Marie didn't answer.

"I figured you didn't want anybody to know we were related, especially Stella. But I'm not okay with this, Marie. Tell me what you're up to."

"You're so smart. You tell me."

Sky touched the brake, letting a rabbit race across the road. The sun was up, the day already getting hot. "That's not how it works," he said. "I've got a job and a reputation on the line. Since you're bent on dragging me into your mess, I need to know what's going on."

"Why should I tell you when you don't give a shit about our family?"

"That's not true. I tried to help Lute. He ended up setting a fire, stealing two horses, and sending a little girl to the hospital. But even then, when he was cornered, I tried to save him. That's what got me shot."

"Well, what about now?"

She was leading up to something. Sky met her words with silence, hoping she'd say more. At last she spoke again.

"Lute called me a couple of days before he died. He said Stella meant to kill him—she wouldn't do it herself, but she'd send somebody else. That was her way. Do you believe that?"

"Pretty much," Sky said. "But there's no evidence against the woman. She can't be arrested and charged without proof."

"I don't need proof." Marie's voice was leaden.

"Lute was my brother and she had him killed. I'm here to make the bitch pay."

The pickup's engine rumbled in the silence. Sky shifted into low gear as he turned the truck onto an unpaved side road. The going would be slow and dusty from here.

"How?" he asked.

"That depends. Right now the plan is to win her trust, take the time to learn all I can about her operation, then strike where it'll hurt her the most."

"You could do it legally. Find enough evidence to turn her over to the law."

"I could." She rolled up the window to keep out the billowing dust. "But I don't have to if there's a way to do it fast and dirty."

He had to give her credit, Sky conceded. Legal or not, going after Stella Rawlins took a lot of guts. But did Marie understand the depth of the danger?

"Be careful," he said. "Stella's like a black widow spider with webs in places you'd least expect. Cross her and she can be deadly. Look what happened to Lute."

"Lute didn't know what he was getting into. I do. And I'm smarter than he was."

"I always thought you were smarter than all of your brothers put together," Sky said. "And speaking of brothers, how does Coy fit into your plans?"

Marie leaned back in the seat and put one dusty boot on the dashboard. "Wasn't my idea to bring him along in the first place," she said. "Sometimes I think I'd be better off without him. But he's here, and it would be a shame not to put him to use. Any suggestions?"

"Don't ask me." In the distance, Sky could see the stand of mesquite that marked the boundary of his land. The uncleared scrub made it perfect for hiding an illegal crop. He could only hope Coy would leave without putting up too much of a fuss.

But knowing Coy, anything could happen.

Stopping fifty yards short of the property line, Sky parked in the open and pulled the hand brake. "Hope you don't mind getting out first," he told Marie. "If Coy sees it's you, he's less apt to react."

"No problem." Marie swung out of the truck and strode across the expanse of dry grass. Sky took a moment to holster the pistol he'd brought. He didn't plan to shoot his cousin, but if Coy needed a little extra persuasion, a gun might come in handy.

"Coy, it's me!" Marie called out. "I've brought Sky!"

There was no response. She called again as Sky came even with her. Again, there was no answer.

"I don't like this," Marie said. "Coy's usually up by now, and he's pretty alert."

"Stay behind me." Sky drew the pistol and cocked it. Moving into cover, he edged forward. This wild country, within easy reach of the border, was the haunt of illegals, fugitives, and drug gangs. He needed to be ready for anything.

Warning Marie to stay back, he stepped into the clearing, where a makeshift tent—little more than a tarp on some sticks—stood with the flap partway lifted. A magpie glided onto the peak of the ramshackle structure, scolded the newcomers, then took wing again.

"Coy?" Marie pushed past Sky and flung back the tent flap. There was nothing inside but some crumpled food wrappers, empty beer cans, and a dirty, rumpled blanket.

Through the trees Sky could see the marijuana

patches, scattered among clumps of mesquite, each one watered by a black plastic hose. Without water, the finger-high plants wouldn't last long.

"Coy! Dammit, where are you?" Marie's voice had taken on a frantic note. She raced past the marijuana and up a faintly worn path that probably led to the latrine. She was back a moment later, a stricken look on her face.

"I can't find him anywhere," she said. "He's gone."

CHAPTER 8

Sky and Marie took a few minutes to scout the area around the camp. They found no sign that any strangers had been there.

Sky made a last scan of the horizon. "Could Coy have taken his motorcycle somewhere? I don't see it."

"That Harley's mine. It's parked behind the Blue Coyote," Marie said. "I drove Coy into town for a burger and some snacks yesterday and dropped him off back here when he was done."

"So that was you I heard driving up. I thought you'd be working at that hour."

"My shift doesn't start till four-thirty on weekdays. Coy gets antsy out here alone, but it makes more sense for me to keep the bike in town. I'd just as soon not have him roaming around, getting into trouble." Marie lifted her hat and raked a hand through her sweaty hair. "I heard somebody riding off on a horse as we pulled in. I was wondering if it might be you."

Sky reached into the tent and lifted out a moth-eaten, red wool blanket. The butts of a half-dozen marijuana joints dropped to the ground as he shook it. There was nothing underneath but a couple of well-thumbed girlie magazines.

Sky tossed the blanket aside. "I don't see any guns. Where would Coy have kept them?"

"Right here in the tent. All he had was a little lever-action rifle and the shotgun we took off the old man."

"Could he have taken the guns and gone hunting? There are plenty of rabbits and birds out here."

"Maybe. Coy likes to kill things. But he's so lazy, he'd have to be starving to skin and cook anything he shot. Besides, we agreed that a campfire might attract attention."

"In this drought, it could start a range fire, too." Sky holstered his pistol and glanced back toward the spring. "How about helping me dismantle this hose setup and throwing it all in the truck? Maybe by the time we're finished, he'll show up."

He seized one of the black hoses and yanked it free of the bent wire stakes that anchored it to the ground. It came up easily. Walking forward he coiled the length between his hands. After watching him a moment, Marie pulled up a second hose and began looping it over her arm. Sky studied her for some sign of anger or regret—after all, she'd likely helped Coy buy the pump and hoses and set up the watering system. But her sharp Comanche features might as well have been chiseled in stone.

It didn't take long to coil the hoses, pull the pipe out of the spring, and disconnect everything from the pump. By the time Sky backed the truck up to the site and tossed everything into the bed, the small cannabis plants were already wilting in the heat— and there was still no sign of Coy.

Marie gave Sky a questioning glance, as if to say, *What about him?*

Sky thought of the work waiting back at the ranch. After opening the cab, he gave several loud blasts on the horn. "I can't wait here much longer, and I can't leave you without a ride. I'll give him ten minutes. If he's not back by then, we're leaving. Coy can figure things out for himself."

"I can come back and check on him later," Marie said. "But he'll need shelter. Can we leave the tent?"

"For now." Sky slid his wallet out of his Wranglers and counted out four twenty-dollar bills. "If Coy needs food or a place to sleep, this'll help. But anything that's still here by tomorrow night is getting torn down and hauled away. Understand?"

Marie gave him a sullen look. "You've gotten mean in your old age, Sky."

He thought of Lute. "Life does that to you. Something tells me you've figured that out by now."

She sat on the lowered tailgate, her thin, muscular arms hugging her knees. "D'you plan to tell anybody about this?"

The drone of insects filled the silence as Sky pondered his answer. Maybe he could forgive the marijuana on his property. But he owed Jasper the chance to face the man who'd nearly killed him. The trouble was, with warrants hanging over him in Oklahoma, Coy would run from any involvement with the law. Maybe he already had.

"I told you, the shooting was an accident," Marie said.

"If that's true, maybe we can clear it up without calling in the sheriff. Coy could go to the Tylers, explain what happened. It's worth a shot."

"Sure it is." Marie's voice twanged with sarcasm.

"If you've got any better ideas, I'm all ears. But know that if Coy runs, the offer's off the table. That's tantamount to an admission of guilt."

"What about me?" she asked. "If Coy wants to leave, I can't stop him. But I'm staying in Blanco Springs, and you know the reason why."

"Get Coy to cooperate—or tell the truth yourself if he runs—and I'll stand up for you," Sky said. "If Coy had the gun and shot Jasper by accident, the only thing you'd be guilty of is trespassing."

"And the weed?" she asked.

Sky lifted an eyebrow. "What weed?"

"Thanks," she muttered, "I'll think about the rest."

"There's a pen in the cab. I'll jot down my cell number for you."

"I'll take it," she said, "but I don't usually carry a phone, and I can't risk anything that might make Stella suspicious. If you need to talk to me, come in and order a beer. We'll work it from there."

She was quiet on the way back to town, maybe worried about her brother, Sky thought. He let her off behind the Shop Mart, where he unloaded the hose parts and tossed them into a Dumpster. Why stir up a fuss when no harm had been done?

Driving home, he forced his attention back to the ranch. If the colts he was training could save the Rimrock, nothing could be allowed to distract him from his vital job—not Marie and her problems, and not even the sexy, red-haired hellion who kept stealing into his thoughts.

Lauren could drive him crazy if he let her, but that wasn't going to happen. Sure, if she wanted a roll in the hay, he'd be glad to give her one, no strings attached. But he'd seen her kind before—a spoiled princess having a little fun with a cowboy, not caring who got hurt. Sooner or later she'd face the fact that he could never give her all she wanted, and she'd move on. He was already prepared for that. As far as he was concerned, she was already gone.

As the house and barns came into sight, Sky glanced at the clock on the dashboard. It was barely ten-fifteen. Plenty of time left to work with the colts. But the sun would be blistering hot. He would need to give his four-legged pupils plenty of water and maybe shorten their training intervals.

Still shifting mental gears, he came up to the house. He'd resolved not to look, but his gaze was drawn as if by a magnet to the gravel strip out front. There was Lauren's Corvette, the dust still settling on its shiny black chassis.

The sudden thought of her, in that room, at that desk, in those jeans, triggered a jolt of lust. A curse escaped his lips as heat forked through his body like an electric jolt.

Damn the woman!

Sky tore his eyes away and kept on driving.

Lauren switched off the computer, rose from the desk chair, and stretched her arms above her head. She'd put in a long day at the Rimrock. Beau would be pleased with what she'd managed to get done.

Beau had dropped by earlier for a quick hello. "I see you found your earring," he'd said, casting an impish glance at the little gold stud she'd replaced in her earlobe. "For what it's worth, Sky's under strict orders to let you work today."

"Fine." Her hot-faced glare had warned him not to say more. Beau Tyler was an incorrigible tease, but he seemed to know when he'd pushed far enough.

At lunchtime, Bernice had brought her a chicken sandwich and some icy lemonade. She'd mentioned that her brother, Jasper, was home from the hospital and already chafing to be up and around. Aside from that—and the brief distraction of Sky's truck passing the house—Lauren had worked undisturbed.

Now it was late afternoon and time for a decision. She could go home now, or she could swallow her pride, find Sky, and apologize for yesterday's behavior. After picking up the hat she'd left on a chair, she closed the office and wandered outside to the front porch.

There was nobody in sight—only a red-tailed hawk riding the updrafts and a dust cloud swirling across the sun-parched yard. Heat waves blurred the near distance where the long barn stood, with the corrals and horse paddock on its far side. Would she find Sky there if she went to look for him? Would he be civil, or would he simply ignore her and go on with his work?

Maybe she should just get in her car and leave. Anything would be better than withering under the contempt in those proud cobalt eyes. A man like Sky could get any woman he wanted. If he'd decided Garn Prescott's daughter was more trouble than she was worth . . .

Lauren dismissed the thought. She had her own pride. And if all she needed was a male body in her bed, there was always Josh Hardesty, who would be back at the beckoning crook of a finger. But Sky had stirred something she hadn't felt since Mike's death. Not that she was in love with him—that would be too much to expect, as well as a disaster for them both. But for the first time in a year, she'd begun to feel something besides grief.

Without having made a conscious decision, she was walking across the open ground. Whorls of dust rose from under her boots. The slanting sun beat down on her straw hat as she came around the barn.

The horse paddock, which had its own windmill-driven watering system, was an island of green in a sea of sun-parched brown. Mares and foals clustered in the shade of a big cottonwood on the far side, their tails whisking flies out of one another's faces. Separated from the mares by a fence, Sky's colts drowsed in the heat or gathered around the water trough. A half-dozen older cows, kept around to accustom the colts to the presence of cattle, grazed along the far fence.

Lauren's pulse quickened as her eyes found Sky. He was on the near side of the paddock, working with Erin and her young palomino. Moving closer, Lauren leaned against the log fence to watch. She'd gotten to know Will's daughter over the past few weeks and found the girl delightful. Today Erin and Sky were working with a length of rawhide rope, not trying to lead the foal but simply letting him smell it, laying it across his back and draping it lightly around his neck to give him the feel of it.

Lauren knew better than to speak. She stood still and watched, amazed by Sky's gentleness. Here, in his own element, he was different from the gruff, driven man she'd come to know. With Erin and Tesoro he was all patience, his manner firm but tender, as if the girl and the foal were the most precious things on earth. What a wonderful father he'd make, Lauren thought, then brought herself up short. Where had that thought come from?

No doubt Sky was aware of her—he was alert to everything around him. But he gave no sign that she'd caught his attention. He was focused on the lesson he

was giving. His manner told her that any other business—even hers—would have to wait.

He took his time before ending the session, releas-
ing the foal with a pat on the rump. With Erin at his
side, Sky walked back to the fence.

"Hi, Lauren." The girl grinned up at her. "Isn't
Tesoro looking good? Sky says he's really smart."

"I can tell," Lauren said. "He's growing, too."

"Sky says that if Tesoro's going to be a stallion, we
have to make sure he's well trained, and that he
knows I'm his boss."

"Well, it looks like you're well on your way." Lauren could feel Sky's gaze on her. He looked as if he'd
been out in the hot sun all day. Sweat had plastered
his cotton shirt to his lean-muscled torso. Below the
brim of his Stetson, moisture beads trickled down his
sun-burnished face. The salty man-aroma of his body
seeped into Lauren's senses, arousing, despite the
tension between them.

Erin caught the top rail of the fence, swung a leg
over, and jumped to the ground. "Guess I'll go see if
Jasper needs anything," she said. "Thanks, Sky. I
know you were really busy today."

He gave her a quicksilver smile. "I can always make
time for you and Tesoro."

"More tomorrow?" she asked. "Just for a little
while."

"Sure."

Lauren watched the girl race back toward the
house. Pulse tripping, she turned back to face Sky. Was
he going to welcome her, or chill her with a look?

His gaze found her. His chiseled face was unreadable. "Hell but it's hot," he growled. "Hand me that
empty bucket next to your feet."

Puzzled, but knowing better than to question him,

Lauren passed the bucket over the fence. He moved to the nearby watering trough and filled the bucket to the brim. Tossing his hat aside, he lifted the bucket high and emptied it over his head. Lauren watched the cool water spill over him, plastering his black hair to his head, flowing down his face and body like a cascading stream over a rocky ledge.

With one hand, he raked his hair off his face. His dripping clothes clung to his body. His breath eased out in a long exhalation. "That's more like it," he said. "Now what was it you wanted, Lauren?"

His voice was as cold as his look. Lauren was on the verge of excusing herself and walking away when a crazy idea struck her. Taking a reckless chance, she placed a boot on the middle rail and swung over the fence to stand facing him. With a nod, she pointed to the bucket in his hand. "I could use some of that myself if you wouldn't mind," she said.

"But you aren't—" He broke off, raising one ink-black eyebrow. His expression had become knowing, half-amused. With a deliberate move, he stepped to the trough and scooped the bucket full of water. Lauren braced herself, closing her eyes as he lifted it above her head.

If he hesitated, it was no more than an instant. She felt the shock of the cool water, breathed the mossy smell of it as it poured over her, soaking her hair and her shirt, dripping down over her jeans and boots.

When she opened her eyes, Sky was grinning down at her. "You look damn good wet," he said. Then his eyes went hungry.

Lauren didn't reply. She'd become sharply aware of the way their clothes clung and the way their gazes devoured each other's bodies. The ache that rose in her was sweet and hot and raw. If he so much as touched her she knew she would topple past the edge of all common sense.

But nothing was going to happen here, in the sun-lit paddock where anyone coming out of the barn or passing the corrals could see them. They stood in mute frustration, moisture steaming off their hair and clothes.

Sky cleared his throat. "Let's go for a ride," he said.

They saddled Storm Cloud and Belle, mounted up, and headed west into the rugged canyon country. Riding single file through the scrub, hat brims lowered against the glare of the late-day sun, they said little until they'd reached the lengthening shadows of the escarpment. It was cooler here, the trail more open. The first rays of sunset cast a glow over the rocky buttresses and hoodoos.

"I had no idea it would be so beautiful here." Lauren caught up with Sky, who'd paused on a level spot to wait for her.

"People can miss a lot with their heads buried in their computers," he said.

"I'll try not to take that personally." Lauren let her hat fall back against her shoulders. Her hair and clothes had dried in the heat. A light breeze cooled her face.

Storm Cloud snorted and tossed his handsome head. They made a striking pair, Lauren thought, the black horse and the hawk-proud, black-haired man. If she'd been an artist she'd have chosen to paint them like this, with the setting sun and the canyon behind them.

"Storm Cloud seems to be behaving today," she said.

Sky patted the gelding's shoulder. "I haven't had much time to work with him, but he does seem more relaxed. If he's calm enough by the time we're ready to go back, I'll let you ride him."

"No perfume today, I promise." Lauren laughed, thinking this was as happy as she'd felt in months.

"There are some petroglyphs up that steep-sided canyon. It's not far. We should have enough daylight left to see them."

"Then let's go." Lauren nudged the mare to a walk. The uneven ground here was slow going, but the pace made it easier to talk.

"I want to apologize for yesterday," she said. "I was trying to smooth things out for my father's sake. It turned out to be a bad idea."

"I don't own you, Lauren." Sky's voice had taken on a slight chill. "I've no right to judge your choice of company."

"Not even if that company turns out to be a horse's ass?"

He sucked in his breath as if her choice of words had shocked him, then exhaled with a chuckle. "I won't have you insulting some poor innocent horse."

"Sorry." Lauren had to laugh. "I'll say no more, except that my father went rushing to the bank this morning to make sure the man hadn't stopped payment on his check. I've learned my lesson. No more political favors for me."

Sky was silent for a moment. "I take it your father doesn't know about us—not that there's much to know."

The last words stung. Lauren shook her head. "I'm a big girl. I don't have to tell him everything."

"He wouldn't be happy." It wasn't a question.

"No, he wouldn't. But since he chose not to be part of my life, why should it be any of his business?"

Sky didn't answer. His eyes had taken on a veiled look, as if his thoughts had wandered elsewhere.

"What about your parents?" she asked him. "Do you have family somewhere?"

"My mother died when I was three. My father . . ." The words had taken on an edge. "My father's dead, too. They weren't married."

"I'm sorry," she said.

"Don't be. It is what it is. I was raised by my aunt and uncle in Oklahoma. I still touch base with my cousins, even though I can't say much for the way they live."

"And what you do with horses? How did that come about?"

"My grandfather was good with horses. He died when I was twelve, but I owe everything I know to that old man. The most important lesson he taught me was to look at every situation from the horse's point of view."

"Empathy, then."

"I guess that's the fancy word for it. But I'm not much for talking about myself. How about you?"

Lauren hesitated, knowing she needed to share but unsure where to begin.

"Beau told me you'd been engaged. If that's too personal—"

"No, I need to say it. He died last year. Jumped off a bridge. He even left me a note—as if that would help." Lauren was startled by her sudden surge of anger, the first she'd felt toward Mike since his death. What a horrible, selfish thing to have done to the people who loved him.

Sky didn't speak. Anything he might have said would have been inane.

"That night in the Blue Coyote—it was the one-year anniversary of Mike's death. I'd had an ugly fight with my father, and it had all come crashing in on me. I just wanted to forget."

"I figured something like that."

"I never thanked you for making sure I was all right."

Sky's mouth twitched in a hint of a smile. "As I recollect, you weren't in a grateful mood."

She glanced down at her hands. "Just so you'll know, it wasn't the first time I'd done something like that."

"We're all human, Lauren. Sometimes being human hurts."

They rode in silence for a time, taking in the stillness of the canyon. The shadows were longer now, the sky like a river of flame above the canyon walls. Clumps of cedar, fed by deep roots, grew green in the hollows below the cliffs.

The trail had narrowed. They were riding single file again, but Lauren was sharply aware of Sky's presence and the heat that flowed between them. Shivers of anticipation rose in the depths of her body. Would he have brought her this far just to look at the petroglyphs?

Where the trail branched off into a side canyon, he paused and waited for her to come even. "Has your father ever mentioned that little canyon?" he asked her. "It used to be part of the Rimrock, but years ago Bull Tyler sold it to your grandfather for one dollar. Nobody knows the whole story, except maybe Jasper, and he's not telling."

"So that's the place." The opening to the side

canyon was screened by brush. If Sky hadn't pointed it out, Lauren would have ridden past without a second look. "My father told me Will had offered to buy it back."

Sky nodded. "It's the only piece of Rimrock land that's ever been sold. I know Will wants it in the family. But he said your father couldn't—or wouldn't—sell. Something about a deathbed promise to your grandfather."

"I wouldn't know about that. But I've heard of the Spanish gold that's supposed to be buried there."

"Will says that's just a story. Old Ferg—your grandfather—sifted through every inch of ground and never found it." Sky glanced upward. "It'll be dark before long. Come on."

She followed him along the winding trail into the depths of the main canyon. Halting the horses, he swung off the gelding and dropped the reins. Lauren dismounted to stand beside him on the smooth sand at the base of the cliff.

"Look there." He guided her gaze upward. Stylized figures of men, women, and animals were etched across the cliff face, cast into relief by the slanting light. Lauren could make out war-bonneted chiefs, deer, cougars and bison, birds and horses—dozens of horses, their leaping, galloping poses frozen in time.

"Beautiful . . . and so sad," Lauren murmured, recalling the history she'd read, how the Comanches had been the finest horsemen on the plains until the army had defeated them in these canyons and slaughtered all their beloved horses—slaughtered them by the hundreds and hundreds—to make sure the tribe would never rise up again. Here in this place, the heartbreak became real.

Without a word, Sky turned and pulled her into

his arms. His kiss was rough and hungry, his sex a straining ridge against her belly. Frantic with need, Lauren melted against him. She wanted his hands on her skin, the weight of him between her legs. She wanted the feel of him thrusting inside her, filling her, owning the secret depths of her body.

Clumsy with eagerness, her hands fumbled with the front of his shirt. With a mutter of impatience he ripped the garment open and tossed it onto the sand. When he took her in his arms again the feel of his golden skin was like being wrapped in sunlight. She breathed in his mossy aroma, her tongue tasting the subtle, salty sweetness in the hollow of his throat, her fingers ranging over his body, coming to rest on a nipple. He groaned as it puckered and hardened beneath her touch.

Freeing the hem of her shirt, he slid his hands up her ribs. The front fastener of her bra came apart with a skillful twist. Lauren's breath caught as his hand closed over one breast, cupping its weight, stroking its sensitive surface. She butted against him, grinding like a stripper to heighten the shimmers that were already rocketing through her body. She was spiraling out of control, and she didn't care. All she knew was that she was dripping wet and she wanted him— every splendid inch of him.

"Please . . . don't wait," she muttered.

He chuckled against her ear. "Does that mean the same as *don't stop?*"

"That comes later—" She gasped as he yanked her jeans and lace panties off her hips and lowered her onto the shirt he'd flung to the sand. While she wriggled the rest of the way out of her jeans and boots, he dropped his Wranglers and paused to add protection.

Lauren lay back on the shirt, gazing up at him. Standing there naked with the sunset glowing on his skin, he took her breath away. He was all power and grace, all muscle and sinew and jaw-dropping sex. If ever there was a magnificent figure of a man, it was Sky Fletcher. And for the moment, at least, he was all hers. A freshly healed pink scar, deep and ugly, marked his left side below the ribs. Lauren remembered what Beau had told her about his being shot and almost dying. Right now it was as if his life was a gift to her.

For the space of a breath he turned away to kick his clothes aside. Only then did Lauren see the other scars, faded and white, that streaked across his back like the marks of a whip. The awareness struck her that there was much more to this man than she knew. But right now all she could think of was wanting him.

Her fingers stirred, beckoning him. "Come here, you," she whispered.

With a raw laugh he dropped between her out-stretched legs. Her knees came up to clasp his hips as he pushed into her, gliding on her slickness, his swollen size filling her so tightly that the first climax rushed through her body even before he began to move.

"Oh . . ." she breathed as the wave ebbed.

He grinned down at her transfixed face. "Finished already?"

Giggling like a schoolgirl, she pulled his head down for a kiss. His tongue teased hers in a playful dance. With Sky there were no complications, no promises, no guilt, just pure, giddy, mind-blowing pleasure.

He began his thrusts with exquisite restraint, pulling back and sliding in deep, giving her time to feel every subtle change in the contact of their bodies. Soon what began as a delicious tingle rose, swirled, turned urgent.

Her breaths became whimpers of need. Her hands clasped his taut buttocks, driving him harder.

She felt his control shatter. Breath rasping, he thrust like a stallion, driving into her deeper, faster, their wild ride ending in a burst of fireworks that would put the Fourth of July to shame.

Sky lay still for a moment, his breath easing out in a long exhalation. Pushing forward, he feathered a kiss on the tip of Lauren's nose. His smile was shameless. "Next time I'd like to show you what can happen when we don't have to hurry," he said.

Next time.

From a man like Sky Fletcher, that was as close to a commitment as she was going to get.

"Where the hell have you been, Lauren? I've been calling your cell for the past couple of hours."

As she walked in the front door, her father's demanding voice shattered the mellow aura that had floated around her all the way home.

"I went to work at the Tylers'," she said. "I told you I was going. And if nobody answered my phone it was because I left my purse in the car."

"You didn't check for messages?"

"Sorry, no." After a twilight ride back to the car with Sky, checking her phone had been the last thing on her mind.

"Well, Josh Hardesty called me. He's still willing to push for the governor's endorsement, and he wants to take you out again. I gave him your number, but when he couldn't reach you, I said I'd try you and get back to him."

"You gave Josh Hardesty my cell number? Can't you get it through your head that I never want to see him again?" Biting back anger, Lauren stepped out of the entry and into the lamplight. Her father's eyes widened at the sight of her tangled hair and rumpled shirt.

"Lord almighty, you look like you've been rolling in a horse trough. What've you been up to?" His eye narrowed. "Never mind, I can guess. Hardesty mentioned that when he picked you up at the Tylers' you'd just come back from a so-called riding lesson with that half-breed cowboy, Fletcher."

Lauren had turned to go to her room, but she swung back to face him. "*Half breed?* Good grief, what century are you living in? That term went out with the horse and buggy!"

His face had turned florid. "What I call that Comanche bastard doesn't change the fact that you've got sand in your hair, girl! Of all the men you could've let between your legs, why *him?* Did you do it to spite me—to drag the family name through the mud?"

Lauren knew better than to lie. She straightened and squared her chin. "My personal life is my own business. I'm over twenty-one. I don't have to answer to you."

Color deepening, he took a step toward her. Lauren braced herself, half expecting him to raise his hand and strike her. But then he halted, the breath hissing out of him.

"Maybe not. But whether you like it or not, your behavior reflects on my reputation. If I find out you're still seeing that man, so help me I'll ruin him! I'll blacken his name all over Texas—and don't think I can't. I'm a U.S. congressman. I have influence, connections, people who'll believe me."

Lauren was trembling by now, but she stood her

ground. "Say one word against him and you'll never see me again!"

His face contorted into a sneer. "Right now I'm not sure that would be much of a loss. You're exactly like your mother—a slut!"

He flung the word at her and stalked out of the room.

CHAPTER 9

By dinnertime the following Sunday, Jasper was strong enough to be up and around. He was already demanding to ride his ATV and move from the spare bedroom in the house to his side of the duplex he shared with Sky. Bernice, who'd cared for her brother with saintly devotion, declared that she'd reached the end of her rope.

"Now I know why I never took on another man after my Andy died, God rest his soul." She punctuated her words with downward strokes of the potato masher. "One more day of fetching and carrying for that old grump, and I'm going on vacation!"

"Then why not let Jasper go back to his own place?" Sky used a towel to lift the heavy roasting pan out of the oven and set it on the stovetop. The kitchen wasn't his job, but Bernice had been favoring her back lately and he worried about the strain.

"You know how rambunctious he is, Sky. If he gets hurt out there again, I'll never forgive myself."

"He'll be fine, Bernice." Sky began carving the succulent prime rib. "I'll look in on him every chance I get. And Will's locked up the keys to the ATV, so Jasper won't be taking it anywhere till he's ready."

"I just don't know." Bernice scooped the mashed potatoes into a bowl and added a dollop of butter. "When you come that close to losing somebody . . ."

The words trailed off as Erin scurried into the kitchen, took the bowl of potatoes, and headed back through the swinging door to the dining room.

"It's time you took care of yourself for a change," Sky said. "Otherwise you'll be the next patient in the house. Leave Jasper to me. He'll be happier in his own place."

Sky put the meat on a platter and carried it to the dining room table before he took his seat. Sunday dinner was a tradition at the ranch, a chance for the family to get together, feast, and talk. Jasper and Bernice were included, as was Sky, although, more often than not, he kept busy elsewhere. He'd never quite felt he belonged at the Tylers' table—not even now. But since today was a celebration of Jasper's recovery, he'd made a point of showing up.

As they waited for Bernice to take her seat, Sky glanced around the table. There was no rule about who sat where, but the arrangement seemed to fall into a natural order. Will was in his customary place at the head, with Erin on his right. Tori, who came most Sundays to be there for her daughter, sat between Erin and Jasper. Beau was seated on Will's left with Natalie and Sky filling in that side of the table. Bernice's place was at the end, closest to the kitchen. She eased her plump body onto her chair with a weary smile.

Beau and Natalie sat close enough to touch shoulders. Without looking down, Sky assumed they were holding hands—or maybe fondling knees—below the table. High school sweethearts, they'd been apart for eleven years when Beau came home. Now it was as if they were trying to make up for lost time. They couldn't seem to get enough of each other.

Sky was happy for them. But he couldn't imagine Lauren looking at him the way Natalie looked at Beau. Oh, Lauren was having fun. But sizzling sex tended to burn out like a Roman candle. It had little to do with the kind of love that flowed between Beau and his fiancée.

For all Sky knew, Lauren was already having second thoughts. He hadn't heard from her since the night of their sunset ride. Sky had to admit he was getting worried. If she wanted to cool their relationship, that was fine. But why hadn't she told him? What if something was wrong?

The *Amen,* murmured around the table, pulled him back to the present. Lost in thought, he'd brooded right through the blessing on the food. Sky wasn't a religious man, but he tried to be respectful of others' beliefs. He could only hope no one had noticed his lapse.

Discussions around the Tylers' table could be intense, even heated. This afternoon, as the dishes were passed, the conversation was relaxed, punctuated by easy laughter. There were serious issues hanging over the family—the drought, the cattle, the money, and the questions surrounding Jasper's shooting. For now these were set aside in the spirit of celebration.

"A toast!" Will rose and tapped his glass for attention. "To our great friend Jasper, the guiding spirit of the Rimrock. We've missed him, and we're happy to have him back."

"Hear, hear," Beau echoed. Glasses of iced sweet

tea were raised and clinked. Jasper harrumphed, clearly delighted by the tribute but trying not to show it.

Beau waved a hand for attention. "Natalie and I have an announcement to make," he said.

Will raised an eyebrow. "I hope this means you two have set a wedding date."

"Not quite, but it's going to be soon." Beau squeezed Natalie's shoulder. "It seems we're expecting."

The beat of silence around the table was shattered by a whoop from Erin. "Awesome! I'm getting a little cousin!"

Blushing, Natalie ducked her head. She wasn't a shy woman, but Sky, who knew her well through her work, sensed that she might've liked to keep the news private a little longer.

"Can you tell us when?" Tori asked.

"The best guess is late February or early March," Natalie said. "We'll have a lot of decisions to make before then."

"Well it's never too soon to celebrate good news." Will's mouth smiled, but his eyes showed concern. Natalie had worked for years to build her veterinary practice in town and would fight to keep it. But Beau was needed on the Rimrock 24–7 for responsibilities that didn't run on the clock. A baby in the picture would only deepen his need to be in two places at once.

Sky hadn't been privy to the problems that ended Will and Tori's marriage, but it made sense that Tori's law career had been a factor in the breakup. Was Will worried that his brother's marriage might suffer the same fate? Or was he even more fearful that Beau might choose Natalie and their child over his duty to the ranch?

Years ago Will had faced a similar choice. Now, when he looked at Tori and Erin across the table, did the ranch boss regret the price he'd paid?

After dinner, before Bernice could rise from her chair, Tori stood and began gathering the plates. "You've done enough, making this wonderful meal," she told the older woman. "Go put your feet up and rest. The girls and I can take care of the dishes."

Taking their cue, Natalie and Erin pitched in, running the leftovers into the kitchen, covering them, and putting them in the fridge. Too tired to protest, Bernice thanked them and retreated to the peace of her tidy apartment off the kitchen. Will, Beau, and Jasper wandered into the den to watch a rodeo on TV. Sky had already gone back to work.

Once the table was cleared and the food put away, Erin excused herself. Natalie scraped the dishes while Tori arranged them in the dishwasher and pondered the right thing to say.

The news about the baby had come as a happy surprise. But as close as she was to both Beau and Natalie, she couldn't help feeling hurt that they hadn't told her first. It wasn't personal, Tori knew. But since their engagement, Natalie and Beau had been so wrapped up in each other that she often felt like an outsider.

Now she and Natalie were alone in the kitchen. With a baby on the way, Tori knew her friend was going to need her.

"Congratulations." She took the last glass from Natalie's hand. "I'm thrilled about your good news."

"I'm thrilled, too." Natalie sank onto a wooden

stool. "But I didn't know Beau was going to share it with the family so soon. I was floored when he made that announcement."

"You know Beau. When he's excited about something, he can't wait to tell the world." Tori paused to put the glass in the dishwasher. "Is everything all right, Natalie?"

"With the baby? Yes, the doctor says so far everything's perfect. Funny, with Slade I never could get pregnant. I'd assumed the problem was mine. That's why Beau and I weren't more careful." Natalie gave a little laugh. "Surprise!"

"You sound like you're still in shock."

"I guess I am." Natalie swept her dark curls back from her face. "I always wanted a big family. It's just the timing—so unexpected and so many things to be decided. We don't even know where we're going to live."

"Relax. You've got plenty of time to work things out." Tori started the dishwasher and took a seat at the kitchen table. She'd wanted a big family, too. But in the years after Erin's birth, things with Will had become impossible.

"I was away at school for most of the years you were married," Natalie said. "You and Will lived in this house the whole time, didn't you?"

"Yes. We lived here—with Bull. It was a mistake." Reaching across the table, Tori laid a hand on her friend's arm. "One word of advice. Whatever you do, if you want a life with Beau, don't let him move you into this house."

Natalie's chocolate eyes widened. "Not that it would be my first choice, but why are you telling me this? There's plenty of room here, and if Bull was the problem, he's gone now. He can't cause any more trouble."

Tori shook her head. "That's where you're wrong. Bull Tyler is still running this ranch—or might as well be. If you move into this house, he'll take over Beau's life—and yours."

"I think I understand." Natalie glanced down at the Texas-sized diamond Beau had placed on her finger. "What if you and Will had moved into a place of your own? Do you think it would have made a difference?"

"Maybe," Tori said. "I wanted him to move out—begged him to. But Will wouldn't do it. His father needed him, the ranch needed him, and that was that."

After Natalie had gone upstairs to rest, Tori finished straightening the kitchen and walked back to the den to say her good-byes. From the hallway she could hear the sounds of the rodeo on TV and the whoops and cheers of the watchers. Erin's voice blended with the men's deeper tones. Her daughter fit right in here—as Tori never had.

The sectional sofa, with its back toward the door, faced the big-screen TV. Standing in the doorway, Tori could see Erin's dark blond head resting against Will's arm as they relaxed on the couch. Will was a devoted father, just as he'd been a dutiful son. But he was stamped in Bull Tyler's mold, raised with the ethic that men were here for the land and the livestock and women were here for their men and their babies. Anything else was unnatural and not to be tolerated.

Had she done the right thing, warning Natalie about the pitfalls of marrying a Tyler? Beau was nothing like his iron-willed father, but he had his own brand of stubbornness. Pushed too hard, Beau had left home and stayed away for more than a decade.

So far, Beau and Will seemed to be getting along. But how would Will take to sharing his brother's time with a wife and child—especially under the same roof? And how would Beau take to Will's playing the patriarch and lording it over his family?

If things went wrong, the painful drama of the past could replay with new characters. But it was out of her hands, Tori reminded herself. She'd spoken her mind to Natalie. All she could do now was be there for her friend and for the family she still cared deeply about.

She walked to the back of the couch, then bent forward to brush a kiss on Erin's cheek. "Call me, okay?" she said.

"Sure." Erin tore her attention away from the bull riding long enough to return the kiss. "Love you."

"Love you back." She ruffled her daughter's loose hair.

Will looked up at her, his eyes so deeply blue that, even after all this time, they could still stop her breath. "Same time next week?" he asked.

"Same time, or I'll let you know. Thanks."

"Thanks for coming." His gaze held hers for an instant. Then he turned back to the TV, leaving Tori to walk outside alone. These days their friendship was little more than an act, staged for Erin's benefit. Something about Will still quickened Tori's pulse. But it wasn't enough to heal the hurt, and never would be. Over the years they'd become different people—strangers, almost, with nothing to link them except the beautiful child they both adored.

With a last look back at the house, Tori climbed into her station wagon and headed back to town.

Sky and Jasper sat on the front porch of their duplex, watching the twilight deepen above the caprock. Crickets chirped in the shadows. The Border Collie curled at Jasper's feet, his nose resting on the old man's boot.

Sky had moved his chair to Jasper's side of the porch so they could be close enough to talk. He had missed the old cowboy. The thought that Jasper might have died from the gunshot wound and the pneumonia still raised a lump in his throat.

Jasper reached down to scratch the dog's ears. "Thanks for gettin' me back here, Sky. That sister of mine was bossin' me near to death."

"And you were wearing Bernice to a frazzle," Sky said. "I figured both of you were ready for a break."

"How about bringin' my ATV around tomorrow? I'm itchin' for a ride."

"Sorry, but that's up to Will. He's got the keys and he won't let you ride till you're stronger. But I can take you out in the pickup tomorrow. If you're up for it, we can take a look at the place where you were shot. Maybe it'll help you remember."

"You told me it was your no-good cousin that shot me. And that now he's lit out somewhere. So what's to remember?"

"Maybe nothing. But if you can help me, I'd like to make sure Marie's telling the truth about it being an accident."

"Marie? That's the cousin who's waitressin' at the Blue Coyote, right?"

"Right. I should probably check in with her. She hasn't been in touch since her brother disappeared."

Jasper spat off the edge of the porch. "Well, after knowing Lute and hearing about those other two birds, I can't say much for that side of your family."

"They're no angels. But after my mother died, they were all the family I had. At least they didn't turn me away. I guess I owe them something for that."

"What about the other side of your family? What have you done about that secret I told you?"

Sky's pulse lurched. Knowing Jasper, he should have expected the question and had a response ready. Instead he felt as if he'd been punched. Seconds ticked by before he answered.

"Nothing. It's like that Pandora's Box I read about in school, Jasper. Open it, and all the troubles come flying out into the world. I'm fine with things as they are. What would I have to gain by telling Will and Beau that their father slept with a Comanche woman and I'm their bastard brother?"

Jasper gazed at him with a puzzled frown. "I was hoping it would give you some peace. But you don't sound very happy about it."

Sky leaned back in the chair and crossed his booted feet. The call of a coyote echoed through the twilight. "Bull Tyler knew all along who I was. He never acknowledged me, never said a word. And he never helped my mother. She died poor, without the medical treatment that might've saved her life. Which part of that should I be happy about?"

"Blast it, Sky . . ." Jasper's words trailed into silence. His chin settled on his chest. He was quiet so long that Sky thought he'd fallen into a doze, but at last he spoke. "Bull had his reasons. You might not understand them, but I could tell you more if you want to know."

Sky weighed the invitation, then shook his head. "Right now I figure the less I know, the less I'll brood about it. If I change my mind, I'll ask."

"Don't wait too long. I'm an old man. I won't be here to answer your questions forever." Jasper ruminated for a moment, then changed the subject.

"Heard about Hoyt Axelrod dyin' in jail. Can't say I'm sorry. Would've plugged him myself if I'd been there when he shot you in the back. Have they figured out what killed the bugger?"

"Last we heard, the official cause of death was 'undetermined.'"

"Sure it was. If you believe that, I've got a piece of oceanfront property in Arizona to sell you." Jasper spat over the porch rail. "An' now Abner Sweeney's the sheriff. Hellfire, Abner's got about as much sense as a jackrabbit. Tag, here, would make a better lawman than that fool, wouldn't you, boy?" He scratched the dog's ears. "Say, did you ever find that shotgun of mine?"

"The one that was missing after your accident?"

"Yeah. Damn good bird gun. Hate to lose it."

"Marie said her brother took it. Wherever he is, he's probably got it with him."

"Well, I hope the dirty snake shoots his foot off with it. If you find him, I want it back." Pushing out of the rocker, Jasper stood. "Reckon I'll turn in now. It's been a long day. Wake me in the mornin'. I'll ride out with you in the pickup."

"Feel free to sleep in if you're tired. We don't have to go tomorrow."

"I'll be fine." He hobbled across the porch, his gait

still unsteady. The accident—or whatever it was—
had taken its toll on the old cowboy. There was no
guarantee he'd ever be as strong as before.

After Jasper had gone inside, Sky sat in the darkness, listening to the night—the drone of crickets in
the dry grass, the mellow *co-hoo* of a burrowing owl,
the muted whinny of a horse in the paddock. Sky's
ears and mind processed the sound. No alarm there,
only restlessness.

Over the past few days, he'd spent most of his
spare time working with Storm Cloud. The black
gelding was making good progress—especially since
Sky had discovered the sore mouth that was causing
him to fight the bit. The change to a snaffle bit
seemed to be helping. But if Lauren wasn't coming
back to work with her horse, Sky couldn't justify the
time and expense of keeping him here.

The situation had become awkward. If Lauren
wanted to break off their relationship, that was her
choice. But something would need to be done about
returning her horse. Much as Sky disliked involving
Beau, having him contact Lauren would be the simplest
solution. A phone call or e-mail should be enough to
set things up. If she was busy, or didn't want to come
over, she could always send a ranch hand with a
trailer.

Leaning farther back in the chair, he propped his
boots on the porch railing. The dog nudged his
hand, wanting to be petted. Sky stroked the tangled
fur, taking a moment to loosen a cockle burr and toss
it off the porch. He and Lauren had been good together. But that was the way of most good things. They
tended not to last. Damned shame, though, when he
thought of all the things he'd wanted—and still

wanted—to do with that leggy, red-haired hellion in
bed.

Muttering a curse, he stood and stretched his saddle-
sore muscles. An evening breeze had sprung up,
smelling of dust and promising another blast furnace
day tomorrow. He would plan to start with the colts at
first light, in the larger of the two round pens. If things
went well, he could get in a few hours of training before he took Jasper out in the pickup.

His job was vital to the ranch's survival. This was no
time to let any distraction interfere with his work—not
Marie and her problems, not the questions about his
father, and not even Lauren.

Especially Lauren.

Garn Prescott propped his bare back against the
pillows and clicked the remote. The flat-screen TV at
the foot of the bed flashed on, lighting up the dark
interior of the motel room.

"Honey, do you have to turn that thing on now?"
Stella ran a teasing hand up his inner thigh. Lord,
the woman was insatiable. Not that he was complaining. She knew every trick in the book, and enough
others to write a book of her own. They'd driven into
Lubbock for dinner and spent the past two hours in
bed, having the kind of sex that boggled Prescott's
imagination. It was a good thing he'd gulped down
some Viagra before they got started. He'd needed it.

"This won't take long," he said. "I just want to make
sure the station is running my new campaign ad."

Prescott had paid top dollar to have the ad run just
before the nine o'clock news. Bankrolled by Stella, the
ad had been done by a slick agency with background

music, a professional script, and a combination of lighting and makeup that made him look ten years younger.

He sighed with satisfaction as the ad came on. It was already making a difference in the polls, and contributions were flowing, if not exactly gushing, into his war chest. He'd lost track of how much Stella had given him, but it had to be coming up on sixty or seventy thousand dollars. How a woman who ran a grungy little bar in a backwater town could spare so much money was a question Prescott didn't ask. His instincts told him he was better off not knowing.

Stella took the remote out of his hand and switched off the TV. "It's not like you have to watch the whole thing," she said. "Come here, honey. Maybe next time we can spend the whole night together. But for now we both have places to be. One more round and it's bye-bye time."

Her hand slid higher, fingers stroking with a skill that drove him wild. Prescott would never have guessed he had it in him but, wonder of wonders, the Viagra was still working.

Balancing the tray above her head, Marie made her way through the crowd. With the Texas rodeo finals on TV, the bar was packed. And Stella had chosen tonight, of all nights, to be gone.

Squeezing past a table, Marie felt a pinch on her bottom. Turning, she fixed the cowboy with a chilling glare. As the seconds passed, his grin faded and his bold gaze dropped. "Sorry," he muttered. Marie moved on. She knew how to handle jerks like that cowboy. Once they got a look at her scarred face, they always backed off.

She'd been twenty when her husband Eddie had come home nasty drunk, kicked her across the floor, and slashed her face with a knife from the kitchen. A neighbor had driven her to the hospital, where she'd lost the baby she was carrying. Probably just as well. She would never have been a candidate for Mother of the Year.

A couple of her brothers had gone after Eddie, knocked out his front teeth, busted his right hand, and threatened worse if he ever came near their sister again. After the divorce she'd kept her married name—Marie Johnson—because in Oklahoma there were advantages to not being known as a Fletcher. She'd kept the scar, too, though not by choice. The operation to fix her face would cost thousands of dollars—more money than Marie could ever earn at the shitty jobs she was forced to take.

But if things went as planned, all that was about to change.

Behind the bar, Stella's brother, Nick, was filling orders as fast as Marie could pick them up. "Where's Stella?" she asked as she stacked a fresh tray.

Nick shrugged, his bland expression unchanged. Despite his shaved head and biker tattoos there was an air of shyness about the man. Early on Marie had tried flirting with him just to see what would happen. But she'd gotten nowhere. Maybe he'd been put off by the scar, or maybe he just wasn't interested in women.

Stella doted on her younger brother. He seemed to be the one person in the world she cared about. Marie could understand that. She'd felt much the same way about Lute. That was why her revenge would be so fitting and why carrying it out would be so sweet.

She would have that bitch Stella right where she wanted her.

Killing Coy hadn't been part of her original plan. But between his marijuana patch and his big mouth, she'd figured that sooner or later he was bound to get them both in trouble and ruin everything. She'd never liked Coy—the way he'd teased her and tormented the stray animals she befriended. But she hadn't thought of killing him until a few weeks ago when she'd come across the loaded 9 mm Glock Nick kept in the back of the drawer below the cash register.

Staring down at the gun, Marie had felt a thrill as her scheme came together. After meeting Sky that first night in the parking lot, she had taken the gun with gloved hands, ridden the Harley back to Coy's camp, and done what she needed to. It had been easier than she'd expected, leaving her with scarcely a twinge of regret.

Now all she had to do was wait.

CHAPTER 10

Sky was pulling off his dusty boots when his cell phone rang. He willed himself to ignore the leap of his pulse as he saw her name. Nearly a week had passed since Beau had e-mailed Lauren at the Prescott Ranch office, asking about her horse and whether she planned on returning to work. Neither he nor Sky had heard back from her.

Lauren was impulsive, to say the least. Sky wouldn't have been surprised to learn that she'd had it out with her father and decided to fly back to Maryland. He couldn't imagine she'd leave without telling him or Beau. But then again, how well did he really know her?

Reminding himself of that, he dropped his boots and took the call.

"Sky?" Her husky voice sounded uncertain, as if she was afraid he might be angry.

"Lauren? Are you all right?"

"Yes, I'm fine." She didn't sound fine, he thought.

"Where are you? I've been worried about you." *Worried* was an understatement. He'd lain awake nights wondering where she was and what might have happened to her. But he'd be damned if he'd let her know that.

"I'm at the ranch. I left for a little while. It's . . . complicated."

"I'm listening."

There was a long pause. "My father found out about us. He threatened to ruin you if I saw you again."

"That's no surprise. We should've known it might happen." Sky willed himself not to feel—no anger, no disappointment. It was what it was.

"I saw Beau's e-mail about Storm Cloud. Do you still have him?"

"I've been working with him. He's doing fine. But he needs to go home."

"Sorry about that. I'll pay his expenses, of course, or Beau can just take it out of what he owes me." Again, there was a beat of silence. "My father went to Lubbock tonight. He told me he wouldn't be back till morning. I think he must have a girlfriend somewhere."

Sky waited, sensing she had more to say, guessing at what it might be.

"I need to see you," she said. "If you could ride Storm Cloud over here, we could put him up and I could drive you home."

Sky glanced at the bedside clock. Eleven-fifteen. Was the woman pulling his strings—keeping him on edge for days, then expecting him to come running like a besotted puppy at her call? It would serve her right if he turned her down and sent Storm Cloud home in a trailer tomorrow.

And what about her father? Who was to say Prescott wouldn't change his mind and come home early?

But why was he arguing with himself? The urge to see Lauren, even just to talk, was driving him like a whip.

"Sky, are you still there?" How long had he kept her waiting for an answer?

His free hand reached for his boots. "I'm on my way. Just tell me where to find you."

By the time she ended the call, Lauren was trembling. Phoning Sky had crushed her pride and drained her courage. Facing him would be even harder, especially given what she needed to say.

Sinking onto the porch swing, she struggled to make sense of the past few days. As the plane had lifted off the runway, bound for Baltimore, she'd told herself she was doing the right thing. The idea of a caring relationship with her father was nothing more than a fairy tale. The longer she stayed with him, the worse his abuse was bound to become. He might even break down and hit her, the way she remembered him hitting her mother. There was no way she would stand for that.

As for Sky, he was better off without her. They'd had a few laughs, but trying to make it last would be like hanging an anvil around his neck. She was doing him a favor, she'd told herself. Even without the damage her father could do, the last thing Sky needed was to be saddled with a neurotic mess like Miss Lauren Prescott.

Leaving without telling him good-bye had been the coward's way out. But any attempt to explain would have been a disaster. She'd planned to write him a letter from Maryland, a nice, polite one, thanking him for what they'd shared and wishing him the best.

What they'd shared . . .

But she'd known better than to go there.

At some point in the flight she'd remembered Storm Cloud. It had been irresponsible on her part, leaving the horse with Sky. At least the black gelding was in good hands. But she'd only borrowed him from the Prescott Ranch. She would need to send money for his keep and instructions for his return.

Her grandparents' home outside Baltimore had been even gloomier than Lauren remembered. Much of the land had been sold to real estate developers. Even her grandfather's horses and stables were gone. Her grandparents, both in their eighties, rarely left the house or even looked past the heavy drapes that kept out much of the light.

The kindly servants Lauren remembered from her teens had been replaced by brusque strangers who clearly viewed her as an intruder. Concerned, Lauren had contacted the family lawyers, who'd confirmed that on her grandparents' deaths the remainder of the estate would be sold to pay its debts, leaving next to nothing for her. The only surprise had been how little she cared.

After three days of filling out applications for jobs she didn't want, she'd driven to see Mike's parents in North Carolina. Arriving at their home, she'd learned from the gardener that they'd left on a cruise.

Just one place remained for her to visit. After buying a bouquet of blue Dutch irises and lilies of the valley from a florist, she'd gone to the cemetery to leave the flowers on Mike's grave.

The last time she'd been to the place was the day of the wrenching, emotional funeral. A year later, climbing out of her car, she'd braced herself for a surge of love and grief, along with newfound anger for all the people Mike's suicide had hurt. But as she kissed the bouquet and laid it at the base of the granite headstone, all she'd felt was a surprising sense of quiet, calm acceptance.

She'd moved on.

And she didn't belong here anymore.

Driving back to Maryland, visions of open space, golden grass, cattle, horses, and a tall, lean cowboy with coal black hair and riveting blue eyes had flooded her memory. Lauren wasn't blind to the risks. Sky was a loner. The odds of a happy future with such a man were slim to none. Reaching out to him would mean setting herself up for heartbreak. But if there was a chance for them, any chance at all, she couldn't walk away until she knew for sure.

Two days later she was on a flight back to Texas.

The distant sound of approaching hoof beats roused Lauren from her musings. If it was Sky, he'd wasted no time getting here. Heart pounding, she rose and walked to the top of the porch steps. She'd told him to come to the house. From there she could show him the way to the stables.

When the syndicate had bought the ranch from Garn Prescott, they'd agreed to leave the main house, with its surrounding lawns and gardens, for the Prescott family. A new house for the ranch manager, along with an office and some outbuildings, had been built some distance away, on the far side of the original barns and stables. The arrangement gave the Prescotts the privacy they needed to live their lives undisturbed, as well as shared use of the stables and other facilities. Since Lauren had worked in the ranch office, she was familiar with the layout of the place, and most of the employees knew her. Coming onto the property in the middle of the night, Sky would need her with him.

Now she could see him riding into the moonlit yard. He slowed the horse to a walk, then swung toward the house as he saw her. Checking the urge to run to him, Lauren forced herself to wait. Time seemed to crawl before he reined up at the foot of the steps.

"Where are the stables?" he asked as if speaking to a stranger.

She felt the chill in his voice. "Through those trees, maybe a couple hundred yards. I'll need to go with you. Otherwise you could end up getting arrested or even shot."

"I thought of that. Come on." He leaned out of the saddle, offering an arm. Lauren clasped it, feeling the steel of his muscles as he pulled her onto the horse. She settled herself behind the cantle, resting her hands against his ribs.

She fought the urge to melt into the warm, solid feel of him, to fill her senses with the smell of sweat and dust, sagebrush and horses, blending in a manly fragrance that was uniquely Sky—an aroma she'd come to love. It was all she could do to keep from wrapping her arms around him and squeezing him close. But this wasn't the time. His body was rigid between her hands, his manner cold and formal.

He probably thought she was playing some kind of game with him—disappearing for days, then calling him in the middle of the night just to see if he'd come running. If that was what he believed, Lauren could hardly blame him. Sky was a proud man. If he thought he was being manipulated, he wouldn't take it well.

She could apologize. But would an apology be enough?

He cleared his throat. "You said you needed to talk. So talk."

"Aren't you going to ask me where I've been?"

"Only if you want to tell me." The chill in his voice was like being jabbed with an icicle. It was too much.

"Stop it, Sky Fletcher!" Lauren punched his ribs, hard enough to make him grunt with pain. The horse snorted and danced beneath them. He soothed the big gelding with a touch.

"That was uncalled for, Lauren," he said.

"Was it? So why are you treating me like a bad case of the chicken pox?"

He halted the horse outside the range of the security lights on the barn. "Because I've been worried sick about you, dammit, that's why! One night you're all over me, and the next you're gone without a word. What if you'd been in some kind of hellish accident? Who'd know enough to tell me about it?" He shook his head. "And then you show up like nothing's happened, you call me in the middle of the night and say you need to talk. If this wasn't the twenty-first century, I'd turn you over my knee and spank you!"

"That might be fun. I'd like to see you try it."

"Don't, Lauren. You're driving me crazy, and this isn't a joke." He exhaled forcibly, the tension whooshing out of him. "Let's put this horse away. If you want to talk, we can do it on the way back to your car."

They stabled Storm Cloud, giving him a rubdown along with some hay and water. "He's doing a lot better," Sky said. "But if he's mishandled, or if he's left alone for too long, he'll be right back where he was. Ride him every day if you can, so he won't forget what he's been taught." His unspoken message was clear. As far as Sky was concerned, neglecting a horse, as she'd done, was as serious an offense as neglecting a person.

They left the barn and walked clear of the bright floodlights. He matched his long strides to her shorter steps but made no move to reach for her hand. "I take it I'm still in trouble," she said.

"With me or with Storm Cloud?" At least he'd mellowed enough to needle her.

"I'm guessing I'm in trouble with both of you. So how can I redeem myself?"

"I've already told you what you can do about the horse," he said.

"And you?"

"No promises, but you might want to start by explaining." He glanced down at her. "You said your father found out about us."

"He guessed after talking to Josh Hardesty. I didn't deny it. He wouldn't have believed me if I had. There was an awful scene. He called me names—names I won't repeat out loud."

"We both knew it was bound to happen. I'm sorry, Lauren. I should never have let things go as far as they did."

The words Sky spoke weren't the ones Lauren had come home to hear. Torn between cursing and weeping, she willed herself to speak calmly.

"He threatened to spread lies about you, to ruin your reputation if I saw you again. I knew he wasn't bluffing. My father has powerful connections. He would have used them to destroy you. I couldn't let him do that. I was on a plane to Baltimore the next day."

"And you didn't think to tell me, or even to tell Beau?"

"I didn't know what to say. I was going to e-mail you when my plans came together. They never really did."

They walked in silence, their moon-shadows falling long over the dusty ground. She'd spent most of the return flight thinking about what to say to him. But face-to-face, none of it had come out right. So far she'd played it badly, saying all the wrong things, making a fool of herself. And now it was too late to take it back and start over. All she could do was stumble on.

"Just one more question," he said. "After being in such an all-fired hurry to leave, why did you come back?"

For you. That was how she'd planned to answer. But she should have known Sky wouldn't be ready to hear those words.

"I came back after I realized there was nothing for me in Baltimore. I'd moved beyond that place and the things that happened there. But I wasn't through with Texas—and Texas wasn't through with me." Good answer, even if it wasn't the whole answer.

"What about your father?" Sky asked.

"I'm back in the house for now, staying out of his way. But I won't stay there any longer than I have to. I'm already checking the ads for a place in Blanco Springs, to rent or even to buy. If I can't find a decent job, I'll start my own accounting business."

He frowned. "I can't say there's much call for an accountant in Blanco, except maybe at tax time. You might find things pretty lean."

Lauren tossed her hair, feeling his eyes on her as she brushed it back with her hand. "That's the beauty of the Internet. I can work anywhere, with clients from all over the country. All I need to do is connect with them."

His flicker of a smile warmed her. "You're one smart lady, I'll say that for you. But why Blanco Springs? It's nowhere."

"Because I can still do work for the Prescott Ranch from there, and for Beau as well, if he hasn't fired me by now." Lauren had realized early on that her only chance with Sky was to get her own place in town, away from her father, but she wasn't about to tell him that.

"I guess Hoyt Axelrod's old house is still vacant. His kids are long gone. They'd probably be glad to sell it."

"I'll think about it. But the idea of living in that place sounds kind of creepy."

He laughed. "I know what you mean. If you want, I can ask Tori, Will's ex, for the name of a good Realtor. She'll know somebody."

"Thanks." They'd passed the back corner of the house and were headed for Lauren's car—not what she wanted. She put a hand on his arm, stopping him. "When was the last time you had a moonlight dip in a nice, cool swimming pool?"

He hesitated. "Can't say as I recall. Is that an invitation?"

"If you want it to be." She tugged his arm. "It won't

take long. Besides—" She wrinkled her nose in mock distaste. "You don't exactly smell like a rose garden. What makes you think I'd allow you in my car?"

"I'm a cowboy. I've put in a long, hot, honest day's work, and I'll be damned if I'm going to apologize for how I smell."

She laughed, pulling his arm toward the back gate to the patio. "Come on, it'll be fun."

He gave her a wicked glance as she locked the gate behind them. "Sorry, I didn't bring a bathing suit."

"What a coincidence. Neither did I." Lauren tried to sound playful and confident, but her voice quivered. She'd laid everything on the line, coming back to Texas and Sky—and she'd just handed him an open invitation to break her heart.

He was like a wild mustang, proud but wary of being penned. Even if she could rope him, could she keep him? Or would his natural urge to be free draw him away?

He undressed without a trace of self-consciousness, tossing his boots and clothes onto one of the poolside chairs. His splendid body gleamed like a blade as he cut the water in a clean dive.

Seconds later his head broke the surface. He was grinning, water drops streaming like liquid diamonds off his ebony hair. "Not bad," he said. "I hope you're coming in."

Lauren had stripped down to her underclothes. His expression changed subtly as she undid the front clasp of her bra. Letting it fall away, she slid her panties off her hips to drop around her ankles. He lay back in the water, watching her.

"Don't move an inch," he said. "Let me look at you."

Lauren felt the heat rise in her body, flooding her face with color. She was aware of the way a lock of her long hair curled to frame one small, firm breast. In an era when half the girls she knew were getting breast implants, she'd become overly aware of her modest size, but that seemed to be where Sky's gaze was fixed.

Shying away, she made a leaping dive into the pool and came up a few feet from him, where the bottom was shallow enough to touch with her toes. She held out her arms. "Come here," she said.

Kicking into the shallows, he gathered her close. The feel of his cool, bare skin against hers was heaven. They kissed hungrily, Lauren nibbling his lower lip and thrusting with her tongue. Their bodies pressed, legs tangling deliciously as his sex rose and hardened against her. She wiggled closer, her blood racing.

"Lauren." There was an edge to his voice. He disentangled himself and pushed her away from him, his hands resting on her shoulders.

She stared at him. "What—?"

"Listen to me, beautiful lady. Tempting as it might be, I'm not going to make love to you tonight."

To demand to know why not would be crass. She studied him, waiting for an explanation.

"For one thing, sex underwater doesn't work anywhere near as well as it seems to in the movies."

He must have tried it, of course. But this was about something else. "What's the real reason?" she asked, feeling wounded.

"Because I don't want to take this any further in your family home. And because, before we get any more involved, you need to get your feet on the ground."

"I'm not sure I understand."

"Look at yourself. You run away. You come back. You talk about moving out and getting a place in Blanco, but it's not a very practical idea, and there's no guarantee you'll do it. If I didn't care about you, it wouldn't matter. But I do care—and what we're doing here is only complicating things."

The water, which had felt refreshing at first, was becoming chilly. Lauren suppressed a shiver. "Are you trying to break up with me? Because that's the way it sounds."

He shook his head. "All I'm saying is let's put things on ice till you get settled. I've got work to do and you've got a life to put in order. If this is something more than a summer fling, we'll find out. If not . . ." He shrugged his gleaming shoulders. "If not, at least we'll know." He traced a fingertip down Lauren's cheek. "Friends?"

Lauren checked the urge to fly at him and leave knuckle bruises on his manly chest. Sky had gotten through to her. He was right, of course. But it still hurt like crazy. She blinked away a tear and forced herself to speak the word.

"Friends."

His hand released her shoulder. "Then what do you say we get dressed and you drive me home?"

No, it was too abrupt, she thought. She needed time to let go of him, to adjust to this new reality with Sky at a distance. "There's chocolate cake and cold milk in the kitchen." She seized on the first thing that came to mind. "Are you hungry?"

"Lauren, it's after midnight—" he began, then seemed to sense what she needed. "But I never turn down good chocolate cake."

"Great." She pulled herself up the ladder. A laundry basket of clean towels stood next to the pool. After wrapping one around her body, Lauren snatched up her clothes. "I'll leave the kitchen door open. Come in when you're ready."

Feeling like a sixteen-year-old at the end of a bad prom date, Lauren fled into the house.

Sky climbed out of the pool, toweled himself dry, and began pulling on his clothes. It had been tough, rejecting Lauren like that. As she stood naked in the moonlight, her beauty had left him breathless. And then in the water she'd been so eager, so vulnerable—and his body had been more than ready for her. Taking her and doing what they'd both wanted would've been the most natural thing in the world.

But he'd forced himself to be noble—and he'd seen the glimmer of her tears. Hurting her had been like slapping a puppy.

It had to be done. Until Lauren figured out who she was, what she wanted, and how to deal with her father, she wouldn't be ready for any kind of stable relationship.

Not that he'd ever been ready himself. When it came to getting a commitment from him, most of the women in his past had thrown up their hands and walked away. But Lauren wasn't like most women. She was stunningly beautiful, scathingly honest, and smart enough to challenge him at every turn. He wanted to get to know her better—both in and out of bed.

But before that could happen, she had some serious growing up to do.

Cursing under his breath, he buckled his belt and yanked on his boots. She'd thank him later on. But right now Lauren probably hated him. For all he knew she was going to spit on that chocolate cake she'd promised him. But he'd just have to take his chances.

The kitchen light was on. Lauren was standing at the cluttered counter cutting generous wedges of chocolate layer cake. She was fully dressed, her damp hair twisted up and fastened with a silver clip.

"Sorry about the mess," she said, as if nothing had happened between them. "Miguel's a terrific cook, but he's not the tidiest. Go on into the dining room and have a seat at the table. That's where we serve our guests."

Sky passed through the swinging door into the dining room, where a chandelier fashioned from deer antlers dangled above the long table—probably Ferg Prescott's idea of good old Texas decor. The brown walls were hung with family photographs. Sky gave them a passing glance before he sat down at the head of the table, where Lauren had set two places. Sky was filling the glasses from a carton of milk when she came in with two saucers of cake. As she sat down and passed him his slice, she gave him a smile. Her eyes looked watery, as if she might have been crying. Sky felt like a jerk, but he couldn't cave in now. His decision had been made with the best intentions. He had to believe he'd done the right thing.

"Good cake." He washed down a bite with a swallow of milk.

"Thanks. I made it myself. From scratch." Her expression was bland, totally believable.

"I didn't know you could cook."

"You'd be surprised. I'm a regular little domestic goddess. I even sewed the curtains for my bedroom. And I'm knitting Daddy a sweater for his birthday. I have lots of hidden talents."

The deepening of a dimple gave her away. "Lauren—"

She dissolved into giggles. "Admit it! I had you going, didn't I?"

"Only for the first few seconds." Damn her, the woman was an adorable rascal. He had to restrain himself from grabbing her and kissing her silly. "Something tells me the most domestic thing you do is order takeout."

Lauren took a dainty forkful of cake. "I'm a good decorator, given enough money. Take this ghastly dining room. I've sat here imagining what I'd do with it. That god-awful chandelier would go first. I'd keep the photos, because they're family history, but I'd put them in matching black frames, with pearl gray linen mats—" She broke off. "What is it, Sky? Is something the matter?"

Sky had barely heard what she was saying. He was staring at the large black-and-white group photo above the far end of the table. His throat had gone dry as ash.

"That woman in the Reagan picture." He forced himself to speak in a conversational tone. "The tall, dark one on the far side, with the tray. She looks familiar. Do you know anything about her?"

"Not much, I'm afraid. I noticed her earlier and asked my father. He couldn't even remember her name. He said she was the maid and that she'd left while he was away at school. That was all he could tell me. But isn't she beautiful? A woman like that could be a supermodel or even a movie star." Lauren glanced at Sky. "You say she looks familiar. Do you know her?"

"No. She looks Comanche. Maybe she's some distant relative." He had to lie. How could he tell Lauren the truth when he could barely process it himself?

His mother, Marie Joslyn Fletcher, had worked as a maid for Ferg Prescott's family.

Sky had done his best to listen to Lauren's small talk as she drove him home. Lauren was a classy lady. She was trying to put a good face on things, and he respected her for that. But it was hard to focus on what she was saying when his thoughts were milling like cattle on the verge of a stampede.

What had happened between Bull and his mother? Had Bull met her on a visit to the Prescott ranch? Had she come to him willingly or, heaven forbid, had he forced himself on her? Had they cared for each other at all?

Bull must have found out she was pregnant. How else would Jasper have known? And how else, when Sky had shown up sixteen years later, could Bull have been so sure that the boy was his son?

Jasper had offered to tell him everything. But did he really want to hear it? He hated the way his gut clenched when he thought about the things he'd already learned. What good would it do to know more?

Maybe someday he'd be ready to hear the whole story. But would Jasper be there to tell him, or would the old cowboy, Bull's one steadfast friend, take the secrets to his grave?

Lauren had turned the car off the paved road, onto the long gravel drive that led up to the house. She'd put the top down on the Corvette and unpinned her long, coppery hair to let it blow in the moonlight. She was putting up a good front, but Sky knew the hurt was there.

"Where'd you get this car, anyway?" he asked, filling the silence. "I can't imagine you bought it around here, and I know you didn't drive it all the way from Maryland."

Her laugh sounded fake. "You didn't know about my grandfather's collection? Ferg Prescott left behind a whole garage full of vintage cars, most of them still working. That's where my father got his Cadillac. I chose this little Corvette to drive while I'm here."

"That collection must be worth a lot."

"A small fortune. But I can't imagine selling even one of them. They're like the family treasure."

Looking at her, thinking how lovely she was, how warm and tender and open, Sky felt an unaccustomed ache. Right now he needed her in a way that had nothing to do with sex. The idea of stopping the car, cradling her in his arms, and sharing his burden with her—who he was, where he'd come from, and why he was so troubled tonight—was tempting. But no, he'd be almost certain to regret telling her. If he needed to talk to anybody, he could talk to Jasper. Or better yet, he could keep his conflicting feelings to himself.

Lauren pulled up to the house without switching off the engine. The message was clear. He was to get out now and let her go.

Sky opened the door and climbed out of the low-slung car. "Call me if you need anything, Lauren," he said, quietly closing the door. "I'll be here for you."

"Will you? How charitable of you!"

Those were the only words she spoke before she gunned the engine and sped back down the drive.

CHAPTER 11

Three weeks had passed since Lauren's return. The drought that had started as a cause for gut-gnawing worry had become a hell of burning sun and blowing dust. The governor of Texas had applied for federal disaster relief and was likely to get it. But no amount of government money could coax rain from the heavens.

With little water to fight them, wildfires were breaking out to race across the tinder-dry grasslands. So far the Rimrock had been spared, but Beau had posted a notice that any cowhand caught smoking outside the gravel bunkhouse area would be fired on the spot. Though the order made sense, it heightened the strain among the men. Yesterday Beau had broken up a fistfight between two cowboys, sent them packing, and put the rest on notice. Everybody was on edge, even Jasper.

"Hellfire, I've seen it bad but never like this!" The old cowboy sat in his rocker on the porch, sharing a cup of pre-dawn coffee with Sky. He'd survived his brush with death, but the episode had taken its toll. He would never be as strong as before. "It'll damn near break Will's heart to sell those steers off early. I know he was countin' on a good price for them this fall."

"Better than watching them starve," Sky said, "or going broke buying more hay to feed them. Blasted hay's become like green gold. At least somebody's making money."

With even the paddock drying up, the ranch was buying extra hay for the horses as well as the cattle. Given the demand everywhere, the price of hay had skyrocketed.

He glanced toward the house. There was a light on in the kitchen, where Will and Beau would be finishing breakfast. From the bunkhouse, the faint breeze carried the aromas of coffee and frying bacon. With daytime temperatures soaring past a hundred degrees, it made sense to start work in the cooler hours of early dawn.

"How're them colts coming along?" Jasper asked. "You've been working 'em pretty hard, 'specially since that little Prescott gal stopped comin' over."

"The colts are doing fine. I'll be taking a few of them out today. As for the girl, no comment." Sky hadn't seen Lauren since the night she'd driven him home. She'd had Beau send her the remaining files so she could finish the work on her own computer. Her message was clear, and Beau was discreet enough not to question Sky about it.

"Right pretty thing, 'specially for a Prescott." Jasper sipped his coffee. "Beau mentioned that she'd taken quite a shine to you."

"Like I said, no comment." Setting his empty cup on the porch, Sky strode down the steps. "Time to get to work. Take it easy, Jasper. Stay out of the sun."

"Oh, stop mollycoddlin' me. I'll be fine."

The old man's voice followed Sky as he headed for the barn. He avoided looking toward the drive, where Lauren had always parked her black Corvette. He knew she wasn't coming back, but he couldn't look at that empty space without missing her.

Several of the sharpest colts had finished their training in the round pens, including a few sessions with the docile older cows that kept them company in the paddock. Now it was time for the young horses to be taken out on the open range, to perform their maneuvers on rough ground while dealing with unfamiliar sights, smells, and sounds. After that they'd be trailered up onto the caprock to work the herd, first with Sky, then with other riders. By the time they were finished, they'd know their job almost well enough to do it by themselves. It was a time-consuming process. But that intensive schooling was what made Rimrock-trained cow ponies so prized.

Sky had his hands full, doing it all alone. But finding the right help wasn't easy. He'd hope to train his cousin Lute as his assistant, but Lute had been a disaster from the start. Sky might have considered Marie. She'd always been good with animals, including horses. But she was cut from the same cloth as Lute, and she was already in trouble. As for Coy, even if he were to turn up and beg for a job, Sky wanted nothing to do with him.

The most gifted, natural-born horse handler on the ranch was Erin. She had all the right instincts. But the colts could be dangerous. Will's daughter was too young and precious to risk to their flying hooves and nipping teeth.

By the time Sky hauled his gear out of the tack room in the barn, the dawn was beginning to pale in the east. He was looking forward to taking Quicksilver for his first outing. The cat-footed gray gelding was the smartest of the colts and so responsive that, if the Rimrock hadn't been desperate for money, Sky would have lobbied to keep him.

They rode out across the flat, then circled back across the sun-scorched pastureland, passing the seep where Jasper had wrecked his ATV. A few weeks ago Sky had driven the old man out to the spot to see if it might jog his memory of what had happened. But Jasper could only frown and shake his head. If he'd seen the shooter, the trauma had blotted it from his mind. Now any evidence that remained had blown away with the dust—and Coy Fletcher, the most likely suspect, seemed to be gone for good.

A jackrabbit bounded across their path, almost under Quicksilver's hooves. The gelding snorted but didn't rear or try to bolt.

"Good boy." Sky patted the dappled shoulder. "Let's see what else you can do." Finding an open spot, he took Quicksilver through backing and turning and the other maneuvers he'd learned. With minimal urging, the young horse performed to near perfection. Nudging him to an easy canter, Sky headed toward the escarpment to try the moves again on steeper, rougher ground.

A quarter mile to his right, at the bottom end of the lower pasture, was a foul bog that covered more than an acre. Drying in the heat, the stagnant muck gave off a stench that Sky could smell even at a distance.

The cattails around the bog's edge were brown and withered. Rotted carcasses of lost calves and wild animals, exposed by the receding water, drew buzzards, ravens, and swarms of carrion-feeding insects.

Sky hated that bog. A miasma of evil seemed to hang over the place, like the clouds of gnats that hovered above the brownish water. He couldn't go near it without remembering the young woman, a waitress at the Blue Coyote, whose murdered body he and Lute had found there during spring roundup.

He was turning aside when he noticed the thick flock of buzzards circling the bog, some flapping in to settle behind the screen of cattails, others perching in the bleached cottonwood that rose like a bony hand on the bog's far side. The place was a hangout for the ugly black birds. Sky was used to seeing a few of them. Today there were dozens, and plenty of ravens, too.

Something was going on and, like it or not, it was his job to check it out.

Sky swung the gray gelding toward the bog. Whatever he was about to find, one thing was for sure—it wouldn't be pretty. If some creature was newly trapped, he might be able to free it. If it was alive but beyond saving, he could at least use his pistol to end its misery.

For weeks the bog had been drying up in the heat. By now the water would be nearly gone. But the reeking mud it left behind smelled even worse. Catching the scent, Quicksilver snorted and tossed his head.

"It's all right, boy." Sky patted the satiny neck. "I know it smells bad, but it'll soon be behind us. Let's do our job." Steeling himself against the stench, he rode close enough to see over the cattails. The birds were clustered on a six-foot mound in the middle of the bog. Through the melee of feathered, black bodies, Sky glimpsed long white bones, tatters of faded gray fabric, a pair of mud-encrusted motorcycle boots, and the rusting barrels of two guns protruding from the mud beneath the body.

Turning the horse away, he filled the air with curses. There was no need to go closer, or even to look again. He knew what he'd find.

He'd come across what was left of his missing cousin, Coy Fletcher.

There was no question of keeping the discovery private. But Sky took the time to ride Quicksilver back to the paddock, unsaddle him, and turn him loose before telling Will and Beau about the body. Will made the call to Abner Sweeney, who, for whatever it was worth, was the law in Blanco County.

By the time Sky and Beau returned in Sky's pickup, the land around the bog was fast becoming a three-ring circus. Sirens wailing, Abner Sweeney roared up in his sheriff's Jeep, trailed by a Land Cruiser loaded with deputies and crime scene processing equipment. Hot behind them came the TV news chopper carrying the buxom Mindi Thacker and her camera crew.

Acting Sheriff Abner Sweeney stepped out of his Jeep. Pudgy and fortyish, with carrot-colored hair and a bumper crop of freckles, his attention seemed to be focused on the news crew. While one of his deputies began stringing yellow crime scene tape and the other two pulled on rubber boots and gloves, Sweeney stepped in front of the TV camera.

"Sheriff, what can you tell us about the situation here?" Ms. Thacker, dressed in a spotless white pantsuit, seemed to be vying with Sweeney for screen space.

Sweeney looked directly into the camera. "We're still investigating what happened here," he said. "But I can assure the public of two things. First and most important, with me and my loyal deputies on guard, the good citizens of Blanco County will be perfectly safe. And second, neither I nor my deputies will rest until the monster who committed this crime is brought to justice."

"I'll be damned," Beau muttered in Sky's ear. "The man's a born politician."

"For somebody who's not supposed to be very smart, he sounds pretty impressive," Sky said.

"It's all hot air. I hear he spends most of his spare time reading sexy crime novels." Beau nudged Sky out of camera range. "Let's keep our distance. We don't want to be cornered by Blanco County's answer to Diane Sawyer."

"I'm right behind you," Sky said, remembering the last time Ms. Thacker had covered a story on the ranch. Beau had threatened her with legal action if she didn't take her crew and leave. But with the sheriff and his deputies here, he didn't have that option.

They circled behind the parked vehicles to a spot from which they could watch without calling attention to themselves. The buzzards had scattered, some to the air and others to the branches of the dead cottonwood, where they watched the drama below.

Wearing high boots, arm-length gloves, and face masks, two men were making a circuit of the body. One had a camera, the other a pole he was using to probe the muck. The deputy who'd been stringing tape prowled the outer edge of the cattails looking for evidence.

"There won't be much to find," Beau said. "That body looks like it's been in the bog for weeks. You're sure the man's your missing cousin—the one who allegedly shot Jasper?"

"No doubt about it. I recognize the boots from the tracks I saw earlier. And I'm pretty sure one of those guns sticking out of the mud will turn out to be Jasper's shotgun—see the double barrel?"

"How well did you know him?" Beau asked.

"It's been years since I've seen Coy face-to-face, but I remember he was a mean son of a gun. Not the sort who'll be missed much. But that reminds me, I'll need to go and tell his sister before she sees this on the news."

"Lord, I don't envy you that. Were they close?"

"Nobody liked Coy much, including Marie. She told me she'd only brought him along because he insisted. But things must've been all right between them. She was picking up supplies for him and giving him rides to town and back on her Harley. That's what she was doing when they ran into Jasper."

Beau scowled. "So she was giving him a ride back from town and they cut across the ranch. Where were they headed?"

Beau was no fool. Sky's jaw tightened as reality sank into place with the weight of a two-ton boulder. This mess wasn't just about Coy and Marie. There was the camp and the marijuana patch he'd destroyed but hadn't reported because he'd wanted to give Marie a break. And there was the land—his land, the deed legally recorded in the county office. The truth was about to come out—and it would be best coming from him.

He planned to tell the sheriff, of course. But first he would tell the Tylers.

"Walk back to the truck with me," he said to Beau. "There's something I need to confess."

"So how long were you planning to keep this a secret?" Now that Beau had heard the story, he seemed far more interested in the land than in Coy's camp and the marijuana.

"Only until I'd decided what to do about it." Sky had told Beau about the deed he'd been given in the will. But he hadn't revealed his relationship to Bull Tyler. That was a secret he'd sworn to carry to his grave.

"What's to decide?" Beau demanded. "You get the land, you use it, run livestock on it, even build yourself a home. For once I agree with my father. You deserve that parcel of land. And when we tell Will, I know he'll feel the same."

Sky gazed past the hood of the pickup, to where the white coroner's van was pulling up alongside the sheriff's Jeep. "And what if I *don't* feel the same? The Rimrock gave me a home and a life. All I've ever done is my job—and for that I've been paid a fair wage. I've never taken anything I haven't earned." He shook his head. "That land's worth a lot of money. It just doesn't feel right."

Beau muttered a curse. "Dammit, Sky Fletcher, if I live to be a hundred, I'll never understand what goes on in that crazy Comanche brain of yours. So, what would you do with the land if you didn't keep it?"

"Donate it to the Rimrock—or sell it and donate the money. I know the ranch could use it, especially this year. But to tell you the truth, I've been too busy to do anything about it."

Beau's response was cut off by a shout from the young deputy who was circling the bog.

"Hey, over here! I found something!" He'd raised his camera and was leaning close to snap photos. Belly jiggling, Abner Sweeney pounded around the side of the bog. He'd taken a handkerchief out of his pocket and was holding it to his nose. Mindi Thacker, in high-heeled sandals, sprinted after him followed by her cameraman. Sky and Beau watched from a distance. If the scene hadn't revolved around a murder inves-tigation, it might have been laughable.

"Here, let's have a look." Sweeney moved in closer, crowding the deputy and inadvertently sinking a boot ankle deep into the muck. He yanked his foot out, grimacing with distaste and spattering mud on the newswoman's spotless white slacks.

"Hope they got that on TV," Beau muttered, then turned his attention to the object the deputy had bagged and lifted out of the cattails. "How about that? Judging from what I can see of it, I'd say that's a nine millimeter Glock. A gun like that could blow a big hole in a man. I wouldn't bet against it being the murder weapon."

"Neither would I, but why would the shooter just toss it here?" Sky stirred, fishing his truck keys out of his pocket. "This is a good show, but I need to go into town and find Marie."

"Go ahead," said Beau. "I'll cover for you here and answer any questions from Abner. Somebody should be willing to give me a ride back to the house."

"Thanks. You can tell them anything you know about the camp and the marijuana. But don't mention Marie if you can help it. If Stella finds out she's a Fletcher, that could put her in danger."

"Fine for now, but we might not be able to keep it a secret."

"I understand," Sky said. "Just give me time to warn her. She can decide what to do."

As Sky climbed into the pickup he could see the deputies and the medical examiner moving Coy's remains to an open body bag on a stretcher. He remembered Coy as a big man, well over 250 pounds. Whoever had killed him, they'd have needed extra muscle to get his body to the middle of the bog—unless Coy had walked there on his own.

Lost in thought, he made the drive into Blanco Springs. It was early in the day. The Blue Coyote would be closed, and Marie would most likely be sleeping.

Worry gnawed at him as he pulled into the empty parking lot. Would he even find her here? He'd given her his cell phone number, but she hadn't contacted him since the day they'd driven out to his property and found Coy missing. She could have decided to leave town without telling him.

He remembered her vendetta against Stella. Could the Blue Coyote's owner have found out who she was and done away with Marie as she had Lute? Given the circumstances and the people involved, anything could have happened.

Sky knew she didn't want to be seen with him. But his news couldn't wait. Deciding not to waste time, he climbed out of the pickup, mounted the back stairs to Marie's room, and rapped sharply on her door.

The long silence was broken by the creak of rusty bed springs and a sleepy voice.

"Who's out there, and what the hell do you want?"

Sky began to breathe again. The voice was Marie's.

"It's Sky," he said. "Open the door. I need to talk to you."

The door chain rattled. The door cracked open. "I told you not to come here. What is it?"

"Bad news, Marie. Coy's dead. We found his body on the ranch."

Seizing Sky's arm, she jerked him into the room, closed the door, and locked the chain. The blinds were down, darkening the shabby little room. Marie was wearing a shapeless, gray tee that fell to the middle of her thighs. She sank onto the side of the bed, pressing her lips together for a moment before she spoke. "Tell me everything," she said.

Sky told her, leaving out the more grisly details. She took the news impassively, as if numb with shock. "I figured something like that must've happened to him," she said. "Coy was probably asking for what he got. But he's still my brother, and I still feel bad. Any idea who killed him?"

"The sheriff's crew found a pistol at the scene, a Glock. They'll have to dust it for prints and do a ballistics test, but if it's the murder weapon, and they can trace it . . ." Sky let the words hang.

"Can they do the testing here in Blanco?"

"There's no lab here. They'll have to send the gun to Lubbock or Amarillo. Most likely they'll send the body there, too."

Marie stared down at her hands. The nails were chewed to the quick. Sky remembered how she used to bite them as a little girl.

"Stella's brother keeps a Glock in the drawer

below the cash register," she said. "I saw it a few weeks ago when I was looking for change. Do you think—?"

"Anything's possible. But a lot of people have those guns. Is there some way to look in the drawer? If it's still there, at least we'll know it isn't the one the deputy found."

"We can look now," Marie said, rising. "I've got a key to the bar because that's where the only bathroom is in this dump. Nobody's here at this hour. Come on."

She yanked on her jeans and shoved her bare feet into her boots. The key, chained to a sheet metal tag, hung on a nail hammered into the door frame. Sky followed her down the dim hallway, which smelled of urine and stale tobacco smoke. At its end, Marie unlocked a door. It opened onto a narrow wooden stairway leading down to the bar.

Motioning Sky back, Marie checked to make sure the place was really empty. Then she moved behind the cash register. "Stella locks up the money every night, but I'm pretty sure the Glock stays . . . here." She opened the drawer, pulling it all the way out and looking underneath. "It's gone."

An ominous chill crept down the back of Sky's neck. "There are plenty of reasons the gun might not be here. When was the last time you saw it?"

Marie checked the other drawers and shelves behind the bar. "I only saw it once—it was about the time you came and found me. That's been . . . what? At least a month." She closed the drawers, putting everything back the way she'd found it.

"Just supposing—and it's a long shot—that this gun turns out to be the murder weapon. What reason would Stella or her brother have to shoot Coy?"

"I was just thinking about that," Marie said. "According to what Lute told me, Stella's got her fingers pretty deep in some illegal pies. Coy did come in here a couple of times, and he's got—he had—a big mouth. If he said anything about the marijuana, she could've seen him as competition and had him blown away."

"I take it she doesn't know Coy was your brother."

"Not unless Coy slipped up and told somebody."

"Now that he's been killed and the law's involved, the relationship's likely to come out. Maybe it's time to think about your own safety." Sky reached for his wallet and pulled out a handful of bills. "Take this," he said. "It should be plenty to get you back to Oklahoma or wherever you want to go."

"Keep your money, Sky. I know what I'm doing." Thrusting the money back to him she glanced anxiously toward the front door. "Come on. You've got to get out of here."

She ushered him back upstairs and locked the door behind them. "Keep in touch with me, Marie," he said. "I mean it. With the chances you're taking, I need to know you're all right. If you don't have a cell phone, I'll buy you one."

She shoved him toward the outside stairs. "Don't worry, I'll be fine. Look around before you go out. Make sure nobody sees you."

Sky left her and drove back to the ranch. By now the sun was well above the horizon, scorching the land with its glaring rays. Ahead of him, on the asphalt, ravens were flocking on a road-killed coyote. Slowing the truck and averting his gaze, he pulled around them and continued on.

He was worried about Marie. She'd insisted she'd

be all right, but the people she was dealing with were as dangerous as Texas diamondback rattlesnakes. One misstep and she could end up like her two brothers.

Had she told him everything? Marie had no reason to distrust him. But Sky had the feeling she was hiding something—maybe something big. His cousin had her own agenda, and she thought she was clever enough to pull it off. But compared to Stella Rawlins, Marie was a bungling amateur. Stella was smart enough to stay one jump ahead of the law and ruthless enough to destroy anyone who crossed her. The thought of what the woman could do to Marie made Sky's blood run cold.

Beau was waiting for Sky on the shaded front porch of the ranch house with two cold Mexican beers. He rose as Sky mounted the steps. "I saw you coming and figured you'd have a powerful thirst," he said, handing one can to Sky and popping the tab on the other. "Sit down and we'll debrief each other. How did your cousin take the news?"

"Like she was expecting it." Sky sank into a chair and opened his beer. "She's one tough lady. I tried to talk her into leaving, but whatever she's got in mind, she's set on seeing it through. I'm worried about her, but I can only do so much toward changing her mind." He raised the can and took a long, easy swig, letting the coolness trickle down his throat. "How about you? How did things go at the crime scene?"

"All right." Beau gazed across the flat to where the sunlight glittered like diamond dust on the dry alkali bed. "While the deputies were finishing up, I went with Abner to look at Coy's camp on your property.

The tent's fallen down and the plants are long dead. Doesn't look like anybody's been there in weeks."

"Am I in trouble for not reporting it?"

Beau shrugged. "Abner didn't say so. I'm guessing he had more urgent things on his mind. But I scored some points with him. When I mentioned I'd been with the DEA, he treated me like a rock star. I told him if he'd include me in the loop, I'd be happy to keep my ear to the ground and report anything I hear. He said that would be dandy as long as I didn't mind his taking credit."

"He actually said that?"

"Pretty much. He wants to build credibility with the voters, and this case could take him a long way."

"At least he's honest about it," Sky said.

"Abner doesn't have enough sense to lie."

"Well, here's a tidbit for you. Marie told me Stella's brother kept a Glock under the cash register. When we went down to the bar to check, it wasn't there."

"Are you thinking the missing gun could be the one they found?"

"I don't know what to think," Sky said. "Maybe we'd better keep that to ourselves till the lab checks for prints. If Stella and Nick are behind the murder, we don't want Abner going in and spooking them too early."

"I agree." Beau's hazel eyes narrowed. "But one thing keeps chewing on me. Stella's a smart broad, and I get the feeling Nicky doesn't even blow his nose without her giving the order. So if they killed Coy, why would they be sloppy enough to toss the murder weapon at the scene?"

Sky was about to respond when Will's pickup

came roaring around the house and pulled up to the porch, braking in a cloud of dust. After swinging to the ground, Will strode to the foot of the porch steps. His disapproving glare made words unnecessary. Sky rose, ready to spring into action if needed. Beau remained where he was, sipping the last of his beer.

"If you two have finished your *break*, I've got some news. Wildfire, a hundred miles to the south of here. It's already burned a house and a barn. The owners were lucky to get their stock out in time."

"You're not thinking it'll make it this far?" Beau was instantly on alert.

"From what I heard on the news, they stopped it from jumping the highway. But if a fire can happen there, it can happen here. If it does—and we have to assume it will—we've got to be ready."

"Tell us what you've got in mind." Sky was already thinking of his horses, every one of them precious.

"For now, we'll put every man we can spare to digging a firebreak around the barns and buildings— that means clearing away anything that'll burn. Beau, I'm putting you in charge. Get Jasper's advice. He's fought fires before. Take the backhoe, any equipment that will make things go faster. Sky, you draw up an evacuation plan for the horses and other stock on the lower ranch. I'll want to see a priority list—which ones to get out first and which ones to leave behind if there's no time to save them all."

No time to save them . . .

Leaden-hearted, Sky headed for the long barn. He'd seen what range fires could do to stock, seen the horror of it, and knew what had to be done. Starting with the most valuable, the animals would be trailered out in relays, probably to the cattle pens on the caprock. Any horses set free to run could be trapped by the fire or become lost to starve or die of thirst.

In his head, he was already assembling the priority list for Will, with Erin's palomino foal and its parents at the top, to be followed by the other brood mares with their foals, the studs and the colts Sky was working to train. The older animals, like the paddock cows, docile old Belle, and the burro that kept the stallions company in their barn, would be left for last, perhaps even shot if the fire was closing in.

The process of moving so many animals would have to begin at the first whiff of danger. But there was one thing Sky knew. Regardless of Will's orders, if a fire threatened the ranch, no matter how close it burned, he would not be leaving any animal behind, no matter how old or feeble. He would stay until every last one was safe.

Any fire that threatened the Rimrock would also imperil the Prescott Ranch. Did the syndicate-hired manager who was running the place have any experience with fires? Would he know what to do?

Sky hadn't heard from Lauren since the night she'd driven him back to the house. She'd done a good job of hiding her anger until the very last. But her parting question, after he'd promised to be there for her, had betrayed her true feelings.

Will you? she'd demanded, then gunned the car and shot down the drive without giving him a chance to reply.

Sky couldn't say he blamed her. He'd tried to do the best thing for them both, but clearly that wasn't what she'd wanted. He missed her more than he'd ever thought possible. There'd been times when he'd almost called her. Pride had stopped him, but now he had a reason. If Lauren was still on the ranch, she would need to be warned about the fire danger.

Maybe it was a lame excuse. But the urge to hear her voice and know she was all right drove him to punch in the number and press the call button. The phone rang on the other end—once, then again and again before the recorded answer voice came on.

"You have reached . . ."

Never mind. The fire danger was on all the news broadcasts and in the paper. There was no way anybody with eyes and ears could miss it. He'd only been using it as an excuse to make an unnecessary call, and Lauren would have seen right through him.

Sky ended the call without leaving a message.

CHAPTER 12

Lauren slid into the booth at Burger Shack and greeted the smiling blond woman who waited for her on the other side of the table.

"Thanks for meeting me, Tori. When I called your number, all I wanted was the name of a Realtor. I certainly didn't expect to be having lunch with you. Since you're doing me a favor, I hope you'll let me treat you."

"Only if you promise to let me treat next time—and that there will be a next time." Will's ex-wife sipped the Diet Coke she'd ordered along with the mushroom pizza they'd agreed to split. She was a stunning woman, tall and slim, her loose, sun-streaked hair anchored by the sunglasses she'd pushed up onto her head.

Lauren had put off phoning her, hoping she could find a place to rent or buy on her own. But after weeks of scanning the ads in the paper and finding nothing, she'd summoned her nerve and called the number Sky had given her. Tori's friendly manner had put her at ease right away.

The teenage waitress came to take Lauren's order—a Coke to go with the pizza. Lauren had turned off her cell phone in the car. She didn't want this visit interrupted by a call, especially from her father, grilling her about where she was and whom she was with.

"As I told you," Tori continued, "Blanco Springs is a small town. There's not enough business here to support a Realtor. But my work helps keep me on top of what's happening. If you'll tell me what you're looking for, I can at least keep an ear to the ground."

"Thanks," Lauren said. "Things have become non-stop crazy with my father. He's started tracking my every move. And he keeps pressuring me to date men who can help his campaign. I've got to get out on my own."

Tori nodded. "Knowing your father, I can understand that. But you could go anywhere. Why would you want to stay here?"

Lauren swirled the ice in her Coke, hesitating before she answered. "Funny, Sky asked me the same question."

"And I believe you just answered it." Tori's smile was warm and knowing. "You're actually blushing."

"It's a redhead thing. So embarrassing. I've always hated it."

"Don't you dare change the subject. Beau did mention there were some sparks between you two."

"There were, but not anymore." Even saying it hurt, but Lauren wanted to be honest. "We're not seeing each other. His idea, not mine."

"Why am I not surprised? I've known Sky since he was a teenager. I don't know what you'd call it—

pride, maybe, for want of a better word. But if you offer the man something wonderful, he'll come up with a whole litany of reasons why he doesn't deserve it and shouldn't accept it. Usually he'll end up walking away, which is probably why he's not married—though, heaven knows, some very sharp ladies have tried to land him."

"The way you make it sound, the breakup was his fault. But it was really mine—because I ran away without telling him, and because of my issues with my fiancé's death and with my father. Sky told me to call him when I got my life together. So that's what I'm trying to do. Even if I never get him back, I need to do this, Tori. Sky was right about me. I'm a wreck."

"But he *did* tell you to call him. He left the door wide open. Coming from Sky, that's a lot. Did he tell you anything else?"

"Yes. The very last thing he said before I drove away was that if I needed him, he'd be there for me." Lauren blinked away tears. "I was hurting, so I just blew him off. Oh, blast it, I didn't mean to unload on you like this. I'm sorry."

"Don't be." Tori reached across the table and patted her arm. "There's one more thing I want to say, and then we'll talk about something else. Sky had a hellish childhood before he came to the Rimrock."

Lauren remembered the scars she'd glimpsed on Sky's back. "I suspected something like that," she said.

"He learned to guard his feelings," Tori said. "He's still so protective that he has a hard time letting anyone in. But underneath that lone-wolf, tough-man shell, Sky Fletcher is one of the gentlest, most compassionate people I've ever known."

"I know," Lauren said. "I've seen how he is with the horses, and with your daughter."

"Then you've seen the real Sky. And you have to know that if he says he'll be there for you, he means it."

Only the distraction of the waitress bringing their pizza kept Lauren from crumbling. "That's all well and good," she said. "But for now, I have to be a big girl and move on as if I never expect to hear from him again. Who knows? Maybe I won't—and maybe that's for the best, at least for him." She was putting on a brave face. But even saying the words was like jabbing herself with a cold steel knife.

"But you're here—for now, at least." Tori scooped a slice of pizza onto her plate, giving it a moment to cool. "So tell me what you need."

"Two things," Lauren said. "A place to live and some steady work. I've got money in a trust fund from my mother, enough to live on for a while, maybe even make a down payment on a little house. But I could burn through it all too easily, and I don't want to do that."

"Of course you don't."

"Buying a house would tie up my cash, but it would be like an investment. I could always sell it later, maybe at a profit."

"True, but given how uncertain things are for you, wouldn't you be better off renting?"

"Maybe. But as far as I know, there's nothing out there." Lauren shook her head. "I know it would make more sense for me to leave. But I've been running away from my problems for too long. I need to stop and face them, and Blanco Springs is as good a place as any."

"So it's not just about Sky."

"Right now it can't be." Lauren slid a pizza slice

onto her plate. "As for the work, I'm pretty much finished at the Tylers' and the bookkeeping I do for the ranch syndicate is only part time. Living at the ranch, it's been enough. But to get by on my own, I'll need more clients, or a full-time job somewhere."

Tori sipped her Coke. "I might have a few connections. I'll ask around. But about the rentals—there's an apartment complex on the edge of town. I'm pretty sure it's full, but I know the manager. I can ask her if anybody's given notice."

"Thanks. I'll cross my fingers."

"There's another possibility. I'm settling Hoyt Axelrod's estate for his children. I could ask them if they'd be interested in renting the house until it sells—maybe with an option for you to buy it."

Lauren shuddered. "Sky suggested that, too. I just don't know . . ."

"I understand," Tori said. "But keep an open mind. You never knew Hoyt. He was a decent man, upheld the law, raised a good family. His wife was a lovely person. But after she died, something went dark in him. I'm not usually one to spread gossip, but I think Stella Rawlins, the woman who owns the Blue Coyote, had a lot to do with it. What happened to him in the end was a tragedy."

"Beau told me the story. He murdered three people and almost killed Sky."

"Yes, he did." Tori's expression was sad but wise. "But the home is a nice little place, well kept, probably cheaper and certainly more private than the apartments would be. I have the key anytime you'd like to look at it."

"I'll keep it in mind. But—"

"No pressure." Tori smiled. "Just think about it."

Lauren thought about it all the way back to the

ranch. In some ways the Axelrod house would be perfect for her needs. But the idea that a murderer had lived inside those walls would haunt every hour she spent there. She could get rid of the furniture, repaint the walls, replace the fixtures and floor coverings. But even then there was no way she would feel at ease. For now she would trust to luck and hope one of the apartments, or some other place, would open up.

When she reached the house, her father was waiting on the porch, a glass of bourbon in his hand. Fighting the temptation to turn the car around and drive away, she pulled into the shade and switched off the engine. Her father rose as she mounted the front steps.

"I tried to call you, but evidently you'd turned off your phone. If you were with that half-breed Fletcher—"

"I was having lunch with Tori Tyler," Lauren said, holding back her temper. "I asked her to help me find a place to live in town."

"Live in town? Hell, you live here!" he snapped. "This is your home! Why should you pay good money for some rat hole in Blanco? And since when do you know Tori?"

Lauren willed herself not to lash out at him. He'd been hard to live with when she'd first arrived. Now his behavior was becoming erratic. While he tracked her every move, or tried to, he guarded his own secrets almost obsessively. She'd begun to worry about his mental state. She might have pushed him to see a doctor, but with the primary and the general election coming up, she knew it wasn't going to happen. She owed the man nothing, Lauren reminded herself. But he was her father and, in spite of everything, she couldn't help worrying about him.

"I need to be on my own, Dad," she said. "Someone at the Tylers' suggested I call Tori. I met her for the first time today. She's a nice woman—seems to know more than a little about you."

He took a swig from his bourbon glass. "What Tori knows about me is none of your damn business. And you're not fooling me, girl. The only reason you want to be on your own is so you can screw that bastard Fletcher."

Lauren gasped. She'd tried to remain calm, but his last accusation had sunk home—maybe because it was at least partly true. She drew herself up. "Maybe I should be the one asking questions. You're coming home at all hours, sometimes staying out all night. When you walk in, the smell of that awful perfume leaves a trail behind you all the way down the hall. Your car reeks of it. Who's the woman, Dad? Is she married? Is that why you won't tell me?"

His hand came up. For an instant Lauren thought he was going to strike her. But then he lowered his arm, turned away, and with a muttered curse stalked into the house.

Lauren's legs were quivering. She sank onto the top step, fists clenched on her knees. With the primary election coming up next month, Garn Prescott had become a walking pressure cooker—and just now he'd nearly exploded.

Since they'd never had a real father–daughter relationship, she didn't know him as well as she might have. Even so, she could tell something was terribly wrong, and it wasn't just politics. He was behaving as if he'd bargained his soul and the buyer was about to demand payment.

Call me if you need anything, Lauren. I'll be here for you.

Lauren fumbled for the cell phone in her purse, then pushed it aside. How many times had she recalled Sky's parting words? How many times had she reached for that phone, then stopped herself before she could punch in his number? Tori had reassured her that Sky meant what he'd said. But that didn't mean she could go running to him every time she needed a shoulder to cry on. She had to prove that she was strong enough to handle things on her own—not only to Sky but to herself.

"What do you mean, it's gone, Nicky?" Stella faced her brother across the bar, a cold knot tightening in her stomach. Her survival had always depended on making sure nothing fell through the cracks. Now, three days after the discovery of a murdered body on the Tyler ranch, something had. The Glock she'd given Nick for protection in the bar was missing—the Glock that was legally registered to *her*.

Nick cringed under his half sister's withering gaze. Older by seven years, Stella had always protected him. She alone understood that beneath the skin of the tough-looking biker was a scared, vulnerable man, too slow-witted to survive a lawless world on his own.

He was the one person she truly cared about.

"What did you do with it?" she demanded.

"N-nothing, I swear to God," he stammered. "I haven't touched that gun since I loaded it and put it in the drawer."

"When was the last time you saw it?"

"A while ago." He shrugged, eyes lowered. "Don't really remember."

"Nicky—" Her eyes narrowed. "I know when you're hiding something. Tell me the truth. When did you first notice the gun was missing?"

"A few days ago. I thought I must've moved it and forgot, and that I'd find it somewhere. I knew you'd be mad if I told you."

Stella exhaled, feeling the knot tighten in the pit of her stomach. "Did you notice anybody looking at it? Anybody opening the drawer?"

"Nobody." He picked up a glass and began polishing it with a towel.

Unable to contain her anxiety, Stella turned away and walked back down the hall toward her office. Abner Sweeney, her eyes and ears in town, had mentioned that his deputy had found a Glock not far from where a body had turned up on the Tylers' ranch. It didn't make sense that the pistol could be the one missing from the bar. But if it was, the serial number could be linked to her, and the prints on the gun could be linked to Nick.

Opening her desk, she took out a pack of Marlboros and a lighter. Hands shaking, she lit the cigarette and inhaled the bitter, calming smoke. Abner had also told her the dead man was a cousin of Sky Fletcher's—Lute's brother, most likely—and that he'd been growing weed on Sky's land. None of that had anything to do with her or with Nicky, but if the murder weapon could be traced to the bar, who was going to believe it?

Sinking into the chair, she leaned back, blew a smoke ring, and watched it dissolve against the low ceiling. This was no time to panic, she told herself.

She hoped it wouldn't be too late for some damage control.

At this stage, Acting Sheriff Sweeney was little more than a friend. Solidly married, he wasn't a candidate for seduction. But in exchange for Stella's loaning him interest-free money for his new SUV, he'd delivered a gift-wrapped box of chocolates to the attendant at the county jail. Sweeney had no clue what had been hidden under the chocolates, let alone that it had any connection to Hoyt Axelrod's death. But over the past few weeks Stella had made sure he owed her some small favors. Maybe it was time to call them in.

Blowing one last smoke ring, she snubbed her cigarette in the ashtray and punched in Sweeney's number on her phone.

"What can I do for you, Stella?" His voice was cordial enough, but she sensed a note of discomfort in the question. Maybe he wasn't alone.

"I'd like to report a theft," she said. "A pistol—a Glock—was stolen from the Blue Coyote a few days ago. I only just now discovered it was missing, but there's a chance it may have been used in a crime."

There was a pause. "Are you talking about that murder on the Tyler place? *That* Glock?"

"We can't be sure, of course—except that the gun's definitely been stolen." Stella felt like a fool. The crazy thing was, everything she was telling him was God's truth. "If there's any way you could—"

"I'm sorry, it's out of my hands," he said. "The gun's been sent to the lab. We can't even be sure it was the murder weapon till we get the autopsy and the ballistics report. But I wouldn't worry. Even if the Glock turns out to be yours, the real criminal's prints should be on it."

Not unless the real criminal was too stupid to wear gloves or wipe the gun, Stella thought. "You'll keep me posted, won't you—as a friend?" she asked.

"I'll do what I can." Abner sounded like a robot. There must be someone with him, maybe a deputy or even that dumpy wife of his who popped out babies like a brood mare. Could she count on Abner to cover for her, or was it, as he'd said, out of his hands?

Swearing, Stella slammed the phone onto the desk. Why now? Just when everything was going so well? She had Garn Prescott under her thumb—especially now that he knew his campaign ads had been paid for with dirty money, and a single anonymous tip to the press could ruin him. Once the organization in Dallas saw proof that she could deliver a U.S. congressman, they'd be begging her to join them. She'd be on her way to having the wealth and power she'd always wanted.

But now she had this mess to deal with. If the gun proved to be hers, and the real murderer wasn't caught, the evidence could cast enough suspicion to bring her down.

The ironic thing was, for once, she and Nick were as innocent as newborn lambs.

Listening in the upstairs hallway, Marie had heard enough to get the gist of both of Stella's conversations. After the crash of the phone, she lurked in the shadows hoping to hear more through the thin planks under her bare feet. But there was nothing except the sound of the toilet flushing in the restroom. After a few minutes she crept back to her room, crawled into her bed, and pretended to sleep. Any time now, Stella was bound to show up and question her about the gun. She would need to appear completely clue-less.

The tiny room was stifling in the late-morning heat. Marie willed herself to lie still and keep her eyes closed. Beneath the ragged cotton blanket, her body was drenched in sweat. Her heart was pounding.

So far everything she'd planned was falling into place. Stella was running scared. If the cops arrested her or Nick for Coy's murder, the bitch would be at her mercy.

She should be happy, Marie told herself. But all she could feel was a stomach-curdling tension that crept into her throat, making her want to gag.

On the way back from shooting Coy, she'd pulled the Harley off the road and thrown up in the grass. She'd always hated Coy, the way he'd tortured the an-imals she loved and the way he used to spy on her through that hole he'd made in the bathroom wall. He'd never touched her physically, but she could just imagine what was going through his mind. She'd told herself that killing him would be a pleasure. But she'd been wrong about that. Whatever happened, the memory of murdering her own brother would never go away.

After meeting Sky in the parking lot that night, she'd known she had to act. Wearing her motorcycle gloves, she'd taken the Glock out of the drawer and had ridden her Harley out to Coy's camp. It had been easy enough convincing her brother that he had to get rid of the two guns—the lever-action rifle she'd used to shoot the old man and the twenty-gauge shotgun they'd taken off his ATV.

Lute had told her about the bog, and Marie had made sure she knew the way. Telling Coy it was the perfect place to ditch the two guns, she'd taken him there on the back of the motorcycle. She remembered the sweaty heat of his body behind her, the familiar, unwashed stench of him. And she remembered the trust in his eyes when she'd told him to take the guns, walk out to the deepest part of the bog, and shove them under the water with a big rock to anchor them down.

Coy had followed her instructions without a moment's hesitation. Marie had waited on the dry edge until Coy reached the middle of the bog. Then she'd drawn the Glock and pumped three shots into his back.

On the way back to her bike, she'd tossed the pistol in the cattails.

A sharp rap on the door jerked Marie's thoughts back to the present. "You in there, girl?" The voice was Stella's. No surprise there.

"Yeah. . . . Just a minute." Marie mumbled the words and made sure Stella could hear the creak of rusty springs as she rolled out of bed. Her fingers fumbled with the chain lock on the door.

"Wha . . . ?" she muttered, squinting at Stella through the narrow opening.

Stella shoved her way in. She was dressed for work in her usual silk shirt and tight denim skirt, but her feet were clad in rubber flip-flops, the toes adorned with corn plasters. Her high-heeled, red cowgirl boots wouldn't go on until the bar was about to open.

"Sit down before you fall down, girl," she snapped. "Look at you! Have you been drinking? You know that isn't allowed here unless you pay!"

Marie sank onto the edge of the bed. "Just tired, that's all. I worked late, and it's hard to get to sleep in this heat. If I could have a fan—"

"You want a fan, buy your own." Stella loomed

over her, hands on her hips. "That's not why I'm here. There's a gun missing from the drawer under the cash register. If you know anything about it, you'd better fess up now."

"Gun?" Marie looked blank. "What kind of gun? Was I supposed to know it was there?"

Stella gave a huff of impatience. "Did you see anybody near that drawer? Anybody opening it or taking anything out?"

"No. Nigel's always right there. How could anybody even get close?"

"What about when the bar's closed? Have you heard any noises downstairs? If you've let anybody inside, so help me—"

"No!" Marie was all wide, innocent eyes. "I'd never do that. But I'm a pretty sound sleeper once I go under. Somebody could've broken in, I guess. Maybe they were looking for money and found the gun."

Stella scowled, deepening the creases in her heavy makeup. "A fine lot of help you are! Let me know if you see or hear anything. Meanwhile, as long as you're up, you might as well get dressed and make yourself useful. The floor could use a good scrubbing before we open, and you can wash the windows, too. I'm not paying you good money to sleep."

"*Bitch!*" Marie muttered as Stella sashayed back down the hall toward the stairs. For two cents she'd tell the woman where she could shove this crappy job. But the stakes had become too high for that. And Marie was too close to getting what she wanted. She would have to be patient a little longer.

So far she'd been lucky. If the gun led the cops to Stella or Nick, and if either of them was arrested, the door would be open to make her move. But luck wouldn't be enough. She would need to be tough and smart. Play her cards right, and she could have it all. Make one mistake, and she could end up as dead as her two brothers.

Four days after Coy Fletcher's body was found in the bog, Will sold off two hundred head of Rimrock cattle. The buyer was a feed lot owner out of Lubbock, the price so low that it made Will heartsick. But at least the money would help feed the rest of the herd for a few extra weeks—maybe until the drought broke, if it ever did.

Was he just throwing good money after bad?

Will asked himself that question as he stood on the porch the morning after the sale, sipping his coffee and watching the cruel sun rise over the plains to the east. The summer's heat had sucked every last drop of moisture out of the soil. The grass had long since crumbled to yellow dust. Even hardy, deep-rooted trees like the cedars were turning brown and dropping their foliage at a passing touch.

The morning breeze stirred the vanes of the old windmill that pumped water from a deep underground well. At least there was wind. But how long would the water last with nothing going down to replenish it? How long could they hold out here if the place became a dust bowl like the one that had sent families trekking out of Oklahoma in the 1930s?

A hundred yards beyond the house he could hear the thrum of the backhoe and see the firebreak Beau had put the cowhands to clearing. The men had been working in shifts through the night, from dusk until chore time, after which the morning sun became too hot to stand. After three nights of back-breaking toil, the eight-foot strip of bare earth made an outward arc on both sides of the drive, giving some protection to the house and other dwellings. The work wouldn't be finished until it fronted the eastern approach to the barns and sheds. On the west, they would depend on the escarpment to keep them safe. Up on the caprock the fire danger was even greater. But God willing, no fire would be able to jump the rocky, bare escarpment in either direction.

On the morning news, Will had seen more wildfires, one of them in the next county to the east. Ranches had been destroyed, stock lost, and two people killed trying to save their property. Would the firebreak be enough to hold back leaping flames? Will could only hope. Gazing out at the seared landscape, he murmured a half-voiced prayer.

He felt a tug on his arm. Erin's fresh young face grinned up at him. "Daddy, Bernice says to tell you breakfast is ready."

He gave her a smile and squeezed her shoulder. Right now his daughter was the only brightness in his world. Nothing mattered more than keeping her safe. Later today he would call Tori about taking her back to town until the worst of the danger was over. Erin would balk at leaving the ranch and her beloved foal, but it was what her mother would want. At least he and Tori saw eye to eye on some things.

Will was finishing his plate when Beau came in to join him. Unshaven and weary, he'd spent the predawn hours on the firebreak. His head and hands were damp from a dousing at the outside tap.

"I got an early morning call from Abner." He slid out his chair and took his place on the opposite side of the table. "He heard from the lab in Lubbock. The three slugs taken from the body are a match to the Glock found at the crime scene. Looks like the poor devil was shot in the back."

"No surprise there." Will downed the last of his coffee. "How come Abner's calling you? Are you moonlighting as his new deputy?"

"Not quite." Beau paused to thank Bernice for the heaping plate she set in front of him. "But Abner's been treating me like his best buddy since he found out I worked for the DEA. Since this is his first murder case, he's pretty stoked about it. Even though it's against protocol, he wanted to share the news."

"What about the gun? Have they tracked the owner?"

"Here's where it gets interesting. The Glock's registered to Stella Rawlins. But there's only one set of fingerprints on it, and they aren't hers."

"How do they know? You told me she wasn't in the system."

"According to Abner, the prints on the grip were weathered and pretty faint. But the prints on the magazine were pristine. Every one of them was a match to Nikolas Tomescu."

"Our tattooed friend Nigel. Does Sky know?"

"Yes. I caught up with him on his way to the tack room."

"How did he react to the news?"

"You know Sky. You can't tell what he's thinking." Beau scooped up a forkful of eggs. "Abner's waiting for a warrant from the judge. Then he'll go with a couple of deputies to make the arrest."

"Damned shame, he's been a good bartender and tough enough to keep the place civilized." Will rose. "Anyway, it's one less thing to worry about. Finish eating and get cleaned up. I'll see you outside."

Will strode out the back door and headed for the barn. The sun was up. He could already feel its heat shriveling his skin. It was going to be a long day.

Stella was sitting at the bar enjoying a smoke while Nick and the waitress—whatever the hell her name was—finished polishing the tables and chairs. The Blue Coyote might not be the classiest place in Texas, but she did like things clean.

They'd almost finished when she heard a business-like knock at the front door. Glancing through the plastic blind slats, she could see Abner in uniform, flanked by two deputies—clean-cut young men who looked like ex-military. A cramp tightened in the pit of her stomach. This couldn't be anything good. But she had to let them in.

Abner avoided her eyes as they walked in and whipped out their badges. Clearly he'd had no choice except to make the arrest. But the little Judas would pay the price later on.

Abner gave a subtle nod in Nick's direction. The taller of the two men stepped around Nick, jerked his wrists behind his back, and whipped out a set of handcuffs. Nick was shaking, his eyes bulging like a frightened animal's.

"Nikolas Tomescu," the shorter man snapped, "you're under arrest for the murder of Coy Fletcher. You have the right to remain silent . . ."

"No!" Nick found his voice. "I didn't do anything! Tell them, Sis! Tell them I'm innocent!"

They shoved him out the door and propelled him to the waiting police vehicle. Stella sagged against the bar. She'd always protected her brother, but right now there was nothing she could do. She'd never felt more helpless in her life.

Glancing back over her shoulder, she saw the waitress standing at the end of the bar. The woman's features quickly assumed a look of concern. But Stella had been quick enough to see the earlier expression on her face.

The skinny bitch had been smiling like a satisfied cat.

CHAPTER 13

By the time they shoved him in the police cruiser, Nick was blubbering like a child. Heartsick, Stella watched the vehicle pull out of the parking lot. She could have argued with the officers but she knew it wouldn't have done any good. The iron-jawed deputies had ignored her. Abner had refused to look her way.

She would deal with Abner later. But not while there was a chance she'd still need him.

Nick was innocent. Stella knew it to the depths of her heart. He looked tough and mean, but he didn't have it in him to shoot a dog, let alone a man. And even if he'd done it, he wouldn't lie to her. He wasn't clever enough for a big lie like that.

Whatever happened, she couldn't let him go to prison. Nick would become a victim in prison, abused and tormented. Prison would destroy him. But she couldn't dwell on that now. She had to focus on how to save him.

He was going to need a lawyer—and not that

blond Tyler woman. Tori Tyler knew too much and there was too much bad blood between them. But Stella had connections. She would use them to get Nick the best lawyer in Texas.

But first it was time to pull some strings. She would make a list of the people who owed her favors and call anyone who might be in a position to help.

At the top of her list would be a certain U.S. congressman.

The waitress was still standing at the far end of the bar. Stella turned on her. "What are you gawking at? Get your lazy butt moving! This bar opens in an hour and you're going to have to run the place by yourself!"

Garn Prescott was driving back from Lubbock, where he'd addressed a women's luncheon. He was congratulating himself on the speech and looking forward to the bourbon waiting for him at home when the jangling ringtone on his cell—the opening notes of "Deep in the Heart of Texas"—broke into his thoughts.

With a sigh, he fumbled the phone out of his pocket. Eyes on a passing hay truck, he pushed the answer button without looking at the name of the caller.

"Hello?"

"Garn, baby, it's me."

At the sound of that smoky voice, his mood tanked. He'd been wary of Stella ever since he'd figured out where those big campaign contributions of hers were coming from. The two of them were still hooking up, and so far she hadn't made any demands or threats, but Prescott knew she'd backed him into a corner.

One word to the right people and he'd be finished in politics, maybe even on his way to jail.

He'd been a fool to accept money from her without checking out the source. But desperation had led to denial, and her generous sexual favors had sealed the deal. He didn't have any solid evidence against the woman—getting it would involve other people and put him at risk. But he'd finally forced himself to face cold reality. There was no legal way she could've gotten so much spare cash—and she'd had no reason to give it to him except to bait her trap.

The anxiety was making him physically sick. He'd sold his soul to a very clever, very sexy devil, who had a grip on him where it hurt the most. Short of murder, there wasn't a damned thing he could do.

"Hi," he muttered. "What's up?"

"We need to talk," she said. "It's an emergency. Where are you?"

"On my way home, about fifteen minutes out of Lubbock."

"I can meet you halfway, at that truck stop with the diner."

"The one with the motel out back, right?" At least he deserved some enjoyment out of this.

"Right, but sorry, honey, it's not that kind of emergency. I'll meet you in the diner. Get us a quiet booth. It'll be too hot outside to talk in your car."

"Sure. See you there." Prescott ended the call, worry gnawing at his gut. Was this the showdown? Was the devil about to demand her due?

The truck stop was ten minutes down the highway. Maybe he should just go on past it and keep driving, or safer yet, turn his big white Cadillac around and go back to Lubbock. But he'd pay a price for that later,

Prescott reminded himself. Better to face the music now. At least he'd know where he stood.

By the time he pulled up to the diner, he'd broken out in a cold sweat. As he walked in the door, the window-mounted AC raised goose bumps on his skin. Glancing around, he found an inside corner booth and settled in to wait.

Not wanting to be recognized, he'd left his jacket and bolo tie in the car, kept his sunglasses on, and used a baseball cap to cover his hair. Still, the middle-aged waitress who took his order for coffee was giving him funny looks. Maybe she'd recognized his car out front.

By the time Stella pulled up in her black Buick, Prescott was ready to bolt. He was going to chide her for making him wait, but then, as she sat down across from him, he changed his mind. Her eyes were bloodshot, her makeup creased. She looked as if she'd aged ten years.

When the waitress came with her order pad and her curious eyes, Stella shook her head. "Nothing for me, thanks," she murmured.

"What is it? Is something wrong?" Prescott asked as the waitress left. His instincts told him Stella was about to ask for a big favor. Even before he knew what it was, he found himself groping for a way out.

She stared down at her hands. Then her fierce tiger-green eyes met his. "That body they found on the Tyler place," she said. "Did you hear about it?"

"I believe so." Prescott spoke calmly. Anything bad that happened to the Tylers gave him pleasure. "Some transient growing a patch of weed. At least that's what I heard on the news. Why? Did you know him?"

She raked a hand through her hair, giving Prescott a glimpse of graying roots. "My brother Nick's been arrested for the murder," she said. "The cops found a gun with his prints on it at the scene. But he didn't do it. So help me God, I'd bet my life on that. Nicky was framed."

"I'm sorry." Prescott could sound sincere when he had to. He reached for her hand across the table. "What makes you so sure he's innocent?"

"I've known him all his life. Pretty much raised him while our mother was off with her boyfriends. Nicky's no angel, but he's not a killer. Besides, he'd never even met the man. Why the hell would he go all the way out to the Tylers' and shoot him?"

Prescott listened as the story spilled out of her—the Glock, registered to her name, missing from the drawer; the finding of the weapon at the murder scene, and her brother's arrest. He knew, of course, what was coming next. She'd want him to intervene. But he couldn't do that—especially not with an election coming up. He braced himself as Stella made her pitch.

"I've done plenty for you, Garn. Those TV ads my money paid for have brought in enough backing to put you out front in the polls. I never meant to ask for anything in return. But now I need your help."

"I'll do what I can," he said, knowing what she wanted. "But—"

"No buts!" Her eyes blazed into his. "You're a powerful man. You know people—the district attorney, the judges, the state attorney general, even the governor. Half of them are your damned drinking buddies. They'll listen to you."

A couple of truck drivers had turned on the barstools to look at them. Prescott was beginning to squirm.

"Stella, it's not that simple."

"I don't care! It's not like I'm asking you to lie. My brother was framed by somebody who stole the gun. He's innocent!"

"If that's true, get yourself a good lawyer and put your faith in the American judicial system. Trust the jury to—"

"The jury will take one look at those tattoos and vote guilty. What's it going to take? More money? I've got that."

"Stella—"

She rose, leaning over the table. "You owe me, Garn! Whatever advantage I gave you, I can take back. You've got twenty-four hours before your magic coach turns into a pumpkin. That's it. I can hurt you. Don't make me do it."

Squeezing out of the booth, she spun away and stalked out of the diner. Seconds later, tires spitting gravel, the Buick roared out of the parking lot.

The two truckers at the bar had turned their backs, making a show of minding their own business. But they'd no doubt gotten an earful. The waitress had probably been listening, too.

Prescott sat still for a moment, feeling the effects of his rocketing blood pressure as his world threatened to implode. Stella had given him twenty-four hours, and he knew she meant business. There had to be somebody he could call—if nothing else, just to show he was trying.

Acting Sheriff Sweeney would be taking credit for the arrest to boost his run for office. He wouldn't want anybody to know he might have jailed the wrong man. Clay Drummond, the county prosecutor, was a hard-nosed s.o.b. who'd rather lose a finger than lose a case. Prescott could cross both of them off his mental list right now. Prescott had played golf and shared drinks with a couple of the judges, but he didn't know who would be on the case. And even if he did, how could he explain his asking a favor on behalf of a woman like Stella? As for the governor or the state attorney general, one word to either of them would be political suicide.

Prescott stood, fished a five-dollar bill out of his wallet, and laid it under his half-empty coffee cup. His skin crawled as he walked out of the diner, feeling as if every eye in the place was fixed on his back. By the time he made it into his car, his knees were threatening to collapse. The Cadillac was sweltering inside, the steering wheel hot enough to burn his hands. Sweating rivulets, he switched the AC on high and pulled out of the parking lot.

He was approaching the turnoff to Blanco Springs when he thought of Josh Hardesty. The man might not have enough influence to save Stella's brother. But if the governor's stepson had a reason to come around, Stella might see it as a sign that Prescott was doing something to help her. Who knew? Maybe Hardesty would be interested enough to look into the case and actually do something.

It was his best chance. Maybe his only chance. But reeling in Hardesty would depend on using Lauren as bait. And so far she'd refused to go out with the man again.

He had twenty-four hours—a little less by now— before Stella brought down his world. No doubt she could do it. All it would take was a whisper in the right person's ear.

His foot stomped the gas pedal. The white Cadillac shot down the road toward home. He could only pray that Lauren would be there and that she would listen to him.

Lauren lifted the saddle off Storm Cloud's back and hung the bridle next to the stall. She took a towel and rubbed down the big gelding, lingering on the spots that made him quiver with pleasure. Following Sky's advice, she'd made it a habit to work with the horse every day, riding him, grooming him, or just stopping by the stable to give him a treat. With time and patience, Storm Cloud had begun to trust her. On this afternoon's short ride, he'd performed beautifully.

"Good boy," she murmured, stroking the satiny neck. "You were broken. So was I. But we're both getting better."

What would she do about him when she moved to town? If she could find a place to keep him, she might be able to buy him from the syndicate. Meanwhile she could at least visit him and ride him as often as possible.

But the horse wasn't Lauren's only concern. She had spent the morning and the early part of the afternoon updating the books in the syndicate office. The talk there, among the manager and the hands who wandered in and out, had been about the fire danger.

As she made the fifteen-minute trek from the stable to the house, Lauren remembered the conversation she'd overheard between the sharp, young ranch manager and an old cowboy who'd worked for the Prescott family most of his life.

"I wouldn't worry if I were you," the manager had said. "The ground is cleared around the buildings, the water tanks are full, and the air drop service is just a phone call away. Being prepared can make all the difference."

"I can tell you ain't never been in a range fire," the old man had drawled. "When them flames come at you, hot enough to turn your bones to cinders, it's like you stumbled into hell, an' you're starin' right down the devil's throat."

Right down the devil's throat. The words echoed in Lauren's head as she entered the house through the kitchen door. The ninety-year-old Prescott family home was made of wood and isolated by distance from the newer buildings and pens used by the syndicate. If a fire came close enough, it would go up like a torch, along with the nearby sheds and the garage that housed her grandfather's priceless collection of antique cars. Would the ranch employees even bother protecting the old home? Why should they?

She was hungry after working most of the day, and the cook wouldn't be in till dinnertime. Finding some leftover chicken in the fridge, she made a sandwich, poured some iced tea, and sat down at the table. She was just finishing her late lunch when her father walked in from the front of the house. The glass in his hand was half-filled with bourbon.

When had Garn Prescott begun to look so old and tired? Was it just that she hadn't noticed, or had some new disaster struck him?

"Are you hungry, Dad?" she asked, trying to be kind. "Can I fix you something?"

"No to both. I had lunch with the League of Women Voters." He sank onto a chair with a weary sigh. "But I do need a favor from my little girl."

She was hardly his little girl. But he looked so down-trodden that Lauren couldn't help feeling sorry for him. "Tell me," she said.

He raised the glass and drained the bourbon in two gulps. His pale eyes were bloodshot. "The details don't matter," he said. "All you need to know is, I've gotten myself into a tight spot and I'm going to need some help getting out of it. One person who might put in a word for me is Josh Hardesty. But he's going to need some persuasion. If you'd care to—"

"Stop right there." Lauren had gone cold. He was up to his old tricks again, peddling her like a pimp to men whose money and influence could help his cause. "Whatever you need, I don't want any part of it—especially if it involves Josh Hardesty."

"Lauren, I need his help or I'm finished in politics! If you'd only listen to reason—"

"No, you listen." Lauren rose. "The first—and last—time I went out with that man, he made it clear what he expected in return for the check he wrote you. Sorry, but I'm not for sale. I'm not that kind of girl."

"Aren't you?" His voice dripped contempt. "You'll spread your legs for a half-breed bastard who'll only drag you down. Why not for a man with enough money and prestige to save your father from ruin? Where's your family loyalty?"

Lauren felt the blood drain from her face. She braced a steadying hand against the table while she found her voice. "You're drunk. If you weren't I'd never forgive you for what you just said."

He studied her with slitted eyes. "I may be drunk, but I know when I'm right. Why him, Lauren? Why a fatherless, half-Comanche piece of trash who stinks of horses and couldn't afford to keep you in a tin shack?"

"Because I love him!"

The words burst out, catching Lauren by surprise. But as soon as she spoke them, she knew they were true. She loved Sky Fletcher. She would follow him anywhere—and if getting him back meant crawling to him on her hands and knees, she would do it in a heartbeat.

"You're a fool," he said. "Just like your mother."

Lauren's chin went up, her spine stiffened. "My mother left you," she said. "And as soon as I can find a place of my own, I plan to do the same thing."

"I'll disown you!" he screamed as she walked out of the kitchen. "I'll sell this house to the syndicate and you won't get a penny!"

Lauren glanced back over her shoulder. "Go ahead. I don't want your money."

Striding out into the hall, she headed upstairs to call Tori. Maybe it was time she took a serious look at the Axelrod house. The thought of staying here much longer was more than she could stand.

Stella waited until the afternoon of the next day. When Prescott hadn't called her by 3:15, she carried out her ultimatum.

Once she'd made up her mind, the rest was easy. All it took was three anonymous phone calls—one to an investigative reporter at the local TV station, one to the campaign headquarters of the opposing party, and one to the state attorney general's office. Stella had laid a careful money trail that could be followed by anyone with the interest and know-how. She'd also made sure that none of the cash she'd given Prescott was traceable to her.

In a way, she knew, she was killing the golden goose. But Garn Prescott could no longer be trusted. Besides, he wasn't the only influential man Stella had on a string. The rest would be put on notice that nobody crossed Stella Rawlins. The only trouble was, none of them were in position to help her brother.

She wasn't through with the congressman. He would have to be silenced before his shame turned to fury. That was why, as she was leaving the diner, she'd placed a tracking signal device under the chassis of his big white Cadillac. It paid to think ahead.

She was still working out the details of Prescott's end—mainly finding somebody to do the job now that good old Hoyt was gone. But right now her most urgent concern was saving Nick.

She'd called a lawyer friend in Lubbock who'd promised to drive down first thing tomorrow. But when she'd described the evidence against Nick, he hadn't given her much hope. Her poor, innocent brother was being held without bail, and she was running out of options.

Now it was almost midnight, and the last customers had cleared out of the Blue Coyote. With Nick in jail, Stella and the waitress had been running nonstop. It was time to go home and try to get some rest. But Stella had a pounding headache and her feet, in their red high-heeled boots, were screaming. Needing a few minutes of peace and quiet, she sank onto a chair, popped the tab on a can of Dos Equis, and lit a Marlboro from the pack she'd laid on the table.

Her clenched nerves were just beginning to unwind when a tall shape blocked the overhead light. The waitress pulled out a chair, sat down across from her, and slid a cigarette from the pack. "D'you mind?" she asked, pulling a pink plastic lighter out of her bra.

Stella shook her head. She didn't especially like the woman, but she'd worked hard tonight and done a decent job. Marie, that was her name.

Marie lit the cigarette and blew a cloud of smoke. "I need to talk to you," she said. "Promise you'll hear me out. I think I've figured out a way to save your brother."

Marie took a long draw on the cigarette. This was it, time for the biggest gamble of her life. Facing Stella was like staring down a hungry tigress, but this was no time for a show of nerves. Her life would depend on playing it cool.

"First, I have a confession," she said. "I've been working under my married name. My maiden name is Marie Fletcher."

Stella's penciled eyebrows shot up. "You're—"

"I said hear me out. Yes, I'm Lute's sister—and the sister of Coy Fletcher, the man who was shot on the Tylers' ranch. That's why I'm the one person who can help you."

"Do you know who killed that man?" Stella asked.

"That doesn't matter. All that really matters is that Nick didn't do it. That's what we have to prove."

"Go on." Stella leaned back in her chair and blew a smoke ring.

"Let me tell you a story. Then you can decide if you want me to tell it to the sheriff." Marie dragged on the cigarette. "I'm not saying it's all true. But if it does the job, that doesn't matter, does it?

"To start with, Coy was a mean, low-down s.o.b. Back in Oklahoma he was in a lot of trouble, with the law and with lots of other people. Lute had told me this was a good place to make money, so I decided to come here to Blanco Springs. Coy wasn't invited along, but he came anyway and set up a little weed farm on some land that belonged to our cousin Sky."

"That hot, black-haired cowboy who works for the Tylers, right?"

"Right. But Sky's not part of this. He's straight arrow all the way."

"So what happened with Coy?"

"Back in Oklahoma Coy hung out with a biker gang—bad news, all of them. When we left there I was hoping those scumbags wouldn't know where we'd gone, but I was wrong. One night, after the place was closed, they came pounding on my door. They said Coy owed them money and threatened to cut me and worse if I didn't tell them where he was. I knew they'd do it, so I told them where his camp was—figured he deserved whatever they meant to do to him."

Stella leaned forward, her green eyes burning like lasers. "Good story so far, but what about the gun?"

"I'm getting to that," Marie said. "They made me let them into the bar. I was too scared not to do it. They took a case of beer from the back, and one of them—he was wearing gloves—checked the cash register for money. When he didn't find any, he opened the drawer, found the Glock, and took it. After that, they finally left."

"I see." Stella's eyes had narrowed to catlike slits. "And you didn't speak out sooner because—?"

"Because I was scared. If you knew I'd let those bikers in the bar, I was afraid you'd fire me, or even have me arrested."

The ash on Stella's cigarette had grown to a smoldering inch. It fell in a shower of sparks to scatter unnoticed on the tabletop. Stella's gaze was sharp and knowing, as if she'd already seen through the lie and was weighing the truth behind it. Marie was just beginning to realize how smart the woman was, and how ruthless. A surge of fear almost took her breath away.

"You know that perjury is a crime, don't you?" Stella said after a long moment's silence.

"Only under oath. I'm hoping it won't go that far."

"The sheriff will have you sign a sworn statement. Are you prepared to do that?"

"Under the right conditions."

"Of course." Stella leaned back in her chair and took a long drag on the stub of her cigarette. "How much?"

Marie forced herself to breathe. "That's the wrong question. I don't want to be paid. I want a chance to earn what I'm worth. Lute told me you had a lot of . . . uh . . . business connections."

"Lute was a little turd. He got what he deserved."

"Maybe so. But I'm older than Lute and a helluva lot smarter. I want to be part of your organization. I want a piece of the action."

Stella dropped her cigarette butt on the floor and stubbed it out with her boot. "Are you smart enough not to double-cross me like Lute did?"

"I'd have to be crazy to do something like that."

Stella rose with a weary sigh. "All right, I'll think about it. But before I take you on, you'll need to prove yourself. My lawyer will be here tomorrow morning. We'll go to the jail and Abner will take your statement. Something tells me he'll choose to believe you. Arresting my brother was . . . let's say, awkward for him. After Nicky's out of jail, I may have another job for you. One question—can you drive a semi truck?"

"I don't have a license, but my ex-husband was a trucker," Marie said. "He taught me how. I used to ride along and spell him when he was too drunk to drive."

"Good." Stella walked partway down the hall toward the office where she kept her purse, then glanced back at Marie. "Clean up that cigarette mess. Then get some sleep. I'll want you down here to meet with the lawyer at nine."

Marie got a wet paper towel from the restroom. "Bitch," she muttered as she scooped up the cigarette butt and wiped away the ash. Stella was still treating her like a slave. But that was about to change. Play her cards right and before long she'd have Stella Rawlins on her knees!

CHAPTER 14

Sky was headed to his quarters for a quick lunch break when Beau hailed him from the back door of the house. "Come on inside. Bernice made sandwiches, and I've got some news you'll want to hear."

After pausing to stomp the dust off his boots, Sky followed Beau into the kitchen, washed his hands at the sink, and sat down at the table. Beau passed him a plate with two beef and tomato sandwiches and then got him a cold beer from the fridge. Sky had been running on coffee since before dawn. He was ravenous, and there was nothing better than Bernice's homemade sourdough bread. He wolfed down the first sandwich before he asked, "Now, what about that news?"

Beau pulled out a chair and sat down across the table. He'd been working on the firebreak and, like Sky, was grimy with sweat and dust. "Actually I've got two stories for you," he said. "They're both pretty juicy. Which one would you like to hear first?"

"How the hell should I know?" Sky took a swig of beer. "Just tell me so I can get back to work."

"Getting prickly, are you?" Beau grinned. "All right, here goes. I got a call from my new best friend Abner an hour ago. Our tattooed bartender has been cleared of all charges and turned loose."

"I had a gut feeling he didn't do it," Sky said. It had been more than a gut feeling, but this wasn't the time to go there. "So why did they let him off?"

"A witness signed a sworn statement that a biker gang from Oklahoma broke into the bar looking for Coy Fletcher. One of them, who just happened to be wearing gloves, stole the gun and evidently used it."

"A witness, you say?"

"Abner didn't give me a name, but it's not like he needed to. Lord, Sky, how'd you survive growing up in that family?"

"Almost didn't. That's why I left." Sky didn't like where his thoughts were taking him. Marie's story was believable except for a few questions. Why hadn't the bikers just shot Coy and left him at his camp? Why toss the Glock near the bog when they could keep it or sell it? And why hadn't they taken Coy's rifle and Jasper's shotgun? Maybe he should ask Marie those questions. But what would he do if he didn't like her answers?

"So what's your other story?" he asked.

"This one's a shocker," Beau said. "I just heard it on the radio driving in. It seems our neighbor, Congressman Prescott, has been financing his campaign with drug cartel money. Somebody phoned in an anonymous tip, and it played out. The funds were traced back to an offshore account under a fake name."

"You're sure it's Prescott they were talking about?" Sky's thoughts flashed to Lauren. Did she know? Was she all right?

"It's all over the news," Beau said. "The opposition is doing a happy dance and calling for him to resign. He could even face criminal charges."

"What's Prescott got to say about it?" Sky spoke calmly, but his worry for Lauren was mounting. Was she safe from any drug dealers involved? Was she being hounded by the press?

"According to his campaign manager, Prescott's unavailable for comment," Beau said.

"And Lauren?"

"I haven't heard anything about her."

Sky cursed himself in silence. When he'd cut Lauren loose, hoping she could resolve her personal issues, he'd told her to call if she needed him. She was going to need him now. But given her pride and how much he'd hurt her, he was probably the last person on earth she'd reach out to.

Whipping his cell phone out of his pocket, he rose and strode out the kitchen door. Beau watched him go, saying nothing. Beau knew what it was like to love a woman. He would understand.

On the back porch, Sky punched in Lauren's number. He heard her phone ring once, then again and again before the recording came on. This time Sky left a message.

"Lauren, I'm here. Call me."

"So what do you think, Lauren?" Tori asked as they drove away from Hoyt Axelrod's former home. "If you didn't know about its history, would it work for you?"

"It's not bad, especially for the price," Lauren conceded. It had taken a couple of days for Tori to reach Axelrod's son and make sure they'd be willing to rent the place with an option to buy. The small three-bedroom house was clean, well maintained, and very affordable. But could she make it her home without being haunted by the thought of the murderer who'd lived here?

"Were you able to check on the apartments?" she asked Tori.

"I called the manager, but they're full. If you want a place anytime soon, this could be your only option."

Lauren sighed. She had to get away from her father. And her need to work things out with Sky was becoming more and more urgent. Maybe if she got rid of the rugs and furniture and painted the walls, the house would be livable. "Can I sleep on it and give you an answer tomorrow?" she asked.

"Take as long as you like. Unless somebody else comes along and wants the place, it'll be here." Tori swung her station wagon onto Main Street. "Are you hungry? The Burger Shack makes great milkshakes. Besides, I need to talk to you about something else."

"Sure," Lauren said. "Make mine strawberry."

Over tall, cold milkshakes, Tori brought up her next order of business. "You said you needed more work, so I did some checking for you. My friend Natalie, who's engaged to Beau, could use some part-time help with her billing and accounts. She could give you a few hours a week, and so could I. You could do most of the work on your home computer. The woman who manages the apartment complex was interested, too. When word gets around, you shouldn't have trouble finding enough clients to keep you busy."

"That's wonderful!" Lauren reached across the table and squeezed her new friend's wrist. "I feel like I've found a fairy godmother!"

Tori laughed. "I may have unlocked a few doors, but walking through them will be up to you. It won't always be easy, but if you really want to, you can make a new life here."

Lauren drove home with the top down, the hot wind raking her hair. She was in high spirits. She'd spent most of her life under somebody else's thumb— first her mother, then her grandparents and the trust fund they'd controlled, and finally her father. Even with Michael, she realized, she'd been looking for somebody to take charge. The idea of making her own way, answerable only to herself, was as thrilling as lifting off the ground in a hot-air balloon.

Maybe she should just take the house and make it hers. Surely a few weeks of scrubbing, painting, arranging, and refurbishing would help her forget that an evil man had lived there. She would paint the living room in cool shades of blue and gray and put a zinc-framed mirror on the wall above the fireplace. With luck there might even be hardwood flooring under that hideous green shag carpet. . . .

Still musing, she switched on the radio. Johnny Cash's rumbling baritone blared out of the speakers. Lauren remembered then that she hadn't checked her cell phone. Never mind, she'd do it when she got home. Any messages would likely be from her father, trying to catch her with Sky.

If only . . .

For an aching moment she was tempted to call Sky and tell him she'd looked at the house. Just hearing his voice would be worth the humiliation. But no, he was apt to think she wanted his advice, or that she was angling for a reunion. Taking charge of her life meant just that—doing it all on her own.

She was halfway home when the four o'clock news came on the radio. Lauren was about to switch to a different music station when she caught her father's name.

"Texas congressman Garn Prescott was unavailable for comment today after an anonymous source claimed that his current reelection campaign was being financed with illegal drug money."

Lauren's pulse slammed. Too shaken to trust herself on the road, she pulled the Corvette onto the gravel shoulder. What she'd heard was just an ugly rumor, she told herself. Her father was far from perfect, but he wasn't a crook.

"When reached by this reporter for comment, the Texas attorney general would only say that further investigation would be needed. But according to reliable sources, the allegations are based on solid evidence. Prescott's colleagues in the U.S. House of Representatives and members of his own party in Texas are already calling for his resignation."

Where was her father now? The gears snarled as Lauren swung the Corvette back onto the asphalt. If he was home, he'd be drinking, hiding from the reporters who would be waiting outside to rip him apart like a pack of yelping, snapping coyotes. Phoning him would be wasted effort. He'd probably turned off his cell and taken the landline off the hook.

Her boot stomped the gas pedal. Garn Prescott might be an abrasive, manipulating tyrant, but he was her father and he was in trouble. Wherever he was, she needed to be there for him.

Garn Prescott sat at the massive walnut desk in his study, gazing at the portrait on the far wall—a portrait of his father wearing a Stetson and holding a coiled bullwhip in one hand. Ferguson Prescott had been a brick of a man—tough, stubborn, and cunning. As his parents' only surviving child, Prescott had never felt he was man enough to win his father's approval. If that portrait could talk, he could just imagine what Old Ferg might say.

You've got nobody to blame for this mess but yourself, you lily-livered fool. You must've been thinkin' with your dick when you let that female tramp lead you down the road. Well, this time there'll be no gittin' up and dustin' yourself off. You're finished, boy. I'm ashamed to call you my own flesh and blood. Hell, a dumb-ass like you doesn't deserve to live!

Prescott poured another three fingers of bourbon in his glass and emptied it down his throat. He was as drunk as he'd ever been in his life, but an ocean of liquor couldn't drown his disgrace. He should've known what Stella was the first time she'd walked up to him and held out an envelope full of cash. Now it was too late. He was ruined.

Glancing outside between the narrow slats of the closed blinds, he could see the news vans and gangs of reporters that crowded the front lawn. Like vultures in the afternoon heat, they were waiting to pounce on him as soon as he showed his face. Too bad. They could damn well wait all day before they'd get any satisfaction from him.

He poured the last trickle of bourbon out of the bottle, emptied the glass, and set it on the desk. That desk had been his father's, as had the vintage Colt .45 Peacemaker that lay next to his hand. The gun was a classic. At least Ferg would approve of that.

One shot would end it all—the humiliation, the scandal, the misery of growing old and weak. Lauren would get all he had, which wasn't a lot by Texas standards but enough to get by. His daughter wouldn't mourn, at least not for long. Why should she? What kind of father had he ever been to the girl?

And Stella? Hell, he'd strangle her with his bare hands if he could. But that wasn't going to happen. She would go on as always, weaving her webs like a spider to catch more hapless flies like him.

His father's stolid features glared down at him from the gilded frame. Ferguson Prescott could forgive sin. But he couldn't forgive stupidity. *Do it!* His expression seemed to say. *For once in your worthless life, be a man. . . .*

Lauren came speeding up the gravel lane to find an army of reporters waiting in the front yard. For an instant she was tempted to turn the car around and drive away. But her father had to be in the house. She couldn't leave him alone. Slowing down and leaning on the horn, she headed the car straight for the front porch. Legs leaped and arms grabbed equipment as members of the press scrambled out of the way. But as soon as she braked at the foot of the steps, they were on her again, thrusting cameras and microphones into her face.

"Miss Prescott, how much did you know about your father's campaign funding?"

"Have you spoken with your father, Miss Prescott? Do you believe he's guilty?"

Fighting panic, she took the keys in her fist, set her jaw in determined silence, and pushed out of the car. It was as if she were drowning in a sea of people, shoving and jostling each other, shouting their questions to get her attention.

"Is your father in the house, Miss Prescott? What has he told you?"

Knowing it was better to say nothing than to open her mouth and lose her composure, Lauren clutched her purse and fought her way onto the porch. Her shaking hand thrust the key into the lock. The door swung open. Stumbling over the threshold, she locked it behind her.

For a moment she allowed herself to lean against the closed door and breathe until her heart stopped pounding. The house was dim and quiet.

Too quiet, even with the cook gone at this hour.

Where was her father?

"Dad?" She moved through the entry, listening for a voice, a footstep, the sound of running water or the opening of a door. All she could hear was the low rasp of her own breathing.

He had to be here. Where else could he go?

"Dad?" She made her way down the hall to his den, the most likely place to find him. The door, usually left ajar, was closed. As her hand touched the knob, a cold dread crept from the pit of her stomach into her throat. Willing herself to move, she opened the door.

She could smell the bourbon from where she stood. Red-eyed and rumpled, his tie askew, her father sat behind the desk. His left hand clutched the empty bottle. His right hand held Ferg Prescott's heavy Colt revolver. The muzzle was pressed against his temple.

"Please don't do this, Dad." She took a step toward him, speaking softly. "Put the gun down. We can talk."

"Too late for talk, Lauren." The words slurred drunkenly. "I'm finished. Ruined. This is the only way out."

She took another step, reaching out with her hand. "I know we've had our differences. But you're the only parent I've got. For my sake, if nothing else, put the gun down—or better yet, give it to me."

Something akin to madness glinted in his eyes. "You hear those bloodsuckers outside? They want t' rip me t' pieces. But they can't have me. I won't put myself through that."

"And what will you put *me* through if you pull that trigger?" Lauren kept moving toward him. "I'll be the one to see the blood, the one who has to call the police and wait for them to come."

"I'm gonna do this, Lauren. Get the hell out if you don't want t' see it."

"If you pull that trigger, I'll be left without a father." She felt her anger stir and rise until she was almost shouting at him. "But you don't care about that, do you? You've never cared about anybody but Garn Prescott, you selfish son of a bitch!"

As his face froze in shock, Lauren flung herself

across the desk. The impact knocked his arm back, shoving the gun away from his head. She'd hoped to knock the weapon out of his hand, but he was more determined than she'd realized. Keeping an iron grip on the pistol, he struggled to get the barrel in position for a fatal shot.

Belly down across the desktop, Lauren was at a disadvantage. But she fought him like a wildcat. He was as drunk with self-pity as he was with bourbon. She had to save him from this insane act that, once done, could never be undone. Mike's death had taught her that lesson all too well.

His free hand smacked the side of her face. Pain shimmered down her jaw, but she didn't let go. Lunging with her weight against his arm, she forced his gun hand downward, hoping to pin it to the desk. But he was too strong for her. His hand twisted, angling the pistol upward, aiming it toward his throat. His index finger tightened on the trigger.

In a surge of desperation, Lauren sank her teeth into his wrist, biting down with all her strength. She heard a yelp, a curse, and then, inches from her ear, the deafening bellow of the big revolver.

Head ringing, she collapsed across the desk. For a moment she lay still, too dazed to stir. At last, knowing that whatever had happened was hers to face, she opened her eyes and raised her head.

Her father sprawled in his leather banker's chair, his face ashen, his jaw clenched. Blood streamed from an ugly wound below his collarbone.

"Damn it all t' hell, girl," he muttered. "Why couldn't you jus' let me die?"

Lauren could barely hear him over the ringing in her ears. Scrambling to her feet, she rushed around the desk, pulled the chair back, and slid him to the floor. So much blood. The den's wet bar had a store of clean towels. After grabbing the stack of them off the shelf, she wadded them over the wound and pressed down hard. He groaned and swore.

"Hold this in place," she said. "I'm going to call nine-one-one."

"No!" His hand clamped her wrist. "With those buzzards out front, just waitin' for somethin' like this, I won't have the medics come screamin' in to haul me away."

"But you're losing so much blood." Pulling her hand free, Lauren leaned her weight over the towels, which were already seeping red. "You'll die if we don't get you to a hospital."

"Then I'll die, dammit! Rather bleed to death than give those shit-eaters a feeding frenzy!"

And he would do just that if she let him, Lauren knew. But she wanted him to live. He was her father, and time was running out.

Her purse had fallen to the floor in the struggle. Finding it within reach under the desk, she opened the clasp. One bloodstained hand found her cell phone. Whether her father liked it or not, she had to get him to emergency care.

She was about to punch in 911 when she saw the message from Sky. Taking an extra second, she pressed the key.

Lauren, I'm here. Call me.

His voice was like clear water, calming her frantic mind. In that instant there was one thing she knew. Much as she wanted to be strong, she couldn't do this alone. She needed help. She needed Sky.

He answered on the first ring. "Lauren, are you all right?"

She struggled to keep her emotions under tight rein. "My father's shot himself. We've got to get him to the hospital. The reporters are out front. Can you come around the back in your truck?"

"I'm on my way." No questions, just enough words to say he would be there. That was Sky.

Sky gunned the pickup, raising a plume of dust behind the wheels as he flew over the rough back road. Lauren hadn't told him how badly her father was hurt, but if Garn Prescott was refusing to let paramedics come because of the press, how seriously wounded could he be?

Sky's main concern was for Lauren—alone, scared, and innocent of any wrongdoing. How could Prescott have laid this mess in her lap?

Through the haze of dust he spotted the stately Lombardy poplars that bordered the Prescott home. Driving closer, he could see the small army of vans, equipment, and people from the news media out front. There was even a chopper from the TV station—a chopper capable of getting Garn Prescott to the hospital in a matter of minutes except that, even if asked, they probably wouldn't do it because of liability.

Short of the house he swung onto the road that circled behind the residence, leading to the working part of the ranch. From there he cut back toward the pool and parked outside the kitchen door. Again he called Lauren's cell phone.

"I'm out back. Tell me where you are."

"We're in the den." She sounded badly shaken.

"Go through the dining room and down the hall. You'll pass a linen closet on your right. Bring whatever's there." Her breath caught in a little gasp. "Hurry!"

Alarmed by the urgency in her voice, Sky raced inside, cutting through the kitchen and dining room. As he passed the linen closet he grabbed an armful of sheets and towels and rushed on down the hallway.

The door to the den was open. Partly hidden by the desk, Lauren knelt beside her father, pressing a blood-soaked towel to the front of his shoulder. Her clothes and arms were streaked with crimson.

"Thank God you're here," she breathed.

Sky crouched beside her, his hand brushing her shoulder. "We'll need to stabilize him before we move him. Have you got scissors?"

"In the desk." She stood unsteadily and moved to open a drawer. "Right here."

He tossed her the folded sheet he'd found. "Cut the edge and tear this into strips. I'll check the wound."

As Sky bent close, Prescott's eyes fluttered open. "What the hell are *you* doin' here, Fletcher?" he muttered.

"Trying to save your life—and the less you talk, the better." Sky lifted away the blood-soaked towels, being careful not to touch the bullet hole with his hands. The bullet didn't appear to have struck a critical spot, but Prescott was in danger of bleeding to death.

After laying clean towels over the wound, Sky applied pressure with his weight over his flat hands. Prescott groaned and swore. "Feels more like you're tryin' to kill me," he rasped. "An' then you'll take my girl . . . take it all . . ."

"Keep still." Sky took the strips of sheeting Lauren had torn and began wrapping them around Prescott's chest to hold the towels in place. Lauren knelt at her father's head, lifting his shoulders so Sky could circle his back. There was no sign of an exit wound. Maybe the bullet had lodged against his shoulder blade.

Prescott clenched his jaw, glaring up at Sky with hatred in his eyes. Sky couldn't help wondering what had happened before he got here, but that story would have to wait.

He knotted the last strip of sheet, holding the towels in place. Prescott's face was the color of alkali dust. Clearly he'd lost a lot of blood. Somebody should have called for Life Flight, the press be damned, Sky thought. But this last shred of dignity was all the man had left.

"Can you make it to the truck?" Sky asked him.

Prescott nodded, clenching his jaw against the pain. With Lauren bracing his wounded side, Sky pulled him to his feet. His breath reeked of bourbon. Only now did Sky realize how drunk Lauren's father must be. Cursing and reeling, Prescott allowed himself to be supported through the kitchen and out the back door to Sky's truck, where they loaded him into the backseat with his head cradled in Lauren's lap.

Sky passed her a water bottle. "Try to keep him hydrated. What's the best way past the press?"

"Up toward the main barn, then cut back to the highway. You'll see the road when you get there."

Minutes later they were on the main highway, headed for the hospital in Lubbock. Would the congressman thank him for this rescue? Sky wondered as the aging truck's speedometer climbed toward eighty. But why ask a stupid question? Prescott despised him for who he was and because of Lauren. Nothing about that was going to change.

At the hospital, the emergency team took over, shifting the congressman to a gurney and rushing him back through the double doors to prep him for surgery. While Lauren gave his information to the desk, Sky moved his truck to the parking lot and walked back to the emergency entrance. Glancing inside, he saw that she was still busy. That gave him a moment to leave a phone message for Will, telling him where he'd gone. The details could wait till he knew more.

When she joined him in the empty waiting room a few minutes later, he was still on his feet. Red-eyed, disheveled, and bloodstained, she walked into his arms. For a long, silent moment they held each other. She was quivering like a frightened animal, her heart pounding as he cradled her close. The tenderness that surged through Sky was so powerful that it shook him to the core. There was nothing he wouldn't do to protect this woman.

"I'm here, Lauren," he whispered, his lips brushing her hair. "I'm not going anywhere."

"Thank you." Her arms circled his rib cage, holding tight. She buried her face against his shirt. "I don't know what I'd have done if you hadn't come."

"You'd have managed. You're tougher than you give yourself credit for, Miss Lauren Prescott. But right now you're as shaky as a newborn colt. Let's sit down."

He guided her to one of the couches. While they sat with their feet up and her head cradled against his shoulder, she told him what had happened at the house.

When he heard how she'd dived across the desk to grab her father's gun hand, then bitten his wrist in the struggle to deflect his aim, Sky was horrified. "Good Lord, he could have shot you by accident. He could have killed you."

"I know that now. But at the time, all I could think of was saving him."

"I don't know what you think you owe the man, Lauren, but you don't owe him your life."

"Maybe not. But whatever else Garn Prescott is, he's the only father I've got. I couldn't just stand there and watch him kill himself." A shiver passed through her body. "And then when he was losing all that blood, and he wouldn't let me phone for the paramedics because of the press outside—that's when I knew I had to call you." She glanced up at him. "Do you think he'll be all right?"

"He made it all the way here, still conscious and cussing. Once the doctors get some blood in him and patch up that hole, I'm betting he'll be on his way to recovery." Sky could speak with confidence. Earlier that spring, after being shot by Hoyt Axelrod, he'd been in far worse shape than Prescott. But the same team of doctors had pulled him through. "I take it he doesn't want anybody to know he's here."

"I made sure they understood that at the desk," Lauren said. "He'll have enough to deal with when he gets home."

Sky's arm tightened around her shoulders. "It could be a while before we hear from the doctor. Why don't you try to get some rest?"

"I don't know if I can," she said.

"Try it. You've been through hell this afternoon. You look done in."

With a sigh of acquiescence, she nestled against him. Sky shifted his arms and body to support her, bending his head to feather a gentle kiss on her lips. "Close your eyes," he said. "I'll wake you as soon as there's news."

With a tired little murmur, she settled close. Sky could feel the strain easing as she relaxed against him. The awareness of her need and her trust raised an ache in his throat. He'd never meant to love this woman—never meant things to go beyond the torrid sex they'd both enjoyed. But she'd crept into his heart and found a home there. He could no longer imagine ever letting her go.

He would never be wealthy, but if she'd have him, he had the means to give them a fine life. He had property, a good job, and enough money in the bank to build a comfortable home. His work for the Tylers could continue while he pursued his dream of raising his own horses on his land—a place where their children could learn to love nature and value honest work.

Was that what Bull Tyler had in mind when he'd bought the parcel and included it in his will? Had the old man been thinking of a way to keep his secret descendants on the land?

A mental slap jolted Sky back to reality. If he proposed to Lauren, he'd be asking her to marry the illegitimate son of a servant who'd worked for her grandparents. How could he explain that to her? And even if she were to say yes, how could he explain it to their children one day?

Maybe it would be better for everyone's sake if he just walked away.

Lauren had fallen asleep, a little feminine snore mingling with her breath. Sky gazed down at her face, already darkening in the spot where her father had struck her. Letting her go would kill him. But he had to make a decision before things went any further between them.

He couldn't make that decision until he knew the full story of where he'd come from—and only one man knew enough to tell him that story.

Tomorrow he would have a talk with Jasper.

CHAPTER 15

The ear-shattering wail of a cranky toddler startled Lauren awake. Flinching, she blinked herself to a blurry awareness of where she was and what had happened.

"Welcome back." Sky was gazing down at her with eyes the color of Texas bluebonnets. Still groggy, Lauren pushed herself upright. They were no longer alone in the waiting room. An elderly man sat in the rocker with an open Bible across his knees. A tired-looking woman with a squirming two-year-old in her arms sat on the far side of the room, watching cartoons on the wall-mounted TV.

Lauren raked back damp tendrils of hair where her head had rested in the warm hollow of Sky's shoulder. "I can't believe I just drifted off like that. How long was I out?"

"Not long. A little less than an hour."

"And no word yet?"

"If there was, we'd both have heard." He squeezed

her shoulder. "Don't worry. These things can take a while. Want some coffee?"

"Thanks. Cream, no sugar."

He rose, walked away, and came back with two steaming insulated cups. Lauren took the one he handed her and sipped the hot brew, feeling the welcome jolt of caffeine. "I let Tori show me the Axelrod house today," she said, deciding to tell him. "It would need some renovation, but it's not that bad, and the price is a bargain."

"So you're really going to make the move?"

"I told you I would. But now it might have to wait. How can I leave my father after something like this?"

Sky's lips parted. Then he shook his head and took a sip of coffee, as if he'd thought better of what he was about to say.

"Tell me," she challenged him. "I want to hear what you're thinking."

He exhaled slowly. "All right, but you might not like it. Your father's not above using this episode to control you. If you can't walk away because you're afraid he'll shoot himself again, or overdose on pills and liquor, he'll have you right where he wants you."

And what would you do then, Sky?

Lauren stared down into her cup, not daring to voice the question. Would Sky have the patience to wait for her? Would he be supportive, or would he throw up his hands in disgust and turn his back?

Before she could voice a reply, the double doors to the E.R. swung open and the doctor walked toward her. He was tall and bespectacled with a beakish nose, his expression telling her nothing.

"Your father's out of surgery, Miss Prescott," he said. "We were able to remove the bullet and close the wound. He should make a full recovery. But for now, with so much alcohol in his system, we're giving him extra fluids and keeping a close eye on him."

Lauren stood. "Is he awake? Can I see him?"

The doctor shook his head. "He'll be sleeping it off tonight. You might as well go home, get some rest, and come back in the morning. He should be alert by then. Meanwhile, don't worry. He'll be in good hands."

"Thank you." She turned to Sky as the doctor walked away. "I guess you might as well take me home. Since you'll need to be working tomorrow, I can drive myself back here. That way I can stay as long as I need to."

They crossed the parking lot in the twilight. Her fingers crept into his big, comforting palm. She felt his hand close around hers. Had things shifted between them? Could they go forward from here, or was he only being kind in her time of need?

Sky opened the door of the truck so she could climb in. Lauren settled back and fastened her seat belt as he went to the other side.

"Hungry?" He started the engine.

Lauren glanced down at her bloodstained shirt. "I can't go into a restaurant looking like this. But you must be starved. We could find a drive-through. Or, if you can wait that long, there's leftover pot roast in the fridge at home."

"The pot roast sounds good." He shot her a sidelong glance, and Lauren realized she'd just invited him in. Had he read more into her words than she'd meant? *Was* there more? Her cheeks warmed in the darkness of the cab. What were the odds they both had the same idea?

The house was dark and silent when they arrived. Sky had driven in the back way, but there'd been no need for it. The news crews had gone. Whether they'd show up again tomorrow was anybody's guess.

"Don't worry about playing hostess," Sky said. "I'm a great hand at rustling up supper with a microwave. You must be anxious to get out of those clothes."

"Thanks. And yes, I am," Lauren said, thinking she'd throw out everything but her boots. "While I'm at it, I could use a shower. Don't wait for me if you're hungry."

"Take your time." He'd opened the fridge and was perusing the shelves. "While I'm thinking about it, where are the keys to those two cars out front? I'll move them around to the back, in case the sharks start gathering before you're ready to leave tomorrow."

"Thanks, they're—oh." A groan escaped Lauren's lips as she remembered. "I left my purse in the den. The keys to the Corvette are in it. And the spare keys to Dad's Cadillac are in the desk. I'm sorry—such an awful mess in there."

"Don't worry about it. For what it's worth, I have an old high school buddy who runs a cleaning business. He specializes in disasters and he's smart enough to be discreet."

"I saw a gangster movie where Harvey Keitel did something like that. Is it that kind of cleaning business?"

His grin flashed. "Go," he said.

By the time Lauren came back downstairs, Sky had moved the cars and warmed the pot roast. His eyes drank her in as she entered the kitchen, dressed in black leggings and a long, white tee that outlined just enough to let him know she had nothing on underneath. With her damp hair framing her fresh-scrubbed face, she took his breath away.

An aching need uncoiled in the depths of his body. It was all he could do to keep from yanking her into his arms and taking her right there in the kitchen. But she'd been through a hell of a time today, seeing her father almost kill himself before her eyes. He couldn't assume that an invitation to supper meant anything more than what it was.

"Oh, you set the table," she said, eyeing the mismatched plates and cutlery he'd managed to find in the cupboard.

"I guessed you might be hungry, too," he said. "Sorry, I looked around for candles and wine, but no luck there."

An impish smile lit her coppery eyes. "I don't know about candles, but I'll be right back. She darted into the dining room. A light flickered on, and Sky heard the sound of rummaging. A moment later she was back with a dark wine bottle, two goblets, and a corkscrew.

"Someone who wanted a big favor gave this to my father," she said, handing him the bottle. "You can do the honors."

Sky glanced at writing on the label. *La Romanee Bochard Pere et Fils, 1988.* He couldn't understand a word of French, but he got the general meaning— the wine was very, very expensive.

"Lauren, are you sure—?"

She thrust the corkscrew into his hand. "Go for it. Daddy's a hard-liquor man. He'd just regift it to somebody else."

They ate their warmed-over pot roast and vegetables on mismatched plates and drank the vintage French wine from crystal goblets. The wine had a nice earthiness to it, but Sky had to confess that, to him, it didn't taste much different from the $20 California muscatel they sold at Shop Mart.

Lauren's laughter was like the forgotten sound of rain. "That's what I like about you. No pretensions whatsoever."

"As long as you like me, I guess that's all that counts." He leaned back from his empty plate, studying her across the table. "Will you be all right?" he asked her.

"Don't worry about me. If I survived Mike's suicide, I can survive this." She took a sip of wine. "I never told you the story behind that, did I?"

"You only told me he drowned. If you feel like telling me the rest, I'm ready to listen."

She poured a splash of wine into her glass. "Mike was an only son, from a long line of achievers. His father was a doctor. His uncle was the lieutenant governor of Maryland. His cousins . . ." She shrugged. "All superstars. You can imagine the pressure. It finally got to him. He started drinking, missing his classes. When he flunked out of law school, it was like he'd betrayed his whole family. He couldn't handle it. I got the call after the police found his body in the river."

"He had you, and he still drowned himself. That's a hard one to believe."

Lauren drained her glass and set it on the table. "I guess that's one reason it hurt so much. Having me and being loved wasn't enough to keep him alive. I'd already bought my wedding dress. I donated it to charity and went off the deep end for a while—as you know. But, yes." A shadow crossed her beautiful face. "I'm a big girl. I'll be all right."

"It's getting late. I know you're tired." He rose. "If

you want to turn in, I can clear the table and load the dishwasher before I go." There it was. Sky had laid down his cards. The call was hers to make. When there'd been nothing but sex between them, it would've been easy just to reach out and grab her. Now, with feelings involved, everything had become more complicated.

"We needn't bother," she said. "Miguel will be here in the morning. He's used to cleaning up when he comes in, and he'll enjoy what's left of the wine."

"You might want to lock the den so he won't walk in on a surprise." Sky turned toward the back door, then turned to look at her. "I'll talk to my cleaner friend. Is it okay if I give him your number?"

"Yes, of course. . . ." She reached for the wall switch, then turned out the kitchen light.

He sensed her hesitation but knew he mustn't push her. Not tonight. Steeling himself against the raw burn of desire, he took a step toward the door.

"Sky!"

He turned at the cry of his name. Back-lit from the hall, she stood with one arm reaching out to him. Even from the far side of the room, he could tell she was trembling.

Two long strides carried him across the floor. He caught her in his arms, molding her body against his. Through the thin shirt he could feel every curve of her, the smallness of her bones, the ripe tautness of her little rump, the firm breasts that seemed fashioned to fit his cupped palms.

Bending, he found her mouth. With a whimper she circled his neck with her arms, pulling him down, binding him close, as if she needed to keep him from leaving her.

His need was a bonfire, but he kissed her with a

tenderness that astonished even him. Lauren could have died today when she flew across that desk to wrestle her father for the gun. Sky was just beginning to realize what he might have lost and how precious she was.

"Don't go, Sky," she murmured. "Stay with me. I don't want to be alone tonight."

He scooped her up in his arms and carried her into the hall. "Show me the way," he said.

In her room he shed his clothes and slipped naked into bed beside her. She came to him, nestling like a child in the circle of his arms. Her lips skimmed his nipples as she pressed her face against his chest.

"I should have showered," he said. "I probably smell like a stable."

"No," she whispered. "One thing I love best about you is the way you smell—like sun and wind and, yes, horses. I love having your scent all around me. It makes me feel safe. And tonight safe is how I want to feel."

He cradled her close, kissing her hair, her closed eyelids, her willing mouth. She'd stripped off her leggings and was deliciously bare below the hem of her shirt. The awareness sent a jolt to his sex, which had sprung to full readiness. But even then, he couldn't let himself forget what she'd suffered today. "We don't have to—" he began, but she stopped him with a finger to his lips.

"Shut up and make love to me, Sky Fletcher," she muttered.

With a rough laugh, he rolled her onto her back and lost himself in her wild, sensual sweetness.

Afterward Sky lay awake in the dark, his arm curled protectively over her sleeping body. He'd bedded his share of women, but never before had he felt as if he'd just made love. It was an experience he wanted to repeat again and again, and only with Lauren.

But making love to her was one thing—offering himself to her as a suitable husband and a father to her children was something else. The last thing he wanted was for this lovely, well-born woman to be ashamed of the man she'd married. Before he'd let that happen, he would walk away and never look back.

A heavy decision hung over him—one he couldn't resolve until he'd found Jasper and learned all there was to know about his beginnings.

When Lauren woke the next morning, Sky was gone. She was disappointed but not surprised. Sky had pressing responsibilities on the Rimrock, and he'd missed part of yesterday taking her father to the hospital. She couldn't expect him to slack off his duties again today.

Reaching for her cell on the nightstand, she called the hospital information desk and asked for the nurses' station outside her father's room. Yes, the nurse informed her, the congressman was awake and doing as well as could be expected. He was still on IV fluids and pain medication, but she was welcome to come and see him anytime.

With a sigh of relief, Lauren swung her legs off the bed and headed down the hall to the bathroom. The twinge at the apex of her thighs brought a smile of memory to her face. Last night with Sky had been heaven. But she'd almost had to rope and tie the man to get him to her bed. Tori had been spot on about Sky's stubborn pride. How could she break down that wall and convince him that she *wanted* him—wanted to brew his morning coffee, do his laundry, and have his beautiful blue-eyed babies?

Twenty minutes later she was ready for the drive back to Lubbock. Downstairs she could hear Miguel cleaning up in the kitchen. A glance out the front window confirmed that the press hadn't shown up yet, but she did need to alert the cook to what might happen today.

"Good morning, Miguel." She strode into the kitchen, glancing around for the car keys, which Sky had left on the counter. She'd already decided to take the big white Cadillac. It was safer and had better air conditioning than her Corvette, which was almost out of gas.

"Good morning, *señorita*." Miguel was a quiet, easygoing man of sixty, whose cooking skills made up for a general lack of organization. The less he knew, the better, Lauren decided.

"We had an accident yesterday with a gun in the den," she said. "My father's in the hospital. He's going to be all right, but we'll need you to keep an eye on things here. If a man comes to the back door and says he's been hired to clean up the room, please let him in. But don't go out front, and whatever you do, don't talk to any reporters."

"Reporters?" He looked puzzled.

"If anybody knocks on the front door or rings the bell, don't open it. And if the phone rings, and it's somebody you don't know, hang up. *Entiendes?*"

He nodded. "You want coffee, *señorita?*"

"Not this morning, thanks. But the rest of that wine is for you to take home and share with your wife."

Leaving him with a smile on his face, she went outside and climbed into her father's Cadillac, which still reeked of his mysterious girlfriend's perfume. Maybe

she had something to do with the trouble he was in.
No woman who smelled like that was fit to be trusted.
But try telling that to a man.

For the first few miles of highway, she drove with
the windows down to freshen the air. But the sun was
up by now, the dry summer heat coming in like the
blast from a furnace. It was only a matter of time before Lauren had to close the windows and turn on
the air conditioner. At least the darkly tinted glass offered some relief from the blinding sun.

By the time she passed the roadside diner, she was
getting hungry. It might not hurt to stop and have a
good breakfast, she reasoned. If her father needed
her at the hospital, she could be in for a long day.
Swinging the car around, she pulled up to the diner
and went inside. A trucker at a table was reading an
open newspaper.

TEXAS CONGRESSMAN TAKES DRUG MONEY.
The blaring headlines on the front page screamed
the story of her father's disgrace. Forcing herself to
look the other way, Lauren found an empty booth,
where she ordered coffee and a cheese omelet. While
she was waiting, her cell phone rang. It was Sky's
friend calling about the cleanup job. By the time the
waitress had brought her coffee, she'd given the man
directions and agreed on a price. One less worry, at
least.

She and her father had never had much of a relationship. But maybe this crisis could be a turning
point—a new beginning. If she stood by him against
the world, maybe he would warm to her. Maybe he
would look on her as a real daughter, not just a tool
to be used in his political schemes. And when she
moved out, as she still meant to, maybe it would at
least be on friendly terms. She'd told herself she didn't

give a damn about Garn Prescott. It had taken this horrific event to make her realize how much she cared.

Sky had mentioned growing up fatherless. Lauren had pretty much done the same. But for everyone's sake, she needed to mend things. If nothing else, she owed her future children their grandfather.

If only Sky would understand that she had to try.

Leaving a couple of bills on the table, Lauren picked up her purse and walked out to the car. The inside of the Cadillac was like an oven. Sweating, she cranked up the AC and pulled out of the parking lot. The dark-tinted windows of the car softened the glare of the sun on the parched landscape. Heat shimmered in waves above the road.

She touched the brake pedal as a lizard dashed across the highway ahead of her wheels. How could any living creature survive this heat, let alone set an unprotected foot on the melting black asphalt? At least the hospital would be cool.

Twenty minutes later she parked the car and walked into the hospital's main lobby. "He's in Room 233," the receptionist told her. "The elevator's just down that hallway. Push the button for the second floor. When you get out, just follow the signs."

Alone in the elevator, Lauren mulled over what to say to her father. Nothing came to mind. She could only promise herself that whatever words she spoke would be gentle and forgiving.

She stepped out of the elevator and rounded a corner to a scene of controlled chaos. From far down the corridor a monitor shrieked its alarm. Nurses and doctors in scrubs were rushing to the sound. A garbled voice blasted over the intercom. Lauren caught the word *stat*. Some poor soul was in crisis. Here in the hospital, the only helpful thing she could do was stay out of the way and try not to look.

Walking down toward her father's room, she checked the number posted next to each door. Lauren might as well have been invisible. She had just reached Room 233 when the door opened partway and the doctor she'd met yesterday stepped out into the hall. For an instant he looked surprised to see her. Then his features shifted into the impassive mask she'd seen the day before.

"I'm sorry, Miss Prescott," he said. "Your father just suffered a massive heart attack. We did everything we could, but we couldn't save him. He's gone."

Sky lifted the saddle off the blue roan and patted her damp withers. A sharp little mare, she'd performed well on the morning's cutting maneuvers with the paddock cows. By next week she'd be ready to join Quicksilver and several other colts up on the caprock, working the herd with the cowboys. Sky tried not to get attached to the young horses he trained. But that wasn't easy. They were the closest thing he had to his own children, and he took a parent's pride in everything they accomplished.

To date, the training had gone well enough. But Sky couldn't help worrying. Will was counting on the sale of the colts to shore up Rimrock finances. But if the drought didn't end soon, what rancher would have enough spare cash to pay what they were worth? Sky knew better than to voice his concerns to Will. The boss of the Rimrock had enough trouble on his plate.

Eyes shaded by the brim of his Stetson, he gazed west. The first clouds of the afternoon were drifting over the escarpment—tantalizing white streaks that raised hopes but brought no rain. Yesterday he'd seen traces of virga, the phantom moisture that formed high and evaporated before it reached the ground. Ghost rain, his grandfather had called it. Sky still missed the old man.

So far he'd had no chance to talk with Jasper. The retired foreman had ridden into town with Bernice that morning and wouldn't be back till later in the day. Meanwhile, Sky had plenty of work to do.

He'd just turned the mare loose in the paddock and was splashing his face at the outside tap when his cell phone rang. Seeing Lauren's number, he picked up. Last night had been good between them. The thought of hearing her voice triggered a riffle of anticipation.

"How's it going?" he asked. "You were sleeping like an angel when I left. Did I wear you out?"

"Sky . . ." Her voice quivered and broke. "Oh, Sky!"

"What is it?"

He listened in shock while she told him about her father's fatal heart attack. "It must've happened just as I was going up to his room," she said. "If I hadn't stopped for breakfast, I might have been there to say good-bye—or even to call for help in time to save him. . . ."

She trailed off. Sky wondered if she was crying. "I'll be right there," he said. "Wait for me."

"No, don't come." She sounded stronger now. "There's nothing you can do here, and I can't leave yet. There's the paperwork, the insurance, the funeral home, and maybe even the police. Nobody was prepared for this to happen."

"Lauren, I want to be there for you."

"No." Her tone was adamant. "You'd just have to wait around. As long as I'm busy, I'll be all right. But if you want, you can meet me at the house when I get home. Walking in the door, knowing he's gone, that'll be when it all comes crashing in. That's when I'll need you."

"I'll be there. Just tell me when."

"I'll have to let you know. I could be tied up for hours. Dad's lawyer is here in Lubbock. I called, and he wants to meet with me while I'm here. I need to coordinate the damage control with his campaign staff and do something about planning the funeral." Sky could hear the strain in her voice. Lauren was walking the ragged edge, but she was holding on. "I'll call you when I'm on my way." She spoke above voices in the background. "Got to go," she said, and ended the call.

Dazed by the news, Sky slipped his cell phone back into his pocket. He should have known Lauren wouldn't fall apart. She was a strong woman. He'd seen that yesterday. But the urge to hold her in his arms, console and protect her, was still there. He would respect her wish that he stay away, but right now he wanted nothing more than to be at her side.

As for the ripple effect of Garn Prescott's death . . . It would be as if an earthquake had struck.

On the heels of the drug money scandal, the news would go national, of course. With luck, Prescott's attempted suicide could be kept out of the press. A heart attack was, at least, a respectable way to go.

The election, already in a tailspin, would become even more frenetic. Until the money scandal broke, Garn Prescott had been the front-runner. Now it was anybody's race; and there'd also be a scramble for the temporary appointment to his seat in Congress.

Other issues hit closer to home. As far as Sky knew, Lauren was Prescott's sole heir. The congressman was far from rich. The Prescott Ranch had been drowning in debt when he'd sold out to the syndicate. But he owned—or had owned—the house and his father's collection of vintage cars and had hopefully left behind some good government life insurance.

Lauren would do fine. So why should she settle for a man with a hundred acres and a little money in the bank?

This was no time for questions, Sky told himself. He loved Lauren, and whatever happened, he would be there for her. But loving wasn't the same as having. The sooner he got that reality through his head, the better.

Looking toward the house, he saw Will's red truck pull up to the porch. Will would want to hear about Prescott's death. And knowing Will, his first thought would be for the canyon parcel he'd tried so many times to get back from the Prescotts. Now that Garn was gone, maybe Will could get Lauren to sell it to him.

Preparing to deliver the news, Sky locked the paddock gate and strode across the yard toward the house.

Climbing into the Cadillac, Lauren took a moment to close her eyes and rest her forehead against the top of the steering wheel. She'd been running on adrenaline all afternoon. Now that she was alone and finally about to head home, she was exhausted.

Shouldn't she be feeling something? This wasn't her first loss. She'd experienced her mother's death and then Mike's with an outpouring of grief and tears that went on and on. But now all she felt was . . . drained.

Today her first priority had been making sure the gunshot wound wasn't leaked to the press. Her father's longtime attorney, whom she'd met at the Lubbock fund-raiser, had come to the hospital to ensure the staff's discretion and the privacy of the medical record. He'd also put her in touch with a funeral director, a personal friend of his, who knew how to handle such delicate matters. They'd spent more than an hour discussing arrangements for the burial. The congressman would be interred next week with the dignity befitting his station and his long service to his country.

Since the death involved a gunshot wound, it had to be reported to the police. Two detectives had come to the hospital, interviewed Lauren and the doctor, then tested Lauren's hands, as well as her father's, for gunpowder residue. Satisfied there was no foul play, they'd left without demanding an autopsy. Thank heaven for that, at least.

Lauren had gone to his campaign headquarters in person to give the news to his staff, mostly volunteers. Still reeling from the funding scandal, they'd taken the news hard. To show her appreciation for their work, she'd taken them to dinner at a nice steakhouse. She'd even managed to choke down a few bites of her prime rib and drink a few sips of wine.

Now the sun had gone down and Lauren had nothing left of herself to give. In the morning she'd write up a statement for release to the press. But right now all she wanted was to go home and lose herself in Sky's arms.

Finding her cell phone in her purse, she called his number to let him know she was leaving. When he didn't pick up, she left a message.

"Sky, I'm on my way. I should be home by nine. I'm going to need you."

Putting the phone away, she switched on the headlights and pulled the car onto the road.

The hulking semitruck, with the Haskell Trucking logo on the trailer, had parked outside the diner with a view of the highway. At the wheel, Marie inhaled the last of her cigarette and tossed the butt out the window. Her tired eyes followed the blinking red dot on the screen of the electronic tracker Stella had lent her. She'd been waiting hours for Garn Prescott to leave Lubbock and hit the highway. Now, at last, the big white Caddy was on the move.

Marie had nothing against Garn Prescott—didn't even know the man. But if killing him would get her in tight with Stella, she was up for it. If she could shoot her own brother in the back, she shouldn't have any trouble ramming a stranger's car.

She knew, of course, why Stella wanted Prescott dead. In any investigation of the funding scandal, the man would sell her down the river to save his own skin. Just like Lute, Prescott knew too much.

And Marie knew something else. This assignment was a test. Carry it out and she'd become Stella's business associate, on her way to taking over when the time came. Fail and she could end up like her brothers.

The signal was in close range now. Looking north up the long, straight road, Marie could see the approaching headlights. If it was Prescott's Cadillac, she was in business.

Traffic was light at this hour. All she needed to do was get behind Prescott's car, follow along until no one else was in sight, and then make her move.

The headlights came close, blinding her for an instant before the car sped past. It was the Cadillac all right. Time to get moving.

Gearing down and switching her headlights on low beam, Marie pulled the truck onto the road and hit the gas.

CHAPTER 16

Lauren glanced at the headlights in the rearview mirror. The big semi had been on her tail since she'd driven by the diner. On this straight road, with little night traffic, there'd been plenty of chances for the truck to pull around her, but the driver hadn't tried to pass.

Were her strained nerves overreacting, or was the situation getting a little creepy?

Testing the driver's intent, she moved to the right and watched the speedometer needle ease down to forty-five. The truck slowed down, too, staying back, making no effort to pass her. A pickup coming from behind honked as it swerved into the left lane, roared around both vehicles, and streaked into the night.

Whatever game the semi driver was playing, Lauren wanted no part of it. Her boot came down on the gas pedal. The Cadillac shot ahead, widening the distance between them.

By the time she dared take a full breath, she'd left

the massive truck behind. She could no longer see headlights in the mirror. Maybe she'd imagined the whole scenario—or maybe she'd seen too many spy movies.

Feeling a slight play in the steering wheel, she eased off the gas. The Cadillac had plenty of power, but it was almost forty years old. There was no telling how long it would hold up at high speed before something broke or came loose. Better safe than sorry.

Once more she glanced in the rearview mirror. Still no sign of headlights. Lauren was beginning to feel foolish. Never mind. She'd be home in another twenty minutes. With luck, Sky would be waiting. She could fall into his arms and put this hellish day out of her mind while . . .

The roar of a huge diesel engine exploded in her ears. From just behind her rear windshield, high-beam truck lights flashed on, flooding the interior of the car, their reflection blinding her eyes. There was no time to think, no time for anything but a jolt of stark terror.

She felt the shock of first impact, heard the shattering crash. The steel chassis of the Cadillac crunched and folded around her. Shards of glass peppered her skin like buckshot. Then she was pitching, rolling sideways, the seat belt digging into her body as she jerked back and forth like a rag doll in a dog's mouth.

By the time the car came to a shuddering stop in the deep roadside barrow pit, Lauren felt nothing at all.

Marie climbed down from the truck, a flashlight in one hand and a heavy wrench, as long as her forearm, in the other. The truck, protected by a thick steel grate on the front, appeared to have suffered little damage. But right now that wasn't her concern.

Garn Prescott had probably died in the crash. But it was part of her job to make sure. If he was still alive she would have to finish him off with the wrench.

She took a moment to check for oncoming traffic. Satisfied that no one was coming, she plunged down the steep bank.

The Cadillac lay upside down on the sand at the bottom of the slope. Its wheels were still spinning. There was less damage than she'd expected, given how hard she'd hit it. But those old '70s cars were built like Sherman tanks. The back was crumpled in like an accordion, the top crushed, the windows broken. With no air bags to protect him, Prescott would be dead, she hoped. Marie wasn't keen on having to bash his head with the wrench.

The top of the car was stoved in. To look inside through the shattered window, she'd have to get down low. Crouching in the sand, she directed the flashlight beam into the car. On the driver's side, a motionless figure hung from the seat belt. Marie moved in closer.

Shit! It wasn't Prescott.

The driver—unconscious or dead—was a slender woman with long, auburn hair that hung over her face. There was nobody else in the car.

Was she alive? Blood dripped from the woman's dangling hair, making dark splotches on the car's headliner. If she wasn't already dead, she was probably dying.

Trying to save her was out of the question. And hitting her with the wrench would involve crawling inside the car to reach her, maybe getting cut on glass or jagged metal. There was nothing to do but get out

of here, the faster, the better, before somebody came
along.

The faint smell of gasoline reached her nostrils.
For a few seconds Marie weighed the wisdom of setting the car on fire. There was no way forensics would
mistake the woman's burned body for Garn Prescott's. But a fire would at least destroy any evidence
and make sure the driver didn't survive to tell the police about the truck.

She'd reached for her cigarette lighter and was
tugging it out of her jeans pocket when she spotted a
set of oncoming headlights in the distance, coming
closer, moving fast. For all she knew, it could be the
Highway Patrol. A fire would attract attention and
delay her escape. Better to just hotfoot it up to the
truck and hit the road.

As she was mounting the slope, a small object
dropped into the dry grass. *Damn!* That would be her
cigarette lighter. No time to look for it now. She could
buy another one in Blanco. Right now what she needed
was to get out of here.

Moments later she was in the driver's seat barrel-
ing back to Blanco Springs. She'd done everything
right, she told herself, even turning off the truck's
headlights so she could sneak up behind the Cadillac
for the kill. With those dark-tinted windows, there
was no way she could have seen who was driving
Garn Prescott's car.

None of this mess was her fault.

All the same, Stella was going to be madder than
hell.

Waiting in his truck behind the Prescott house,
Sky redialed Lauren's number. By the time the ring

switched over to her voice mail message, his gut was in a knot. She should have made it home long before this. Something had to be wrong.

He'd been busy with the horses till after sundown. Somehow he'd missed her phone call. But he'd gotten her message in plenty of time to drive to her house. Now it was after ten. Lauren was more than an hour overdue, and she wasn't answering her phone.

Her black Corvette was parked where he'd left it the night before. But her father's Cadillac was missing. It made sense that she'd take the bigger car—it was safer and more comfortable for the hour-long drive to the hospital. Still, anything could have happened to her. A dozen grim possibilities clicked through his mind.

What if he'd already waited too long?

After scribbling a note on the pad he kept in the glove compartment, he climbed out of the cab and stuck it in the screen door. Back in the truck, he started the engine, switched on the lights, and raced toward the highway.

Twenty minutes up the main road, he spotted his worst nightmare. The flashing red and blue lights of Highway Patrol cruisers, clustered on the opposite side of the highway, could only mean one thing.

Sick with dread, he parked on the shoulder of the road, climbed out of his truck, and crossed to the other side. There were two patrol vehicles, the troopers standing together, looking down at something in the deep barrow pit—something Sky couldn't see until he came up even with them.

The white Cadillac lay upside down, its crumpled chassis gleaming in the moonlight. The driver's side door hung open as if it had been forced. Sky's heart dropped. There was no sign of Lauren.

"Where's the driver?" he asked one of the troopers.

The man eyed Sky suspiciously. "Do you know her?"

Sky struggled to downplay the anxiety that was eating him alive. "I came out here looking for her. Her name's Lauren Prescott. She's the congressman's daughter. That's his car."

The lawman nodded. "We already ran the license, so we know that much. She's on her way to the hospital. The ambulance took her ten minutes ago."

"Then she's alive?" He forced his voice past the icy fear that clutched his throat.

"She was when they took her. But she was unconscious. Looked like she smashed her head pretty bad on the steering wheel. She was hanging from the seat belt, bleeding the whole time. No telling how long she'd been there before somebody saw the car and called it in."

Sky's first impulse was to jump back in his truck and race after the ambulance. But right now he needed to know more about what had happened and why. He stared down at the wrecked car. The front end was battered but pretty much intact. From the doors on back, however, the Cadillac's solid body had been crushed like a tin can.

"That car didn't just roll," he said. "Looks like it was hit from behind, hit hard, by something big enough to do a lot of damage."

"We figured the same—maybe a big truck. She could've braked for something, an animal maybe, while the truck was coming up behind her, going too fast to stop."

"Then where's the truck? The driver had to have known he hit her. Why would he leave?"

The trooper shrugged. "Suspended license, maybe. Or something in the back he didn't want us to find. Or maybe he just didn't want trouble with his boss. Things like that happen out here, with nobody around to see. Since the wreck took place in Blanco County, it'll be up to Sheriff Sweeney to look into any criminal charges."

Abner Sweeney. As if any news could worsen the situation after what had happened to Lauren. But Sky had spent enough time here. Right now all he wanted was to get to the hospital and find her.

As he turned to cross the highway, back to his pickup, his eyes caught the gleam of light on the asphalt. He could see where the Cadillac had torn up the shoulder as it careened off the road. But it was what he didn't see that chilled his blood.

There were no skid marks on the pavement. The driver who'd hit Lauren had made no attempt to stop or swerve.

To Sky, the crash no longer looked like an accident. It looked more like attempted murder.

Lauren stirred and moaned. Her first awareness was pain stabbing her head, pain in every joint, every muscle of her body. Her eyes opened, taking in the white ceiling tiles, the cold lights. A plastic clip on her finger was attached to the monitor above her bed. An IV bag dripped clear liquid into her arm.

"Thank God." The voice was Sky's. His big hand tightened around hers, gripping hard, as if he never wanted to let go.

"What . . . happened?" She had vague memories of shattering glass and crumpling metal, the seat belt snapping against her body. Were those memories real, or was she waking up from a nightmare?

"You were in a wreck," Sky said. "You've got a couple of cracked ribs, a nasty gash on your head, and a concussion."

Lauren's free hand went to her forehead, fingers feeling the thick bandage. She struggled to sit up, then fell back as the pain lanced her ribs. "I'm in the hospital?"

"You are. You're lucky to be alive."

"What time is it? What day . . . ?"

Sky glanced up at the wall clock. "It's five-fifteen in the morning. You've been unconscious almost eight hours." He lifted her hand and pressed a kiss into her palm. "You gave me a bad scare, Lauren."

She turned her head and looked at him. His clothes were rumpled, his eyes bloodshot and shadowed with fatigue. "You were here all night?"

"When you didn't show up, I went looking for you. By the time I got to the wreck, the ambulance had come and gone. I took a minute to talk to the troopers, then got here as fast as I could. I knew you didn't have anybody else." His fingers tightened around her hand. "I'm not a praying man, but I prayed last night. I was so scared I was going to lose you."

Lauren forced back a freshet of tears. "As you once told me, I'm tougher than I look." She tried to smile. Even her face hurt.

"There are signs that somebody might have hit you on purpose. Can you remember anything about what happened?"

Closing her eyes, Lauren groped her fogged memory. "There was this big truck—brown, I think. It pulled out of the diner and stayed right behind me. I

thought it was gone. Then it came out of nowhere
and . . ." She'd hit a blank wall. "I'm sorry. It must've
rammed me and run me off the road. That's all I remember." She opened her eyes. "You're right. The
driver must've done it on purpose. But why?"

"I've thought about that," Sky said. "If the reports
are true, your father could've been mixed up with
some pretty rough people. And since they didn't
know he'd passed away, they wouldn't have realized it
was you, not him in that car. It's the only thing that
makes sense."

"But what if—" She gasped as awareness struck
her. "Oh no! My father, the funeral, the press release—" She pushed herself up, clenching her teeth
against the pain. "Help me, Sky! I've got to get out
of here!"

Rising, he eased her shoulders gently back down
to the pillow. "You're not going anywhere till the doctor says so. The funeral can wait as long as it has to.
And if you'll tell me what to say in that release, I'll
write it down and give it to the press myself—or find
somebody else to do it."

"Traitor!" She gave him a mock scowl. Her sudden
movement had pulled the clip off her finger. At the
sound of the beeping monitor the nurse came rushing into the room.

"You're awake!" Her motherly face brightened.
"Goodness me, but you had us worried, girl. This
gentleman here never left your side. If you're smart,
you'll hang on to him. He's a keeper, and I can tell
how much he loves you!"

Lauren felt the hated blush creep into her face.
Sky had never said he loved her or given her any
other reason to believe he wanted a long-term rela-

tionship. The woman had probably embarrassed him half to death.

"Hang on, and I'll get the doctor," she said. "He'll be glad to know you're awake." She bustled out of the room, leaving an awkward silence in her wake.

"You look dead on your feet," Lauren said. "Go home and get some rest. I'll be fine here."

"I'll do it as long as you promise not to get up and try to leave," Sky said. "You're to stay put, hear?"

"You don't understand," she said. "My father had no family left but me. If I don't take care of things—" She broke off, remembering. "Oh no! Where's my purse? I need—"

"The troopers sent it with the ambulance. It's in the cabinet with your other things. But I'm going to tell the nurse not to give it to you. You need to rest."

"Stop trying to manage my life, Sky Fletcher!"

He gave her a slow smile. "Hey, you've got your spunk back. I can tell you're feeling better already. But you're not doing anything till the doctor clears you."

"He's right." The doctor—a short, balding stranger—strode in the door. "The fact that you're awake and lucid is a good sign, Miss Prescott. But we'll want to run a CAT scan to get a look at that bump on your head. Somebody will be here to take you down to Radiology in the next few minutes. After that, you're under orders to rest. You can plan to be here through tomorrow, at least."

With a mutter, Lauren lay back on the pillow. Her head was throbbing, but the pain was nothing compared to her frustration. It had fallen to her to deal with her father's death and all its messy implications. And here she was, practically shackled to the bed, forbidden to move. If she ever got her hands on the scumbag who'd rammed her off the road, so help her . . .

"Give me the name of the mortuary and I'll call them," Sky said. "They can put the funeral on hold till they hear from you."

"Thanks." Lauren surrendered with a sigh. "It's called Worthington Hills. They're in the phone book. While you're at it, you can call Tori. Tell her what happened and where I am."

Two young men in scrubs had come to wheel her bed out of the room. Sky reached down and squeezed her hand. "I'll be back tonight. Rest."

All she could do was return his hand squeeze before they whisked her away.

By the time Sky was back on the road, the sun was coming up. Braced by two cups of scalding black coffee, he shifted mental gears, preparing himself for a day's work with the horses.

Last night had been the most gut-wrenching experience of his life—sitting by Lauren's bed, his gaze fixed on her battered face and closed eyes—those beautiful, copper-flecked eyes that might never open again. He had told her he loved her—told her more times and ways than he could count. Whispering close to her ear, he'd told her all the things he'd held back—how much she meant to him, how he wanted to build a home for her and their children, how he wanted to begin every morning of his life with the sight of her beautiful face on the pillow beside him.

Now that she was awake, she wouldn't remember a word of what he'd said. But never mind that. And never mind that he'd been up all night, felt like crap, and had a day's work ahead of him. All that really mattered was that Lauren was going to be all right.

His sunglasses were clipped to the truck's visor. He slipped them on to shield his eyes from the sun's glare. He was bone tired, and the day promised to be another scorcher. A dust devil danced over the flat, dying out as it crossed the highway. Up ahead he could see the diner where the truck driver would have waited for the white Cadillac to pass, then pulled out to follow it, waiting for his chance. If he ever caught up with the bastard, Sky vowed, he would rip him apart with his bare hands.

But the driver would almost certainly have been working for somebody else—somebody with reason to want Garn Prescott dead. So it was Lauren who'd paid for her father's mistake. That had to be the truth of it.

A few minutes later Sky slowed down, scanning the roadside until he spotted the wrecked Cadillac. It was lying where it had rolled last night, probably waiting to be loaded and hauled off. Would Abner Sweeney have the sense to inspect it for evidence, or would it go straight to the junkyard?

No one was here this morning. Sky pulled his pickup onto the shoulder and swung to the ground. He needed to get home, but this would likely be his only chance to look at the crash scene. Last night the troopers and paramedics had been focused on saving Lauren. Looking for evidence in the dark would have been the last of their concerns.

A glance in the morning light confirmed that there were no skid marks on the asphalt. Any glass or other debris from the collision would have been cleared off the road by the troopers. But if the driver had meant to kill Prescott, it made sense that he'd stop the truck, get out, and check to make sure he'd finished the job. If he'd done that, he would have left tracks.

The trouble was, there were plenty of other tracks at the scene. Sky identified the standard-issue boots the troopers wore. The paramedics usually wore sneakers. There'd be no way to tell what footgear the trucker had been wearing except by elimination.

The tinder-dry grass on the slope made for poor tracking. But the car had come to rest on a bed of sand, washed down the barrow pit by storms and runoff. Kneeling a few feet back, Sky studied the sand.

Most of the prints would have been made by the paramedics. If the truck driver had been wearing sneakers as well, picking out his tracks would involve calculating which had been made first. But no—there would have been two paramedics, and Sky could see now that there were only two sets of sneaker prints, which left—

His heart slammed as he saw it—the narrow cowboy boot print with the pointed toe. Here was another one, and another, all but covered by the larger sneaker imprints. He'd seen boot tracks like those before, near where Jasper had been shot, and it wasn't hard to guess who might have left them. But how could the truck driver have been Marie?

Sky forced his sleep-starved mind to concentrate. Lauren had mentioned a brown truck. The Haskell trucks were brown. Stella Rawlins owned Haskell Trucking, and Marie worked for Stella. But did Marie know how to drive a semi? Was she capable of using one of those huge trucks as a murder weapon?

There was a lot he didn't know about his cousin,

Sky reminded himself. Marie had come a long way from the little girl he'd left crying in the kitchen the night he ran away.

But maybe he was wrong about the boot prints. Some truckers wore cowboy boots. And not all truckers had big feet. Some were even women. He needed more evidence. And even if he found it, there were still a lot of questions to be answered.

Using his cell phone as a camera, he snapped photos of the tracks, then walked a cautious circle around the Cadillac, taking pictures of the wreck from all sides. That done, he headed back up to his pickup.

Halfway out of the barrow pit, his eyes glimpsed something bright in the yellowed grass. There, at his feet, was a cheap cigarette lighter encased in pink plastic, exactly like the one he'd seen Marie use. After snapping a photo, he took out his handkerchief and picked it up. It was clean and free of dust, which meant it couldn't have been here long.

How many macho truckers would carry a pink cigarette lighter? It wasn't final proof, but if Marie had dropped it, the fingerprints should tell the tale.

With the lighter safely wrapped in the handkerchief, Sky climbed back into his truck. His thoughts churned like black dust in a twister as he started the engine and pulled onto the road.

He'd been cutting Marie slack from the first night he'd seen her in the Blue Coyote. When she'd blamed Coy for shooting Jasper, he'd chosen to believe her, and he'd looked the other way when he found the marijuana patch. Even when Coy's body turned up, he'd kept his suspicions secret, telling himself there was no evidence against her and that the wistful little girl of his childhood memories couldn't be a murderess.

But it was time to face the truth—and time to act on it.

Twenty minutes later he arrived at the Rimrock and parked next to Beau's Jeep. He found Beau alone in the kitchen, drinking his morning coffee.

Beau glanced up as Sky walked in. "You look like you just spent a night in hell," he said. "We got the message you left. How's Lauren?"

"Awake and giving me sass. Those nurses are going to have to hog-tie her to the bed. I promised her that if she'd rest, I'd call the mortuary and write a press release about her father. Maybe you could give me a hand with that."

"Sure. Heart attack, right?"

"Right. Short and sweet. No mention of the scandal or the gunshot. Funeral pending. When it's ready, we can e-mail it to the local TV and radio stations and the newspaper." Sky fished in his pocket for his cell phone and the lighter he'd wrapped in his handkerchief. "Right now I've got something you'll want to see."

He showed Beau the photos he'd taken and the lighter he'd found at the crash site. While Beau studied the evidence, Sky got a lock-top sandwich bag and slipped the lighter into it. "Lauren says she was rammed by a big brown truck. Sound familiar?"

"The Haskell trucks are brown. But we'll need more than this to prove the driver was your cousin."

"How about fingerprints? It shouldn't be too hard to get a bottle or can from the Blue Coyote with

Marie's prints on it. If the prints on that lighter are a match, we can put her at the scene."

"But we'd also have to prove she was driving the truck. For that we'd need to show cause and get a warrant to search the Haskell lot for the truck." Beau glanced at Sky. "You know what this means, don't you?"

Sky gave him a grim nod. "If we want to go ahead with this, we'll need to involve your buddy Abner."

"Leave Abner to me. The fact that he's running for office will put some pressure on him. He might not be the sharpest knife in the drawer, but he's smart enough to know that an arrest will make him look good to the voters." Beau pushed his chair back from the desk and stood. "Marie's your cousin, Sky, the closest thing you had to a sister growing up. Are you sure you can do this without backing off?"

"Damned sure. She almost murdered Lauren. The woman's got to be stopped."

"Then here's what I'm thinking," Beau said. "Hear me out, and feel free to argue when I'm finished. If the truck checks out, we may be able to get Marie for attempted murder. But a smart lawyer could claim the wreck was Lauren's fault and get the charge reduced to leaving the scene of an accident. That's a slap on the wrist—most likely a fine and probation or a few weeks in the county jail."

Sky forced himself to keep quiet and listen. Beau was making sense, he knew. But that didn't mean he had to like what he was hearing.

"Marie had no reason to ram Prescott's car unless she was following orders," Beau said. "What we really want is to get the person behind those orders—and behind a lot of other things. I'd say we give Marie some rope, let her work her way into Stella's organization. As long as she doesn't know we're onto her, she could slip up again. Meanwhile we can look for ways to prove she shot Jasper and murdered her brother."

"So if we wait, there's a better chance she'll get what she deserves." Sky was still skeptical. He wanted this mess over and done.

"More than that," Beau said. "If she knows she's looking at years behind bars, she'll be more apt to make a deal—and give us Stella."

CHAPTER 17

So far Marie had managed to keep out of Stella's way. Last night after the wreck, she'd stayed away from the Blue Coyote until she was sure Stella and Nick had gone. This morning she'd spent a couple of hours at Haskell Trucking, hosing, wiping, scrubbing, and vacuuming every fingerprint and every trace of paint, dirt, and gravel from the semi, including the tires. There wasn't much chance the woman in Prescott's car had survived, and even less chance she'd gotten a good look at the truck. But why risk it?

Now it was time to report back to work and face whatever had to be faced. She'd have little choice except to tell the truth. Letting Stella catch her in a lie would be a bad idea.

She walked in to find Stella, looking sour and suspicious, waiting at the bar. Nick was nowhere to be seen.

"So, are you going to tell me what happened?" she asked in a voice that was like the purr of a cat about to pounce on a sparrow.

Bracing herself, Marie feigned a shrug. "I picked up the signal a little after dark. Prescott's Cadillac came by the diner a few minutes later. I followed it to a spot with a good, steep shoulder and rammed it from behind. It crumpled and rolled down into the barrow pit."

"And?" Stella's eyes narrowed and sharpened, as if she already knew the truth.

"When I walked down to check, it wasn't Prescott. It was a woman with long red hair. She was alone in the car."

"Prescott had a red-haired daughter. Probably her. Was she alive?"

"I couldn't tell for sure. She was unconscious, hanging by the seat belt, bleeding from her head. I figured if she wasn't dead, she soon would be."

"So you *left* her that way?"

A rivulet of cold sweat trickled down Marie's back. "Somebody was coming. I could see the headlights. I figured my best bet was to get out of there before I got caught." Marie could feel herself beginning to crumble. "Give me another chance. This time I'll find Prescott and finish the job, I promise."

Stella's laughter exploded. "No, you won't, dearie."

Marie stared at her, her stomach curdling.

"I heard the news on the radio driving in," Stella said. "Garn Prescott died yesterday in the hospital— of a heart attack."

Marie's legs buckled. She sank onto a chair. "So he was already dead last night when I . . ."

"That's right—not that we knew it at the time. At least you showed willing. But I'd be happier if you'd made sure his daughter wasn't going to wake up. Since nothing's been on the news, I'm guessing she survived. Do you think she got a look at the truck?"

"It was dark. But the parking lot at the diner has overhead lights. She could've seen me as I pulled out. I cleaned up the truck this morning. There's nothing on it that could link it to the wreck or to me."

"Well, I've learned not to take chances. A friend in Lubbock is looking to buy a truck like that. I'll discount the price if he picks it up today." Stella's green eyes narrowed. "So why are you sitting there? No thanks to you, Nicky and I were shorthanded last night and didn't have time to clean up. The floor needs sweeping, and the bar and tables need polishing before we open. Get to work!"

Marie grabbed a broom and dustpan from the hall closet and began sweeping under the tables. For now, at least, it was business as usual. All she could do was wait for Stella to play the next card.

After what had happened to Lute, she knew better than to turn her back on the woman. With the Harley gassed, pistol loaded, and backpack handy, she'd be ready to cut and run at the first sign of trouble.

But she wasn't ready to give up yet—not as long as there was a chance to move up in Stella's world of wealth and power. For all Marie knew, it could be the only chance she'd ever have.

Sky worked the horses till after sundown. He'd climbed out of the shower, about to dress and drive back to the hospital, when his cell phone rang. It was Lauren.

"Hi." He tried to sound casual, but concern for her had dogged him all day. "Sounds like you talked the nurse into giving your phone back. I was just getting ready to come see you."

"That's why I called. You looked dead on your feet this morning. If you haven't slept, I don't want you nodding off on the road. Stay home."

"You're giving *me* orders now?"

"You're darn right I am. And don't worry about me. I'm still hurting, but the scan showed no bleeding on my brain. The doctor wants to keep me through tomorrow night. After that, if all goes well, I can go home the next morning and get ready for the funeral."

"You'll have a lot to deal with," Sky said. "Are you sure you'll be up to it?"

"I can manage—especially if you've got my back. But you won't be much help if you've crashed and burned. You can come get me when I'm ready to go home. Meanwhile, for my sake, if not yours, get some sleep."

"You're sure you'll be all right?"

"Stop babying me. I'm supposed to be a big girl, remember?"

After a moment's good-natured banter, Sky ended the call. Lauren's good news had lifted a dreadful weight. But as he pulled on his sweatpants and a worn T-shirt, the disappointment was there, too. He'd looked forward all day to being with her. But she was right. He was tired to the marrow of his bones—too tired to be driving on the highway. He needed a good night's rest.

Wandering barefoot onto their shared porch, he found Jasper in his rocker, the dog sprawled at his feet. Sky had yet to corner the old man long enough to ask for the full story of Bull and his mother. Maybe now was as good a time as any.

Pulling his chair over to Jasper's side of the porch, Sky sat down. With the sun gone, the twilight breeze felt almost cool on his damp face. The rim of a waxing moon had risen above the rolling plains to the east. The lights were on in the big house.

"Feels good to be off my feet," Sky said. "How about you?"

Jasper stirred with a little snort, as if he'd been dozing. "Hellfire, I'm goin' stir-crazy sittin' around here. Can't get very far on my feet, and Will won't let loose of the key to the ATV. I been goin' and doin' all my life, Sky. I wasn't cut out to sit on my butt like a damned toadstool."

It wasn't the response Sky had expected. Maybe another time would be better to ask the old man for answers to his questions.

"You did make it into town today," he said.

"Runnin' errands with Bernice? That wasn't much better than sittin' around here. She wouldn't even let me drive the truck. What I want is to be out on my own. I want my ATV back. I want to have a gun and go out huntin' like I used to afore I got shot."

"I guess you still can't remember everything, can you?"

Jasper shook his head. "Don't suppose I ever will. Heard the gun, felt the bullet, and then the blasted ATV wouldn't steer. That's all I remember. If I got a look at the lowlife that shot me, I still don't recollect it. But if it was that cousin of yours, the one they found dead in the bog, the varmint got what he deserved. Worst of it was, he took my good bird gun."

"Tell you what," Sky said. "I'll bet Will would let you take the ATV out if somebody was with you. I'll get the key tonight. Tomorrow morning, before it gets too hot, we can take my shotgun and go out for an hour or two. Maybe you can even shoot us a wild turkey for Sunday dinner."

"You'd do that for me?" The old man's voice shook with joyful amazement, then took on a note of suspicion. "Guess I'd better ask what's in it for you."

Sky laughed. "Nothing much. But if you'll tell me what you know about Bull and my mother while we're out there, I'll call us even."

Jasper's grin lit the twilight. "I'll do that with pleasure. It's about time you asked me. I've been half-fearin' you'd make me take the story to my grave."

Will had no problem with giving Sky the key to take Jasper out hunting. "Just don't let him get too tired, Sky," he said. "We don't want the old man back in the hospital."

"I'll take care of him," Sky said. "Believe it or not, I worry as much about him as you do."

"How's Lauren, by the way?"

"Better. They'll be keeping her another day. Then I can drive her home."

"Damned sorry for all that girl's been through," Will said. "First her father, then this accident, or whatever the hell it was. If she's not up to being alone, she's welcome over here. We've got a couple of spare guest rooms in the house, and it's not like she's a stranger. She's more like family, even if she *is* a Prescott."

"Thanks. I appreciate that more than you know." Sky chose not to question Will's motives. The disputed land might be on his mind, but Will did have a kind and generous heart. Sky would give him the benefit of the doubt.

* * *

The ATV was a side-by-side model with a bench seat and a roll bar over the top. With Jasper driving, they set out across the brush-dotted plain toward the seep. In this drought, the meager water supply was the likeliest place to find good bird shooting.

Even at first light the day was warm, with a dry wind sifting across the flat. The streaks of cloud in the east painted the sunrise with slashes of flame and crimson. Startled by the sound of the ATV, a golden eagle flapped off the ground and soared into the dawn.

Jasper parked the vehicle on a low rise overlooking the seep. Sky handed him the loaded shotgun. The old cowboy balanced it across his knees and settled back to wait. Quail piped their calls from the underbrush. But Jasper wasn't here for quail. Sky knew he was waiting for a wild turkey.

For the first few minutes they sat quietly. Sky waited for Jasper to speak, not wanting to push him.

At last Jasper broke the silence. "So, what do you already know about your parents?"

"I know what you told me about Bull," Sky said. "And I know my mother worked as a maid for the Prescotts. She's part of a group photo I saw in their dining room."

"And your mother didn't tell you anything?"

"Not that I remember. I was only three when she died."

"What about money?"

"What money? We were so poor we had to live with our relatives. There wasn't even money for a doctor when my mother got sick. If there had been, she might have lived."

"You've got a lot of anger in you, boy," Jasper said.

"Can you blame me? My mother was a good woman. Bull Tyler got her pregnant and tossed her away like an old shoe. He didn't give a damn about her."

"So that's what you think, is it?" Jasper settled against the back of the seat, his far-sighted eyes watching the birds that flocked around the seep. "It's about time you decided to hear the truth."

Sky waited for the old cowboy to begin, part of him still braced against the pain of knowing. But Jasper was right. It was time for the truth.

"I was with Bull the first time he saw your mother," Jasper said. "It was the day Ferg Prescott's wife, Edith, was buried. You know Bull and Ferg never did get on. But when there's a death in the family, it's only common decency to set bad blood aside and pay your respects. It's what Bull was doing that afternoon, and he'd asked me to come along—most likely to watch his back."

"So my mother would've been serving at the house." Sky filled in the brief silence.

"That's right. And Lord Almighty, she was the most beautiful woman I've seen to this very day. Even in that dog-plain maid's uniform, with her hair in a bun, she was a queen. I reckon every man in the room was givin' her sideways looks. But she wasn't lookin' back. Not till she locked eyes with Bull.

"By then Bull's wife, Susan, had been gone a few years, and Bernice had come to cook and help out with the boys. I know for a fact there was a gal in Lubbock that Bull paid now and again to see to his needs, but there was no love in it. He was still visiting his wife's grave with flowers every Sunday. I don't think he ever meant to remarry. But when he set eyes on your mother, and she looked back at him . . . it was like seein' him come to life again."

Jasper raised his binoculars to scan the brush around the seep, lowered them, shook his head, and then continued. "I saw the two of them talking in a corner that day. After that I never saw them together. But I knew they were findin' ways to meet up. And I could see that, for the first time in years, Bull was happy.

"One day she took that old car she drove and left without a word. Bull never was much of a one to share, but I could tell how bad he'd been hurt. I know for a fact he really loved the woman."

Jasper paused to lift the canteen to his lips and wet his dry throat. "A day or two later, Bull got a call from Ferg Prescott. It seemed Marie had written Bull a letter before she left and put it in the mailbox by the Prescotts' gate. When Ferg came out to mail something else, there was the letter, waiting for the mailman. Naturally the bastard took it. But that wasn't all. The low-down skunk steamed the envelope open and read every word."

Too stunned to curse, Sky listened in silence. No wonder Bull had hated Ferg Prescott. And no wonder Jasper had nothing good to say about the man and his family.

"Ferg offered to make a deal," Jasper said. "He would give Bull the letter and swear not to make a copy on condition that Bull deed him that little piece of canyon land where the Spanish gold was supposed to be hid. Otherwise, he'd keep the letter and use it any way that struck his fancy, maybe even send a copy to Bull's sons when they got older."

"Did Bull know what was in the letter?" Sky was still

struggling to wrap his mind around what he'd just heard.

"Ferg wouldn't tell him. He just hinted that it could do some damage if it came out. Bull would've done anything to keep his boys from bein' hurt, and he was plumb frantic to know why your mother had left. In the end he gave in to Ferg's blackmail and signed over the land. I signed as witness to the contract Ferg drew up. That's how I know all this."

"Did you ever read the letter?" Sky asked.

The old man nodded. "Bull showed it to me before he burned it. Said he wanted somebody else to know, in case somethin' ever happened to him. He made me swear I'd never tell his boys or anybody else. But now that he's gone, I can't help thinkin' he'd want you to hear this."

"So what did it say?"

"About what you'd guess. Your mother was in a family way. But she was a proud woman. She knew how people would talk if Bull married her, and how they'd treat her and their children. She didn't want to put him and his family through that kind of shame. She made it clear that Bull wasn't to come after her or to ever try and get in touch with her. But she told him not to worry, their child would be raised with love." Jasper gave a slight shrug of his bony shoulders. "That's about all I remember."

"So Bull just let her go?"

"Your father was a better man than that. He hired a private detective—gave the man a letter sealed in an envelope, with a check made out to her, for fifty thousand dollars. The detective was to give it to her when he found her. The detective came back a couple weeks later, said he hadn't found her so he'd left the letter with her brother. The man had promised to give it to his sister."

Sky groaned out loud. "I'll bet that check was cashed, wasn't it? With a signature on the back that looked exactly like my mother's."

Now it was Jasper's turn to look stunned. "I saw the cancelled check myself. The handwriting on the back looked just the way I remembered from her letter. When she didn't answer the letter or even send a note to thank him for the money, Bull had to accept that it was over between them. He never tried to contact her again."

"My uncle was a thief and his wife was a master forger," Sky said. "I can guarantee my mother never saw the letter or a cent of that money."

"So those were the two buzzards that gave birth to Lute and to the rascals that shot me." Jasper shook his head. "It all makes sense now. But to cash a big check like that at a bank—wouldn't somebody have to show their ID?"

"My aunt could fake anything. Believe me, ID would have been no problem. I'd guess she opened an account as my mother, deposited the check, and then took the cash out."

The two men sat gazing toward the seep. Sky's thoughts were focused inward on the story he'd just heard. It was still sinking in, the way things had happened. At least he knew that Bull had loved his mother and that he'd tried to do right by her. But Sky couldn't help wondering about the paths not followed. Would Bull have married his Marie if she hadn't left him? Or, if her brother hadn't stolen the letter and the fifty thousand dollars, would his own life have been different?

Sky had few memories of his mother. But when he'd run away at fifteen, he'd recalled her mentioning Blanco Springs and the Rimrock, so that was where he'd headed. Bull Tyler had taken one look at him, asked about his parents, and hired the scrawny, ragged teen as a stable hand. Bull would have known who he was from the first day. But in life he'd never acknowledged his secret son nor shown him the slightest affection. Now, at least, Sky could begin to understand his reasons.

The question that remained was the most urgent one of all. Was what he'd learned enough to justify his asking Lauren to be his wife?

A jab from Jasper's elbow jerked Sky's attention back to the seep. There, strolling out of the scrub within easy range, was a big Tom turkey with his harem of three hens.

Jasper raised the shotgun. Too late Sky remembered that his weapon fired a heftier load than the gun the old man had lost; and when fired, it packed a nasty recoil. They should have taken a few practice shots back at the house so Jasper would know what to expect. Now the birds were here, and it was too late to speak up without spoiling the shot.

Sky had made up his mind to keep quiet when he noticed something. Jasper had the gun stock braced against his shoulder, near the spot where he'd been wounded. The kick from the shotgun would not only hurt, but it might damage healing flesh.

"Stop," he said softly, putting a hand on Jasper's arm. But he was too late. Jasper's finger was already tightening on the trigger. The shotgun roared, the recoil from the blast punching him back against the seat. His yelp of pain was followed by a string of curses as the turkeys scattered, unharmed, into the air.

"Tarnation, that hurt." He clutched at his shoulder.

"Sorry, I should've warned you," Sky said. "I forgot how hard that gun can kick. Are you okay?"

"I'll live. And so will the damned turkeys, no thanks to—" He went silent, a blank look stealing across his face.

"Jasper, are you all right?"

The old cowboy managed to nod. His mouth worked as he tried to form his thoughts into words. "It's that burnt gunpowder smell . . . and the shot, and the pain in my shoulder. Lord, Sky, I remember it all, clear as day! I remember what I saw out here!"

"Calm down and think." Sky's own pulse was racing. "You saw the man who shot you."

"Plain as I see you," Jasper said. "Tall, thin, long, black hair. Only it wasn't a man. It was a woman."

"You're sure?"

"I may be an old duffer, but I know a female when I see one. She had on a black shirt that showed her figure some, and she had a scar on her face."

"Think." Sky forced himself to speak calmly. "When she shot you, could it have been an accident? Could she have been trying to shoot over your head and warn you off?"

Jasper shook his head. "No way in hell. She was lookin' right down that barrel at me. Woulda hit me in the heart if I hadn't gone over a little dip. I swear it, Sky. I don't have a doubt in my mind that woman meant to kill me!"

The gunshot had spooked every bird within a half mile of the seep. "I'm afraid hunting's over for the day," Sky said. "We'll go again soon, I promise. But right now I want to get back and tell Will and Beau what you saw."

"I'd rather be goin' back with a turkey if it's all the same to you." Jasper was still sour about the missed shot. He muttered and grumbled all the way back to the house.

Beau and Will were eating breakfast when they arrived. "Pull up a chair and join us," Will said. "There's plenty."

While Sky and Jasper washed up, Bernice piled two plates with bacon, scrambled eggs, and hash browns and set them on the table. Sky could only hope that a good breakfast would improve Jasper's mood. As they ate, he filled Beau and Will in on what had happened and how the old cowboy had regained his memory of the shooting. Jasper chimed in to add details and answer questions. Sky could tell he was enjoying the attention.

"So it was Marie all along, and not Coy who did the shooting." Will summed up what he'd heard.

"And I'm willing to bet she killed her brother so he wouldn't talk," Beau said.

"That, and to frame Nigel so she could clear him and have Stella in her debt," Sky added. "Marie's a clever woman."

"And colder than a rattlesnake," Will said. "After hearing this, I can imagine she's capable of anything."

Sky put down his fork. "Beau, I know you wanted to give Marie more time in the hope of building a solid case and trapping Stella. But we've got photos of her boot prints at the seep and we've got Jasper as a witness to his own shooting. If nothing else, that should be enough to put her behind bars for attempted murder." He glanced toward Jasper. "Our friend here deserves justice for what she did to him. I say we call the sheriff, tell him what we know, and have him arrest her."

"That gets my vote," Will said. "The sooner that woman's locked up, the better. Go ahead, Beau. Call him."

"All right. I'll call him." Beau stood, resistance showing in the tight set of his jaw. His expression was one Sky had come to recognize. It wasn't the decision to call Abner that rankled him. It was taking Will's constant orders. With the tension and worry brought on by the drought, both brothers were close to the snapping point. Sky could only hope the family—*his* family—could survive the blowup that was building like thunderheads before a summer storm.

Beau walked out onto the back porch to make the call. Sky could hear his voice through the screen door, but Sky couldn't make out what he was saying. Minutes later Beau walked back into the house, an impatient scowl on his face.

"I got Abner on his cell phone," he said. "He's at a law enforcement conference in Austin, won't be back till Monday."

"Can't he just have his deputies make the arrest?" Sky asked.

Beau shook his head. "I told him what we'd learned and what we suspected. But Abner wants to handle this business in person. With the election coming up, you can guess why. As long as Marie doesn't know we're on to her, he doesn't think it'll hurt to wait a few more days."

"Abner's a fool," Will said. "Anything could happen between now and the time he gets back."

"Tell that to Abner." Beau shrugged and sat down to finish his breakfast. "Why don't *you* call him? Maybe you'll have better luck than I did."

Will didn't answer. The air between the two brothers crackled with tension. Sky didn't like it, but he knew better than to interfere. Trying to calm the pair would only make things worse.

And he had his own share of worries. He'd lost all sympathy for Marie. But there were other concerns—the horses that needed training, the evacuation plans in case of fire. . . .

And there was Lauren. Lauren most of all.

On Friday afternoon Sky, who'd been working sixteen-hour days with the horses, took some needed time off to pick up Lauren at the hospital and stay with her. Will had invited her to recover at the ranch, but she asked Sky to pass on her thanks and insisted she'd rest better at home.

"That's fine," Will told Sky over the phone. "But let her know she's expected here for Sunday dinner. The girl might as well know what she'll be in for if she decides to stick around."

Now where had that come from? Sky wondered as the phone call ended. He'd tried to hide his plan to propose to Lauren, but if Will could read him so easily, the secret must be out.

Lauren's cracked ribs were still painful, the gash on her head stitched and bandaged with surgical tape. Sky had hoped she'd have the good sense to lie down and nap, but he should've known better. She spent most of the time going over the details of Monday's funeral—the program for the modest service, the grave in the family plot, which Sky planned to dig with the small backhoe borrowed from the Rimrock, the condition of the house and yard, and the catered buffet to be served after the burial. And she hadn't forgotten Storm Cloud. She wasn't well enough to ride, but she'd visited his stall to groom him and feed him a carrot.

Although flowers and cards were already pouring in, the gathering at the graveside wouldn't be a large one. Most of the senders, including the governor and the Texas congressional delegation, had sent sympathies and regrets. With an election coming up, nobody wanted to be seen or photographed at Garn Prescott's funeral. His campaign staff would likely be at the service in Lubbock, and some of the syndicate crew would drop by the house to pay their respects and sample the buffet. But it was sad to discover how few true friends the man had.

Bernice had sent over some lasagna and salad for supper. As the twilight deepened outside, Sky took the warmed casserole dish out of the oven and set two places at the dining room table and Lauren found another bottle of vintage wine in the cabinet.

Sky had yet to tell her the story of his parents. He'd meant to do it this afternoon, but the right moment hadn't come. As he helped Lauren with her chair, he realized there might never be a better time than now.

But how could he begin? He gazed at the lovely, impassive face in the photo above the table, as if silently asking for help.

"She was very beautiful, wasn't she?" Lauren said.

"She was my mother, Lauren."

Lauren smiled. "I'd already guessed as much. You look so much like her, that dark coloring and those high cheekbones. But where did you get those deep blue eyes? That's what I'd like to know."

Incredibly, she'd opened the way. Sky let the words flow, repeating everything Jasper had told him—his mother's affair with Bull Tyler, how she'd left Texas when she learned she was pregnant, and how Ferg Prescott, Lauren's own grandfather, had blackmailed Bull out of that canyon land. He told it all from awkward beginning to painful end, how his aunt and uncle had stolen the money Bull sent, and how his mother had died, leaving her son to grow up in a family of abusers and criminals. He told her how he'd run away at fifteen and come to the Rimrock, where the father who never acknowledged him in life had taken him in, given him work, and willed him his own piece of land.

When he'd finished, Sky waited in silence, half expecting her to be repelled by the sordid story—and by him, the illegitimate son of her grandfather's servant.

At last she spoke. "So Will and Beau don't know you're their brother."

"If Bull had wanted them to know, I figure he wouldn't have deeded your grandpa that land. They won't hear it from me—and not from you, either, I trust, now that you know."

"Of course not. . . ." Her voice broke on the last word. Tears glimmered in her copper-flecked eyes. "Oh, Sky!"

Lauren rose, walked around to his chair, slid onto his lap, and circled him with her arms. She held him tightly, pressing his face into the warm hollow be-

tween her breasts. For a long time they stayed like
that, both of them trembling. Sky breathed in her
sweet, musky aroma, filling his senses. She smelled
like love, he thought.

He could ask her to marry him now. But no, he
wanted to do it right, after she'd healed and after
he'd had the chance to buy her a ring. The whole
schmaltzy knee-on-the-ground thing—he'd always
thought it looked silly, but he wanted to do it all.

Some things were worth taking time.

CHAPTER 18

Lauren gazed around the Tylers' Sunday dinner table, grateful for the good people who'd done their best to make her feel welcome here. Her eyes lingered briefly on each face. Will, at the head of the table, seemed to have aged since she'd met him. The creases had deepened at the corners of his eyes, and his dark brown hair was showing strands of gray. Worry over the drought was taking its toll on the boss of the Rimrock.

Beau, her first friend on the ranch, sat next to Natalie. With their wedding coming up and a baby on the way, he had every reason to be happy. But today he was uncharacteristically quiet, his expression uneasy, as if he were waiting for a bomb to explode.

Jasper was glancing from brother to brother, clearly sensing trouble. Bernice, who'd labored all morning to prepare a delicious pot roast with all the trimmings, simply looked tired.

Tori sat on Will's right, her lovely eyes casting concerned looks in his direction. What had happened between these two people who seemed to care so deeply for each other? Even though Tori had become her friend, Lauren suspected she would never know the full story.

"But I want to stay here!" Erin was pouting. Her parents had agreed that she should go home with her mother until drought conditions improved at the ranch and Will had more time to be with her. The real reason—the danger of a terrible wildfire—hadn't been mentioned in her hearing. No one wanted to frighten the girl.

"What if something happens to Tesoro? What if he doesn't remember me when I come back?"

"He'll be fine." Will's gruff manner showed the strain he was under. "Stop arguing, Erin. It's time you learned that you can't always have your way."

"I have a suggestion." It was Natalie who spoke. "If somebody would bring Tesoro and his mother into town, they could stay in my corral behind the clinic. Erin could even help out around the place to pay for their board. I really could use her. With the baby coming, I don't have the energy I used to."

Erin's blue eyes lit. "Oh, I'd love that! Please say yes, Daddy! Sky could haul them to Natalie's place in the trailer."

"The horses will be fine where they are. And Sky can't spare the time right now." Will was clearly running out of patience.

Sitting next to Sky, Lauren sensed the tension at the table. Will was Sky's boss. But Sky was partial to Erin and to those horses. Would he speak up? But why wonder? She should have known he would.

"No, listen, Will, it's a good idea," he said. "Think about it. The mare and foal would be fine, Erin would be happy, and Natalie would have the help she needs. It wouldn't take me an hour to load those horses, drive them to Natalie's, and come back here."

"And I wouldn't be stuck with a complaining daughter," Tori said. "I agree, Will, it's the perfect solution. I'll take Erin home with me today, and Sky can bring the horses when he has time."

Will scowled at the faces around the table. "Looks like I'm outvoted. If this keeps up I won't have any say around here."

"How soon can you bring Tesoro and Lupita, Sky?" Erin was all sunshine now.

Sky glanced at Lauren before he spoke. "The funeral for Lauren's father is tomorrow. I won't have time to move the horses till it's over. But I'll shoot for the end of the day, or the day after. How's that?"

"Fine." Erin gave him a grin. Lauren reached for his hand under the table. She'd learned that Sky had a quiet way of making things go smoothly, seeing what needed to be done, and doing it with a minimum of fuss. He'd been a godsend since her release from the hospital, helping her plan the funeral and get the house ready for the gathering afterward. Still in pain and needing a lot of rest, she could never have managed on her own.

Two nights ago when he'd told her his story and they'd held each other, she'd known—as if she'd ever doubted it—that Sky Fletcher was the love of her life and that no force on earth could stop her from marrying him.

The only trouble was, Sky hadn't asked her.

The idea that he was Bull Tyler's son was still sinking in. Glancing at his secret half brothers, Lauren could see traces of resemblance—Will's cobalt eyes; Beau's stubborn, slightly cleft chin. The bloodline and the land Bull had left him might have made a difference to her father. But to her he was just plain Sky, the man she loved.

"Bernice," Will demanded. "How about some of that apple pie I smelled baking earlier?"

"I'll get it." Tori spoke before Bernice could rise off her chair. "Come on, Erin, you can clear and serve."

Erin followed her mother into the kitchen and was soon scampering back and forth, taking the dinner plates and returning with saucers of homemade apple pie, each one topped with a scoop of vanilla ice cream. What a blessed child she was, Lauren thought—happy, secure, and surrounded by love every minute of her life. Lauren could only dream of raising her own children with the same kind of love, in a home on the land she'd seen with Sky. But what if she was jumping too far ahead? What if she was planning a future that could vanish like virga, the phantom rain that fell from the clouds but never reached the thirsty ground?

Tori and Erin had just sat down with their desserts when Beau tapped his glass for attention. Sliding back his chair, he rose. "I have an announcement to make," he said.

"You goin' to tell us it's twins?" Jasper's attempt at a joke fell flat. Beau wasn't smiling. And Natalie's expression appeared more worried than happy.

"I hope you're going to tell us you've set a wedding date." Tori spoke into the awkward silence.

"That's part of it, yes," Beau said. "We're getting married the fifteenth of August."

A smatter of applause went around the table. Will's eyes narrowed. "Congratulations. Now tell us the rest."

"I was getting to that," Beau said. "After the wedding, Natalie and I are leaving. We're moving to DC."

Will's features froze. His color deepened. "The devil you are," he snapped.

"Hear me out, Will." Beau stood his ground. "I said I'd give ranch life a try. But things haven't worked out between you and me, and it'll be even more of a trial to keep you happy after Natalie and I get married and the baby comes. Natalie's found a young vet, a family man, who'll lease her house and clinic and take over her practice. And I've accepted an offer from the DEA. I get my old job back at a higher salary starting September first."

There was dead silence around the table. Will's taut voice broke it. "You know the terms of Dad's will. If you leave, your share of the ranch drops to twenty-five percent."

"I'm aware of that," Beau said. "And I'll get along fine on whatever's left to me. Believe me, twenty-five percent of this place isn't worth my sanity, or my family's future."

"What about Natalie?" Will argued. "She's built up her practice here."

Beau's hand moved to Natalie's shoulder. "We've talked about this. There are plenty of animals around DC, including horses. When Natalie's ready, she'll have no trouble finding work. Meanwhile, she can focus on resting, getting ready for the baby, and being a mother."

Will was silent, but Lauren could sense the explosion building. Erin was close to tears. Lauren knew Will's daughter had been excited about having her new little cousin close by. Tori looked stricken. Surely Natalie would have shared this news ahead of time, but it didn't appear that way.

Will stood, quivering with anger too long held back. "Dammit, Beau, I need you! The ranch needs you! You can't just stomp the dust off your feet and walk away while we're going through a bad time. Who am I supposed to get to take your place?"

Beau's reply was glacial. "Get anybody you want. With you around to boss them like you did me, half the cowboys on the ranch could do my job. Flip a coin. Draw straws. I don't care."

Lauren glanced at Sky. Seen in profile, his face revealed nothing. But he had to be hurting. This was his flesh-and-blood family falling apart, and he had no right to interfere. She ached for him.

Will glared down the table at his brother. "This has always been your way, hasn't it, Beau? When things get tough you walk away, just like you did eleven years ago. Dad never let on how much you hurt him, but I could tell. For all his rough ways, he loved you—maybe because you were the most like our mother. But you didn't care. All you could think about was yourself—and you haven't changed."

"Say anything you want to, Will." Beau's voice was strained tight. "I'm staying until the wedding to help you out—that gives you almost a month to replace me. But you're not going to change my mind."

"Fine," Will snapped. "Do whatever you want. You always have." He took a step toward the front door. "I've got work to do. If anybody needs me, I'll be up on the caprock with the cattle."

He stalked outside, slamming the front door behind him. Seconds later his pickup roared away from the house.

The stunned silence hanging over the table was broken when Erin burst into tears.

* * *

Stella sat alone at the bar in the Blue Coyote, smoking a cigarette and reading the Sunday paper—a day late since it was Monday, but what did it matter? The bar wasn't set to open for more than an hour, but today she had plans to carry out. She would need to make sure everything went down as it should. Split-second timing would be critical.

But it was early yet. For now she could relax a little and fortify her nerves for what lay ahead. After taking a drag on the cigarette, she blew a smoke ring and opened the newspaper to the obituaries.

The front page story about Garn Prescott's death had come out a couple of days earlier. Heart attack. Who would've guessed fate would play into her hands that way? She'd told him to watch his blood pressure, but the strain of having his dirty little secrets aired in public must've been too much. Too bad. She'd had big plans for the man before he let her down. But at least his fate would be an example to others. Nobody, not even a U.S. congressman, crossed Stella Rawlins and got away with it.

Today the news about Prescott had faded to a notice of his funeral service, to be held at ten o'clock on Monday—that was today—at the Worthington Hills Mortuary in Lubbock. Burial to follow in the family plot on the Prescott Ranch.

By now the service would probably be over, the procession headed back to Prescott's ranch. Not that Stella had planned to go—although it might have been interesting to see how many people had the guts to show up after the scandal. Would the governor have been there, or any of Prescott's colleagues in Congress? Would the governor's smarmy stepson,

Josh Hardesty, have shown up to console Prescott's red-haired princess daughter?

The spectacle—or lack of it—would have been interesting, Stella thought. Too bad she couldn't have been a fly on the wall. But never mind. She had other fish to fry.

One of those fish was Marie Fletcher.

Stella had been on the fence about Marie since that fiasco with Prescott's Cadillac. True, the mistake hadn't been entirely her fault. But a professional would've made sure Prescott's daughter was dead and erased every trace of evidence at the scene, something Marie hadn't done. And Marie had seemed almost too eager to make amends. Stella's gut instincts had hinted that something wasn't right.

On Friday Abner had called her from his conference in Austin. His news had confirmed her worst suspicions. The Tylers had solid evidence that Marie had shot that old man on their ranch, and they were pretty sure she'd also killed her own brother—the crime she'd pinned on poor Nicky. Even more dangerous for Stella, they'd found tracks and a lighter that could tie Marie to the wreck that had nearly killed Garn Prescott's daughter.

"Just wanted to give you a heads-up, Stella," Abner had said. "I'll be meeting with the county commissioners Monday morning to report on the conference. After that, I'll be coming around with my deputies to arrest Marie for attempted murder."

And Marie would sing her lying little heart out.

Something had to be done. Abner was a good source of information, and she knew he'd warned her for a reason. But Stella could hardly ask him to get rid of Marie. She'd needed the job done soon,

and she'd needed it done right. That had meant calling her Dallas connection and paying the price for a
good professional hit man.

The man she'd hired was in place now, waiting by
the road out of town. Hearing footsteps overhead,
Stella picked up her cell phone and made a quick
call. "It shouldn't be long. I'll phone you when she's
on the move."

"Fine." The word was followed by a *click* as the man
on the phone ended the call. His voice sounded for-
eign, but Stella couldn't be sure. She'd never met the
man face-to-face. Everything had been arranged
through his boss—half the payment made by electronic transfer, the other half to be sent when the job
was done.

Pulse racing, Stella finished her cigarette and
stubbed it out in the ashtray. She missed the old days
when Hoyt Axelrod would've taken care of a problem like this. But then Hoyt had become the problem. At least this way was simpler and safer.

She was still reading the paper, or at least pretending to, when Marie came downstairs to use the restroom. A few minutes later Marie came out, still
barefoot and wearing the dingy gray tee she used for
a nightgown. As she headed back toward the stairs,
Stella spoke.

"Marie, I need to talk to you."

Marie turned around. "Sorry, I know I overslept.
But I left the place clean last night and I'll be good to
go by the time we open."

"No, that's fine." Stella waved a dismissive hand,
showing off her freshly lacquered blood red nails.
"This is about something else. Sit down."

Marie lowered herself to a chair. Nervous hands

pulled her shirt over her knees, fingers bunching the hem as she waited.

"Cigarette?" Stella held out the open pack and her lighter.

"Thanks." Marie accepted the offering, taking a cigarette and lighting it. Stella, an expert at reading people, noticed the flicker of hope in her dark eyes. Did she think she was about to get another chance to prove herself? Poor, foolish girl.

"I'm about to do you a favor," Stella said. "I owe you this for what you did to clear Nicky of that murder charge." She paused to light another cigarette, giving her words time to sink in. She was playing now, like a cat with a mouse, enjoying the game.

"What I'm giving you is a warning," she said. "I got a call from the sheriff. That old man who was shot on the Tyler place got his memory back. He's claiming it was you who pulled the trigger, and that it was no accident. The Tylers and your cousin Sky are backing him up."

Marie swore and took a long drag on her cigarette. "I was hoping the old fart was dead. I'd have finished him off with another shot, but the dog kept getting in the way. I couldn't shoot a dog."

"You should've shot them both," Stella said. "Abner wanted me to make sure you'd be here this afternoon. He's planning to come by with his deputies and arrest you for attempted murder."

The look of panic that flashed across Marie's scarred face gave Stella a rush of satisfaction. She reached for her purse, which she'd left on the bar. "Here," she said, taking out a fistful of bills. "This should be enough to get you wherever you need to go. I'm sorry things didn't work out here, but what happened happened. The sooner you're on the road, the farther away you'll be when the sheriff shows up."

"Thanks." Marie rose, dropped her cigarette in the ashtray, took the money, and without meeting Stella's eyes turned and walked toward the stairs.

"You're welcome, you double-crossing bitch," Stella murmured as she disappeared. "I'll see you in hell."

Marie pulled on her clothes and crammed Stella's money into her pockets, along with her cigarettes and the new lighter she'd bought. Glancing around the room, she grabbed the few small possessions she'd left out and stuffed them in her backpack. After checking the load in her KelTek P3, she shoved the small pistol into the back waistband of her jeans and pulled the hem of her T-shirt over it.

Without bothering to put on socks, she yanked on her boots. Marie was no fool. She knew Stella hadn't warned her or given her money out of gratitude. Stella Rawlins didn't have a grateful bone in her body. The last thing the woman would want was for her to be arrested and strike a plea deal with the court. Whatever Stella's motives, there was only one thing to do—take the money and run. Maybe if Lute had done that, instead of getting greedy for more, he'd still be alive.

No need to say good-bye. Marie raced down the back stairs and found her Harley under the lean-to where spare chairs and empty crates were stored. The bike was old but well maintained. She'd put gas in the tank a few days ago. A quick check showed that it was still full—no scumbag had siphoned it out like the last time.

Stowing her backpack, she sprang onto the seat,

switched on the ignition, and opened up the throttle. The bike rumbled to life, shot out of the parking lot and down the street toward the main highway.

The wind caught her hair, blowing it out like a black banner behind her. It felt good to be leaving this garbage dump of a town behind—even though she was also leaving behind some big-time dreams. She'd blown her chance to be rich and powerful like Stella. But things could be worse. At least she wasn't in jail. At least she wasn't dead. She could go someplace else, start over, maybe find a decent man who wouldn't mind the scar—or better yet, would pay to have it removed. She had a good figure. With her face fixed, and some pretty clothes, she'd be a woman any man would be proud to have on his arm.

She'd turned onto the highway and was headed west when a black SUV pulled out of a side road behind her. The big vehicle was following too close. That was nothing new. A lot of drivers behaved as if motorcycles on the road were invisible. Still it was annoying. Marie was tempted to give the jerk behind the wheel her middle finger. But if he was prone to road rage, that could be a bad idea.

Giving the old Harley full throttle, she roared ahead. She'd outdistanced the SUV by a quarter mile when she heard it coming up behind her again, gaining fast. Cold terror clutched her as the truth struck home—this wasn't just any vehicle or any driver. She'd been played. Stella had sent somebody to kill her.

Did the driver mean to run her down or shoot her? With no time to think, Marie's survival instincts kicked in. Swerving left, she rocketed off the highway and headed across the scrub-dotted landscape. On the paved road she wouldn't stand a chance. But running loose amid rolling hills, clumps of mesquite, and sandy washes, she might be able to outmaneuver the lumbering SUV, either keeping out of sight or leading the big vehicle into a spot where it could high center or get stuck. She had her pistol, but the driver—she'd glimpsed a lone man in a dark hat—was bound to have a more powerful weapon. She couldn't risk letting him get a clear shot at her.

The SUV had turned off, too, and was coming after her. With its off-road tires and four-wheel drive, it would be hard to stop. Marie cut a zigzag route, keeping to the lowest path she could find. The long, yellow grass that carpeted the ground was so dry that it crumbled beneath her wheels, raising a plume of dust that trailed behind her in the wind. She could no longer see her pursuer, but she knew he was close on her trail and that he wouldn't give up the chase until she was dead.

The lay of the land looked familiar. She'd been here before. This was the eastern boundary of the Tylers' ranch, the area she'd cut across on the way to Coy's camp.

Not far ahead there should be a narrow wash with a sandy bottom. Marie's shifting mind calculated what little she recalled of its width and depth and the upward slope leading to its edge. Did her bike have enough power to make the jump to the other side?

If she tried and failed it would be all over for her. Either she would die in the crash or the man coming from behind would finish her off with a single shot to the head. But it was the best chance she had, maybe her only chance.

She scanned the horizon in a frantic search for the dip that marked the rim of the wash. The SUV

was gaining on her, its engine blasting in her ears. If
she didn't find it soon . . .

Suddenly there it was, a straight shot, not fifty yards
ahead. Rising off the seat like a jockey, Marie opened
up the aging bike to the limit of its power. The Harley
roared forward and upward, passed over the rim of
the wash, and went airborne.

The breathless sensation lasted only an instant.
Then she felt the shock of solid ground beneath the
wheels. Incredibly, she was unhurt, the bike still
speeding forward. Without looking back, she made a
beeline for a nearby rocky outcrop. The driver might
be slowed down by the wash, but if he had a long-
range rifle and a good aim, he could still climb out of
the vehicle and drop her with a shot.

Protected for the moment by the rocks, she let the
bike idle while she checked it for damage. From the
wash behind her came the sound of a racing motor
and spinning wheels. Evidently the driver had tried
to go through the shallow wash and become stuck in
the sand at the bottom. But with those big tires and
that powerful engine he wouldn't be stuck long.
Over time and distance there was no way she could
outrun him. There had to be something else she
could do to stop him and get away.

*Her nerves were shot. Dammit, if only she had time for a
cigarette. . . .*

The thought triggered a desperate plan. The wind
was blowing out of the west, back toward her pursuer.
Yes, it could work.

Except for a few scratches, the Harley appeared
undamaged. Opening one of the panniers, she took
out a box of cookies she'd picked up days ago at
Shop Mart. Dumping the cookies on the ground, she

tore the box open flat, clicked her lighter and touched
the flame to one corner. As the cardboard caught
she tossed it under a tinder-dry bush. In the seconds
it took to rev up the bike and speed away, a wall of
fire flared behind her, wind blowing the flames toward the wash.

She'd covered a good half mile when she heard
the blast of a fiery explosion. Behind her, a tower of
black smoke rose against the sky. Marie's mouth tightened in a satisfied smile. She hoped the scumbag
who'd tried to kill her had been inside the SUV when
it blew, but she wasn't going back to find out.

With a war whoop of victory, she swung back toward the main road. She'd done it. She was safe.

By the time the wind shifted direction, blowing
smoke and flame back toward the Rimrock, Marie was
too far away to care.

CHAPTER 19

Sky stood next to Lauren as her father's casket sank into the sunbaked earth. The brief service in the family plot was sparsely attended. Will and Beau were there to support Lauren and pay their respects to their lifelong neighbor. Natalie was working, but Tori had come, leaving Erin at a friend's. A few near neighbors, along with Randall Clawson, who managed the ranch for the syndicate, and Reverend Bunker Sykes from the Blanco Springs Community Church rounded out the small gathering.

Jasper had refused to go, declaring that anything good he had to say about Garn Prescott would be a lie. Bernice, who'd sent over some fresh banana bread, had chosen to stay home and look after her brother.

Sky glanced at Lauren's downcast profile. Beneath her narrow-brimmed, black straw hat, a lock of mahogany hair that the hot wind had loosened fluttered across her cheek. He'd seen no tears today. She and her father had barely had a civil relationship, let alone a close one. But he knew she was mourning all the same for what might have been and now could never be.

During the final prayer her hand had crept into his, fingers holding on tight. He was all she had now. He wanted to let her know he'd always be there for her. But before he complicated her life with a proposal, Lauren would need time to heal and let go of the past.

It was a relief to get out of the burning sun and into the air-cooled house. Lauren lifted off her hat and tossed it onto the back of a chair. Only Sky knew how deeply the day had drained her strength.

"Sit," he ordered, guiding her to the couch. "I'll get you a plate and some cold lemonade."

"Thanks." She gave him a wan smile. "I'm going to sleep around the clock when this is over."

"Do that. Anything else can wait till you're feeling a hundred percent." Sky walked to the buffet table, where he filled two plates with cold ham and turkey sliders, some potato salad, and some fresh strawberries. Will and Beau were on opposite sides of the room, their backs toward each other. Will was talking to Randall Clawson, the syndicate manager. Beau had cornered the reverend, maybe to discuss arrangements for his August wedding to Natalie. Since the news that he was leaving, the two brothers had barely spoken to each other. They'd even driven separately to the service, Will having made the excuse that he might have to leave early.

Returning to Lauren's side, Sky found that Tori had joined her. After pulling up an extra chair, he set the plates and glasses on the coffee table between them. "Anything I can get you, Tori?"

"No, thanks. I'll be going out with Natalie when she gets off work." She sipped her lemonade, her gaze shifting from Will to Beau. "What are we going to do about those two? This can't go on."

"Beats me," Sky said. "They're both as stubborn as . . . mules." *As stubborn as their father,* he'd almost said. "Beau won't be leaving for a few more weeks. Maybe between now and then they'll work things out."

"I don't know about that," Tori said. "I keep remembering the last time, when Beau quarreled with his father and didn't come back for eleven years. Erin's heartbroken. She was so excited about having a little cousin to play with. Now . . ." She shook her head. "I'm afraid this might be my fault. Not long ago I warned Natalie not to let Beau move her into the ranch house. Heaven knows, I meant well. I didn't want her marriage to go the way mine did. Now I realize I should've kept my mouth shut."

"You can't blame yourself, Tori." Lauren laid a hand on her friend's arm. "It was Beau's decision to take his old job back."

"But don't you see? If I hadn't given Natalie that advice, maybe she would've talked Beau out of leaving."

"Don't beat yourself up, Tori," Sky said. "Beau and Natalie are grown-ups. We can't make their decisions for them."

"Speaking of decisions," Tori said, changing the subject. "I apologize for the bad timing, Lauren, but I need to ask you this. There's a family interested in buying the Axelrod house. I told them they were second in line. Do you want me to hold it for you?"

Lauren hesitated, but only for an instant. "No, that wouldn't be fair. Not with—"

The rest of her response was cut off by the jangle of Will's cell phone. He'd turned it off for the grave-

side service, but he must've switched it on again.
Heads swiveled toward the sound as Will grabbed the
phone out of his pocket.

"What is it, Jasper?" He stepped into a quiet corner of the room, his fingers tightening on the phone.
"What? . . . How close? . . . Hang on. We're on our
way."

He turned back toward the people in the room.
"Fire on the Rimrock, this side of the east boundary."
Will's voice and manner were amazingly calm. "Jasper's called nine-one-one, but it might take the fire-
fighters some time to get here. In the meantime, our
first concern is to get everybody safe."

"You can count on me to help, Will," one of the
ranchers said.

"No, Sam, you've got your own property to protect," Will said. "If the wind changes, the fire could
go anywhere. Randall—" He glanced toward the
Prescott Ranch manager. "This place is the closest to
ours. It could go next. You'll want to get your buildings hosed down and your stock out of the way."

"Can I make it back to town?" Tori, in her black
court suit and stiletto pumps, was already headed for
the door.

"If the fire's jumped the main road, you could be
driving right into it," Will said. "You'll be better off
coming with us to the Rimrock."

She looked stricken. "Erin—"

"She'll be all right. Call her before she hears about
it. Tell her not to worry."

"I'll come with you folks." Reverend Sykes was in
his sixties but still fit and active. "Since Tori was the
one who gave me a lift, I can't get back either. Might
as well make myself useful."

Beau was already outside. They could hear his vehicle starting up. Sky stood with Lauren, knowing he had to leave, too. "Go," she said. "I'll be fine."

"You can't stay here," he said. "If the fire comes this way, this old wooden house will go up like a torch. Go with Clawson to the syndicate headquarters. There'll be plenty of water there and people who can evacuate you if it comes to that. I'll have my hands full with the horses. I can't be worrying about you, too. Promise me you'll stay safe."

"I will." She took his hand and squeezed it hard. "And you stay safe, too. Now go."

I love you, Lauren. Sky felt the words, but this wasn't the time or the place to speak them. All he could do was tear himself away from her and race outside to his truck.

The reverend piled in beside him. Through the row of tall Lombardy poplars that formed a wind break around the house, they could see columns of smoke rising against the hot, blue sky.

"Looks like a big one," Reverend Sykes said. "Too big."

"Any fire's too big." Sky stuck the key in the ignition and turned it. The engine made a clicking sound and died. Sky swore and tried again. This time the engine coughed, turned over, and started. Sky revved the motor to give it plenty of gas and charge the battery. The truck shot across the yard toward the road.

"Sounds like maybe a low battery or a bad solenoid," the reverend said.

"Yeah, I've been meaning to replace both. But who's got time these days?" Sky used one hand to drive and the other to call the cowhand he'd left in charge of the horses. "Start loading them up and trucking them out," he told the man who answered. "Mares and foals first. Like we talked about."

"Got it. Trailers are hitched up and coming around now," the man answered.

"Thanks, I'm on my way." Sky ended the call. When he'd gone over the evacuation plan with the hands, he'd never imagined how soon that plan would have to be carried out.

Reverend Sykes gazed at the smoke through the open window. "Don't see any sign of air support yet," he said. "I heard tell there's a big blaze down south of here. Maybe that's where the planes and choppers are."

"Well, until they come, I guess we're on our own." Sky swung onto the turnoff to the Rimrock, tires squealing in a cloud of dust.

"Are you scared, Sky, when you think of what could happen?"

"Scared?" Sky eased off on the gas as the house and barns came into sight. "Hell—excuse me, Reverend—if I let myself think about it, I'd be scared spitless. So I don't think. I just do my job. Right now that's all I can do."

"Hurry, Lauren! Blast it, we've got to get out of here!" Randall Clawson's wife and daughter, luckily, were out of town, but he was anxious to get away and get back to his duties. Lauren couldn't blame him. The smoke was close enough to sting their eyes and nostrils. A single spark, carried on the high wind, could turn this house into an inferno, destroying everything in it and around it—the stately poplars, the garage with her grandfather's priceless vintage auto collection, and the history of a family.

She'd encouraged Clawson to go on ahead and let her follow in the Corvette when she was ready. But the good man had insisted on staying until she was safely out of the house. If she wanted to take her little car, then she could follow him.

The funeral director and catering staff had packed up and taken the back road to the main highway, bound for Lubbock. Lauren had changed into her jeans and filled a valise with a change of clothes, some personal papers and jewelry, and a few toiletries. But she knew she could be seeing this house for the last time. She wanted something else—a memory to keep. As soon as she laid eyes on it, she knew what it had to be.

"Step on it! The fire won't wait!" Clawson stood framed in the open front doorway, his car keys in his hand. Smoke was drifting into the house. Lauren could taste it, bitter and burning in her throat.

"One more thing and I'm coming." She raced to the dining room and seized the framed photograph that showed her grandparents, her father, and Sky's beautiful mother. More than all the expensive furnishings in the house, this picture was the one thing she wanted to save for her children. "Let's go," she said.

As they came out onto the front porch, Lauren could see the hellish glow of the fire through the trees. The shifting wind was blowing it straight toward the Rimrock. She imagined Sky, working feverishly to load the horses as the flames swept closer. So many horses—and they were like his children. She knew Sky wouldn't leave until every last one was out of danger.

As she sprinted out to her car, her lips moved in silent prayer. *Please . . . please keep him safe.*

With nothing in its way, the wildfire stampeded across the tinder-dry grassland. Searing flames leaped higher than a man's reach. Smoke billowed upward, darkening the sunlight. Swift-moving animals—rabbits, coyotes, and deer—plunged ahead of the burning grass in a desperate search for safety. Snakes, lizards, mice, and prairie dogs took refuge under the ground. Birds took to the air. Some animals would survive. Many would not.

On the Rimrock, the mares and foals and the first of Sky's colts had been loaded into the two longest trailers and were on their way up to the fenced pastureland on the caprock. It would be rough going, the gravel road steep and narrow, the loaded trailers heavy, the horses frightened.

While they waited for the trucks to bring the empty trailers back down, Sky and his crew of a half-dozen men loaded the stallions into the smaller vans. The horses snorted and tossed their heads, smelling the smoke and sensing the danger. Some panicked, bucking, screaming, even biting. Others refused to budge.

Alert for any sign of trouble, Sky moved among them on foot, pausing where he was needed to soothe a terrified animal, prevent an injury, or coax a stubborn horse up the ramp. Vaquero, the champion chestnut stud, wanted nothing to do with the one-horse trailer that would haul him to safety. Eyes rolling, ears laid back, he was snorting and dancing, becoming more agitated by the second. The two mounted

cowboys holding the big stallion on double lead
ropes were in danger of losing control.

"Easy, boy." Sky stepped to his head, one hand
clasping his halter, the other stroking his powerful
neck. "I know you're scared. We all are." Leaning toward Vaquero's ear, Sky murmured the horse song
his Comanche grandfather had taught him. It was a
song the stallion had heard many times before and
recognized as a signal. *Be calm like the water. Be steady
like the earth. All will be well. All will be well. . . .*

Vaquero lowered his head. His ears pricked forward. With a last defiant snort and a swish of his tail,
he trotted up the ramp into the trailer.

Sometime soon, Sky thought, he would teach that
song to Erin.

With the stallions loaded and the trailers waiting
for the trucks, Sky took a moment to catch his breath
and glance around the yard. Tori's station wagon was
parked at the back corner of the house with Bernice,
Jasper, and the dog inside. Dressed in baggy jeans, an
old shirt, and work boots—most likely borrowed from
Jasper—a rumpled Tori staggered into sight lugging
a wire cage full of Bernice's precious red laying hens.
She was smudged head to toe with dirt and chicken
manure. Sky could imagine her chasing down each
one of those hens and herding them, or stuffing
them, into the cages. Bernice would have wanted her
to save them all.

After hefting the cage into the back of her vehicle
next to another one like it, Tori closed the tailgate,
piled into the driver's seat, and headed off toward
the road that climbed the escarpment.

From across the yard Will had paused to watch her
load the car and drive away. The boss of the Rimrock

seemed to be everywhere at once, coordinating things in the yard, directing the men hosing down the house and outbuildings, and using a walkie-talkie to communicate with Beau on the fire line and the men up on the caprock. The preparations he'd made ahead, which both Sky and Beau had viewed as his usual overmanaging, were paying off.

Now he stood with fiery smoke billowing behind him into a sky still empty of any help from the air.

Sky walked over to his side. Will was gazing after Tori's wagon as it vanished up the road. "She's quite a woman, isn't she?" he said. "Chicken poop up to her eyebrows, and she wears it like a million dollars. Take my advice, Sky. If you ever find a woman like that, don't be as stupid as I was. Hang on to her. Don't ever let her go."

Sky kept silent, thinking of Lauren, wanting to call her but forcing himself to wait. "What do you hear from Beau?" he asked.

"The fire hasn't reached the break yet, but it's moving fast. Beau's crew's working to beat back the new flare-ups with shovels, but they can only do so much. Best they can hope for is to hold it off till help gets here." He glanced upward through the smoke. "*If* help gets here."

"How much water have they got?"

"Tanker truck's full. But that's all, and it's not much. They'll be saving it in case the fire jumps the break."

Will sounded as if he could be talking about the weather or a story he'd heard in town. But Sky wasn't fooled. Behind his easy manner the man had to be heartsick. Even before the fire, the ranch had been in trouble. Now, even with insurance, he'd be forced to sell off the cattle and most likely the horses, too.

Will had given his life to the Rimrock. Now, in a matter of minutes, everything he and his family had worked for over the years could go up in flames.

The two long horse vans were rolling into the yard. Sky sprinted back to help unhitch them and hook the small trailers to the trucks. While the stallions were being relayed up the road, the crew would be loading the rest of Sky's colts-in-training. Those would be followed by the older horses, the paddock cows, and Pedro, the old donkey who kept the stallions company in their barn. Only when the last animal was safe would Sky feel free to look to his own needs and worries.

The wind had risen to an ungodly howl, driving the flames faster than any man could run. Glancing up, Sky could see the hellish glow spreading across the horizon as far as the Prescott ranch. Anytime now, Lauren's old home could become a torch. There was no way she'd be there, of course. He had to believe she'd fled to safety. The thought of anything else would have driven him crazy.

A pale shape flashed by as Quicksilver, the finest of his pupils, thundered into the trailer. The cowboys were moving the horses fast now, shouting and waving their hats to herd them up the ramps as the smoke billowed overhead. Sky led gentle old Belle into the last empty spot. This would be the final run for the long trailers. The mounted cowhands would ride their horses up to the caprock. Then the remaining animals—the paddock cows and Pedro—would be loaded into the smaller trailers and carted to safety.

Once the animals were gone, Sky would join Beau's crew on the fire line, doing what he could. If the blaze jumped the firebreak—and it would unless help came—the men would have to be evacuated, too. After that there'd be nothing left except to watch the ranch burn.

Beau's cell phone rang. He thrust his shovel blade into the ground and slipped off one grimy glove to fish the phone out of his pocket. The caller was Natalie.

"Beau, are you all right?" He could barely hear her voice over the roar of wind and fire. Flying sparks had burned holes in his clothes and peppered his skin. His eyes stung so bad from the smoke, he could barely stand to keep them open. The other men were the same.

"Hang on. I'll find a quieter spot." He walked a dozen paces back from the fire line and turned up the volume on his phone. The last time they'd spoken was right after he'd left the Prescott place. Conditions here had turned nightmarish, but he didn't want to upset her. "I'm fine," he said. "But I can't talk long."

"I understand." And Beau knew she did.

"We're trying to hold the line till the fire crews arrive," he said. "But don't worry, we're not taking any chances. If things get too bad, we'll pull back." *They were already too bad, but he wasn't going to tell Natalie that.*

"I talked with Tori," she said. "Now I can't get through to her phone. When you see her, tell her I've got Erin here with me."

"Does Erin know her foal's all right?"

"She does. We've been watching the news, but it's all about the big fire down south. Nothing about the one at your place."

Beau muttered a curse. Where the devil was the press when you needed them? "Gotta go," he said.

"Be careful, Beau."

"I will. I love you, Natalie."

"Don't . . ." Her voice broke. "Hearing you say that just scares me."

Shouts were coming from down the line. Beau ended the call, dropped the phone in his pocket, and ran in that direction. Fifty yards down he saw what he'd dreaded most. A shower of sparks, blown by the wind, had crossed the firebreak and ignited the dried grass stubble on the near side. The men were shoveling dirt on the fire. It had worked with smaller flare-ups, but this time it wasn't enough. The fresh blaze roared to life, racing over the ground in a widening pool of flame.

"It's moving too fast!" Beau shouted. "Go! Get out of here now!"

Hearing his order, the men grabbed their tools and fled back toward the ranch yard. Beau watched them go. He'd done the right thing, he told himself. The fire had become too dangerous. He couldn't risk losing even one of their lives.

He pressed the talk button on the two-way radio. "We're done here, Will," he said. "Fire's jumped the break. I'm sending the crew in. I'll be along shortly. Over and out."

Beau knew he didn't have much time. But there was one chance left, and he had to take it. The tanker truck stood a hundred yards back, ready to be brought in if needed. The tank was meant for small blazes and didn't hold much more water than a horse trough, but if he moved fast, there might be enough to douse the fire on this side of the break.

He dove in the truck and drove it as close to the

fire as he dared, jumped out, and unwound the hose.
While he had two legs to stand on, no fire was going
to burn the ranch his family had worked so hard to
build—the ranch that meant so much to the people
who lived and worked on this land, *his* land and his
children's land.

With the pressure on full force, the hose was hard
to handle alone, but he directed the stream at the
fire and held it steady. He should have known better
than to try. Within ten minutes the tank was empty,
the fire still spreading. And now the flames were racing toward the tanker truck. With no time to get to
the vehicle and move it, Beau could only back away
and watch as the truck began to blaze.

Only then, as the gas tank went up in a *whoosh* of
flame, did he realize the trouble he was in. By now
the fire had jumped the break in other spots and was
roaring toward him. For a short distance he might be
able to outrun it. But he couldn't run forever and he
had nowhere to escape.

Natalie's face flashed through his mind. He had to
get away, had to be there for her and their child.
Beau's legs sprang into action. In high school he'd
been all-state in track, but that had been decades
ago, and now his lungs were burning from the smoke.
The fire was already gaining on him. With each stride,
he felt his legs getting weaker. This was the race of
his life, and he was losing.

"Beau!" The familiar shout reached his ears. Will's
bulky form, running toward him, materialized through
the smoke. "You damn fool!" Will's strong arms caught
him, pulled him toward the pickup that waited ahead.
"What the hell did you think you were doing?"

"Trying to . . . save your ranch. But I couldn't . . ."
Beau was out of breath. His feet stumbled as Will

dragged him the last few yards and piled him into the pickup.

"*Our* ranch, you knucklehead," Will growled. "We can talk about that later. Right now let's get us both out of here."

Seconds later they were rocketing back toward the ranch yard with a wall of smoke and fire towering behind them.

From outside the barn, Sky watched the fire sweep closer. The last of the trailers had vanished up the road, the men from Beau's fire crew riding along in the trucks. But there was still no sign of Beau, or of Will, who'd gone looking for him.

The blaze was a monster now—an unstoppable juggernaut, burning everything in its path. It was time to get out of its way. But he couldn't leave without knowing what had happened to Will and Beau.

Relief swept over him as Will's pickup burst through the smoke with two men in the front seat. The ranch might burn, but at least his brothers were alive and safe.

Will swung the pickup close to where Sky stood, hit the brake, and rolled down the window. His smoke-reddened eyes were like burning coals in his soot-black face. "Jump in. Let's get out of here," he said.

"Go on," Sky said. "I want to check the place one last time. I'll follow you in my truck."

"Fine. Don't take long." Will gunned the engine and disappeared up the road to the caprock.

Sky raced through the barns, checking each stall to make sure no animals were left inside. Jasper's ATV was in the shed behind their duplex. Sky would have liked to save it for the old man, but he didn't have the key and the fire was roaring close now. There'd be no time to rig the ramp and push the ATV into his pickup. There were some valuable saddles in the tack room but no time to take them and load them in the truck. Flames were shooting up beyond the bunkhouse and the commissary. Soon the sparks would ignite the barn and the wooden roof of the house. He could smell the acrid smoke, taste it. His stinging eyes burned with it. He had to get out—now.

His silver-blue truck was parked in the open. Sky grabbed the key ring out of his pocket. Flinging himself into the driver's seat, he thrust the key into the ignition, touched the gas pedal, and gave the key a turn.

There was a faint *click,* then silence.

He pumped the gas pedal, jiggled the key, and tried again.

Nothing.

CHAPTER 20

Lauren's babyhood home was gone. From the shelter of the brick and metal syndicate office, she'd watched the flames in the house shoot up higher than the tall poplars. Then the trees themselves had caught fire, blazing like candles around an altar.

Losing the house saddened her. But it was Sky's safety that had her frantic. She'd tried again and again to reach his phone but had gotten nothing but his answering message.

Finally, after several desperate tries, she managed to call Tori on the caprock. "Everybody else made it out ahead of the fire," Tori told her. "But we're still waiting for Sky. He wanted to check the barns before he left."

"Can't somebody go back and make sure he's all right?"

"Not anymore," Tori said. "The fire's burned past the bottom of the road. We can only hope he's headed up here or that he got out some other way. Don't worry, Lauren. Sky's too smart to get caught in the fire. As soon as he shows up, I'll have him call you."

Minutes after the call ended, Lauren's phone rang. She shook with relief when she saw Sky's name and heard his tired voice. "I saw the smoke when your house went up," he said. "I just wanted to make sure you were safe."

"I'm fine. I'm at the syndicate office. I've tried and tried to call you."

"Sorry, I've been busy. And I left my phone in the truck." Something in his voice set off a warning. A cold premonition crawled up her spine.

"Where are you?" she asked. "Tori said you weren't with the others."

"I'm still at the ranch. But I don't plan to be here long."

The fear sharpened, cutting deep. "Sky, what is it? Are you all right?"

"I'm fine." In the background, behind his voice, she could hear a sound like wind, but more than wind. "I just wanted to tell you something, that's all. I'd planned to wait till everything was perfect and I could get down on one knee with a diamond ring in my hand. But I think I need to say this now. I love you, Lauren. I'll always love you. Whatever happens, never forget that."

"Sky, what's going on? Tell me—"

But there was no reply. She'd lost the connection. When she tried again there was no answer.

Lauren's heart slammed. She should have sensed the truth the instant she heard his voice. Sky had known he was in life-threatening danger. The call had been his way of saying good-bye. By now he could be dying, or even dead.

The urgency was a scream inside her. Whatever it took, she had to go to him.

Her Corvette was in the parking lot, but the low-slung car wasn't made to go off-road, and if it got too near the fire, it would burn. She'd have to take a horse.

She ran to the metal-roofed stable, where she grabbed a saddle and a bridle with side-blinders from the tack room. One horse was hers to take—a horse strong enough to carry her where she needed to go. But that horse had a strong will of his own. She could only hope Storm Cloud was in a mood to behave.

She'd used a silk scarf to tie back her hair when she'd left the house. Pausing, she pulled it free and stuffed it in her pocket. There was a chance she'd need it to blindfold the horse. She couldn't risk letting the wind blow it away.

The big, black gelding was in his stall. He was nervous, most likely spooked by the smell of the fire, but he allowed her to saddle and bridle him and to climb on his back. She walked him out of the stable and looked around to make sure the way was clear before digging her heels into his flanks.

Storm Cloud responded as if a gunshot had gone off behind him. They rocketed out of the yard. Lauren crouched over his back like a jockey, planning her route as she rode. Trying to pass through the smoke and flames would be too dangerous, and the ground already burned would be too hot to cross. She would have to circle wide and come into the Rimrock from the north, ahead of the fire. That would mean trusting that the wind would hold—a risky bet, but one she would have to take.

"Hey! What're you doing!" a male voice shouted somewhere behind her. "Come back here, you crazy woman!"

Without a backward glance, Lauren kept on riding.

After calling Lauren, Sky had taken the loaded revolver out of the glove compartment and stuck it in his belt. He'd rationalized that he might find some poor burned animal and need to put it out of its misery. The real reason for having the weapon was one he didn't like to think about. If the flames cut him off from all hope of escape, a quick bullet to the head would be better than burning to death.

But things hadn't come to that yet. He still had a fair chance of surviving this fire. All he had to do was find it.

The well and reserve tanks had been drained in an effort to water down the house and barn. Turning on the outside tap, Sky wet himself down from the trickle that remained. Blown by the wind, the fire was burning from east to west. The escarpment on the west would be the safest place, but he'd never make it on foot. No man could hope to outrun a roaring, windblown fire for any distance. There was an unburned break to the north, but even if he could make it that far, the fire would get there first.

The bunkhouse was already burning, and the water-soaked roof of the long barn had begun to steam. Soon it would be smoldering. Staying in the open, away from the buildings, wasn't an option. When the full force of the fire swept through, it would suck all the oxygen from the air.

Sky scanned the yard for shelter. The house was stone, but once the roof caught it would be an inferno. The same for the sheds and the duplex he and Jasper called home. Was there a root cellar? Lord, he couldn't remember. Even if he could find it, would it give him enough protection? Would anything?

Sky's frustration exploded in a string of curses. He didn't want to end his life like this. He wanted to live out his years with his brothers in this place that gave him all he could ever need. He wanted to build a home on his land, to marry Lauren and fill her sweet belly with their children. It wasn't right that it should all end here—he couldn't let it happen. Dammit, he *wouldn't*.

An unexpected sound made him turn. There, galloping hell for leather down the open strip to the north, was a big black horse. At first he couldn't make out the rider, but when he caught a glimpse of flying red hair, he knew.

Lauren was risking her life to come for him.

The unburned gap was narrowing. Anytime now, with a fresh breath of wind, it would close. Lauren could be trapped by the flames.

What if that were to happen? Sky had the pistol. He could shoot the horse if he had to. But could he shoot Lauren?

"No! Lauren, get back!" Sky raced toward her, trying to wave her to safety. But she kept coming, urging the horse ahead. Sky could tell Storm Cloud was terrified. He could easily throw her to the ground and bolt.

With the fire closing in, they met halfway. Still gripping the reins, Lauren slid to the ground. Sky caught her close, but only for an instant. He knew they were running out of time. Without a word, Lauren handed him the reins. The black gelding was tossing and snorting, on the verge of panic.

Springing onto the saddle, Sky pulled Lauren up behind him. As she settled into place, her arms around his waist, he spoke to calm the horse. "Easy, boy, it's all right." Storm Cloud seemed to recognize his touch and voice. His agitation lessened. But when Sky turned the horse back the way Lauren had ridden, he saw the danger. The unburned gap had closed. They would have to leap the fire to get away.

"Protect your head," he told Lauren. "Press your face against my back and hold on tight. We're going through."

He took an instant to pat the gelding's lathered shoulder. He knew he was asking a lot of the horse. He could only hope Storm Cloud would trust him. "You can do it, boy," he said. "Let's go!"

Communicating with his knees, weight, and hands, Sky urged the horse to a thundering gallop, then to a soaring leap that carried them over and through the flames. A searing breath of heat brushed past them. Then they were clear and running, the fire blazing behind them.

Sky swung the horse toward the safety of the escarpment. They were gaining distance on the fire now, but Storm Cloud was tiring. Sky slowed the gelding's pace to an easy canter. They had a little time now.

He freed a hand to reach back for Lauren. Her fingers caught his and held on tight. Later they would talk and make plans. Right now no words were needed.

They were nearing the escarpment when the whirring, droning sound of aircraft reached their ears. "Sky! Look!" Lauren cried.

Sky turned the horse. Behind them, above the ranch, planes and choppers were swarming in to dump their loads of water and fire retardant. Sirens wailed as the ground crews moved in from the far side of the fire. The flames were already losing the battle.

As the sun set over the caprock, Sky halted the horse in a shadowed canyon by a spring, dismounted, and gathered Lauren into his arms. The fire had done plenty of damage. But grass would grow again. Fences and buildings could be repaired. Only lives were irreplaceable. Lives and love.

EPILOGUE

August Fifteenth

Will and Jasper sat on the front porch, listening to the sound of the cool rain drizzling off the eaves. They were waiting for Beau and Natalie's wedding, which would take place in the family parlor as soon as Sky arrived with Lauren and Reverend Sykes, who suffered from a mild narcolepsy that kept him from driving safely.

Will glanced at his watch. "Damnation, where are they? I need to get out of this blasted suit and get back to work on the bunkhouse."

Jasper's mouth twisted in a half smile. "Stop your gripin', Will Tyler. Look around you. The rain's fallin', the grass is growin', the barn's got a new roof, and your brother's gettin' hitched to a fine woman. For Pete's sake, relax and enjoy the day!"

Will exhaled and shifted his legs. True, he had plenty to be happy about. The fire had spared the house and the duplex, and only damaged the long barn. The machine sheds and their contents had been saved, as well as the four bungalows for the married hands a half mile away. With the rains, the land was greening fast, both here and up on the caprock. Soon there'd be plenty of feed for horses and cattle. Meanwhile, Sky had opened up his untouched acreage to the Rimrock for grazing.

And Beau would be staying—that alone was enough to celebrate. He and Natalie would live in one of the bungalows until their new house on the ranch was finished. Natalie would work part time in partnership with the new vet who was renting her house and clinic.

There was another house going up, this one on Sky's land. Proud as always, he'd insisted on putting off his wedding to Lauren until he could offer her a suitable home. For now she'd found a small apartment in town, where she was working to grow her accounting business. But the two were already spending most of their nights together.

"Did Abner ever figure out what happened to start that fire?" Jasper asked, making conversation.

"Not Abner," Will said. "As you know, we all figured that the fire came from that burned SUV down by the east property line. But when the deputies found a body in it, the FBI got involved. We didn't hear anything for a while, but Beau made some calls. They'd traced the rented vehicle to a hit man for the Dallas mob, and the DNA was a match. But nobody seems to know how it caught fire in the first place."

"What about Sky's cousin, that woman who shot

me? Maybe she got burnt up in the fire, too. It'd serve her right!"

"The FBI didn't find any sign of her or her motor-cycle. A clerk at a truck stop in Wichita Falls remembered selling cigarettes to a woman matching her description—hard to forget, with that scar. But she's in the wind—until she gets caught, which is bound to happen sooner or later."

Jasper spat off the porch. "Never mind. We all know who was behind this mess."

"We do." Will thought of Stella, like a black widow spider with a network of webs, too crafty and too dangerous to get caught. "Her day will come, Jasper. And when it does, Blanco County will be a better place."

"Hope I live to see it." Jasper peered through the rain at the new dark blue truck that had turned the corner onto the long, graveled lane. "Well, I'll be damned. Here they come, and right on time." He glanced at Will. "Sky and Lauren make a right handsome couple, don't they? And those looks they give each other—" The old man gave a low whistle. "I'm guessin' there'll be another wedding before long, maybe sooner than we think."

"And I'm guessing there'll soon be more little Tyler cousins to run around the ranch." Will let the words hang, fully aware of what he'd just said.

Jasper's jaw dropped. He stared at Will. "How long have you known?"

"I've suspected all along—those blue eyes, the little mannerisms, the way my dad treated him. But I didn't know for sure until Sky got shot and we had to give him blood. How many people have AB negative? Sky knows, doesn't he?"

"He didn't for a long time. I finally told him, but he'd never say anything to you or Beau."

"He wouldn't, of course," Will said. "I do plan to tell him, but in my own time, whenever that is. Maybe on his wedding day."

Jasper grinned. "Remind me. When you've got time to listen, I'll tell you the whole story."

The pickup stopped at the foot of the porch. The reverend got out of the backseat and hurried up the steps through the rain. Sky climbed out of the truck and went around to Lauren's side. She handed him an umbrella, which he held over her until they reached the cover of the porch.

The two of them were so much in love. Will remembered when things had been like that between him and Tori, before his world crashed and he'd lost her. What he wouldn't give to have that feeling back. But as Jasper would put it, there'd been too much water the bridge. Too much time. Too little forgiveness on both sides.

The front door opened. Tori and Erin came out onto the porch. Erin looked heartbreakingly grown-up in her simple blue sheath dress, her hair twisted up and pinned with a silk flower. At some point she'd gotten her ears pierced—how could he have missed those little pearl studs? And was that lip gloss she was wearing? Now that was a shock.

Tori had put aside her black court suit for a flowing, flowered dress that made her look like a young girl. Her golden hair was loose, falling over her shoulders, and she wore gold gypsy hoops in her ears. She looked delicious—and so sexy that Will felt that old, familiar stirring. He forced himself to ignore it.

"Come on inside," she said. "Everybody's ready. Beau's just waiting for his best man. Isn't that you, Will?"

Will followed his ex-wife and daughter into the house, where the wedding was about to begin. As the vows were spoken, he would stand with his two brothers and the women they loved.

And he would ache for what he'd lost.

Don't miss the next exciting novel in
Janet Dailey's Tylers of Texas series,
Texas Tall,
available in hardcover from
Kensington this September.

She can't forget him.

The born rancher who stole her heart, her ex-husband, the tough, tender father of her child . . . Tori Tyler can't let Will Tyler go to prison for a crime that was a simple accident. But she can't deny that her feelings for the man run much deeper than loyalty, and her desire for his strong, sure embrace has never died. Protecting him is second nature, until an unexpected terror threatens to shatter them both . . . and Tori needs Will's fierce love more than ever before.

He can't let her go.

The sassy, sexy wife he never meant to drive away, the gorgeous woman who haunts his memory and his fantasies . . . Will can accept the blame for the destruction of his marriage, but he can't believe that he and Tori won't have a second chance to make it right. With the ranch in trouble and his freedom on the line, somehow fighting for her is the only thing that matters.

The first November chill had painted the Rimrock ranch with a golden brush. From the glint of sunrise on the high escarpment to the sweep of yellow grass across the plain, from the fading willows along the creek to the bursts of saffron where the cottonwoods grew, the land was the color of Spanish gold—the gold that, legend whispered, lay hidden in a canyon on the border of the ranch.

By day, flocks of migrating birds swept southward. Meadowlarks settled on the pastures and brightened the air with their calls. Ducks, geese, and sandhill cranes traced elegant V formations across the autumn sky. By night the stars were diamond sharp, the harvest moon ripe and mellow above the horizon.

A man with an easy mind would have savored the season's rich beauty. But Will Tyler's mind was far from easy. Wherever he looked, what he saw was not so much beauty as trouble.

The grass was weak, still recovering from the summer drought and the raging wildfire that had charred the lower pastures. Even if the winter turned out to be mild, would there be enough to feed the calves and breeding stock he needed to sustain the ranch? Or, with finances strained to the breaking point, would he be forced to buy more hay at a cutthroat price for the cattle he'd kept after selling off most of his herd?

Will had counted on the auction of Sky Fletcher's superbly trained colts to shore up the ranch's funds. But the drought-impoverished Texas ranchers, who would have scrambled to buy the lot, were, like Will, too cash-strapped to pay. Only a few young horses had been sold, and those at cut-rate prices.

Worries gnawed at Will as he drove his twelve-year-old daughter Erin home to the ranch for the weekend. While school was in session, the girl lived in Blanco Springs with her mother, Will's ex-wife Tori. But her weekends and summers were Will's. These days Erin, who loved the ranch, was the only bright spot in his life.

Will drove his pickup carefully, with the headlights on high beam. It was late, almost eleven, and the narrow, two-lane road from town was unfenced here, with a narrow shoulder and steep barrow pits on either side. Deer, coyotes, even cattle and horses, had been known to wander onto the asphalt at night and cause serious accidents. He would've brought Erin home before dark, but she'd gone to a friend's house for a birthday party. She'd phoned him when it was over and he'd picked her up there.

Erin had turned on the pickup's radio. The local country music station added a twanging underbeat to the thrum of the truck's engine.

"So what's new with you?" Will asked, breaking the relaxed silence between them. "Anything happening at school? Got a boyfriend yet?"

The boyfriend question was an ongoing joke between them. At two months shy of thirteen, Erin was more interested in horses than in boys. And Will would've run off any boy who got within a dozen yards of his daughter.

"Not yet. But Mom might have one. She's got a date tonight."

A knot jerked tight in the pit of Will's stomach. He and Tori had been divorced for eight years, but some part of him still claimed her. The marriage may have been a disaster, but they'd made Erin together—the best thing they'd ever done.

"You don't say?" He feigned a casualness he didn't feel. "Who's the lucky man?"

"His name's Drew Middleton. He's the new principal at the high school."

The knot pulled tighter. "What's he like?"

"He's okay. Seems nice enough."

"Think it's serious?"

"Maybe. Mom hasn't dated anybody in a long time."

"Uh-huh." Will swallowed hard. If Tori had found a man she wanted to date, that was her business. She deserved to be happy. But damn it all, he didn't have to like it.

With Erin at the ranch, Tori would have the house to herself for two nights. The thought of what could be going on there was enough to make Will grind his teeth. *Drew Middleton.* The name tasted like sawdust in his mouth. He'd never met the man, but he already wanted to punch him.

Will had paid scant attention to the radio, but when the signal for an emergency news bulletin came on, it caught his attention. "Turn that up," he told Erin.

The voice came through a crackle of static. *"The*

sheriff's office is asking for your help in tracking down a man who held up the pharmacy in Blanco Springs, took cash and drugs, and shot a clerk. The suspect fled on a motorcycle going north. He's described as a white male in his thirties, wearing a black leather jacket and a black motorcycle helmet. He is armed and dangerous. If you see him, call nine-one-one."

"Hey!" Erin exclaimed as the music came back on. "What if that guy's out here, on this road? What would we do if we saw him?"

"I'd keep driving and let you make the call," Will said. "Somebody like that, with a gun, I wouldn't take a chance on playing hero, especially with you along."

"But what if—" Her words ended in a yelp as the pickup's right front wheel slammed into something solid and stopped dead. Only her seat belt kept her from flying into the dashboard.

Will switched off the key, cursing under his breath. He wasn't sure what he'd hit. It hadn't felt like an animal, but just in case, he pulled his loaded .38 Smith & Wesson revolver from under the driver's seat. If he'd struck some unlucky creature, he'd want to put it out of its misery—or defend himself if it had any fight left.

He found a flashlight in the console. "Stay put," he told Erin as he opened his door. "Whatever happens, don't get out."

Climbing to the ground, he closed the door behind him and turned on the flashlight. The night air was chilly through his denim jacket, the full moon veiled by drifting clouds. The distant wail of a coyote echoed across the sage flats as Will walked around to the passenger side of the truck.

The pickup had come to rest at a cockeyed angle, probably blown a tire, which he'd need to change. In the beam of the flashlight, he could see what he'd hit. It was the engine block of some kind of vehicle, most likely fallen off the back of a flatbed because the fool driver hadn't bothered to tie it down. Heavy and solid, its edges were sharp enough to puncture a tire, which was just what had happened. If he hadn't been distracted by the announcement on the radio, he might have seen it in time to stop.

Erin rolled down the window. "What is it?" she asked. "Is it an animal?"

"No, just a big, nasty chunk of metal. But I'll have to change the tire."

"Can I help? I can hold the light for you."

"No, just stay put. I'll be fine."

He'd stuck the .38 in his belt and was walking around to get the spare and the jack when he saw it—a single headlight approaching fast down the long, straight road from the direction of town, maybe half a mile away. It looked like a motorcycle, sounded like one, too.

Will turned off the flashlight and laid it on the ground. One hand drew the weapon out of his belt. "Close the window, lock the doors, and get down," he ordered Erin. He caught the flash of her frightened eyes as she obeyed. He'd probably scared her for nothing, but he couldn't take any chances.

The motorcycle was slowing down. Maybe the rider was just some Good Samaritan wanting to help. But Will couldn't lay odds on that. He might be safer inside the truck, but that could expose Erin to more danger. Right now, his daughter's safety was the only thing that mattered.

A few yards ahead of the truck, the motorcycle pulled onto the shoulder and stopped. The rider swung off his machine. He wore a black leather jacket with a dark helmet, the visor pulled down to obscure his face. His right hand held a small pistol with the look of a cheap Saturday-night special. It had to be the robber. Will waited in the shadows, gripping the .38, as the man approached and spoke.

"What the hell happened here? We were supposed to meet down by the cross-road." His whiny-pitched voice sounded vaguely Eastern, and strangely familiar. "Never mind, I got the package on the bike. Show me the money, and we're good."

Will stepped into the moonlight, his pistol leveled at the man's chest. "Hands where I can see them, Mister. Now, nice and slow, drop your weapon. Then kick it over here toward me."

"Shit, you're not—" The motorcyclist froze in surprise. He dropped the gun on the ground. As he kicked it toward Will, his hand flashed. Suddenly there was a knife in it. As his arm flexed for the throw, Will pulled the trigger. The .38 roared, striking the man squarely in the chest. He toppled backward, dead by the time he hit the ground.

Will stared down at the bleeding body, cursing out loud. He'd never meant to kill the stupid jackass, but he'd had little choice, especially with Erin to protect.

"Daddy?" Erin had rolled down the window partway. Her voice sounded thin and scared. "Are you all right?"

"I'm fine, honey. Close the window and stay in the truck. Try not to look. I'll come around." Leaving the body where it lay, he circled behind the truck to the driver's side. Once inside, he reached across the console and gathered his daughter in his arms. She clung to him, trembling.

Will felt shaken, too, when he thought about what he'd just done. His brother Beau, who'd been an

Army sniper in Iraq, had never revealed how many
kills he'd made. But for Will, this was a first. He'd
never taken a human life before. Now, even though
he'd killed a criminal in self-defense, the thought
sickened him.

Erin pulled away as he released her. She'd be all
right, Will told himself. She was strong, like Tori.
"You need to call the sheriff, Daddy," she said.

"I know. But first I'm going to call your mother."

Will reached for the cell phone in his pocket. As
an afterthought, he climbed out of the truck again
and closed the door. His conversation with Tori
could easily get emotional. It might be better not to
have Erin listening.

His legs felt unsteady. Leaning against the side of
the cab, he scrolled to Tori's number and pressed
the call button. The phone rang, once, then again.
Maybe she'd turned it off, the better to enjoy her
new boyfriend. But no, it wouldn't be like Tori to do
that, not even on a date. She had clients who needed
her. More important, she had a daughter.

Will was waiting for his ex-wife's voice message to
come on when she picked up. "Will?" He could sense
her tension. "What is it? Is Erin all right?"

"Erin's fine," Will said. "But I need you to come
and get her. There was an . . . incident on the way to
the ranch. The truck's stuck on the road with a
blown tire, and I can't leave."

"An *incident*, you say? What happened, Will? What
are you not telling me?"

"I'll explain later. Erin said you had a date. Hell,
bring him along if you want. I don't care. Whatever
you're doing, just drop it and get here. Now."

"I'm on my way. Tell Erin I'm coming." She ended
the call without saying goodbye.

Will waited a few minutes, then called 911. The night dispatcher who answered his call was a woman whose voice he recognized.

"Carly, this is Will Tyler," he said. "Tell the sheriff he can stop looking for that drugstore robber on the motorcycle. I just shot him."

"Is he dead?"

"Dead as a doornail. I need somebody to come, pronto."

"Where are you?" There was an odd note to her voice.

"About ten miles out of town, on the road to my ranch. My pickup's got a blown tire."

"I hear you. Stay in your truck and don't touch anything. Somebody will be right there."

She hesitated, as if weighing her next words. "There's something you need to know, Will. Whoever you shot, it wasn't the pharmacy robber. The man was picked up a few minutes ago, headed for the freeway on his motorcycle. The drugs and cash were on him. They're bringing him in now."

More from Bestselling Author
JANET DAILEY

More by Bestselling Author
Hannah Howell

Available Wherever Books Are Sold!

Check out our website at
http://www.kensingtonbooks.com

Books by Bestselling Author
Fern Michaels